Yes No Maybe

a novel

JESSICA SHERRY

Published by Jessica Sherry

Copyright © 2024 by Jessica Sherry

jessicasherry.com

ISBN: 979-8-9887254-5-9
Book Cover Design by ebooklaunch.com
Printed/Published in the United States of America

Dedication

To everyone who puts on a brave face. You're perfect, scars and all.

Author's Note

Dear Reader,

Though the story you're about to read is a feel-good contemporary romance, it features realistic, wounded characters and sensitive subject matter that may upset some readers. If you'd rather not know any spoilers, ignore the next paragraph and skip to chapter one with my thanks for reading.

For those who prefer to know, this book deals with the following difficult topics: burn scars, assault, grief, toxic relationships, and child abuse (bonus content). There is profanity and some mild sexual content.

Please know that I did my best to handle these topics with respect and sensitivity. Thank you for reading.

Jessica

One

ROWAN

It's the final, sold-out night of Coastal High School's reboot of Shakespeare's *Taming of the Shrew*, and I'm staring down the mother of all zits, as if my intimidating glare might convince it to vacate the premises.

It's the Mount Vesuvius of acne—positioned at the base of my student's nostril. Its yellow pus crater stretches bigger than a fingertip. Pus moves under the skin window like cells under a microscope, devilishly multiplying. It's the most heinous pimple I've ever seen, and working with teenagers every day, that says a lot.

"Ms. Mackey, I can't perform," Eddie Speck proclaims. "Not with this *booger* crusted to my face."

I offer my most reassuring smile. "A little makeup, and no one will know."

"We've tried that." Eddie motions to the baffled make-up team standing by and Julio, another student, who plucked me from the audience for this emergency. "Nothing adheres to this thing! It's makeup-resistant!"

Of course, it is. As someone with permanent burn scars across her left cheek, neck, and hand, I know better than most that makeup fails to hide everything.

"Um, you should pop it. If it's flatter, it'll be easier to hide."

Julio and Eddie look horrified.

"What? You've never popped a zit before?"

They shake their heads. Eddie swipes a tear. "Julio... notify my understudy."

"You don't need your understudy. Just squeeze it between your fingernails."

Eddie holds up his hands. His nails are bitten down to useless stubs.

I glance at Julio, who shakes his head. "Don't look at me. The entire make-up team refuses to touch it."

"Fine." I send a hurried text to my sister Mira, who I'm holding five extra seats for in the packed auditorium. *Third row. Right side. Look for my stuff.* "Boys, let's find a bathroom."

"We're popping the zit," Julio announces into his walkie.

Eight years in a high school classroom have taught me many universal truths about teaching—the most surprising is that a teacher will do almost anything for her students. Not just the obvious things like tutoring and extra credit, but a daring litany of the unexpected that, if asked in college... *would you ever...* you would've said *hell no* with the emphatic certainty and luxury of someone who thinks she knows everything, especially herself. *Silly younger self... so naive.*

Consequently, a teacher must be prepared for anything. Teenagers are smart—they'll sniff out the unprepared, attack, and reduce the teacher to a glorified coat rack to ensure getting away with murder for the rest of the semester. It's *Game of Thrones* in there. Once you lose control, it's impossible to get back.

But nearly anything else can be fixed—a lesson plan, a scheduling conflict, a bad attitude, a heinous zit—and I'm the Fix-It Queen, a behind-the-scenes problem-solver.

Even so, this is the weirdest thing I've done for a student. That includes holding a trashcan for Tonya Jeffers while she got sick from the cafeteria's "clean-out-the-fridge" nachos. And chasing a thuggish ninth grader after he grabbed a student's butt during carline. Adding zit-popping to the list is unexpected, but the show must go on.

"At least *someone* looks amazing," Eddie says with jealousy as I wash my hands.

I grin. "Buttering me up to do this?"

"A little, but it's true."

"Thanks." A short twirl in my emerald green chiffon dress ripples the sheer overlay. "Dean, I mean, Mr. Maddix, suggested dressing up. I must've changed four times."

Julio's eyes pinch, but the caboodle-toting makeup artists flash coy grins. "Very pretty," one says.

"I feel pretty," I admit—a rare feeling. My eyes travel along my burn scars in the mirror—the spotted beginnings at my lower left cheek from chin to ear, the warped fault line at my jaw, the lumpy coral-esque texture running down my neck, and the pink and red splotches covering my left hand and wrist. *"Freddie Krueger face,"* a student once called it, prompting my mac-n-cheese story—a fictionalized version of what happened to answer students' bold questions. I never tell the real story. She exaggerated, anyway—most of my face is unscarred, and from the right side, it's not seen at all—but the scars create such a strange juxtaposition between woman and "monster" that sometimes I wonder if it stands out more next to unblemished skin. It's shocking when people discover it, like my scars jump out at them from behind a corner.

I turn away to grab paper towels. "Okay. Let's do this."

"Deep breaths," Julio advises, bracing Eddie against the sink.

My right hand trembles as it meets the enemy.

I love my students. I love their energy, honesty, and creativity. I love them for who they are, what they'll be, and what they're going through. I was them once—still am in most ways. If I can help, I will.

But this tests my love like never before.

My fingernails pinch the gooey-thin skin, and my breath holds. Gasps follow *ewwws* and finally switch to applause as the pimple drains. Julio administers the paper towels, eyeing a speck on my green dress. I wipe it quickly, wondering if it'll stain.

Eddie checks the mirror, sinking with relief. It looks better already. "Ah, Ms. Mackey, my hero. Thank you."

Returning to the auditorium, I carry inexplicable nerves with me. Ginormous zits aside, something seems off tonight.

I reach my reserved seats in time to stop an unfamiliar woman directing her brood of middle schoolers into my row.

"Um, these seats are taken," I say, though I shouldn't have to. The six seats holding my scattered belongings should've been a clue. No one drapes her sweater, umbrella, teacher bag, purse, and annotated copy of *Heart of Darkness* over multiple seats just to have a row to herself, not even an introvert like me.

Huffing, she escorts them away, and I resume my position in the inner seat against the right wall, my unease growing with the crowd.

The student-written, directed and produced play, aptly renamed *Ten Things* as a nod to the nineties movie *10 Things I Hate About You*, was modest until tonight. The first performance filled half the auditorium—mostly parents and friends. The second drew slightly more students, perhaps curious how Shakespeare's *Taming of the Shrew* might be redone to feature a trans student and a school's small LGBTQ+ community. With that show and students taking to social media, interest grew. Co-star Ashley Morrow's father, Kent Morrow, a meteorologist from Channel Twelve, upped the exposure by mentioning it on the 11 o'clock news, calling it *"A performance everyone should see."*

It seems people listened. I spot three school board members, two Channel Twelve anchors, and nearly all of Coastal High's administration.

The kids deserve the attention. They've done an amazing job with the rewrite, keeping the humor and charm while adding present-day themes and language everyone understands.

Many good things have come from the project, despite my initial reluctance. When go-getter assistant principal Dr. Evelyn Tate assigned teachers a vague *Inspiration Project* to enhance the curriculum and bolster student interest, I was peeved. Inspiring students is a daily endeavor—not a novel idea. Another truth about teaching is that I still *always* have a million things to do and don't need more tacked on by ambitious administrators.

I glance up from the play's program and see the woman herself—Dr. Evelyn—working the crowd like a classically trained schmoozer. Her dress is gorgeous, understated and elegant, even though it's shimmery gold and matches her hair's blond ribbons. *How could she have that lying around for a show she hadn't been interested in attending two days ago?* My shoulders slump... I hate her a little. She's annoyingly perfect, as if inspiring envy is *her* personal inspiration project.

Holding these five empty seats is about as much envy as I've ever inspired. Two couples nearby fixate on my object-clad seats like they might enact pirate rules and toss my things aside. One man makes eye contact, ready to ask the obvious question, but he notices my cheek and neck—*people can't help it*—and decides against it.

Finally, Mira edges into my row, picking up objects as her family settles behind her. Her wife, Jane, and their adopted kids, Kenan, Izzy, Beth, and baby Aster, wrapped against Jane's chest like a kangaroo pouch, look like a modern family showcased in a car safety commercial or Walmart ad. They're exactly the chaotic, messy, beautiful family I want someday.

Well, except with a guy. And for the first time in years, I'm seeing someone who might be a contender—Dean.

"Dang girl," Mira coos. "That dress is *banging*."

"If I'd known it was a fancy affair, I would've worn my pearls," Jane laughs. "Ooh la la."

I blush, glad they don't see the pimple pus stain. "Thanks. It was Dean's idea to dress up on the last night."

My sister-in-law and real estate agent, Jane, hands me a keychain with the words *Beach Bum* in silver dangling with the single key. "The key to your little house. Kenan picked out the keychain."

"It's perfect." I smile down the row at him while relieving Mira of my gear and tucking it under my seat. "But it's too early for a keychain. I haven't decided on the house yet."

Jane waves her hand and purses her lips. "Girl, you're buying that house, and the owner was fine with handing over the key for your final walkthrough after I told her how much you loved it."

"You aren't worried about Dean, are you? You should've told him you were house-hunting," Mira says, as she has throughout the four-month process with Jane as my realtor. "His dark side's sure to come out when he learns you've been keeping it from him."

Mira believes everyone has a dark side.

"He doesn't have a dark side," I say dismissively. "And if my omission bothers him, I'll fix it."

She rolls her amber-hued eyes. "You can't fix everything, Rowan. And why should you? Some things are meant to be broken."

Well, I just fixed the Queen Mother of all zits, I want to argue but don't. "Nothing will need to be fixed. He's not... like that. Besides, he knows my lease is nearly up. He's been swamped with rehearsals. I didn't want to burden him or make things weird."

"You buying a house shouldn't be weird," Mira says.

"Oh, right. Guys *love* it when the girl they've been dating wants to look at houses together—that would *never* scare him off. We'd only been dating a few months when I started looking... Who knew we'd make it to seven?"

"Not *together*, together. Just... together," Mira clarifies, badly. "If he's scared off by an independent woman, then you don't want him. He's too showy anyway."

"Not showy. Extroverted, as any good theater teacher and actor should be. After the play, I'll take you backstage to his office so you can see his Wall of Fame," I suggest, thinking of the first time I saw the humble display. Dean had explained, *"When I'm not teaching, I work in community theater or as an extra in TV shows and movies. I post my credits here, so kids can see that even average guys like me can follow their dreams."*

Dean's acting dreams have not amounted to much by typical standards. Not yet, anyway. But that makes the photos more endearing. He's played a dead body in a failed Hulu production. In DC's *Swamp Thing*, he played a rowdy bar patron, later edited out, but he met Ian Ziering. *"A super nice guy,"* he said. Dean's played a bum, a sheriff's deputy, a drag queen, a redneck, and a white rabbit sex plushie with devious eyes, all featured on his office wall. When I asked if his students made fun of him—*what teenager could resist teasing a teacher in a sex plushie outfit?*—he admitted, *"Sometimes. But that's when I teach them a great lesson. There are no small parts, only small people."*

My favorite highlight on his Wall of Fame is a photo from his sophomore year in high school. He'd been a miserable teenager so uncomfortable with his weight that he didn't want to be seen, evidenced by his raised hand blocking the camera—a familiar move that makes me rub my scarred hand.

"That wasn't who I was meant to be," Dean explained once, *"so I fought like hell to change. By senior year, I was a hundred pounds lighter and a million times happier."*

This is why I love Dean. He's beautifully honest about his weight loss with his students—and that he's been through something difficult warms me to him more than anything could. He understands struggle; he understands *my* struggle or will someday.

"You'll be impressed," I promise, despite Mira's skepticism. "And after, I'll tell him about the little house. Thanks for letting me borrow the keys, Jane, so I can show it to him after the play. He'll be so surprised. With the deal all but done, he won't feel like this is a trap."

"He should be so lucky." Mira has universal disapproval for the men I date, a strong sisterly vibe often softened by Jane, who tends to be more gracious. Sure, there's a short list of things I don't love about Dean. He doesn't read much. He's allergic to my cat, Edgar Allan Poe. And he treats my scars like a nuclear test site—best to avoid. Still, Dean's a prince compared to others I've dated, and the closest I've come to believing in a Mira-and-Jane happily-ever-after for myself.

Besides, there's so much to love about Dean. He's magnanimous, a bundle of handsome positivity—Rob Lowe meets *Ted Lasso* and Lin-Manuel Miranda (also one of Dean's role models). Dean wants me at his side, regardless of my obvious imperfections. Some people wince at the sight of me, so finding an attractive, decent man who wants me on his arm feels miraculous.

"I'm surprised Dean didn't rope you into being assistant director, Rowan," Jane says.

"Oh, no. *He's* the drama department. He understands that I prefer being behind the scenes."

"Or in a corner." Mira pats the armrests.

"I like the corner." I point to the side door where Julio retrieved me earlier. "There's an easy escape if anyone needs it."

"The play isn't that bad, is it?" Mira chuckles.

The lights blink twice and then dim, quieting us.

The show goes on without a hitch. Not one flubbed line or misstep. Eddie's massive, deflated zit is invisible from the seats, even under the bright lights. Perhaps we should've done *All's Well That Ends Well*, I think, with amusement as the play draws to its lovely conclusion and the audience jumps into a standing ovation.

Jane dabs her tears while Mira squeezes my hand. "Wow, Rowan. Just… wow."

Dean emerges from backstage, his crisp black suit making him look handsome and important. Between charming jokes about wrangling teenagers and trying to keep up with them, he highlights each subset of the production. He mentions our partnership but doesn't make a big deal, as we agreed. Finally, it's the actors. Ashley Morrow and Eddie Speck's double bow receives another standing ovation before they join hands with the remaining cast across the stage.

A deep breath releases my trapped nerves. Soon, we'll enjoy the cafeteria cast party before I show Dean the house I'm buying. My fingers wrap around the beach bum keychain in my dress pocket, imagining how loving and supportive he'll be about me, making my dream of home ownership a reality.

But Dean doesn't end the show as usual.

He frees the microphone and steps around the podium. Behind him, Julio appears, looking worried while holding a gigantic spray of red roses. Ashley and Eddie don devious, giddy grins as they descend stage right.

"What's going on?" Mira's voice cuts through Dean's as he spouts words I can't string together. *Serendipity... companionship... love.*

"I don't know." Panic rises through my disbelief. *Is he...? He can't be.*

"Soon, the play was no longer the thing. She was."

Ah's wave across the audience, bringing hundreds of eyes to me.

"Shit." I sink into my chair, wishing for a black hole, a rabbit hole, or a sinkhole—*anything* so I can disappear. Heat surges through me volcano-like, surely turning my face more hot-pink than usual, especially when he says...

"Rowan Mackey, will you join me up here?"

"You don't have to go." Mira leans in, blocking the crowd. She glances toward the side exit. "Escape door?"

"It's a gorgeous proposal," Jane says.

"It's social blackmail," Mira corrects dryly.

"It's stage fright," Dean laughs it off with the audience. "Rowan, please."

The *please* forces me to my wobbly feet.

Undeserved applause hides my awkward bumbling and whispered curses down the aisle. My game face comes out, locking eyes with Ashley and Eddie, waiting for me at the row's end. I latch on to their extended arms, grateful for the support like I'm Dorothy, linking arms with Scarecrow and Tin Man and about to face the dreaded wizard.

"Don't look so horrified," Eddie whispers. "You can handle anything, Madam Zit Popper."

Only I can't. My heart pounds so violently it might rip itself from my chest. They escort me up stage right, exposing my scarred side to the audience. Dean's gregarious smile falters when he notices his bad staging.

Even worse, this is my personal drama playing center stage with my students and hundreds of people watching! It's against the unsaid rules of teaching to hijack the students' limelight. I don't like attention—Dean *knows* this. I get enough stares already. There is no mental space to be calm or in control—not with my chest tightening, my breath gasping, and my high heels dragging like concrete bricks against the wood floor.

As Ashley and Eddie guide me into place, my eyes meet Dean's, blue and brilliant under the shimmering lights, and for a second, I think it's okay. I imagine a hazy future of us in bed, faces against our pillows, talking before the kids wake up. *That's* the life I want, and I've never been closer to it than *right* now.

The audience coos as Dean takes a knee. Baby Aster cries from the darkened rows behind me. Dean says lovely things, I'm sure, but anxiety pulls me in like a monster gripping my leg underwater, clogging my ears, and preventing my breathing. He asks me to marry him—*he must have*—because everything goes silent, and he holds a ring at my fingertip.

I *know* what I'm meant to say—what I *want* to say. Popping the question should make a girl squeal, hop up and down, and shout her clear *YES* from the hilltops, rooftops, or high school theater stages like it's the only word she knows, especially *this* girl. *YES! A thousand times, yes!*

"Yes. No. Maybe" comes out, like I'm being cattle-prodded to keep changing my answer. *Zip. Zap. Zing.*

Eddie drops the mic positioned at my mouth, causing it to screech. Then, all goes silent like the air's been sucked from the room, and no one breathes.

My eyes fix on Dean's—he looks crushed like a bug underfoot, all the moment's joy squirted out and the ring hanging limply in his fingers.

Fix this! I grab his ring hand, pulling him up. "I mean, yes. Yes! I meant yes!" With a momentary fumble, I slide the ring onto my finger and hold it up to convince the gawking crowd.

"She, um, she said yes." Dean puts on a happy tone like he would a mask, and the crowd plays along, cheering and clapping. But it's clear in his obligatory kiss—I've hurt him.

Two

ROWAN

The sky opens like a busted water balloon on the drive to my little house. Well, not *my* little house, but the one I thought *could* be mine. It's spring on the coast, which doubles storm chances and creates sudden explosions of rain and lightning, as if the sky has anger management issues and can't control itself. But anyone living in Wilmington, North Carolina quickly grows used to weather-related outbursts.

My grip on the steering wheel tightens as a car passes—its headlights highlighting my bare ring finger. *How can I miss something I wore for less than an hour?* Dean's words backstage recycle in my thoughts. "I'm so goddamned embarrassed. I'm heartbroken, Rowan. Seven months together, and... I think... I should go on that trip with my acting buddies. I need to get away, let the smoke clear. Three months of traveling for extra work will do that... I need space."

Space. The word sounded menacing, like a hissing snake. And ridiculously vague like Ross and Rachel and their infamous "break."

"You want *space* over my *one* stupid mistake? I get nervous in crowds. My answer is yes—how many times can I say it? How can I fix this if you aren't here?"

He had no answer. Only he marked us as *to be continued* like a TV show that may or may not get picked up for a new season. I didn't bother telling him about the little house, knowing he'd see it as more evidence of my uncertainty.

The thing is—I *want* to marry Dean. But his proposal shocked me. We'd never discussed marriage, and I've learned not to expect it anyway. One abusive relationship and many horrid first dates have turned the hope of my twenties into jaded resignation in my thirties—some people are meant to be alone. I figured I was one of them.

But my mistake turned his *yes* into a *maybe*, and pulling into the driveway under a curtain of rain, I wonder if it's still possible.

I race to the porch under an umbrella, heels clicking in puddles and hand fumbling for the beach bum keychain. A motion-censored light helps guide the key in the door.

It's muggy inside, as an empty house with closed windows and no AC running should be. I leave my drenched raincoat and umbrella hanging on the door handle and move inside, switching on lights as I go.

Seeing it like this is good—when darkness hides its charm, the heat feels oppressive, and the storm gives it a creepy vibe. Tomorrow, I'll return the key to Jane with a confident, "No, thanks. I've changed my mind."

She'll understand, though Mira won't. I'll stay where I am, extend my lease, and wait for Dean to return, hoping we can buy a house together.

But I *do* love this little house. It reminds me of my favorite picture book, *The Little House* by Virginia Lee Burton. The house in the story looked like a cozy, quaint oasis—the perfect home to retreat to, away from the world. But the world built up around the quiet country house, sending it into disrepair and sadness until the family moved it back to the country where it could be a happy little house again. With Mom in the military, I always wanted a moveable house—something small and cozy that we could take anywhere. This place reminds me of that home, and I long to be the change that makes it happy again.

But Dean's happiness overrules my nostalgia. He'd never want this—too small and too many projects. That's why most people don't want it, according to Jane.

Still, this place ticks all my boxes. We must've looked at a hundred houses before this came on the market. Everything else felt too new, too sterile, too *not me*. The little house hasn't seen new carpet or an appliance upgrade in at least thirty years, but I like that about it—it's a testament to how good things last. It's small with a manageable yard. Close to school. In a quiet, established neighborhood. And oozing with charm and possibilities. There's even a porch swing!

Most importantly, it would be *mine*. Grandpa Ro used to call property ownership the American dream, and sharing it with others made it even better. For him and Betty, that meant foster kids and me when Mom was deployed. *"Renting a tiny apartment is money down the drain,"* he often told me. *"You deserve a real home, Rowan."*

Everyone does, but as an army brat with a single mother who moved twelve times in as many years, his words felt especially true. Mom made our nomadic life the best it could be, but I'm more determined as an adult to be rooted in a place I love. With Mira here and the beach nearby, choosing Wilmington to be my hometown was a no-brainer. Picking this place to be my home felt just as easy.

I plop onto the fireplace's brick hearth, exhaustion mixing with confusion. And sadness. I accidentally broke Dean's heart tonight, and now, mine's breaking, too.

Rain pelts the windows and roof in an angry drumbeat, the sky dumping its frustrations—wish I could do the same. Lightning flashes brightly through the unobstructed windows, and thunder shakes the foundation.

But I scream when a *pound, pound, pound* rattles the front door.

"We know you're in there! Open up!" an angry male voice orders as I rush to the door. "It's the police!"

"Vernon!" a woman chides. "You can't say that!"

Dumbfounded at the entryway, I peer into the hole *hesitantly*. In my first apartment, I went through a mystery phase, during which I deduced that the perfect way to murder someone would be to shoot them through a peephole. It's the efficiency of it, you see—quick with no blood spatter.

Answering doors always incites my anxiety anyway.

A small army of hooded rain jackets and flashlights stand on the other side, one holding a frying pan. But no guns in sight, thankfully.

"Who are you, and what do you want?" I demand, my voice cracking.

"Neighborhood watch, and if you don't open this door, we're calling the police."

So, not the police. I slip out my phone, wondering if I should call them myself. I peep again to see them in a whispered argument, the smaller one waving the frying pan. There are four of them—the two animated ones in front, a tall one with his arms crossed directly behind them like a bouncer, and a fourth, leaning, as if bored, against a porch column. The bouncer steps between the arguers and gently taps on the door.

"Ma'am, this house should be vacant. We saw the lights and grew concerned. If you can alleviate those concerns, we can all go home to bed."

Swinging the door open prompts their flashlights. I twist to the right and raise my left hand to block the beams. Spotlights on my scarred side make me want to shrink away, but I straighten myself and force a smile. *Game face, Rowan.*

"I'm Rowan Mackey. My sister-in-law and real estate agent, Jane Freely, lent me the key for a final walkthrough. I apologize that it's late, but I didn't think anyone would notice... or care if they did."

"Oh, are you putting in an offer?" The one with the frying pan, now lowered, is a woman. And British. But I can't see their faces, for the lights still blinding me and their hoods shadowing them. Her light rolls over my green chiffon dress and wet toes, peeping from my strappy black heels. "Oh, fancy frock. You look lovely, dear!"

"Have you just enjoyed a night on the town?" the man beside her asks conversationally.

The leaning raincoat pushes off the column with urgency, slapping down their flashlights. "This isn't an interrogation. The house is fine. The neighborhood's safe. Criminals don't look like her."

I grimace with offense, assuming he means my scarred face.

"I'll have you know that *some* criminal masterminds dress up," the other man says, finger raised. "This bank robber in the fifties wore a black suit and tie to every robbery. Oh, and a very nice hat. Started a trend, he did."

He meant my clothes. Of course. My shoulders dip with relief—I'm being oversensitive.

"Oh, come now, Jack," the woman says. "What's the harm in a little chat? It might rustle you up some story ideas. What do you do, Rowan?"

"I'm a teacher."

She gasps while the man at her side steps forward. "Teachers are the unsung heroes of society. My mother, God rest her soul, taught for nearly fifty years."

"Vernon, hush."

Lightning flashes, and thunder drowns her next words. With rain spitting into the porch sideways, it seems proper social protocol to say, "Would you like to come in?"

The frying pan lady steps in first. "Rose McGinty." She drops her raincoat at the door, revealing a mop of gray-red curls. "Me and Vernon live across the street."

"It's a great neighborhood," he says, following his wife's lead—raincoat discarded—and moving inside after a firm handshake.

"Tom Goodman. My wife Marcy and I live across the street, diagonally. A pleasure to meet you, Rowan," says the radio-voiced bouncer.

The fourth man, Jack, ducks by me with a grunt, not removing his raincoat or lowering his hood. His gruffness feels like an icy draft through an old castle, sending a shiver through me.

The regular living room light reveals that Rose and Vernon are in their sixties and wearing button-upped pajamas with rain boots. Tom is younger, but his white-gray ponytail suggests not by much. The only thing I discover about Jack is that he's tall and annoyed. He keeps his hood on and lurks near the front door as if desperate to run out of it.

"Forgive our intrusion, dear." Rose sits on the fireplace hearth. "But we thought you might be a vandal or using the place as a sex den."

"Are vandals and sex dens frequent problems in this neighborhood?" I ask, only half-serious.

Rose gasps while Vernon stutters, "What? Oh, goodness. No."

"Relax, Vern. She's only kidding," Tom says.

I stifle a chuckle. "Well, it's good to know you're looking out for the place."

"There's safety in numbers," Vernon says. "When Rose saw the lights—"

"I was up late reading." Her girlish grin makes me wonder what book.

"We called Tom for backup and Jack for muscle," Vernon explains.

"I'm not the muscle." Jack's gruffness sounds less sharp.

"I'm the muscle." Rose holds up her frying pan.

"Right. Jack's got the best knees. He's supposed to run for help," Vernon says.

"You were saying, love? About teaching?" Rose prompts.

"Oh, high school English at Coastal."

"That's Jack's alma mater." She bounces, clapping her frying pan. "A proper English teacher. The neighborhood could use one of those."

"A shrink would be better," Jack mumbles.

Rose waves a dismissive hand. "Don't mind him. Writers can be so irritable."

I'm about to ask him what he writes to forge a connection like I would with a disgruntled student. *The only way to break a bad attitude is to get them talking*, Grandpa Ro used to say.

But Vernon chimes in with, "They don't make 'em like this anymore. Solid." He pounds his fist on the brick above his wife's head as if proving his point. "But I suppose you'll take a sledgehammer to it."

"Gosh, no. I'd pull up the carpet and paint the walls, but no major renovations. I love the old brick and fifties tiles in the bathrooms. I even love the kitchen—the antique gas stove and small fridge. The little green tiles with pictures of fruit remind me of my grandparents' house. They had a kitchen banquette, too—that's where I did my homework when my mom was deployed. It makes the kitchen feel like a retro diner, don't you think? I'd reupholster the cushions probably. I don't know what I'd do with the converted garage yet, but I'm okay with not having one. I have so many books. Maybe I'd use it as a study."

Their mystified stares force my mouth shut. Rose gives Vernon a pleading look before both turn to Jack like they're seeking his approval. He folds his arms over his chest.

"The previous owners, Margot and Ben, turned it into a music room," Vernon explains. "She was a piano teacher. Students came and went nearly every day. In the evenings, they'd open the bay door, Ben'd get on his fiddle, and they'd have mini-concerts. We'd come over with our lawn chairs and listen from the driveway. Those were... good times."

His head droops. I suspect the good times ended not by choice but by a change no one wanted. Grandpa Ro pops to mind, along with a quick montage of friends, neighbors, and houses left behind in moves growing up. "I'm sorry. It must've been hard to say goodbye."

Vernon waves off my sympathies, his gray eyes looking slightly damp. Jack peers out from under his raincoat curtain, letting me see him for the first time. He's younger than I expect, given his cohorts. Dark hair brushes pinched brown eyes that are more thoughtful than menacing and bookended by fine laugh lines he'll one day call wrinkles. But not yet, even though his face seems permanently fixed in a scowl. Heathcliff meets Rochester meets Severus Snape. His inexplicable contempt drips off him like the raindrops on his coat. *Who wants to live next to that?*

"Ben and Margot loved this place," Rose coos. "Lived here fifty years. Raised Corey here. He—"

"Don't go there," Jack warns sternly.

Rose winces and rethinks. "I was going to say that they used to have living room campouts with their grand-babies and read to them until they fell asleep."

Vernon chuckles. "They called it *The Little House*, you know, after that picture book."

My hand covers my mouth, like surprised women in old books overcome by emotion (and super tight corsets). *Gosh, Rowan, what's next? Will you faint?*

"Oh, you know it?" Rose perks up. "That's an old one."

"Well, books are her business, being an English teacher," Vernon laughs. "Right, Jack?"

He groans while I say, "Mom used to read it to me. It's what I call this place, too. *The Little House.* Growing up, I wanted a house I could take with me. We moved so often that home felt like a shapeshifter. As soon as we settled into one, we traded it for another. Gosh, I'm sorry. I just love that book."

Tom steps forward with hippie-like authority. "Well, if that's not a sign, I don't know what is."

Now, I stare, a little baffled. Identifying with this house the same way its previous owners did strengthens my connection to it, especially when Rose fumbles around the built-in bookshelf and pulls a worn copy of *The Little House* from the cabinet.

"See, love? Margot left it behind for the new owner."

She hands it to me, and in a room full of strangers, I hug the book that made me want this house in the first place.

A bit breathless, I manage, "But I don't believe in signs." Lightning and then thunder join my declaration, making my shoulders tense.

"*Everyone* knows that book," Jack says sharply. "It's not a sign. It's a damn coincidence. Can we go home now?"

"Don't mind him. He's always like this when he's not writing, and this house is special," Rose whispers, though he still hears her. He cuts her a narrow-eyed look of warning. "So, how soon can you move in? ...You *are* moving in, right?"

"I love this house. It's totally me. And you're lovely people. *Mostly.* But it's been one of those surprising, exhausting, exhilarating, and confusing days that changes everything."

"Oh, do tell, pet," Rose implores sweetly. Jack's face twists again like he's about to scold her.

To cut him off, I say, "I botched my boyfriend's surprising public proposal by blurting *yes, no, maybe,* before saying a definite *yes,* and now he's asking for space. *Space?* Like I'm a helicopter girlfriend or a child hanging onto his leg—an irony because I'm not needy."

Jack huffs. "All women are needy."

I square my shoulders. "Ha, with that narrow-minded attitude, I bet you're single."

Rose, Vernon, and Tom laugh.

"He's as single as the day is long," Vernon confirms.

"Do go on, Rowan. This is stimulating," Rose says.

"A *needy* woman wouldn't buy a house without telling her boyfriend, which I *almost* did. He doesn't even know I was house hunting. I didn't want him to feel trapped or obligated to share the responsibility. But leave it to me to get engaged and nearly broken up with on the same night, not that anyone would ever predict the former, least of all me." I motion casually to my face.

"Why not, hon?" Rose asks, looking straight at me.

I smile like she could be my new best friend, though I wonder about her eyesight. "I don't get many dates. Not that I'm complaining."

She looks confused while the others stay silent.

"Anyway, he's leaving for three months to pursue his acting dreams—he's an actor, well, and a teacher. Hopefully, when he returns, we'll pick up where we left off, as if my verbal hiccup didn't happen. Buying a house without him would hurt my chances of convincing him that I mean *yes.* So, this won't work for me anymore."

"Eh, if you love something enough, you find a way to make it work." She pats my hand as she says it—a trick I pull with distracted students when I see them daydreaming—and it works on me, too. I love Dean enough to make us work, and I love this house enough to wonder if it might fit into that equation. *Could it?*

Vernon steps closer, locking eyes with sternness. "Think of your children, Rowan, and the school district."

A laugh surfaces at his strong conviction—though he's right about the district, *my* district. It's the best in the area. "You'll have other buyers, ones who have children. Maybe even a shrink or a nice... podiatrist or something." I don't know why I said podiatrist, but they graciously overlook it—except Jack, who looks almost amused.

"Oh, people with children don't want the place," Rose says. "Too small, they say."

"Too much work," moans Vernon.

"No garage," Tom adds.

"If it doesn't sell soon, Margot'll resort to renters." Rose whispers *renters* like it's a bad word.

"We *renters* aren't all bad," I say.

"I'll buy the place," Jack huffs. "Can we go home now?"

Rose leans in. "See how he is? Complains the whole time when he could've popped off as soon as we knew you weren't an ax murderer. He's not that bad once you get to know him." Rose turns to him and sternly says, "Devin and Corey would approve. She's delightful and honest and hardly wants to change the place. What more do you want, Jack?"

He stiffens bitterly before heading for the door.

"We should go, too," Tom says. "Thanks for indulging us, Rowan."

"Oh, yes, and if it helps, we have no homeowner's association fees and are within walking distance of the cross-city trail. Do you bike or jog?"

"Let's go, Vernon." Rose pushes him to the front door.

I follow behind, anxious for home now that the rain's let up and ready to put this day and the little house behind me.

Rose flashes a demure smile on her soft, pink face as we exit. "This doesn't happen every day, you know."

My head cocks, wondering what she means.

"Falling in love with a house," she grins. "Saying yes should be easy."

Three

JACK

I know that woman. Rephrase—I don't *know* her. I've *seen* her.

I cut across the yard through the rain as the memory replays.

Two years ago. I sat in the corner booth at George's Bistro, taking advantage of the restaurant's busy Saturday night vibe to stoke my writing. Sometimes hearing conversations, music, and clinking dishes makes my fingers fly, not that I needed the help *then*. Back then, I had no problem filling pages. I was three-quarters done with *The Other Us*, coming out this summer, and two deadlines ahead with my agent. The damn book had practically written itself—I just needed one more pivotal scene to finish it.

So, three hours and three beers in, my laptop on the table, I'd written all around the scene, even finished the epilogue. My readers love epilogues. But the scene proved elusive—I couldn't get the feeling right. I needed heartache and agony, the novel's lowest point, but it came out as mildly upsetting. Not good enough.

I closed my laptop and asked for the bill.

That's when I saw her.

She sat alone at a two-seater table in the middle of the crowded dining room, back to me. She had dark Cleopatra hair and legs I'd love to wrap myself in, long and athletic. They were crossed under the table and leaning sideways, her heels resting together. Her silky green dress dangled off the sides of her chair, revealing more thigh than she probably realized, and her toned arms begged for fingers to run up and down them. She had a sexy air of confidence, even from behind. A jealous pang ripped through me toward the guy she was meeting—and she was definitely waiting for her date. The cliched rose on the table was a dead giveaway for a first meeting.

Is this what love's been reduced to, I remember thinking. Padded online profiles and awkward meetings with trite red roses? Real romance is dead. Before long, it'll come down to an algorithm—love will be a science, not a head-spinning, heart-racing adventure. Even the best romance novels like mine will become archaic fantasies, crowding clearance bins.

The waitress brought my bill, but I ordered another drink, much to her disappointment. A lone guy hogging the best booth—I understood her frustration.

But I tip well.

Cleopatra adjusted the rose for the fifth time, sipped her wine, and then realigned her silverware. Mostly, she fiddled with an emerald scarf around her neck—the only thing about her look that didn't fit. Scarves are for winter and old ladies. On sexy women, it's just another annoying thing to take off. Unless that's all she's wearing... No, still annoying.

A man approached, his gray eyes fixed on the rose before landing on her. He looked like a former frat guy with a trust fund, daddy's lawyer on retainer, and a dead body buried in his backyard. I imagined his rich mother drunkenly waving a martini around and saying, "Boys will be boys," when confronted about her son's behavior *again*. I laughed, opening my laptop. He'd make a fun villain—a piece of shit I could drag through fictitious mud and have readers cheering for his demise by the end.

An ass-beating in an alley?

A flesh-eating virus? That starts on his dick?

Or should he suffer a long, mental manipulation?

So many choices...

It's my universal truth in writing—see things, ask what if, write it down. From the tiniest, inconsequential detail to the most meaningful and profound moments, my experiences are reflected in my stories like warped funhouse mirrors of what-ifs. I couldn't separate the two if I tried—that's how creativity works. Or at least, that's how it used to work.

Another universal truth of writers—fucking writer's block. But that came later...

At her table, an awkward beat passed. I knew the date would fail—he wasn't good enough for her. I've always been an expert at people-watching and making predictions. I expected him to sit, thankful his hot date wasn't a lying ogre, and spend the next hour talking about himself between chewing an expensive steak, mouth open, before she politely told him her version of *this-isn't-going-to-work-out*.

But he never sat down.

He gawked, wide-eyed, nearly laughing as he took her in. *What the hell?* Words were exchanged before he shook his head, gave her a dismissive wave, and left.

Cleopatra's shoulders sunk a fraction but rose again with a deep breath. She stopped the waitress delivering my drink, dropped the flower on her tray, and pointed to the menu, determined to enjoy a good meal despite the dickhead. *Atta girl.*

The waitress delivered my beer, and I motioned toward the woman's table. "What happened there?"

"He didn't like her face."

Her face? A quick trip to the bathroom solved that mystery, but initially, I didn't see her scars—just a poised, well-dressed woman with electric blue eyes that stood out next to her dark hair like stars at night. When I passed her table, she glanced up and even smiled. Not a desperate *please-save-me-from-these-assholes* smile but one of polite resignation. *This-is-my-life-and-I'm-getting-a-good-meal-out-of-it.*

Her scars caught my attention like an afterthought. I looked twice—I can't believe I did a double-take like an asshole. Her eyes rolled slightly as she turned away, and I crept by her table, mapping out her scars. They started on her left cheek and disappeared into the scarf around her neck—ah, camouflage.

While I'd never pull a dick move like her asshole date, I understood his vanishing act. That guy wanted a quick lay or a potential trophy wife. Maybe both. But she's neither—whatever happened to her can't be ignored. For some, scars are off-putting, as are the stories that come with them. Guys don't want drama or imperfections. They want an unrealistic ideal propagandized by TV, magazines, music videos, and movies. Everyone wants Taylor Swift, but the truth is only the top one percent of men could or *should* be contenders. And *never* a guy like that.

At least he didn't waste anyone's time.

Still, I felt bad for her. The guy was no loss, but that twenty-second encounter must've added another jagged tear to her inner agony. I tried to imagine that rejection—conjuring feelings I'd never understand but wanted to capture anyway.

I wrangled the psychological jabs inflicted—her hope dashed in a glance, and then her dignity trampled by his cold amusement. How could she sit there? And eat dinner in defeated solitude? No anger. No tears. No desperate race to the door. Nothing.

Her fake indifference intrigued me. Tormented by an injury she can't hide and the trauma of whatever happened to her, life's slings and arrows had built her an impressive shield. But her cold demeanor was bullshit, too.

"She screams on the inside," I said, typing ideas as they flooded me. Under the right conditions, with the right person, her iron defenses would crumble.

That's what I needed for *The Other Us*—screaming on the inside. And the right conditions for my characters to break down. It played out in my head in all its heart-wrecking glory. My fingers twitched across the keyboard.

My waitress returned, eyeing my half-gone beer with annoyance. "Get you anything else? Food?"

"What wine is she having?" I motioned toward the woman's table.

"The house merlot. Want me to ask if you can join her? I don't mind." Her eyes lit up at the prospect of freeing the booth. "She'd probably like the company."

"She's been screwed over enough already. I'll take my bill and hers—add a bottle of your expensive merlot and your best dessert. Don't tell her it's been paid until I leave, and don't tell her who paid it. Just that it *wasn't* the prick."

At home that night, I wrote my best scene yet, finishing *The Other Us*.

But nothing since. Days later, my neighbor, Ben, keeled over in my driveway, grabbing me and his chest at the same time and soon becoming the second guy to die in my arms, and only yards away from the first. I'd known Ben all my life. He'd been a second father to me and my brother Devin. Now, they're both gone, taken out in a sentence when there should've been many more chapters ahead. Fucking unfair.

I duck inside my house, shedding my raincoat at the door. I promised Tom that I wouldn't interfere with selling the little house. An empty house isn't good for anyone's property value, and buying it myself would've turned it into a shrine. Still, I ignore Tom's hippie-dippy nonsense most days, but he has a strange point—as long as that house has been empty, I haven't written a damn thing.

Not a chapter.

Not a paragraph.

Hell, I couldn't even pen an anonymous *Yelp* review for the dudes I hired to power-wash the deck. And they did a fantastic job!

I am ridiculously blocked. Rephrase—I am utterly fucked.

So, Tom might be right—a new neighbor might spark ideas. But I don't care—I hate it anyway. That's Ben and Margot's place... and Corey's. He's the reason my brother Devin spent as much time there as he did in our house.

He'd say I'm being a prick right now, that change is good. But not when it's a change you didn't want.

Hell, Devin would probably even argue for *her* specifically—he understood damaged goods. He'd compare her to the moon—cratered and marked but still beautiful.

There *is* something about her.

Not that it matters. If she moves in, she'll be off-limits. I can't have a casual fling with the girl next door—it's too close to home. She's probably too Hallmark-channel to hook up or be cool about joining the rotation.

"You're not cool about your hookup rotation." I hear Devin's voice as if he's standing next to me.

"I've curated a list of beautiful, attachment-free hookups—that's every guy's dream," I argue, but it's half-hearted. If Devin existed, he'd see right through me.

Especially as I retreat inside my dark, quiet house—the same house we grew up in.

And grab my half-empty glass of whiskey...

And stare at the blank notebook left open on the counter.

I imagine him flashing his dopey grin while shaking his head. "Sadness has made you numb. That's why you can't write about love anymore. Love is the best part about living, and you keep yourself from both."

I toast the air. Devin is still annoying, even in my subconscious. He's wrong—I don't *keep* myself from anything. I've spent time with amazing, accomplished, gorgeous women, but I've never found that sweet spot of connection I write about in my books. Not even close. Maybe I am numb. But love isn't for everyone.

Besides, I appreciate the beautiful, agonizing irony of it. I can write love but can't have it.

At least, I *used* to write love. Now, I can't do anything.

A new neighbor will only heighten my frustrations. No matter what she says, she'll make changes and slowly erase all the home's beautiful history, like heavy paint rolled over smudged handprints on walls. Margot, Ben, Corey, and... Devin will be blotted out by a few trips to Lowe's and Ikea.

The idea of her—of *anyone* moving in next door—makes me bristle. I pour another drink. With any luck, her latest asshole will get that ring on her finger and keep her away from me and our close-knit corner.

Four

ROWAN

"It's a great house, Rowan. A *really* great house." Mira twists in the passenger seat of the fifteen-foot U-Haul as I back into the driveway. "A much better investment than marrying Dean."

"I'm still going to marry Dean." A low-hanging tree branch scrapes the roof as I park. "I'll make this place so homey and comfortable that he can't help but move in when he comes back. Besides, we discussed it at length. If he needs three months away to feel better about us, I told him I need this. He's pursuing his dream, and so am I."

"Sounds like you both *dream* of being apart."

"No, we're independent together," I say, using his words. "Our autonomy has been the best part of Dean and me. He's the first man I've dated who hasn't thought of me as *Silly Putty* meant to shape-shift around his life."

Mira scoffs. "Sounds like two separate lives to me. Are you still engaged? Because I don't see a ring."

"We are... together. That's all that matters. Please, don't give me that look."

"What? There's no look!" she defends futilely. "I'm freaking ecstatic that you bought the little house!"

"But?"

"But..." Her light brown eyes fix on mine. "I don't think he's coming back, Rowan. And you shouldn't take him back if he does."

I suppose saying what you think is a universal truth of sisters because that's what Mira has done since she became my grandparents' foster the same summer I moved in with them, too. It was Mom's first deployment after I incurred my injuries, and despite my grandparents' best efforts, I would've been miserable if not for Mira. We've called each other sisters ever since.

Still, sometimes, using a gentler friend filter on her remarks would be appreciated. I force a smile. "Well, lucky for us, what you think doesn't dictate what will happen. This is just a temporary separation before permanent coupling. You'll see."

Along the street, my students park in front of the house. We slide out of the U-Haul and meet them on the driveway.

"Now, for the fun part," I say, eyes wide with new-home-owner giddiness.

"The fun part was seeing you drive this tank. You look like a twelve-year-old behind the wheel, especially in those overalls," Eddie Speck says, snapping a picture.

I look down at my faded jean overalls, cuffed at the ankles, white t-shirt, and white and black Adidas, and second-guess my moving-in outfit.

"Madam truck driver *and* insane organizer," Ashley Morrow adds with a slight valley-girl twang. She holds up my clipboard, which contains a list of all my furniture and boxes, color-coded by rooms. Green for kitchen (to match the tiles). Yellow for bedroom. And so on. "This is why I'll never be a teacher—I'm not organized enough. Well, and the money."

I sigh, unable to argue. Behind us, another carload of generous teenagers with nothing to do on a Saturday pulls in, bringing extra hands, and Edgar Allan Poe, my long-haired black cat, looking stressed in his carrier.

He meows frantically when we lock eyes as if saying, "You let me ride with *them*?"

Mia Danvers hands him over with a short smile. "I don't think Edgar likes car rides, Ms. Mackey."

"Thanks for letting him tag along. And thanks to everyone for volunteering to help. It's much more fun doing this with you than movers."

"Cheaper, too," Julio says, grinning.

"Much cheaper, but I've got a cooler full of sodas, snacks, and pizza on the way." My teaching career has taught me that students are more willing to work when pizza's involved. Hoots and claps precede the students jumping to action. The truck door rolls open with a screeching slap. Ashley supervises them into an assembly line to start unloading.

Julio grabs a box labeled Edgar's supplies and follows me inside. The small laundry room offers a quiet space for Edgar to hang out away from the chaos. Julio helps me arrange his litter box, water, food, and a plush bed.

His forehead creases with soft lines. "My grandfather says that if you're unsure about your answer, then maybe it's the wrong question."

An internal sigh slumps my shoulders. Nearly a month's gone by since the proposal, and no one but Dean has mentioned my *yes, no, maybe* answer. Not to me, anyway. It was all anyone could talk about after it happened. Dean and I surfed the gossip wave professionally, but it created more tension at school and between us.

"I'm sure about my answer now. At the time, I was nervous."

"Mr. Maddix told us his plan before the show. I should've warned you."

"But it was meant to be a surprise. No need to worry. He asked the right question. I messed up my answer, but I fixed it—I am fixing it."

Julio seems unconvinced but nods anyway. "And next year's Inspiration Project? Will we team up with Mr. Maddix again?"

The second-most talked-about thing at Coastal High School has been me and Dean's joint Inspiration Project. Dr. Evelyn Tate took full credit for our play's success and doubled the pressure on us for next year. Curious students like Julio added more pressure. As their AP English teacher for their junior and senior years, I needed an even better plan than our Shakespeare reboot to meet their high expectations.

"Um, no. He's teaming up with the history department for a *Hamilton*-style musical," I report, trying to sound excited. "I'll go solo this year, but I don't have a plan yet."

His eyes widen in shock. "You without a plan? That's a first."

I release Edgar as we hear a loud "Ms. Mackey!"

Clipboard in hand, Ashley awaits me outside the laundry room. "The guest bathroom toilet won't flush. Guests have arrived, and a cute, old couple is wandering around with a bottle of wine."

As she speaks, I slide the clipboard away from her and retrieve my laminated sign. *Keep closed. Cat inside.* I affix it to the laundry room door with Scotch tape in my pocket. Then, remembering what my mom advised last night over FaceTime, I take one thing at a time.

The toilet handle hangs loose in the pink-tiled bathroom. The chain has broken, which means a trip to Lowe's. I create a new sign. *Out of Order.*

In the backyard, Mira's kids take turns on the rope swing dangling from a blooming magnolia tree. Jane watches with baby Aster in her arms while Mira nudges my shoulder.

"Grandpa Ro would love this house. I can almost see him here, lugging his toolbox and looking for things to fix."

I laugh. "Me, too. I already have a bum toilet, so he'd have his first assignment."

"Well, how 'about me? Where do you want me?"

"Don't forget me," Kenan says, leaving the swing to his sisters.

"Technology setup?"

Kenan salutes, and we head through the sliding glass doors to the living room. We stop short at the small, stunned crowd gathered around the fireplace, including Rose and Vernon McGinty from across the street.

"What's wrong?"

"Shh. Listen," Julio says.

Scratching follows gentle cries and rustling from inside the brick fireplace.

Vernon sits on the hearth and leans inside the opening with a flashlight, as if he always carries one in his pocket. "Yep, you've got some unexpected roommates up there. Raccoons probably. Sounds like the mamma's made a nest on the damper."

Rose shimmies over, holding out the bottle of wine. "Welcome to the neighborhood, dear."

"Thanks," I say unsurely.

With an ashy smudge on his forehead, Vernon pulls out of the fireplace. "Alright, which of you young lads wants to hop on the roof for a look-see?"

"None of them. I can't let them do that," I say quickly, imagining broken legs and angry parents.

"I'd do it myself, but my knees won't let me," Vernon says.

"Let's call Jack," Rose says excitedly.

"No need. I'll handle it myself." My words bust out with more confidence than I have, but the last thing I want is to be indebted to the grumpy guy next door.

"Who's Jack?" Mira cuts in.

"Jack Graham. The author," Rose coos. "He lives next door."

"The romance author?" Mira gushes. "Rowan, you didn't tell me you were moving in next to a celebrity. Jane reads all his books."

"I don't." Still, I know his name. Jack Graham's edgy romances made front displays in *every* bookstore alongside the latest by Stephen King, James Patterson, and Colleen Hoover. He's not just an author but a bestselling one. It's a shock that he'd live in this modest neighborhood. "I don't read romance, classics excluded."

Rose looks offended, as if I've shunned her homeland. "But it... can't be true."

"Rowan's too jaded for romance," Mira says, "but it's only because she hasn't found her soulmate yet."

I groan. "There's no point in calling a romance writer to deal with critters in my chimney. I'll call someone... a professional."

"Hello?" Tom, the gray ponytail from across the street diagonally, enters from the hall, carrying a mason jar filled with something red and accompanied by a petite, sandy-haired woman ten years younger and a foot shorter than he is. "Oh, there you are, Rowan. Welcome to the little house."

They shake my hand, and his wife says, "I'm Marcy Goodman. Nice to finally meet you."

"Likewise. Please excuse my mess." I introduce Mira and my students as they go by.

Tom hands over the mason jar. "It's homemade BBQ sauce."

"Thanks. How thoughtful." I set the wine and sauce on the kitchen table behind us as Tom and Marcy list ways to use it.

"Best on grilled meat, though," Tom decides, finally.

When scratching and crying interrupt our pleasantries, Vernon points to the fireplace, informing Tom, "Critters."

"Shall I get on the roof and check it out?" Tom asks.

"No, thanks. I'll call a professional. I wouldn't want one of my kind neighbors falling off the roof... not on my first day."

I laugh, but the rest aren't amused.

An awkward silence falls over us. I'm a bit befuddled about what to do with them. *Offer them something? Make conversation? Put them to work?* It feels strange to play hostess on move-in day.

"It has happened once or twice," Vernon says, breaking the silence.

"What has?" I ask.

"Neighbors falling off roofs," he says as if it's obvious.

The chimney noises kick up to a frenzy, spiking my nerves. To have baby creatures die in one's new fireplace on the first day seems a terrible start to home ownership. I half-wonder if I'll be cursed thereafter, and a weird story of a vengeful clan of raccoons wreaking havoc on me plays out in a mental movie.

Under her reddish-gray curls, Rose zeroes in on me like she's trying to read my mind. "Got any tea, love?" She loops her arm in mine.

"Um, yes," I sputter as she steers me toward the kitchen.

As I'm escorted away, Mira says, "I'll ask Jane who to call for the chimney. She'll have a guy for that."

"Make yourselves at home," I call to the others, but they've already moved on to Kenan and my entertainment system.

Rose sets me in the white and sage banquette as if I don't have a million things to do. *One thing at a time.* Mom's words recycle through my thoughts, and I realize I *always* have a million things to do—moving-in day or not—and they'll get done regardless of tea breaks. Rose rummages freely through my labeled boxes, finding what she wants quickly.

"Ah, ginger tea." Rose sorts through my small collection. "Soothing and good for the tummy." She fills the kettle from the same box and heats it over the stove. Grabbing mugs from the MUGS box, she says, "Trash and recycling day is Thursday. We do a caravan to church on Sunday and beach outings. I'll need your email for our weekly newsletter and your number for text alerts."

She slips me her phone. "Add yourself as a contact... And, oh, Jack'll be by later to talk about the tree."

Her side glance tells me this is her main tidbit of information, and it comes across like a warning. "What tree?"

She motions to the backyard through the window. Thick hedges separate our properties, flat-topped as if he keeps them at head height but wild on my side, in desperate need of trimming. In the far back corner, a large pine tree caps off the hedges like a bookend and stretches tall with billowing needle branches cresting its peak.

"It's on both your properties, and he's anxious to get it taken down," Rose explains, fixing our teas with sugar and cream without asking. "If he shows up, go easy on him, love. It's been hard on him—"

Blaring music interrupts, luring me to the backyard to uncover the culprit. "Just Don't Give a Fuck" by Eminem blares from next door and is joined by laughter, splashing, clinking bottles, and basketball thumps against the concrete.

Mira edges between Rose and me as we peek over the shrubbery. With its extended deck, pool, mini-basketball court, bar, and outdoor kitchen, it isn't a backyard but a party zone. Men in various states of thirty, some with the start of dad-bods and receding hairlines, drink beers and comment on the inflatable big screen airing a baseball game.

"Oh, yeah, he seems very broken up about it," I huff sarcastically.

Rose shrugs. "We all have different ways of coping, love."

"Holy shit, is that him?" Mira gapes through the bushes with enlarged eyes and a devious laugh.

"He's the hottie with the tatts, dear," Rose confirms.

I peer closer and see Jack sitting on the pool's edge. Wild, thick-lined, colorful tattoos pull my stare into his chest and arms. The diamond cuts of his arms, shoulders, and ab muscles ripple like the water's surface dancing around his legs. He is cologne-model attractive—like he should be shirtless next to a horse in a black-and-white photo advertising a scent called *Man* or *Muscle*. More surprisingly, he's smiling—a crooked, playful thing that looks almost easygoing and inviting—unlike the brooder I met on proposal night.

"Rowan, send Dean a picture of that guy and say you've moved on," Mira chuckles.

I scoff. "Dean doesn't need to worry, especially not over a guy like that."

As soon as the words fall out, I want to suck them back in, especially when Mira's coy grin transforms into a scolding stare-down. "Why *not* a guy like that?"

This is an argument we have often—Mira gets upset with me for knowing *from experience* that men like him don't look twice at a woman like me (not in a good way), while she argues that I'm gorgeous and shouldn't settle or sell myself short. Then, I argue that the last semi-hot guy I dated before Dean ended up being an obsessive psycho, so looks aren't a good indication of anything. She counters by bringing it back to Dean and our perfectly fine, but, yes, *slightly* routine sex life. *Sex shouldn't be like getting an oil change, Rowan—it should be better than maintenance.* To which, I protest that regular oil changes are key to the health and longevity of a vehicle. And certainly better than never getting my oil changed at all.

We argue like this at least once a season, sometimes more if dating is a hot topic of conversation.

For now, our back and forth comes across in our stare—no words necessary.

From the outside looking in, I understand what *she thinks* she sees. Her decade-long relationship with Jane has been a passionate one. They are the sweetest, closest couple I know, cute to the point of annoying, especially since they think everyone else should be like them. Even half of what they have is more than enough for me. And in ten years, Dean and I will undoubtedly grow into each other as they have.

But there's no use trying to convince her what time will surely prove.

She points across the hedge. "A guy like that knows how to curl a woman's toes—you need some toe-curling."

Rose giggles, giving Mira's shoulder a gentle bop. "I like you. You're saucy."

They share devious smiles, like they're kindred spirits.

Turning to Rose, I wince. "Please tell me I haven't moved beside a man-baby who parties all the time."

Rose's slight brow pinches. "Well, I wouldn't say man-baby."

My shoulders slump at her unwillingness to negate the partying.

Five

ROWAN

Honking wakes me. Obnoxious, lay-on-the-horn honking. When it doesn't stop after a solid minute of burying my head in my pillow, I jolt from bed, surging with angry energy.

It's Sunday—the only morning I let myself sleep past seven. I need the rest. A monster list of to-dos has swallowed the week. Ripping up carpets, scrubbing the endless grout, painting the walls (white in the bathrooms and sage everywhere else to match the kitchen tiles), and finally organizing and arranging—I expected these.

But another monster of must-dos snuck in with the unexpected. Jane's contact transplanted the raccoon family, cleaned the chimney, and fixed the upper cap to prevent more settlers, punching an unexpected, six-hundred-dollar hit to my bank account.

Then, the dryer conked out, the AC unit's motor died, and a toilet leak in the guest bathroom required a plumber. The latter resulted in an awkward encounter with a brutish man who smelled of beer and cheese and visibly shuddered at the sight of me. Two-hundred-fifty to him, $700 to Best Buy, and another thousand for the motor replacement, and my savings reflected my energy level—drained.

As is my tolerance for deliberate honking before eight on a Sunday morning.

My front door swings open with the force of my annoyance and sends waves across my nightgown. Yes, that's when I realize—*I'm standing outside in my nightgown.*

The offender locks eyes with me from across the lawn, where he sits smugly in the driver's side of an older model white van like a pedophile looking for targets. He honks the horn again, smirking at me as he presses it. With my arms folded across my skimpy tank gown, I trudge barefoot through the high grass, determined not to retreat now that I've been spotted.

The window rolls down at my approach.

"Jack Graham... why are you honking?"

He motions behind him, where the back seats are nearly full of senior citizens.

Rose bats her blue-gray eyes at me. "Didn't you get my emails? It's the church party bus. Want to join us?"

Their newsletter, *Daisy Chain, Connecting Our Streets Since 1997,* had reached my inbox—seventy-seven back issues and counting. It's named for our street, Daisy Lane, not the slang term, thank God, although a sex den was mentioned when we first met, so who knows? The headlines, often shorthanded with emojis, boast merit badges, honor rolls, church concerts, medical appointments, and proper lawn maintenance. I've only skimmed a few issues.

Spotting my ignorance, Rose giggles. "A teacher who doesn't like homework, aye?"

I deflate like an undone balloon gone flaccid, anger gone, and embarrassment taking over. "You drive the church bus?"

"Keen observation, Miss Marple." A snide look accompanies his jab. *He thinks I'm an old busybody.* "Hop on. You'll give the preachers plenty to sermonize about in that get-up."

His brown eyes burrow into mine, daring me for a rebuttal that doesn't come.

"Sorry, Jack. Forgot my readers." Vernon climbs into the open door on the right side.

"Oh, do come, Rowan. It's such fun." Rose claps.

"No!" My brain floods with excuses as if I need any, and these compile awkwardly into, "Shoes... clothes... sleep... Just go."

I step back, and Jack gives me a shameless once-over. Legs, hips, chest—bra-less, of course. I feel like a cut of meat ogled by a hungry wolf. But his amusement vanishes at my scars, though he slowly studies them, too. He glances at the little house behind me before peeling away.

My face falls into my hands, and I wish I could erase the last five minutes. Better yet—that I could erase buying this place at all for how it has zapped my energy, drained my money, and put me in *that* man's periphery.

This is not my first awkward encounter with Jack Graham. It's not even the first time he's woken me up.

Often, I hear him late at night, playing music, moving around his deck, splashing in his pool, or taking shots on his driveway basketball court. Once, when this happened at 3:30 in the morning, I slipped outside and peeked over the hedges, thinking something must be amiss. No one in his right mind would be gallivanting at this hour.

But there he was, half in the pool, hovering over a composition notebook that was surely getting wet as he scribbled into it. Beside him, a glass of brown liquid served as inspiration. Before long, he tossed the notebook aside, downed his drink, and dove under. I seized the moment to scratch my leg—something was biting me—and when I looked again, he stared in my direction. I ducked and back-stepped, nearly tripping over an unruly garden bed, and then dashed inside, hoping he hadn't *really* seen me.

But he did. The Miss Marple remark surely confirms it.

One morning, returning from a run, I slowed outside his house and wit-nessed him escorting a gorgeous brunette to her car between groping and kissing her. It was the second woman I'd seen him with that week. His eyes met mine over her shoulder, and he tossed me a wave, as if boasting about his virility.

The worst encounter, though, was Friday night. Returning from Mira's around ten, I pulled up behind five unsteady bicyclists, balancing beers on their handlebars and taking up the entire road. It took a short honk for them to notice me, even though I drive a convertible 1977 VW Bug that anyone sober would hear coming a mile away. Clumsily, they made room for me to pass, and one said, "Dude, is that your new neighbor?"

Jack snorted with derision. "Unfortunately. Wish I'd bought the damn place myself."

"Why? She's pretty."

"She's pretty fucking annoying."

"Bet you still bed her," another man prodded, bringing the rest into a howl of laughter.

"Hard pass," I muttered at the same time Jack said, "Hell no."

I sped away, leaving them in a plume of old car exhaust, which wasn't nearly satisfying enough.

Over tea one afternoon, Rose shared that Jack's house is where he grew up. After his first bestseller, he bought it from his parents and moved them to a swanky place on the water. He's been renovating and tweaking it since. Contractors show up almost daily for estimates or upgrades. The house—the biggest on the block—is an ashen brick two-story colonial that looks regal (and normal) from the front while being a full-on man-cave in the back. It's the house version of a mullet haircut.

Despite his partying, playboy, asshole persona, he's a meticulous homeowner. He keeps no discernible life or work schedule, but I see him daily hunting for weeds in his professionally groomed flower beds, sweeping cobwebs from his front porch, or cleaning his pool. Once, I spied a long branch emerging from the top of the hedge on his side, and by the day's end, he'd trimmed it.

And the neighborhood *adores* him, as evident in the emoji and GIF-covered pages of the *Daisy Chain* back issues I peruse over coffee. "Jack's Writing Block

Holds at Five Months"... "Six"... "Ten"... "Jack Tells Reporter in Neighborhood to 'F@#k Off' Refuses Interviews & Appearances"... "Jack Saves Motherless Opossum" (with picture)... "Jack's Release Party for *The Other Us* Planned for August."

Though two months away, his upcoming black tie release party headlines every recent newsletter alongside media buzz about the book. Less exciting are the smaller articles on the neighborhood's annual Fourth of July oyster roast. Though I like that the neighborhood celebrates together, it's disconcerting that it's Jack they celebrate most.

In the most recent edition, I find a small corner about me under the headline "Our Charming New Neighbor, Rowan." The couple shares how I fell in love with the place based on the book *The Little House*, and how Margot, who now resides with her son Corey and his husband in Asheville, teared up with the story and called my new ownership, "Meant to be."

Rose also elaborated that I'm "a proper English teacher with a snazzy wardrobe, a black cat named Edgar, and *perhaps* a fiancé on an acting hiatus, from which he might return at the end of summer (Rowan's sister, Mira has doubts)." *Puzzled emoji followed by the shocked face of Kevin McAllister when he applies aftershave*

I groan.

Another email snatches my attention—Dr. Evelyn Tate requests an appointment to discuss my Inspiration Project.

I don't know which bothers me more—my nonexistent Inspiration Project or my absent boyfriend.

I need a beach day.

It's my favorite thing to do—spend the day at the beach with a book. I contemplate my library, wondering which classic might spark an idea for my Inspiration Project. But my brain feels dried up like a desert with tumbleweeds rolling over it—completely uninspired.

A text from Mira interrupts. *Hey, free around lunch? I'll bring over wine and subs. I have a favor to ask.*

Mira would understand if I said no. But she rarely asks for favors, and whatever it is takes priority over me getting my beach on.

Sure. See you then!

So when my doorbell rings just before lunch, I expect Mira on the other side. My smile falls into surprise and, quickly, disappointment at Jack Graham shadowing my doorway.

He thrusts a bottle of whiskey toward me and says, in a dry, robotic voice, "Welcome to the neighborhood."

He glances behind him, pulling my attention to Vernon and Rose staring at us through their living room window. Quickly, they turn their heads upwards. Rose even points to an imaginary thing to look at as if she can hide their obvious nosiness.

I burst into a laugh. "They're the absolute worst spies... I assume they put you up to this. No—wait. Don't answer that. Another one of my *keen observations*, right? Look, I'm not a nosy Miss Marple. Yes, I saw you swimming through our hedges, but that's only because you were making a lot of noise, as you *often* do. At all hours. When something wakes me in the middle of the night or early on a Sunday morning, for that matter, I get out of bed to investigate."

His hands go into the pockets of his khaki shorts. "Investigate. Like Miss Marple."

I grunt, rolling my eyes. "Thanks for the whiskey." I turn to retreat inside.

"Rowan, wait. Can I have five minutes to talk about the tree?"

I nod begrudgingly. He waves me to his property and leads me along the hedges toward the back until we reach a towering pine tree at the corner, mostly on my side. Slightly tilted toward the street, it reminds me of the Leaning Tower of Pisa.

"Yes, it's a tree."

"It's a dying tree." He points to the branches with their bursting needles and drooping pinecones. "The needles should be green. Not brown. My tree guy confirmed it. It's rotting from the inside. If we don't have it taken down properly, the next hurricane will do it for us."

Living on the North Carolina coast makes hurricanes a frequent problem. He shows how the tree will fall—directly between our houses, surely damaging both.

"It's mostly on your property, making it *your* problem, but I'm offering you the same deal I had with Margot and Ben before... well, before. I'm willing to pay half. I've already gotten estimates."

"How much?"

His broad shoulders bounce in a careless shrug. "Fifteen hundred."

Everything sinks—my jaw, my shoulders, the nervous knot in my throat.

"It's not only a safety concern. It's a nuisance, dumping needles in the pool and housing squirrel nests, which means more yard fleas."

I think of my itchy ankle the night I spied him swimming. But still—*$1,500?*

"Your yard needs work," he continues. "Your grass is high. Trimming the overgrown shrubs and cleaning the garden beds will prevent mosquitoes, fleas, and other pests from infiltrating *my* yard. It's a common courtesy for your neighbors on both sides. I can recommend a lawn service if you're too busy."

My hand goes up, stopping him. "I'm not hiring a lawn service, and the tree will have to wait."

"We're already in hurricane season. Sooner is better."

I don't doubt he's right about the tree. It seems unhealthy, though, at first glance, I never would've noticed its dingy gray bark flaking away in odd splotches or its needles losing their luscious green color. As a lifelong renter, things like tree health aren't on my radar. So, this information is useful.

But this man irks me. As a teacher, I've encountered many off-putting personalities—rich, entitled kids, cocky athletes, and all sorts with angry chips on their shoulders. Even so, I've never truly disliked a student or failed to find a way to work together.

Jack Graham seems like a bad combination of the worst qualities—rich, entitled, cocky, *and* angry. Besides, it's hard to get along with a guy who clearly doesn't want me living next door to him.

"I'll add the tree to my long list of to-dos." I force a smile. "Thanks for bringing it to my attention."

"You're brushing me off?" His head cocks as he scrutinizes me.

"Yes, for now. I want to think about it." *And do research. And get my own estimates. Is it normal for homeowners to have a "tree guy"? I'll have to ask Mira.*

Jack looks insulted. He folds his muscular, tatted arms and chews on his inner lip. He needs a haircut. And a shave. Whenever I see him, he's sporting a five o'clock shadow and dark, wispy hair that constantly falls into his daring brown eyes, as if he prefers the messy look. Or refuses to be bothered with such mundane things—not when there's partying to do. Finally, his hand goes out like he's about to handle something delicate.

"What's there to think about? I have the estimates inside if you want to see them and the report from my tree guy. All you have to do is agree. I'll set it up. I'll even front the money, and you can pay me back." His eyes narrow. "In installments if need be."

I don't want to owe this man anything. "Since you *must* have an answer this minute, it's no. I'll take care of the tree myself, but thanks for not being condescending or pushy about it. Oh, and here." I push the whiskey into his stomach. "I don't need your *heartfelt* welcome gift."

An audible grunt emerges as he presses his lips together, and it's satisfying—not giving in to his demands. I turn to storm off properly. But the desired effect doesn't happen with flip-flops on grass.

"Rowan, what the hell?" He stops me between the windowed side of what looks like a library and the neatly trimmed hedge. "Look, I'm sorry. I didn't mean to sound condescending. I'm trying to be helpful. That's all."

I seek some sincerity in him, but it's like panning for gold in a sandbox. Meanwhile, I carefully edge around him, determined not to be penned in—a move that amuses him. I imagine him thinking, *"What's this? A woman who doesn't want to run her tongue over my chest muscles? It can't be."*

My throat clears. "Helpful, huh? If that's true, I appreciate it. But I'll handle the tree on my own. Like you said, it's *my* problem."

He takes me in like a puzzling grammar mistake—he knows I'm wrong but can't figure out why. "What about the yard, Miss Independent? Ben and Margot loved their yard. They took good care of it."

My head cocks as I scrutinize him. I *really* don't like this man.

"So will I. In my own time, not yours. Not getting your way must be so hard for you. *Unfortunately*, I can't help but be *pretty fucking annoying*, right?"

My words emerge slowly and with surprising confidence, which sticks even when he looks confused. I don't wait for a response but twist on my flip-flops and beeline toward my driveway as Mira's SUV pulls in.

Six

Jack

Shit. *Pretty fucking annoying?* The words jingle a vague bell—*did I say that? Aloud? To her?* The stress of not writing has turned me into someone I don't even like, and, for some reason, my new neighbor gets the brunt of it.

I take my rejected whiskey inside and wander to my office. A highlight reel of the night in question replays in my head.

The call from my agent about my publisher's threats to drop me and take their advance back...

All day staring at a blinking cursor and blank page...

My friends showing up for a baseball game we got too drunk to watch...

And a bike ride—five drunk idiots doing laps around our street like we're twelve. Chris put credit cards in the tire spokes like baseball cards. Bryan rode Mom's old pink bike with the tassels on the handlebars, basket and all. It would've been funny if they hadn't spent the time complaining about their wives and chauffeuring their kids to games and practices all the time.

"Wish I had your life, Jack," Bryan said.

No, he doesn't.

I remember her loud-ass VW puttering up the road. My face lands in my hands as my words echo. *Pretty fucking annoying... bet you still bed her... hell no...* Damn it.

My tabby, Harper Lee, saunters up with what sounds like a chiding meow. I wonder if cats can read minds—I've always felt she can. Her golden eyes narrow in what looks like disappointment. I deserve it. I plop in my reading chair beside the open window and hear a thwack outside. A voice comes next.

"Are you okay?"

"Yes, peachy," Rowan answers sharply, suggesting she isn't. Table legs scrape against concrete. They sit at her embarrassingly small, pizza-sized metal table with matching ass-numbing chairs. They're close enough for me to hear the wine being poured.

In hindsight—not the best idea, adding on to my house so close to hers. But Ben and Margot rarely used that dinky porch, and I never considered that they wouldn't be there. With only a few feet and a shrub separating her porch from my office and being higher up, I see everything, even through the window over her kitchen sink.

I'll have to put up a fence, tall and solid.

I reach to close the window but stop when Rowan says, "This isn't about Dean, is it?"

And my ass is glued to the seat. Rowan's shitstorm love life has inspired me before. I can't afford to miss a second opportunity.

"—Please, Mira. It's been a bad day already."

"It's not about Dean. I need your help with something."

"Sure, anything."

"No, hear me out first. You're allowed to say no. This isn't something you should agree to because you're being asked. Understood?"

"Fine. Just tell me what it is already."

"Now that you have the house and an extra bedroom, I wondered if you'd be open to fostering a teenager—"

"Yes. Absolutely."

They laugh knowingly, like it's an understanding between them, before Mira asks, "Maybe I should give you all the details first?"

"Sure, but I'll do it."

I watch through the corner of the window where they can't see me, even though this conversation has veered into a category that I don't care about. If not for the irony, I'd already be on the phone with my fence guy. She couldn't give a straight answer to her boyfriend's proposal but couldn't give her yes fast enough to a stranger living in her house. This woman is strange.

"Her name is Sara Sweet. She and her father, Eddie, live on the other side of The Pines, inherited from his mother. He's a landscaper. Good guy but doesn't make the best choices. He was caught with stolen property stashed in his garage. Sara says he was duped into storing it by a no-good relative, which is probably true, but he wouldn't come clean. So, he's about to do ninety days, and there's no guardian for Sara."

"So, she needs a temporary placement."

"Yes, but one in *this* school district, which is impossible to find. She's starting her sophomore year at Coastal. I don't want to force her to switch schools."

"Well, now she won't have to. I'll get a bed, dresser, and desk for my spare room—I have a little money set aside. We'll ride to and from school together. It'll be great!"

"It'll be *hard*, Rowan. She won't want to be here. She's pissed at her dad, and she's got a very bad attitude."

"I've handled bad attitudes before—"

"Yes, but not under your roof. It's different."

Rowan huffs with irritation. "It almost sounds like you want to talk me out of it."

"No. I only want you to have realistic expectations. This won't be a three-month slumber party. Sharing your space with an angry teenager will be challenging."

"Yes, and I'm up for it. Trust me."

A beat passes before Mira sighs. "I do. I knew you'd say yes. Thanks for being willing to try it. Do you want to talk to Dean before starting the process?"

Their pleasant back and forth stops abruptly.

Rowan recovers with a weak, "No, it's fine. I'll let him know."

"You *are* talking to Dean still, right?"

Another hesitation makes the air feel hollow around them. "He asked for space. I'm respecting his wishes... I broke his heart, Mira. I didn't mean to, but I did."

"So, now he gets to break your heart every day. Is that it?"

I nearly trip over Harper Lee to grab a notebook from my desk—that's a damn good line.

"When was the last time you heard from him?"

"The day he left."

"No texts? No calls?"

Rowan shakes her head. So do I. Whatever esteem I had for the woman devouring her meal after being rejected by sight fizzles. She isn't confident or strongly indifferent. She's a fucking pushover.

Mira says, "You deserve better, and you don't have to put up with it."

"I love him. I don't have a choice."

"He's not showing you any love. And you *always* have a choice. I know you think that Dean seems nothing like the assholes of your past—"

"Seems?"

"Yes, *seems*. You don't *know* him, Rowan, and men have turned on you before. I don't need to remind you—"

"No, you don't," she snaps. Her fingers flutter with her napkin, nervously folding it into triangles. "I really don't want a history lesson, okay?"

Oh, please, give us a history lesson, I think, pen at the ready.

"Fine, I'll just say this—The men of your past... You didn't *deserve* them, Rowan. You *survived* them. Don't settle for Dean because you think he's as good as you'll get."

I capture Mira's words verbatim, and they repeat in my head. She *survived* them. She survived *them*. *She* survived them. The rusty wheels of my creativity sluggishly start to turn.

Their silence compounds the tension, making it thick like humidity. Mira's quick to laugh it off. "Tell me you got him for breaking your no-romance rules with the proposal, at least. We worked hard on those."

My writer senses tingle again. If done right, romance is sweet and sexy, the thing that separates one person from all the rest. Who doesn't want to feel that beautiful attention? That adoration? That love?

Rowan's nerves scatter in a chuckle. "That was... quite the night."

"After Trent, we needed it. Your no-romance rules were useful at the time. No more wine and roses."

"No PDA or fancy dinners," Rowan tacks on, like they're playing a game.

"No flowers or gifts. Always splitting costs."

"No damsel-in-distress moments."

"No big romantic gestures." Mira laughs.

"Proposals are the exception."

"Maybe, but you made dating *way* too easy on him."

"No, the rules helped. Despite what you think, I feel like I really know Dean."

I nearly laugh. She's delusional. Yeah, she really knows the guy who's ghosting her?

Mira's smile vanishes into a sigh. "Here's the problem with Dean—You're not *desperate* for him, Rowan." Her words come quickly as if uncaged. "He's not desperate for you, either. It's like you're both only halfway in. And if it's only halfway, why do it at all?"

I can't write fast enough, but still, I peek through the window to see Rowan's reaction—the slight fall of her shoulders, the confused, maybe hurt pinch between her brow, and her typically bright blue eyes turning a shade paler.

"Don't hold on when you should let go," Mira says more softly.

"Letting go means giving up, and maybe it's hard for you to understand, but I can't do that. That's the only proposal I'll ever get, and dating is... torture for me. I can't go through it again. It's Dean or nothing."

"How perfectly unromantic," Mira says playfully.

Rowan stays stoic. "No one wants to be alone. I'm *desperate* for something more."

Her words resonate in ways I don't like. I love my solitude... when I'm writing. Otherwise, the empty space around me is a vise squeezing my chest. My perpetual blank page has strangely revealed other blanks like my life's a warped Mad Lib waiting for words I, once again, can't deliver.

Mira breaks the long silence. "Desperate for something more? You should try the hottie next door."

Spit catches in my throat, making me cough.

"What was that?" I hear Rowan ask.

I pin myself to the wall, feeling like a dumbass.

A non-busted dumbass, I realize once they return to their conversation. Rowan redirects them to Sara and the process ahead of them, and my mind goes elsewhere.

A young girl running down city streets at night, fumbling over her feet as she glances over her shoulder. Scared. Trying to survive. And desperate for something more, for the one person who makes her feel safe—if only she could find him.

I can't reach my laptop fast enough.

I enact my ritual—ass in my desk chair, pencil tucked behind my ear, notebook and laptop open, and music blaring. I hit play on the remote, letting Method Man's "Bring the Pain" surround me.

It's an old-school choice, but Devin and I used to do a ridiculous rap dance to it before baseball games. It's the song I play whenever I start writing a new book.

Holy shit, that's what I'm doing! Starting a new book!

I bend and crack my fingers. Then, I'm tapping out a scene that will fit into a plot I don't know yet with a character I've only just met. An outcast. A survivor.

I don't know her full story yet, but I'm in the scene with her—a ghost witnessing and documenting her messed-up life. That's how it works. I smell the stench of stale Chinese food and piss in the alleys and hear the buzz of neon lights and distant traffic. I feel her trembling fingers as she holds tight to her school bag—the only thing she had time to grab. Her body is cold from sweat and the night air. She has no idea where she's going—only away. He can't hurt her if he can't find her.

Hours pass before I come up for air, and only because I hear scraping outside my study. A glance at the bottom of my screen reveals a miracle—3,327 words. I stand, stretch, and peek out the side window.

Rowan drags a large branch between our houses, its extended limb tickling the sides of her house. I snort-laugh, eyeing a leaf plastered to her back thigh.

I groan. "Should be wearing gloves, newbie."

With trouble, she finally deposits the branch streetside between our houses, her tone arms flexing with the effort. She's created an impressive pile, and it's *slightly* endearing to see the poised, perfectly put-together woman sweaty and dirty over yard work. Endearing *and* sexy. Her damp tank clings to the curves of her chest, leaving little to my imagination, especially when she bends to adjust the pile and her full breasts dangle against her bra.

Dick-thoughts aside, she *listened* to me.

She returns to her backyard and retrieves another fallen branch—bigger than the previous one. She grits her teeth as she pulls it through the gap, like a stupidly cute puppy playing tug-of-war. Outside my corner window, she loses her grip and falls on her ass. She pops up quickly, glancing around to make sure no one saw. I duck from view, laughing.

Maybe I should help her. Or, at least, stop watching her. But it's too amusing. Hell, watching that leaf on her back thigh is enough to keep me entertained.

But I don't have time.

Craving a drink, I consider my shit-gift. I knew she wouldn't want whiskey, but I didn't want to welcome her despite Rose and Vernon's insistence.

But after 3,327 words, I can't exactly hate her either.

When she vanishes into her backyard again, I grab an expensive chardonnay from my wine rack, scribble out a sticky note—*More your style, princess?*—and leave it at her front door.

Conscience cleared.

Then, with the relief and joy of someone being rescued from a long-ass stay on a deserted island, I go back to writing.

Seven

JACK

My no-name character ends up in a city park and takes solace in moonlight and grass underfoot, if only to avoid thinking about the shadows lurking in the woods—

A loud chime yanks me from the scene. I glance at my phone, *motion at the front door*, and see Rowan. She takes one step closer to the doorbell, doesn't ring it, and then takes a step back, reconsidering.

Time has gotten away from me—it's nearly dark. I'm at 6,277 words.

Tina Turner's "Better Be Good to Me" blares from the speakers—my badass Cinderella playlist—but it's interrupted as the chime alerts me again. *Motion at the front door*, but still, no doorbell.

I leave my desk.

She jumps when the door swings open.

"Um, s-sorry. I didn't ring the bell yet."

"I know, Miss Marple." I point to the Ring camera beside us. Then, I pause the music via a remote in my pocket. "I decided for you. What's up?"

Her brow pinches like she's second-guessing her visit. "Thanks for the wine. It *is* more my style... though I could've done without the *princess* remark."

I *almost* smile. "You're welcome. Anything else?"

She's cleaned up since her experiment with yard work. Shorts show off her long legs—leafless—and a soft teal tank brings out the blue in her eyes. Her hair is down and wavy. She's not bothering to pull off Cleopatra tonight. Nor is she wearing make-up, but a soft shimmer on her lips makes me think she went for lip gloss before coming over here. Is she taking Mira's words to heart about the hottie next door? Would I actually be down for that?

No. Off-limits. I reach for the pencil tucked in my ear and braid it through my fingers.

"You're writing—I get it. Rose sent a *Do-Not-Disturb* text alert to the whole neighborhood, which feels slightly ridiculous, but... I saw you in there, working. I mean, I didn't intend to." She motions to the narrow path between our houses. "Couldn't help it. I've always been fascinated with how authors create their stories. You were antsy, pacing the room. *Think. Type. Think. Type.*" She looks amused before her pale cheeks turn pink. "Um, sorry. I'm *really* not a Miss Marple. And I don't want to hold you up. It's just... we've gotten off on the wrong foot. You didn't want a new neighbor, but I'm here. And you're... *you*. Can we just get over each other and—"

"Fine. Whatever. Fine." My words spurt out only because I need to end this as soon as possible. Inspiration's quickly turning into distraction. And not at all in the way I expect.

"Fine?"

"Yes, fine. Is that all?"

"No, actually. I want the paperwork on the tree, if it's not too much trouble."

I groan. "Any other time, yes. Not now. I'm busy."

Her shoulders sink a fraction, just like they did with the trust-fund asshole and the mere mention of her bad ex earlier. But she straightens. "Are you this rude to your mother?"

She gets a laugh out of me. Not only does she ask the weirdest question, but her hands go to her hips like she's about to lecture me. Every clenched muscle in me relaxes. I lean against the doorframe and tuck the pencil against my ear. "Um, yeah. Sometimes. She doesn't tolerate it, either."

"Good. Maybe the next time we interact, you can use your mom filter and cut out anything she wouldn't tolerate. We'll probably get along better that way."

"Think of you as my mom. Got it." Fat chance, given where my head's going already. I remember her racing across her lawn in her nightie—no make-up, no bra—and imagine things I shouldn't. *Stop it, Jack.*

Her eyes narrow into icy slits like she's reading my mind.

"My apologies for being rude, Rowan." For fun, I use my bedroom voice.

She softens in a blink. Still, she looks unsure, like she expects me to be the bad guy in a story she's reading. I don't like that bullshit vibe. I'm no villain.

Eyes locked on hers, I say, "Sorry for what I said with my friends, too. It was drunk-no-filter-Jack talking, and I honestly didn't think you'd hear it."

She stiffens again. "I bet your mom could explain what's wrong with that apology... but I'll take it. Um, I'll get the paperwork later. Get back to writing."

She leaves so abruptly that I miss her when she's gone. *What the hell?* I don't go inside until I hear her slam the door to her place.

Then, I resume my playlist. "Build a Bitch" by Bella Poarch blasts from the speakers as I pour myself a drink—water, no alcohol tonight.

My phone chimes—a text from Amber, a frequent companion. *Running a little late, but I'll be over soon.*

I completely forgot about our plans. I text back. *Don't bother. Can't tonight. Working.*

She responds with a simple *Maybe next week, then* like it's no big deal. It *isn't* a big deal—we have a mutual understanding. We occasionally enjoy each other's company for fun, uncomplicated sex. No dating. No plus-one favors. No meeting friends or families. No gifts or expectations. No obligations. It's an arrangement that works, and most women appreciate the honesty and convenience of it.

So, I get it—Rowan's not the only one with rules against romance.

I also appreciate her anti-damsel-in-distress clause. Sure, there are some things that *might* be easier for a woman with a dude around, like reaching something high on a shelf or loosening the lug nuts on a tire. But that's why the world invented step stools and mechanics. Women can solve their own problems.

Still, some women intentionally play the damsel like a commitment test to see if her guy will come running when she calls. It's a manipulation I see through in a heartbeat and end things quickly. Being there for someone you care about is an honor. Getting roped into "saving" someone who can save herself just because she has boyfriend ideas isn't.

Even so, many men fall for playing the hero—they even like it. For some assholes, it makes them feel superior. I imagine that's why it made Rowan's list—she can take care of herself and doesn't want to be with someone who thinks otherwise.

That I understand... respect, even. If I ever fall in love—highly unlikely—it'll have to happen without the usual bullshit. No games. No manipulations. No romance.

I stand by my office window, overlooking the little house, and glimpse her kitchen. Rowan's washing the wine glasses from earlier. Her hair is in a messy bun, not hiding her scars but showing off her slender neck. A lock of her dark hair falls over her eyes, and she blows it back, smirking when it returns to the same place. I shouldn't watch her, but I like seeing her this way, graceful and relaxed. There *is* something about her.

I turn away from the window, hating that the neighbors are right. *She's ending my writer's block.* And I'll need more material, more grist for my mill.

More of her.

My pen wants what it wants, but damn—I don't like this. She's annoying, stubborn, and too much trouble.

"Just like you," I imagine Devin saying, but I don't engage. I've got work to do.

Returning to my desk, I imagine Rowan getting ready for bed soon. She's one of those irritating people with routines and schedules. She'll soon hate living next door to me, if she doesn't already.

The repercussions of not writing for over a year is that I'll write all night, as long as I can, until my fingers ache and my brain feels like mush in a blender. Music will serve as my companion, with Olivia Rodrigo, Billie Eilish, Selena Gomez, and Rihanna headlining. My badass Cinderella playlist will keep the princess next door up all night.

Now, back to my no-name character in the shadowy park...

Eight

ROWAN

A week later and the night before my dreaded meeting with Dr. Evelyn Tate about my non-existent Inspiration Project, I stroll toward the Fourth of July oyster roast, knowing I've already ruined my evening.

Stress over my lack of a plan has built over the last twelve hours—I've pored over my old lesson plans and novel notebooks since dawn with nothing to show for it.

On top of that, a twisted and unwarranted fantasy that Dean might show up has not only delayed me by a half-hour—and I detest being late—but has also heaped disappointment on my shoulders like I'm a pack horse overloaded with foolish expectations. He never said he could make it or even that he'd try.

But he called three nights ago after a rough day on set. He vented about working with elitist stars who kept delaying the production, which meant hours of boredom and a scolding he received from the assistant director because he looked too "normal."

"I don't know what I'm doing," he said.

"Come home," I suggested—no, I begged. "Take the weekend off, at least. I miss you."

I told him about the oyster roast—Dean loves a party. It's only a six-hour drive from Atlanta. With airports in both cities, it's even more doable by plane—less than two hours and only two hundred bucks. Mira would hate this, but I even offered to pay for his ticket.

He only responded, "I miss you, too," before he had to go. I never had the chance to talk to him about Sara.

With my steps feeling heavier the closer I get, I consider taking my freshly baked chocolate chip cookies (a classroom favorite) back home and eating them all while on my couch with Edgar Allan Poe. But I push on as I have all week, determined to offer my cookies, chat with a few people, and leave early.

The Pines is a huge neighborhood bordered by schools, grocery stores, and churches in equal measure. Our corner is a neighborhood within a neighborhood. Two parallel streets, Daisy Lane and Daffodil Drive, form a closed H and are linked on either end by short side streets. These are bordered by extra-large ditches that lead to a massive retention pond behind our properties. Our loop is an island—a quiet pocket protected from the city while still a part of it.

The block party occupies the middle of the H—a short and superfluous road linking the main streets. It's quiet and heavily shaded with stretchy live oaks, magnolias, and towering pines—the namesakes of the neighborhood.

A small band plays "Zombie" by the Cranberries—*The Daisy Chain* advertised that the neighborhood's cover band, *The Hurricanes,* would feature '80s and '90s hits. The invitation also promised a food smorgasbord to accompany the oysters—pop-up tables house casseroles, salads, and chips.

Between the band and the food, dancers sway to the slow song. Mismatched tables and chairs fill the rest of the space with people chatting and kids running around.

Twinkle lights canopy the road, like walking into a gorgeous gazebo. I'm surprised at how lovely and casual it is, like a scene pulled from a cheesy Hallmark movie—the social event that brings the town (and the inevitable couple) together at the end.

I pass by the oyster tanks—large metal drums heated by propane—and say hello to the men supervising the roasting. Behind them, another set of newspaper-covered tables awaits the shelling extravaganza.

I make room for my cookies near other desserts and grab a beer from one of the coolers. I spot Rose, Vernon, Tom, and Marcy quickly, but the rest blur into unfamiliar faces.

I stand there feeling self-conscious and uneasy. My navy sundress and blue ombre wrap, strategically draped high on my shoulders to cover my neck scars, feel too dressy compared to everyone else's shorts and t-shirts. The crowd is so engaged and familiar with each other that I go unnoticed—not that I'd know what to say if they did.

Mom says I've always been shy, but I argue that life's made me this way.

"Beer drinker, huh?" Jack Graham emerges behind me like he may've been hiding in the trees. "That's surprising."

"I'm surprised you've given it thought."

He shrugs. "It's good to know your neighbors. What someone drinks says a lot about them."

"And you thought I was exclusively a snobby wine princess?"

His dark eyes catch mine. "Aren't you?"

"Usually," I admit sheepishly. "But I've been less discriminate about what I drink since moving next to you."

"I have that effect on people. Let me know if you want the whiskey back." A wide grin bookends his words, easing my discomfort.

"Hmm, I might need it if your writing streak continues... to put me to sleep."

His head cocks. "Is the music a problem?"

"No, I'm kidding. I've lived in apartments so long that I'm used to noise. But a softer playlist after midnight might be nice on weekdays."

"I'll keep that in mind."

The conversation dwindles into a strange silence, but he doesn't disappear. He stays at my side, his upper arm brushing my shoulder when kids crowding the food table move us closer.

"Congrats on the writing, by the way. I hear that's a huge deal for you."

He looks almost shy, glancing at his feet at the mention. "Yeah, thanks. I haven't written like this in over a year."

"How does it feel?" I ask rather than question the writing itself, which feels too personal.

"Like a fucking relief," he breathes out before taking a long swig of his beer.

"Even if the whole neighborhood knows?" My head bobs toward Rose and Vernon's table. They've sent daily text alerts about it. "It seems like a lot of pressure. Do they report everything that happens around here?"

"Just about, but it's meant to bring the neighborhood together, and the support is nice.... Most of the time."

Again, I expect him to make a quick exit. But he lingers. So, I tilt my bottle to the crowd. "Okay then, what can you tell me about the other neighbors?"

He points to a burly man standing near the roasters. "Ed is strictly a beer drinker. Head of the neighborhood watch. You've probably seen him in his golf cart."

"The one always checking the perimeter?"

"Right." Jack nods to the woman beside him, whose loud laughter suggests her mixed drink isn't her first. "That's Renita, who's married to him and Mary Kay."

"Ah, the anemic pink Cadillac."

"She's good. I've even bought shit from her."

"I'll definitely avoid her then." I laugh lightly.

"Absolutely. Then, steer clear of our Girl Scout cookie supplier and those three Boy Scouts. They'll get you for popcorn sales," he says, pointing them out.

"Oh, is that the porch couple?" I ask, motioning to an older couple dancing, who are on their front porch no matter the hour or the weather like they're cursed fixtures, cemented in place. "It's the first time I've seen them away from the porch."

"Yes, Dan and Diane. One time, I went on a walk at, like, 2 a.m., and passing their dark house, I heard someone say, 'Good morning, Jack,' and I nearly shit myself."

"Creepy."

"Fucking diabolical. I told 'em so." Jack's eyes meet mine. "And they laughed."

I grimace, imagining it. "I will limit my runs to the daylight hours, then."

Jack motions toward our end of the street. "If you cross the concrete bridge over the gully next to my place, you can hop on the cross-city trail and avoid the neighbors altogether."

"Good to know." The song changes to "November Rain" by Guns N' Roses, and a sigh putters from me. "I love this song."

Eyes fixed on the band, I sway, mesmerized. Jack eases away my dwindling beer and reaches for my hand.

I must look as confused as I feel because he says, "A neighborly dance. What's the worst that could happen?"

"Us killing each other?"

A smirk rises on his left cheek. "We aren't that bad, are we?"

"I'd call us... cordially volatile."

"I like that. *Let us read, and let us dance; these two amusements will never do any harm to the world.*"

I gawk. "You're quoting Voltaire to me? Is that how you typically get women to dance with you?"

"Not typically... but I'm impressed that you recognize Voltaire. Did it work?"

My hand slips into his while his fingers circle my waist. "Such tactics only work on the nerdiest subset of the population."

"Then, we have that in common." He drags me close by the waist, but not too close.

"A property line and nerdiness—I suppose that's something." My hand rests on his shoulder, but it's a struggle, forcing it to stay there. It wants to roam down the hard hill of his bicep like I'm a hormonal teenager discovering muscles for the first time.

Stiffly, I lock my hands in their places and try to keep an acceptable distance. We're like awkward cousins forced to dance at a wedding.

"This isn't so bad," he says, as if convincing himself. "This way, when you bail on this party, like you've wanted to do since you got here, you can honestly say that you were here *and* you danced, earning you a participation award from anyone who asks."

Mira and Mom will. "How'd you know?"

"I'm a writer. I see people. You fiddling with your scarf is a dead giveaway for nerves."

As he says it, it falls off my shoulders, tangling around our joined arms. I tug it back into place over my neck marks.

"I'm not nervous, just... new and alone," I say.

"Where's that elusive fiancé of yours?"

"Acting in Georgia until the end of August."

His eyebrow cocks with a glance at my ringless left hand, fixed on his shoulder. Then, he surprises me with an unexpected twirl that swooshes the subject away but brings me closer, latching onto his neck and falling against his stony chest. He smells like cedar, cocoa butter, and bad ideas. And my head's suddenly riddled with images of gladiators, knights, and even sexy elvish fighters, like Legolas from *The Lord of the Rings.*

His soft lips curve into a playful grin as he takes me in. I don't know whether to be grateful for his company or more nervous. Dancing with a neighbor at an oyster roast is innocent enough, but I wonder, *briefly*, what Dean would think of me dancing with a neighbor like *him*—the hot, rich playboy of The Pines. With the music, twinkling lights, and the amber flecks in his eyes, his dark eyes look like galaxies full of stars and questions, easy to get lost in, like the immersive experience at a planetarium.

He holds my gaze like he knows exactly what I'm thinking. "His loss," he says. "Besides, you're never alone on this street, even when you want to be."

He nods to a nearby table where Rose and Vernon stare at us while nibbling chips like they're watching a rom-com.

I laugh, shaking my head. "The worst spies. Do you think we'll make the newsletter?"

"It'll be their top story."

"'Beauty Befriends the Beast'?" I ask, looking snide because clearly, I'm the beast in this scenario.

His eyes narrow as if challenged. "Only if they want a lawsuit for calling me a beast. More like... 'Lady Befriends Tramp and Tramp Removes Huge Chip from Shoulder'."

"That may be a little long for a headline."

With another spin, his grin deepens. "Not when it's half-done with emojis."

Laughter erupts, imagining Rose and Vernon coding out emojis on their newsletter template. Tension vanishes, too, as if laughing overrides nerves. Maybe he's not so bad after all, and I'm guilty of the wrong first (second, and third) impressions.

His fingers walk across my back, inching me closer, like maybe he's thinking the same thing. I stop worrying about keeping a safe distance and just hang on. The song's pace quickens, and he leads us in a surprisingly poetic and strangely synchronized waltz, *of sorts*, toward the more official dance floor. My wrap escapes my neck again, sliding to our arms.

"You don't need this." A gentle tug on one end slides it off me, leaving me exposed. He tosses it to Rose, who catches it with a giddy scream like a band groupie.

Then, like he's reading my mind, he says, "We've all seen your scars. No one cares."

I'm about to argue, but he quickly says, "You aren't hard to look at, you know. Not even a little. When you're not pissed at me, you're damn lovely. But truthfully, if you're worried about it, hiding them makes it more obvious."

I only gawk. *Lovely* is an adjective never used for me, and certainly not by someone like him. Not just *lovely*. *Damn lovely.* Did showing up at this party pull me into an alternate universe? Is this a portal story? *The Upside Down*?

My stunned expression makes him curious. "What? Are we not allowed to talk about it? Mom explained where I went wrong with my apology, but should I consult her again about being too direct?"

"Um, no," I say with a small laugh. "I'm okay with directness. I prefer it, actually. But most people don't talk about it. It makes them uncomfortable. Covering up minimizes the attention, usually."

"You should own that shit." He twirls me around again. "I love a song that tells a story."

The subject change and twirling make me dizzy. But weirdly, I like it. "A sad story. Is it better to have loved and lost than never to have loved at all? I wonder."

"Well, Tennyson votes yes. But I say it's better to love and not lose."

"If only."

Jack leans into me at the song's dramatic conclusion, forcing an awkward dip to close it out that has me laughing harder than I have in a long time. He brings me to my feet in a flourish that receives applause from Rose, Vernon, and others watching nearby.

The microphone screeches as Tom approaches it, and his radio announcer's monotone says, "Come get your oysters, ya'll."

A mass migration ensues as partygoers flock toward the oysters steaming on the newspaper tables. I linger where we are and feel relieved when Jack stays, too. Despite our differences, he's put me at ease in the strangest way, like we're unlikely animal friends in an Instagram post.

Amid the chaos, he says, "Another beer?"

"There you are!" A shrill voice cuts through my answer, which would've been yes. Renita beelines toward me through the migrating crowd, wobbling precariously on her high wedges.

"Shit," Jack says under his breath as she corners us. Renita is at least in her fifties, but she's so finely made-up that she looks younger—a solid testament to her Mary Kay business. Her hands give her away, though, showing her years like rings around tree stumps. She holds what looks like a margarita slushy in one hand while she animatedly extends her other to me.

"I'm Renita Dabney. Ed and I live at 412 Daisy. You're Rowan!" Her loudness doesn't hide her slight slur.

"Yes, nice to meet you, Renita." I shake her hand.

"I've heard a lot about you." She wags a bright red fingernail. "Saw you dancing with our Jack here. He's such a handsome devil, right? If I weren't married, I'll tell you what—"

"Yikes, Renita," he says. "How many of those have you had?"

"Oh, honey. That's not the drink talking... She knows what I'm talking about."

I glance at him playfully. "He's not bad... if you like moody-writer-types."

Renita slaps her bare knee in laughter, sloshing her beverage.

"How about those beers?" His hand goes to my elbow to lead me away.

Only Renita grabs my hand. With a sweet but critical look, she takes in my face. I try to escape her, but any pull might cause her to lose her balance, and I don't want to see her fall over.

"I've wanted to meet you, honey. I can help you with your features, you know."

"Renita!" His stern voice only makes her scoff.

"Jack, this is girl talk. Make yourself scarce." She continues her awkward stare. "Have you tried Mary Kay? We have a line of concealers made for people like you."

People like me. Her words close me up like a flower under a hot sun. I glance about for my scarf but don't find it. I force a weak smile. "I'm okay with my... features. Heavy makeup clumps and never looks good on me."

She grunts. "You haven't tried *my* make-up. I bet I can make you look almost normal—"

"Um—"

"—I hear you're gettin' married. You don't want anything to mess up those wedding pictures." She casts me a sympathetic look. "You're a beauty. Don't you want the world to see that instead of, well, *that*?" She motions to the side of my face before lighting up again. "We should schedule a makeover!"

"God damn it! Nobody wants your fucking makeover, Renita," Jack snaps louder than necessary.

His harshness stuns us both. Renita back-steps, nearly tripping over her wedges. He catches her by the arm to hold her up and snatches the drink from her hand.

"Wait, don't…" I say, but he's already marching her toward her husband, Ed.

"Shit," I mutter before leaving.

Edgar Allan Poe is glad to have me home early. He meows on the other side of the door as soon as my key jiggles the lock. Inside, I scoop him to my shoulder and take comfort in his welcoming purrs. We plop together on the living room rug, where he saunters around me, rubbing his face on my hand and curling his tail high. I loved Edgar the moment I saw him in the humane society's cat room—hunched into a loaf in the corner, watching the other, bigger cats with anxiety pinched on his pitch-black brow.

"Aren't black cats unlucky?" Mira had asked when the family came over to meet him.

"Only in their adoption rates." I'd shared how they are the least likely to get adopted because of their less-photogenic color and unlucky reputation.

Always ready to jump on a cause, Mira and the family adopted two black cats the following week.

"Sorry, I didn't score you an oyster, Edgar." I pet his arched back, and he meows his disappointment.

Ready to put the night behind me, I change into a tank top and shorts and pull my tidy hair into a messy ponytail. I put on *Married at First Sight*, something Dean would never watch. I pour what's left of Jack's expensive chardonnay and settle with Edgar on the couch.

Curled with Edgar is where I want to stay—loafing in a corner, wary of the other cats. My history replays from the day it happened, and through every indignity since, as if I need the humiliating recap. Memories haunt me like wicked ghosts that keep multiplying and dragging me back to that day, kicking and screaming. *Always* screaming.

My internal screams turn audible when a gentle knock on the door makes my shoulders pop and my heart thunder in my chest.

Nine

JACK

Rowan isn't the mess I expect to find when she opens the door. No tears. No puffy eyes. No anger. Just Cleopatra from the restaurant—poised and controlled. Her worry lines deepen as she breathes a weak "Hi" and takes me in.

Her wrap is draped around my neck, and I'm holding another bottle of chardonnay as a peace offering, but she isn't charmed by either. *Of course, she isn't.* She's unimpressed and maybe pissed at my reaction earlier—I did exactly what she hates. I assumed she was a damsel-in-distress, so I played the idiot hero.

"Sorry," I finally manage.

"It's not your fault. She didn't realize how she sounded, that's all."

"No, I mean... I'm not apologizing for Renita. She's an idiot, but not *my* idiot. She owes you her own apology, and it better be a good one." A heavy sigh escapes as I struggle with the right words—me, the fucking wordsmith. "I'm sorry for my part in it."

"Your part?"

"Getting pissed and dragging her off to Ed felt good then, but when you disappeared, I realized I made it worse. You were probably ready to handle it gracefully."

Her pouty lips upturn slightly. "Do you mean I would've played the lady if not for you acting like the tramp?"

"Exactly," I smirk. "Forgive me for exploding what could've been diffused... and not leaving it up to you."

Her crystal-blue eyes widen like an apologetic man is a new phenomenon. "You *have* been talking to your mom," she smiles.

And delicate tingles swirl through my chest. Okay, maybe I like this woman. *A little.* I take a breath, studying her. "How do you do it?"

"Do what?"

"Not get angry at shit like that?"

Her worried brow makes a stunning return, sucking in her smile like a black hole. She struggles to answer like she's mentally filing through acceptable responses, trying to find the one that will get her out of this as soon as possible. Finally, she says, "Anger is destructive."

Three words. Vague but intriguing enough for me to know that I want in. Not into her heart or even her bed—God, no. Rephrase—I want into the little house. Yes, I need to flesh out my ghostly no-name character. But more, I need to unlock why my creative side finds this woman so damn fascinating.

In our silence, she gnaws at her inner lip and fixates on her doormat like she's gone wherever the mention of *anger* took her. *Where are you right now?* I want to ask, but I know she won't answer.

Then, a sharp inhale brings on a measured smile, like she's flipped a switch. "Years of practice help, too. It wasn't so awful, Jack—someone standing up for me—as long as you never think I can't do it myself."

My lips curl as we lock eyes. "I wouldn't dare."

Briefly, her forced smile turns genuine. She's damn beautiful, and she has no idea.

"Well, um, thanks—"

"Oh, who's this?" A long-haired black cat circles her feet, giving me a suspicious look. He lets out an exasperated meow as if to say, *we're a little busy, buddy.*

I thrust the wine at her and scoop him up—a move he gratefully accepts. Purrs rumble against my chest as I stroke his silky fur.

"Jack, meet Edgar Allan Poe," she says, sounding surprised.

"A literary cat. What a novel idea." My eyes find hers again, and yes, maybe it's like I'm holding her cat hostage, but I try my luck anyway. "Have a glass of wine with me?"

"Um, I have an early meeting tomorrow."

The excuse drops out like I've hit a lever on the dunking game at the fair. *Game over.*

My eyes narrow. "It's not even nine."

"I have a million things to do."

"Yeah, but don't you always?" My lips coil into a cool smile as I say it—one she matches because she knows I'm right. A million things to do, so busy she can barely breathe—that's her to a T.

Still, I say, in my gentlest voice, "One glass. Please?"

She moves aside and lets me in. "Only because Edgar approves. He's usually skittish about new people."

I nuzzle his nose, and he gives me a playful bop on mine with his paw. "He knows I'm a cat person... and a Poe person."

She snickers, closing the door behind me. I carry Edgar into the living room, trying to hide my double shock—first, that I made it this far, and second, at how the place looks.

A soft sage covers the walls, replacing Ben and Margot's thirty-year beige. She's repainted the trim white, pulled up the old carpet, and refinished the buttery hardwoods. A soft shag area rug makes the living room look cozy and brings out the pops of blues and greens in her throw pillows and decorations.

Her fingers lace behind her back, and she bobs on her bare feet, looking nervous as I scan the room.

"I like what you've done with the place."

"Really?" she breathes out. "Um, thanks. It's coming along."

"It looks amazing. Guess I really didn't think about how dated it looked when Ben and Margot were here. It needed an update." I eye the old copy of *The Little House*, proudly centering the coffee table. "That's nice to see. It really means something to you, this place?"

"My Grandpa Ro used to say owning property is the American dream, and sharing it with others makes it even better. That's what he and my Grandma Betty did—opened their home to me when Mom was deployed, and fostered kids like my sister, Mira. Buying this house makes me feel like they're still with me. That it looks like the house in the story makes it even more special. Mom got sick of reading it, but it was my favorite. The pages were rumpled, and the spine creased, you know? Like well-loved library books?"

I nod, knowing exactly what she means. "*The Hobbit*... that's the most rumpled and creased one in my library."

She lights up. "Ah, definitely a book that should be well-loved."

Holding up the wine bottle, she carries it to the kitchen. I follow, leaning against the white-tiled counter as she gets a glass and the corkscrew.

Edgar gets antsy, so I free him. He saunters away, high-tailed.

She hands over a wine glass, looking hesitant. "I'm fostering soon, too. Sara arrives at the end of the month."

"Holy shit, really?" I say, feigning surprise—I must be careful not to let on that I've eavesdropped. "That's amazing. She'll have the second bedroom?"

"For three months, while her father's, um, working some things out. It's been a long process, but I'm nearly there."

I motion down the hallway. "Can I show you something?"

She nods, and I lead her down the hall like it's my place more than hers. I stop short at the half-painted room, the floor covered in plastic tarps.

"I'm working on it. The home inspection's next week. I haven't gotten furniture yet." She sounds embarrassed, as if I've walked in on the room half-dressed.

I open the closet door, showing her the crudely carved initials inside. *C + D* next to a crooked heart. I run my finger along the rough edges, warmed by memories but chilled by his absence at once.

"Who are they?"

"Corey—Ben and Margot's son—and my brother, Devin. He died at seventeen. Cancer."

"Oh, Jack, I'm sorry." Sincerity wraps her face—it's not an automatic response, but a heartfelt one.

A muted smile pushes through, and for a moment, this isn't about getting material for my book but sharing something important to me.

"They were best friends and in love—not many people know that. I used to cover for him when he'd sneak out. At the time, it was annoying, but after... I was so grateful that he had that. That he loved and was loved back. You know?"

"Better to have loved and lost than never to have loved at all," she repeats from earlier.

"Exactly. Then Ben died, and it brought everything back. Watching someone else move in here... well..."

"I reminded you of the life your brother lost," she finishes for me. "I get it... and I won't let anything happen to that door."

I cover my relief with an uneasy chuckle. Maybe she's not that bad after all. I tug my phone from my pocket and start texting. "I want to do something for you."

"You don't have to do anything."

"It's already done." I hit send and tuck my phone away. "Rose and Vernon will request free bedroom furniture for your foster kid in the next newsletter. The people on this street have so much shit they don't know what to do with."

A warm grin eases up her cheeks. "Thank you... oh, ask for a desk, too?"

I reach for my phone again. "*Absofuckinglutely.*"

Her warm smile tells me I've leveled up, even when she says, "You cuss a lot."

"Yeah, too much rap music as a kid, I guess. Mom doesn't like it either."

"I didn't say I didn't like it. It suits you. Somehow." Her brow pinches as she slips by me as if bothered by her near-flirtatious remark. *Was she flirting?* It's hard to tell.

We retreat to the living room, where I plop onto her couch. She refills her wine glass before sitting on the opposite side. Edgar hops up and snuggles in the space between us.

I point to the screen. "I love this show. Would you ever do that?"

She gives me a look like *of-course-I-wouldn't*, and I suppose it's a dumb question, but I want to get her talking.

"Me, neither." I clink my glass to hers for a gentle ting. "Cheers."

After sipping, she fiddles with a throw pillow before saying, "So, your brother fell in love with the boy next door? That's so beautiful and serendipitous... if you believe in that sort of thing. Is that why you write romance?"

"I used to be a journalist. I loved chasing stories and asking questions. But human-interest stories intrigued me the most. I love hearing people talk about life-changing moments. Few things are as life changing as falling in love, right?"

Her pinched brow reappears, and she stares into her glass.

"My fascination probably started with Devin and Corey—you're right. I'm incredibly influenced and inspired by the people around me. But it works—*Netflix* is starting production on one of mine in Georgia soon. *Cape Moon.* Have you—"

"I haven't read your books."

Books are everywhere—lining the shelves, stacked in corners, and even wedged under the couch. It's a slight punch to my ego that she dismisses mine when she's clearly an avid reader.

"It's romance... I don't enjoy romance."

"It's not for everyone, especially when you have rules against it." I wince at my carelessness.

"Ah, so *you're* the Miss Marple now. Just when I was starting to like you." Her words emerge lightly but with an uneasy twinge. I almost hear her conversation with Mira replaying in her head as she checks it for secrets. She gulps her wine.

"Sorry. I'm a writer. I'm like a sponge around people."

"More like a vampire, sounds like, secretly sinking your teeth into other people's lives." She jokes, but it sounds half-hearted the longer she thinks about it. *I'm losing her. Fast.*

"A vampire, huh? I'm more Team Edward. No one gets hurt, promise," I flash my best grin, hoping to catch her eyes, but she doesn't look at me.

She sits up, sets her glass on the coffee table, and faces me urgently. "Wait, um. This sounds ridiculous—*I know*. Maybe it's the wine talking, but I have to ask... Does your writing streak have anything to do with me?"

My eyes narrow in immediate defense. "Does it matter?"

Air puffs from her like she's been punched in the chest. "Don't write about me, Jack Graham. I mean it."

Her sternness is like an implosion, sucking in everything pleasant.

"What's wrong? Why not?"

She takes a breath, calmly saying, "Is that why you talked to me at the party? Is that why you're here?"

"That's what you think this is? Me using you for fucking book sales?"

"Is it?"

"No! It's me being goddamned neighborly."

"Then you *aren't* writing about me?"

Her crystal eyes turn to gray ice, making me cold and angry.

My frustration meter rises. "Not about *you*. Not specifically."

"But someone *like* me? Are you writing about a teacher, a homeowner, an annoying neighbor, or did you bypass all of that and go straight to someone who's suffered serious burns?"

"It's not like that. I take pieces of people all the time—that's how it works. It's not about *YOU*—Rowan. It's a shade of you, a version in an entirely different world. You shouldn't be insulted. You should be fucking flattered."

"Flattered? Ha! There's the arrogance you've hidden all night! I'm not one of your damn groupies. And this—" She motions to her face. "—isn't a romantic novelty. It's my trauma—one that will *never* go away. How could you try and capitalize on it?"

"I'm not! I don't know what happened to you. I haven't even asked."

"But you will. I can't believe I thought you were being *nice*."

"Rowan." I force myself to calm down like a skilled negotiator in a hostage situation. "We don't know each other well, but come on. We share nerdiness and a property line. Trust me. I'd never trivialize your trauma or violate your privacy."

"You already have." She stands, banging her knee against the coffee table. She swallows the pain and points toward the door. "I want you to leave."

Her words hit me like a freight train, barreling me over. I hate that she thinks of me like that, even if it's partly true.

My wine glass clinks as I set it beside hers. It's all very civil—her escorting me to the door.

But my mind spins with anger at her distrust and the distance she keeps, like I'm a fucking predator or one of her bad-date assholes. Without even letting me explain. *Who does she think she is?*

Determined to change her mind, I turn abruptly at the door. She fumbles backward and raises her hands defensively.

Her reaction stops me cold, contorting my anger into an instant apology.

"Fucking hell, Rowan, I'm not going to hit you. Or hurt you. I would *never* do that. I'm-I'm sorry." My tone is desperate. She can think many things of me, most are probably true, but never that I would physically harm her.

She takes a quick breath, hanging her head as if ashamed. "It's been a long day. Were you going to say something? Go ahead."

"I-I don't want to now."

She holds the door open, waving me onto the front porch. "Oh, come on, Jack. Do you honestly think you can come up with something worse than I've heard before?" She forces a sardonic smile to assure me that she doesn't care.

I don't buy it for a second.

Still, I meet her eyes, locked into giving her exactly what she wants. "Fine. I was going to say... You aren't that fucking interesting."

Her lips coil before she slams the door in my face.

Ten

ROWAN

The slammed door shakes the little house and echoes like a car backfire. I'm not a door-slamming person—I regret it immediately, along with everything else. Attending the party. Letting him in. Buying the little house.

I call Dean. No answer.

I'm up and ready to run at 5:30 the next morning. Using the gully next to Jack's house, I get on the cross-city trail and map out my new routine. It takes me to Magnolia Park, where I do loops without worrying about traffic or neighbors.

But even though it's a lovely run, two thoughts keep recycling through my head—that *I'm not that fucking interesting* and *I should've said no to the little house.*

I don't even *want* to be interesting. Blending in has been my life goal since fifteen. I spent years wearing hoodies to hide under. Becoming a teacher took mental strength I never knew I had, and it's still a daily struggle. The last thing I want is more unwanted attention from an arrogant writer who thinks he can use my pain and dares to believe he can understand it.

Five fast miles later, I race over the concrete bridge toward home. Sweaty and winded, I slow down, spilling into the neighborhood. I take in the little house as the sun speckles its bricks and gray roof. It's not the sad place it was, not with its pansy and marigold flower boxes, freshly repainted blue door, and tidier lawn. With Edgar in the window eyeing my return, the house is postcard-perfect. To me, anyway.

If only I could pick it up and move it elsewhere.

In the shower, I refocus on my inspiration project. The best I can come up with is a vague philosophical approach to classic books—finding the meaning of life through literature. But it feels boring and unimaginative. Still, I make a mental note to grab my annotated copy of *A Tale of Two Cities* for a story of love and sacrifice to introduce it.

Though it's summer and I'm technically off-duty, I dress professional-ly—blue, ankle-length chinos, a pink polka-dotted white blouse with a collar, and my strappy black heels to show Dr. Evelyn Tate that I've made an effort. The magazine-worthy administrator appreciates style. With my dark hair straight-ened into a sleek bob that frames my face and modest make-up covering the bags under my eyes, I'm ready—at least by appearances.

A knock at the door quickens my pulse sharply. It's probably Rose and Vernon with their tea service, ready to dish about last night.

But it's Jack.

"I lied." His hands go up like he's trying to diffuse a bomb. "You *are* that fucking interesting."

"I don't care. I don't have time for this."

"Right, important meeting. You look very nice. Professional. Um, I swear, I come in peace. I-I feel awful about last night."

"Yeah, me too." My coffee pot gurgles behind me, but I stay focused on Jack. His stumbling words and distressed expression strike a slightly sympathetic chord in me. "I have to leave in seven minutes."

"All I need is one. Rowan, please."

He's wearing the same clothes as last night, and the soft skin under his eyes is more shaded than usual. I groan, ticking through a must-grab list in my head. *Coffee. Keys. Bag. Book. Notebooks.* "A minute... but follow me."

"Awesome." He closes the door behind us, and I keep a cautious eye on him.

I click-clack over the hardwoods to the kitchen and prepare my coffee.

"Okay, I've been an asshole—I get that. Yes, you've sparked some ideas. But the party, the dancing—that wasn't some manipulation to get material. I was having a nice time. I had nothing to do with Renita's behavior—"

"I know that." I leave my coffee mug and step into the converted garage.

"Good. Anyway, I could hardly sleep last night thinking about our fight. I'm not a vampire, more of a... scavenger. But I'd never take anything that wasn't freely given. Understand?"

I shrug, focused on my mission. Two large bookcases flank the side wall—one with annotated books and the other with a rainbow of color-coded three-ring binders labeled by unit. Sure, it's all material safely secured in the cloud. But it's comforting and ritualistic for me, beginning a new unit by brushing up on the material in my hands, like going through an old photo album.

"Um, if you say I can't write about you... And by that, I mean someone *like* you... then fine. I'll delete the pages—"

"Really?" I look up from the shelves in surprise. "The first pages you've written in over a year? Do you mean that?"

"Yes," he says with a slight hesitation.

"Good."

"But maybe you'd be willing to read them first?" His usual broodiness shifts into puppy-dog pleading.

Huffing, I pull out the lavender notebook labeled THEMES and a second one on GENRE. He holds out his arms to carry them for me, and I notice a book tucked against his side. I hand him the stack with a sigh, meeting his eyes.

"Maybe... I really can't think about this now. I'm woefully unprepared for this meeting."

He smirks at the notebooks. "It doesn't look like it."

A Tale of Two Cities slides out from the T section of my shelf, and I place it atop Jack's stack. He awkwardly tucks the notebooks under his arm with his existing book to examine mine. "What the hell is this?"

"*A Tale of Two Cities.*"

"No, I mean, what've you done to it?" He thumbs over the multi-colored sticky notes along its top and side. Flipping through pages, he laughs over my underlines and annotations like I'm a foolish child who colored outside the lines. "Is this a social media thing? Bookstagram? BookTok?"

"No, I'm not on social media. I'm a teacher. I annotated it."

He cocks his head before he eyes my crowded bookshelves. "Do you treat all your books like this?"

"I do, actually. It's my job to study books."

"You aren't meant to *study* books. You're supposed to read and enjoy them." He holds the book up. "*This* is the problem with English classes."

My shoulders slump. *Am I really doing this right now?* In the kitchen, I grab my oversized bag, holding it open so he can shove the notebooks inside.

"English classes suck the beauty and life out of books and turn kids against reading. Reading is meant to be a wild adventure, not a fucking dissection. Besides, who wants to read long-dead old white guys or repressed women looking for husbands? It's boring. Over. Done. Do you think Shakespeare would be proud of his *forced* teen readership? Doing this to a book turns a living, breathing organism into a cadaver. It's torture, Rowan."

"I don't have time for this." I grab the book and tuck it into my oversized bag before heading out the door.

At my top-down VW, I toss my bag into the passenger seat. He leans beside me, setting the coffee I forgot into the cupholder.

"I know you have to go, but here." He hands me the book from under his arm. *The Other Us.* The cover is an artsy blend of blues and blacks around a silhouetted couple—close in one scene while separate in the next like an odd tug-of-war that feels intriguing and sad. "It's an advanced reader copy. I know you don't read romance, but can you make an exception? I'd love for you to understand what I do. I promise—it's not a wine and roses story."

My fingers slip over the cover, and my stress moves aside for a light smile. Being given an ARC feels like an honor.

"Well, in that case... I'll give it a shot. Thanks, Jack."

"You're welcome." His smile grows, but he holds up his finger. "But please, read it for pleasure. No highlights or sticky tabs or whatever the hell. Read it as it's *meant* to be read. It's the only way to really live in a story."

In less than five minutes, he's insulted my profession and poked fun at my process.

Still, I love the way he describes it. *To really live in a story.* Part of me wants to blow off Dr. Evelyn Tate for the beach and do exactly that.

With a satisfied grin, he opens the driver's side door. "Don't be late."

"Right!" I get in, tucking his book into my extra-large bag with everything else.

Fifteen minutes later, I arrive at my meeting. Dr. Evelyn Tate's office is as zen and controlled as she is—a peaceful island amid the unkempt sea of florescent lights, painted concrete walls, and the scent of cleaner mixed with feet. Nothing here is standard issue. She doesn't use the overhead lights but full-bodied gray lamps on her rustic wood desk. The room smells like fresh linen, and soft blue curtains shield the dingy blinds. A cushy white leather chair awaits me, sitting opposite her more queen-like one. A plush shag carpet cradles my feet. Peaceful scenes cover the concrete walls, boasting words of encouragement. *Mind over matter... First, be kind... We are all in this together... Be the difference.*

Her perfectly tan face edges into a well-practiced smile. "How's your summer, Rowan?"

"Busy but productive, thanks. Yours?"

She breaks from her script to hold up her left hand. A rock the size of my car glimmers on her finger. "Same here. He proposed on our Caribbean trip on his yacht."

"Ah, congratulations. You and Xander are great together. You're both so accomplished and driven."

She contemplates my words with an amused air. "Yes. We complement each other. I bet you feel the same way about Dean."

"We're a good fit."

"And you're so *cute*," she adds with a girlish grin.

A forced smile covers my annoyance, though I'm sure she doesn't mean anything by it. Dean and I *are* cute. But words are important. It bothers me as if by *cute*, she implies childlike and small, especially compared to her and her ginormous rock.

"Tell me about your wedding plans. Dean says you're holding off for now?"

"We're taking our time. Um, when did you talk to Dean?"

"During our Teams meeting about his project last week. I think we discussed his acting sabbatical more than his project."

"Right, of course. He's been very busy." Last night's sting resurfaces, with my call to him still unanswered.

She eyes my hands, resting on my crossed thigh, and looks puzzled. "Everything alright between you two?"

Game face, Rowan. "Yes, of course. I forgot my ring this morning. I haven't gotten used to wearing it yet... I've started a wedding binder. It's full of ideas to talk about when he gets back."

"The wedding will be lovely, I'm sure. Dean's such a generous soul."

Generous? It's another word that feels like it has a double meaning. Yes, Dean's a generous person, but of all the adjectives one could use to describe him, why pick that one? *Is he generous for loving a woman like me? Generous for still wanting to marry me after I screwed up his proposal?*

With a quiet breath, I disregard my oversensitivity. "He is, thanks."

"Well, I doubt your classroom project is about weddings. Tell me..." She leans back in her soft, white leather chair like I'm meant to blow her away. "How do you plan on inspiring your students this year?"

I don't know.

"Um, well… It's very exciting."

"I'm sure it is." She gives me a look that suggests that her certainty is fading.

"It is." I dig in my oversized bag to buy time. I remember something about exploring life philosophies and *A Tale of Two Cities*, but a glance at her bulletin board of trite sayings muddles my idea. My hand falls onto a book, and I pull it out.

Only it's not *A Tale of Two Cities*. My fingers trace the artsy cover of Jack's book. "The only way to *really* live in a story is… to read for pleasure. My Inspiration Project is to strengthen my students' love for reading so it becomes a lifelong habit. What better way to do that than to give them a choice?"

She sits up. "A choice?"

"Yes. They'll decide what to read, and I'll help them apply their critical thinking skills to whatever they choose. No more dead white guys or women hunting for husbands. No more antiquated language or outdated themes… unless that's what they want. Instead, they'll study heroes outside the white, male, or hetero boxes of classic lit. They can read banned books, modern books, even cheesy romances."

I hold up Jack's book. "To set the example, I'll read this."

Her porcelain face tilts with surprise. "That book isn't out yet."

"It's an ARC," I announce proudly, hoping it might earn me extra points. "Are you a Jack Graham fan?"

Her eyes dart to a bookshelf where three of his books fill the space between her high school swimming trophies. *Cape Moon* is upside down, tempting me to set it right.

"You could say that," she answers slowly. "This is interesting. You want to give them more autonomy. Liberate them from the oppression of high school English classes."

"Um, sure. Testing their literary skills against their choices will motivate them, I think."

"Yes, but how will you grade them? What about their AP exams?"

"They're juniors and seniors. They've already read enough classics to ace the AP exam's open-ended essay. But we'll study the same concepts that'll ensure they score well on the test. As for the classroom..." I take a cleansing breath, the idea forming into something beautifully, irritatingly cogent in my head. "It'll be like a Montessori approach to an English class—the students will guide the learning. The assignments will be based on what they want to learn."

I want her to hate the idea, to tell me—*no, order me*—to come up with something else. My excuses are primed and ready. It's the wedding... the new house... the foster child living with me soon... *I've overextended myself, Evelyn. Please give me more time...* everything I should've said initially.

"Rowan, this is... inspired. It's so simple and yet so engaging and diverse. Our main goal here is to develop lifelong learners. Your idea does that. You have my full support."

"Oh, thanks, Evelyn."

"I will need it in writing, though, with a semester-long plan."

"Of course."

She shakes her golden head. "It's funny. I had a sneaking suspicion that without Dean, you'd struggle coming up with a great idea on your own."

My gaping expression returns.

"—But I'm happy to be proven wrong. I'm looking forward to an inspired year."

She stands, indicating that our meeting is over. Feeling somewhat gutted, I leave her—a grateful smile plastered to my face. But inside, I'm crying for the notebooks that will go unused, the books we won't be reading, and the work ahead of me. I might as well be a first-year teacher with nothing prepared.

That Jack Graham authored this *brilliant* idea makes it even worse.

Eleven

ROWAN

Within an hour, I'm in my beach chair, letting the salty wind and the glittering ocean restore me.

Only it's not working. Tossing out eight years of lesson plans and thousands of hours of hard work means sacrificing my identity as a teacher. I *hate* this plan. Worse, I don't think I can pull it off. *What have I done?*

"A little harmless improvisation. That's all," Dean once said when the kids went off-script. I imagine that's what he'd say now before reminding me what I'm known for, *"Is there anything you can't fix?"*

I slump in my beach chair. *I can't fix us.* I stare at my phone, willing Dean's face to light up the screen. What goes through his head when he sees that I've called? Is he so busy that he doesn't have the time or energy to respond, or does he not want to?

Pulling out Jack's book, I stifle annoying tears. Crying never helps.

I open the cover and flip to the first page. *The Other Us.*

The first scene pulls me in immediately. A young couple sits nervously in a nondescript waiting room. It's unclear what kind of waiting room it is or why they're there, but there's an alluring intensity to the way they are with each other, adoring and anxious. Sweet and tense. And peppered with little intimacies. It's as if whatever awaits them determines their fate.

I reach into my bag for my pencil case, ready to mark the foreshadowing and highlight the engaging imagery. But then, I remember. I left that at home to force myself to try Jack's way—to live in the story.

I groan. *Jack.* I don't know what to think about him. Should I rely on my first impressions—that he's a brooding Heathcliff, a partying playboy, and an obnoxious jerk? Or the brief moments that combat them—his apologies, sharing about his brother, his help getting furniture for Sara's room (Rose has already sent a text alert), and his offer to toss out what he's written? My feelings mix like spilled paint, swirling into icky shades of gray.

I need this beach day. I push thoughts of my enigmatic next-door neighbor out of my head.

But page to page, I trace him through the story like a faint backroad on a crowded map. I see shadows of Jack in his main character—his antsy writing energy, his moodiness, his dark eyes—but they aren't the same people. Like a literary *Where's Waldo* game, I find other familiar caricatures. Tom is a calm, well-spoken therapist. Marcy shows up as the main character's sister. Rose is a nurse, while Vernon is a neighbor obsessed with model trains. Small clues reveal their identities—Tom's voice, Rose's red hair, Vernon's rambling, and Marcy's matter-of-fact way of putting things. But anyone outside the neighborhood wouldn't make the connections. They are pale versions of the originals disguised in Jack's fictional world.

The story revolves around Caulder and Jasmine, a seemingly perfect, passionate couple, magical in the way some couples just are. But they have secrets—Jasmine is bipolar, while Caulder battles depression, insomnia, and alcoholism. So, when they're good, they're *really* good. But when one or both aren't, they're the absolute worst people for each other. And they're rarely "right" at the same time.

It's tragic, sad, and dark but beautiful in how they stay together, regardless of how hard it is. *The Other Us* is the side of them they don't let others see, the side they fight against to return to that sweet spot of mutual "normalcy." And there's hope, *always* hope like this impenetrable chain locked between them.

In a heart-wrenching scene near the end, they push each other away, sacrificing their happiness to help the one they love. They put on brave faces and say things they don't mean, all while screaming on the inside like they're being ripped in half.

I fold the book against my chest—I have to stop reading. I've never known love like that, but the scene hurts in strange ways. The pain I keep locked away rattles my inner cages. That's what I do—put on a brave face when I'm screaming inside.

The sun and breezes bathe my bad feelings, and though fearing an unhappy end to his "not a wine and roses story," I pick it back up.

When I finish, I'm crying. The sun's setting. Nearby sunbathers stare with concern.

"It's a good book," I defend tearfully. "A *really* good book."

Watching the surf, I let the tears come—it feels good to let them out, especially in the mental safety of a fictional world and surrounded by strangers. I'm devastated, but in the best way. Crying helps, after all, I decide as my tension releases in the purge. My personal sadness slips out, camouflaged with the emotions I feel for Jasmine and Caulder's story.

The Other Us has a happily-ever-after but *not really*—the couple tries living apart to better their conditions only to discover they can't and decide that five minutes of happiness together is worth whatever time it takes to get there. So, the ending is sad because things will never be easy for them.

Even so, part of me wishes for a love like that, one worth any struggle. This is what Mira meant about two people being *desperate* for each other. I've never felt that before. But once, when someone felt something *like* that for me, it felt wrong and became my nightmare.

So, my other half understands—*that's why I love Dean.* Safety and comfort are more important than desperation. I can't imagine feeling that, anyway, let alone finding someone who is decent and kind, doesn't mind my scars, *and* wants me *desperately*. That's a fantasy reserved for romance novels and one-in-a-million couples.

During the quiet and thoughtful drive home, I'm still reeling from Jack's beautiful story. I plan to reread it tonight in bed with a glass of wine—I'm shocked at how much I loved it.

More surprisingly, *this is a book I can teach*. His expert use of literary devices feeds my teacher's imagination—not only can I teach the same concepts that I do with Shakespeare or Hemingway, but with *The Other Us*, it'll actually be... fun.

What if I turned my classroom into an everyday book club? With ideas spinning up like a tornado, my wine-in-bed plans will have to wait until after a brainstorming session.

Rose and Vernon rush from their house when I pull into the driveway.

"Oh, Rowan, you're finally home." She claps. "We must discuss Operation Foster Furniture."

"It's an honorable thing," Vernon says, "offering your home. My Uncle James and Aunt Loraine hosted foster children and foreign exchange students for some thirty-odd years. Of course, that was when—"

"Vernon, no. Rowan, we're headed to Jack's for dinner. Join us."

"Um, I need a shower... and to take care of Edgar... and do some things." The more I speak, the worse my excuses sound.

"Come after all that, love," Rose says, unfazed. "We're making BBQ pizzas. Yummy for the tummy. I've been sent loads of furniture pictures. It'd be nice if you could sort what you want."

"Our street is a generous one," Vernon says, "and there's no time like the present to do a good deed. I want to work out the pick-up and delivery with Tom and Jack. But we can't make plans without you. You like pizza, don't you?"

"Of course. But is the *entire* neighborhood invited?"

"Just our little corner. Do say you'll be over."

"Yes, in a little while."

Rose claps giddily again before they take the path between our houses to his backyard.

Almost an hour later, I follow the same path. Twinkle lights and Edison bulbs brighten a surprisingly peaceful setting—this isn't his typical party. My neighbors sit beside the outdoor kitchen at a large round table, laughing, drinking, and nibbling from a charcuterie board and slightly charred pizza from the oven.

Vernon and Tom stand in old-school formality as I join the table. When the typical greetings are out of the way, I say, "Where's Jack?"

"Writing." Rose motions to the lighted, open windows of his office. "Having people around sometimes helps, like background noise at a coffee shop."

Marcy loads a plate for me while Tom pours me an expensive Merlot. I'm about to question these ever-evolving rules concerning Jack—not to disturb him while he's writing and yet come over and enjoy a meal in his backyard while he's writing—but my phone chimes.

I hold it up. "It's Mom from India. Is it okay for me to take this?"

"Oh, yes! We'd love to meet her." Rose lights up, bouncing in her seat.

I accept the FaceTime call and find Mom where I usually do—sipping tea in the small courtyard of her rental. It's morning there, and she's dressed in a silky blouse, sleeveless to highlight her toned arms, and probably black pants, though I can't see them. She's one of few women in the world who can pull off a pixie haircut—it makes her seem taller and goes with her professional vibe. Her signature gold hoops dangle from her ears, and she twiddles with the single pearl necklace around her neck.

Until lately, Mom and I have always been extremely close. Now a consultant for the military and overseas companies, she's busy. Sometimes distracted. But our communication has suffered since Dean came into my life. She doesn't think he's right for me and, like Mira, doesn't refrain from telling me so. Still, given her difficult history with men, I doubt she'll ever approve of anyone.

Circling the table with my phone, I introduce my neighbors. "This is my mom, Christine Mackey."

Vernon stands up, saluting her. "Thank you for your service. My father, God rest his soul, worked a submarine mess hall for fifteen-odd—"

"Vernon, no." Rose pulls him to his seat.

The group chitchats about India, military service, and the weather before I give up holding my phone and perch it against a pepper grinder to put the entire table on-screen.

When Mom asks about the oyster roast, the table goes silent, everyone glancing around to see who might answer first.

"It was fine. Let's not talk about it. Or Jack." My abrupt tone sounds rude, though I whisper the last part.

Rose flashes her most sympathetic look. "Did something happen with Jack?"

"He behaved so admirably last night." Vernon folds his arms.

"Wait. Who's Jack?" Mom leans toward her computer screen.

"Rowan's next-door neighbor." Tom motions at our surroundings. "This is Jack's place."

Marcy leans in. "Jack Graham. The writer."

My mother squeals—a sound I've *never* heard her make. Mom doesn't even read romance.

So, my mouth drops when she says, "*The* Jack Graham? Author of *Cape Moon* and *Edge to Nowhere* and, oh my gosh, *Love and Other Miseries*?"

Okay, I guess she does read romance.

"The one and only," Rose says. "Jack grew up here. He's our resident celebrity."

"A good boy, too," Vernon adds. "He handled the oyster roast situation with care."

"What situation, Vernon?" Mom prompts despite my chiding look.

"Well, our neighbor Renita made some unfortunate remarks about the need to cover up Rowan's, um, well, you know, pressuring Rowan to try her Mary Kay products as a means to..."

"Hide her scars," Rose says plainly.

"Thank you, dear. Jack got angry—"

"I've never seen him so upset," Rose gawks.

"He tried to deal with it quietly. Told Ed that Renita needed to go home. Then, Renita, well—"

"She had a right conniption." Rose's blue-gray eyes double in size. "Ed didn't know what to do with her."

"He attempted to coax her into his golf cart, but she said she was a caged bird finally let free and bringing beauty to the world—"

"She was off her rocker," Rose says. "She gets this way, you see."

"The party was crashing, and we hadn't even reached the second batch of oysters yet. Poor Ed, full of apologies." Vernon shakes his head like these are the larger travesties—uneaten oysters and a man apologizing. "Finally, Jack cornered her. He gently explained that everything was a-okay. *You just need a rest, Renita. Nothing's broken that can't be fixed—*"

"Oh, and that she *does* make the world beautiful in her way," Rose chimes in.

"Renita broke into tears. Then, Jack put his arm around her, and she hugged him, saying how sorry she was, and he said… oh, what'd he say?"

Rose perks up. "Oh, yes. That it's not a party until someone gets drunk off their ass and acts a fool. The crowd cheered."

A snicker bumbles from me, hearing Jack's words in Rose's prim British accent.

"The party went on like nothing happened, and all the oysters were eaten," Vernon concludes, "and that's that."

"No, that wasn't just that." Rose turns to Mom and me. "Jack walked Renita home himself. I thought that was sweet, considering how upset she made him."

"Did everyone know why he was upset? You know, what Renita said?" I ask, though I still don't want to talk about it.

"Oh, no, dear." Rose shakes her head.

"We had no idea," Marcy says, motioning to Tom. "We just thought Renita was being Renita."

"Vernon and I overheard it, you see. But Jack kept it under wraps." Then, she locks her lips with her fingers and tosses the imaginary key over her shoulder. "No one knows she offended you, love."

"I wasn't... *that* offended. Jack was."

"Rowan, why not?" Mom cuts in, looking bothered. "You *are* a beautiful woman. You should object to anyone telling you to hide your face."

Rose turns to Mom. "Christine, to be fair, Jack didn't give her much chance. He's very full-steam ahead when doing or saying what he wants. He strikes people as a cocky grump. That's why he and Rowan aren't besties... yet." She holds up her crossed fingers.

"But facts are facts," Tom begins with authority, "Jack's writing block is over... and it's because of Rowan."

The table falls silent, staring at me while I groan.

"I don't understand," Mom says. "What does Rowan have to do with Jack's writing?"

"Jack hasn't written a word in over a year," Vernon says.

Mom gasps, hand to heart. "Why not?"

"Let me explain," Vernon says with authority. "Jack had an older brother, Devin. They were more like twins, less than a year apart and inseparable. Best friends with Ben and Margot's son, Corey, next door. The three amigos. But in their teens, Devin was diagnosed with acute lymphoblastic leukemia." He shakes his head. "He fought like hell."

"They all did," Rose continues. "But the treatments were a vicious cycle. Jack lived on high alert, waiting for positive change that never came, watching his brother get sicker and sicker, and helpless to stop it."

"Devin died on a rainy Wednesday in spring," Vernon says. "It would've been the boys' last baseball season together."

"That's when he met Evie," Rose groans. "It was the perfect storm—a grieving boy getting a lot of attention for his dead brother meets an attention-seeking girl who suddenly wants to help him through it. Evie became a fixture in Jack's life. Quite a pretty girl."

Vernon's eyes widen. "A stunner. Still is."

"She dumped him when they were in college," Rose says before adding in air quotes, "so she could focus on her studies."

I shrug lightly. "Everyone has tough breakups."

"True, dear. I'm sure you have a few stories to tell... we'll get them out of you eventually." Rose giggles like it's a game.

"But it didn't end there," Vernon says.

"They still hook up," Rose explains. "Friends with benefits, I suppose, but there's a downside. Evie may have inspired his stories, but she's not good for him. Being with her reminds him of what he's lost. Jack's always in a right state afterward."

"Another vicious cycle," I breathe out, "like with his brother."

"Precisely," Vernon says.

"Jack finished *The Other Us* over a year ago," Rose continues. "Then, Corey's dad, Ben, died in Jack's arms—heart attack in the driveway—and when he reached out to Evie for comfort, she refused like he was asking too much."

"And she told him she'd found someone else, someone serious," Vernon adds.

Rose nods, pursing her lips. "He's had writer's block ever since. I think—"

"*We*. We think," Vernon clarifies.

"Yes, we think. Sorry, love. *We* think his sadness has caught up with him."

"It's like *his* cancer!" Vernon decides vehemently.

"Right, dear. All his partying, grumpiness, and empty relationships—it's just sadness disguised. He needs someone who makes him feel hopeful again. He must purge his old muse and find a new one."

Vernon leans up in his seat, squaring his shoulders. "That's you, Rowan."

"Nope! Not it! Jack doesn't need a muse. It's a sexist and demeaning concept—that women are meant to be mystical beings, puppeteering a man's creativity... and that a man's incapable of creating without one. Jack Graham is a successful, well-loved writer. An amazing writer. Evie didn't do that for him; *he* did. He doesn't need a mystical force guiding his hand. He needs a better mindset and understanding of his abilities. A good therapist will help him better than I ever could. And speaking mythologically, Evie's not a muse, more like a siren toying with him. A good therapist will help him through that, too."

Their dumbfounded, wide-eyed expressions—not at me but at the air around me—make me slump. "He's right behind me, isn't he?"

Rose giggles.

Twelve

JACK

Walking up behind Rowan, I suspect I might be in trouble—I *really* like this woman. Her speech about trusting my abilities instead of a mystical force impresses me, but, *of course*, a confident, independent woman like her believes that. So do I, despite what our neighbors think and my writer's block suggests.

It's the small things about her, though. Sharing her mom's call with the neighborhood. The stern way she says my name. The lavender and vanilla smell when the breeze catches her just right. Her tight calves and long legs—*always* those legs.

But most of all, it's the look on her face when she whips around and finds me there. Her cheeks flush pink, and her full lips part in a quiet inhale. Her always-pretty blue eyes widen and sparkle like diamonds at sea. She *wants* to see me.

That's enough to change us from cordially volatile to something else entirely.

She searches for words that don't come. I don't know what to say either. I'm gobsmacked—a word I never use.

"Jack, meet Rowan's mum, Christine." Rose points to the flushed but lovely woman on the propped screen.

I pick the phone up, flashing my best smile. "Hi, Christine. I'm Jack. Nice to meet you."

"Oh, my. You're even more handsome than on your book jackets."

"Mom, geez," Rowan mutters, eyes rolling and cheeks reddening, just like her mother's. *This could be fun.*

"I've read all your books," Christine says. "They're wonderful, Jack. Truly. They make me... believe in love again."

Rowan's brow knits, hearing her say that. *What's with these women and love?*

"Wow, Christine. That's a beautiful compliment. Thank you."

"I can't believe you're Rowan's next-door neighbor!" Christine giggles while her daughter scoffs beside me.

"Me, neither. So, when do we get to meet you in person?" I ask.

"End of August."

"Really, Mom?" Touching my hand, Rowan moves the screen toward her. "Before Thanksgiving? That's awesome!"

"For two weeks... I'll help with the start of school and Sara. I can't wait to meet her. Rowan's going to be a foster mom. Did she tell you?"

The conversation veers into fostering and how they all want to help. I hold the phone, taking Christine around to each speaker and not minding the job.

Before long, Christine sighs. "Oh, this has been absolutely lovely, but I must get to work. It's been a pleasure meeting all of you... And Jack?"

I turn the screen. "Yes, Christine."

"Rowan despises romance. You know all about jaded hearts. Get her to believe in love again, and I'll buy you dinner while I'm there. Hell, I'll buy you dinner anyway!"

"It's a date. I've already pushed my newest on her. We'll see if she reads it, though."

"I'm not jaded. I read it," Rowan chimes in defensively.

I nearly drop the phone, turning toward her. "What? All of it? I just gave it to you this morning."

"I'm an English teacher. Speed-reading is a required skill."

"You've always been a quick reader. She'd go through four or five books a week as a teenager," Christine adds.

"I had little else to do. You're going to be late, Mom."

Everyone says their goodbyes, and the phone flashes to the home screen. The table chatter returns in a wave as if nothing interrupted them. They discuss dinner plans for Christine's visit, which kicks off a discussion about local restaurants, good and bad.

Rowan doesn't return to her seat but stays beside me, watching the others with amusement like they're a life-sized diorama of a pleasant evening or a Norman Rockwell painting.

A soft touch along her upper arm brings her attention back to me. My hand stays there, gently holding her in place as if she might run off rather than end my agony.

Taking me in, she asks, "What's wrong?"

I try sounding cool. Relaxed. But the words come out hurried and flustered. "You finished my book? What'd you think?"

Her breath catches. "Jack, I loved it. I can't stop thinking about Caulder and Jasmine—their passion, their fragility. I've been holding them in my heart since the beach like they're wounded birds I've scooped up and want to protect, though I know they'll never be the same again. *I* won't be the same again."

Tears threaten her eyes. *Has she been crying?* Her free hand grabs my other forearm, right between the tattooed conch shell from *The Lord of the Flies* and the rebel alliance symbol from *Star Wars*. Her fingers tighten to my skin like she's bracing herself against her uncharacteristic emotion now spilling into our odd circle.

And for once, she holds nothing back—I *really* fucking like this woman. Really like her touch, too.

"That scene..."

I know exactly what she means before she explains—the one I wrote thanks to her.

"—when they try to end things, though it rips them apart. You captured their inner pain despite their outward appearances—that resonated. I feel that way often. Anyway, I did what you said. I lived in that story. I'm still there. And tonight, I'll read it again."

I think to tell her—*you're the reason that scene is so good*—but it's too weird. The woman who doesn't believe in muses and has more shields than an army might find the news that I've "bled" her for ideas disconcerting.

It's sure as hell disconcerting for me.

Instead, I release a trapped breath, relieved. She hates the genre, so maybe that's why it feels like a tremendous win, turning the un-romance-able into a fan. But that she loved my book feels like a walk-off home run; her sparkly, tearful eyes and tender smile match the ecstasy of the home team crowd, cheering as I round the bases.

I'm in serious trouble here.

"Let me write about you—not *you*, but shades of you, whichever sides you'll let me see."

Her hand falls from my arm. "I don't know. I'm really not that interesting."

"Course you are. More interesting every second. Let me talk to you and ask you questions. I'll give you veto power over anything I write, and you can read it first."

She looks distressed, but her eyes stay on mine as she deliberates, probably running through every conceivable pro and con in her head. I think of her *yes, no, maybe* proposal debacle and wonder if I'll get a similar non-answer.

My hand drifts down her arm before letting go. "Give the answer *you want*, Rowan. Don't overthink it."

"Yes." The word falls out with surprising ease, and she seems happy to let it go. "But I need something, too."

"Tell me."

"I have a confession to make. It stuck with me when you explained your hatred for English classes this morning. So when I met with the Ice Queen—um, she's my boss, err, one of them anyway—I panicked over not having a solid idea for my Inspiration Project and used yours."

"My what?"

"Your idea about tossing the usual curriculum aside and letting students read for pleasure." She pauses for air, her arms flailing in an awkward shrug. "I want to see if I can foster a true love of reading in my students. It'll be up to them—what they read and what we do in class. A guided learning adventure... or a disaster. Not sure yet."

"A teacher relinquishing control to her students? That's not a disaster. That's a fucking miracle. How can I help?"

"I don't know yet. How do I have a plan when there's no plan? I'll have to be prepared for anything in case it comes up. I may want feedback on my ideas... once I have them. Gosh, I can't believe you talked me into this. You saw my notebooks, Jack. How can I teach without them?"

"Eh, you don't need them." With a smile, I tap her left temple. "It's all up here, anyway, right?"

She smirks lightly while her shoulders bounce in a shrug.

"Don't think about it like teaching," I say. "You get to talk books with a bunch of cool kids every day. What could be better than that?"

Her unease shifts into a slow smile. "You're right. It'll be refreshing. Perhaps *I'm* a little tired of explaining why we must decipher Shakespeare and why finding a husband topped every heroine's priority list back then." A breath escapes her. "I can do this... and it might be amazing."

My grin widens watching her—*I inspired this?* "Looks like we might be mutual muses. No harm in that, right?"

Her head tilts, considering it. "I'm not sure yet, but perhaps it's better than being cordially volatile."

I feign disappointment. "Aw, I like cordially volatile."

Her soft giggle is downright addictive.

"Jack, you should visit her class." Tom draws our attention back to the group to find them all staring at us—I'd forgotten they were there. "If Rowan's students will be reading contemporary novels, then wouldn't they want to meet a contemporary author?"

"A best-selling one at that!" Marcy says. "They'd love you!"

Rowan's eyes light up again as her gaze lands on me.

Shit.

"Oh, do it, Jack. It's not really a public appearance. More like community service," Rose argues.

"It would mean a lot to the kids... and me," she says.

"Fine."

The table erupts with cheers. Rowan practically beams. There's no getting out of it.

Rowan looks puzzled. "Why do you hate public appearances?"

"I'm lucky enough not to have to sell myself in the media. People appreciate the mystery. Besides, I cuss too much for TV interviews, and book signings are overwhelming."

"Too many women hitting on him at once," Marcy laughs.

"Well, he won't have that problem at school... I hope. I'll make sure it's low-key."

"Then, I'm in your hands," I say, flashing a coy grin.

Her cheeks turn pink, and it feels like another win.

Damn.

Thirteen

ROWAN

Walking home from Jack's place, I feel befuddled. The same man I slammed the door on after the oyster roast is now something like a friend. How did that happen?

His book certainly altered my opinion of contemporary romance novels, but that's not why I'm warming up to him.

I smile over his charm with Mom. Hearing her say she believes in love again thanks to his books fills me with gratitude. I never wanted her to stop believing in love, but she hasn't dated since my injury, perhaps in solidarity with me. It's amazing to see her so hopeful… and giggly.

Besides that, he charmed me, too. His intense focus on my thoughts about his book sent tingles down my spine—I still feel them like tiny aftershocks. Jack-shocks. Jack-tingles. Ugh. I don't know what to call them, but neither should've happened. He shouldn't care about my opinion—the world loves him. Still, his touch, his rapt attention, his eyes burrowing into mine, I felt valued in a way that I haven't in ages. It's beautifully strange to think I might matter to him.

Equally exhilarating and scary is our deal. It forced a mental debate with two drastically different sides. I thought of Trent and how open I was with him, just for it to be used against me in his wicked manipulations. On the flip side, Dean knows so little about my past that it's almost laughable, and it's only hurt us for the added distance it's caused.

But neither applies to Jack—it's literature, not love. A simple favor between neighbors. He's a hot book nerd and author, so *of course*, I'll have Jack-tingle-shocks on occasion. But I'm aware of the fleeting nature of such things and entirely capable of ignoring them.

Weeks go by, and not much changes.

At random, Jack pops over with a bottle of wine. He's a Magic 8-Ball of questions, seeming to snatch them from a cluttered, nonsensical list. A benign list—I'm grateful to discover.

Why do women apologize so much?

What clubs were you in in high school?

How many places have you lived?

What's your favorite book of all time?

In turn, I ask about his former English classes—what he loved and hated—and his book history. Talking books with Jack helps conceptualize my teaching strategy. With the whoosh of an email, I send Dr. Evelyn my semester-long plan, glad to get back to my summer.

And Sara's imminent arrival.

The neighborhood provides a wrought iron daybed (courtesy of the Mueller family), a tall wood dresser (thanks to Tom and Marcy), and a small desk with a wooden rolling chair (from Ed and Renita, who also gave me a basketful of free Mary Kay products as an apology). Vernon, Tom, and Jack supervise the deliveries, and though I could easily help move items into the house, they are insistent on doing the heavy lifting.

Men.

With the money I don't have to spend on furniture, I splurge on a full-length mirror, a cute desk lamp, and a shag rug. I go with lavender curtains to compliment the sage walls and bed linens. A short bookshelf completes the room, which I stock with some of my favorites as a teenager. *Little Women. Anne of Green Gables.* Titles by John Greene, Kiera Cass, and *The Hunger Games.* She'll have plenty to read and a lovely room to retreat to.

Sara Sweet arrives on the last Tuesday of July. I greet them in the driveway, where Mira unloads an old, beach-blue bicycle with a basket and a single suitcase from her SUV.

"Oh, we can go on bike rides...once I get a bike, that is," I say as I think it. "It's a great neighborhood for it."

"I know. I live here, too," Sara says with an eye roll and a huff.

She is a head taller and thirty pounds heavier than me, wearing mostly black and donning long, lavender-colored hair that looks so thick and different I wonder if it's real. A nose ring and brow stud tell me she's brave, perhaps keen on attention, while the dark smudges on her right fingers suggest she's an artist. I adore her *instantly.*

"Right. I forgot that. I'm Rowan." I extend my hand.

She keeps her arms folded and looks disgusted. "God, your face."

Dropping my hand, I gape while cueing up the story I give my students. "Well—"

"I don't care." She steers her bike to the porch, propping it against a column.

Inside the house, I give her the full tour. Sara isn't impressed by the snack-filled pantry or soda-lined fridge, though both are stocked with things teenagers love. She turns her nose up at my freshly baked chocolate chip cookies and sandwiches on the kitchen table.

She ignores the lavender-hued towels in her bathroom, which I point out are, coincidentally, the same color as her hair. The cozy vibe I created in her room with sage bedding, light green walls, twinkle lights around the window, and a soft desk lamp doesn't impress her either.

Grunting, she eyes the Squishmallow on her bed—Danielito the Starry Cat—before tossing him into the trashcan by her desk. "I'm not five."

"Sara, don't be rude," Mira says gently. "We talked about this."

Rescuing Danielito, I shrug. "That's fine. I'll take him. He reminds me of Edgar."

I force an indifferent smile, hugging the soft, stuffed cat. Whatever pride I have left in my work shrivels in her contempt.

Edgar saunters into her bedroom to see what's happening. Animals make for excellent icebreakers, and he's such an adorable cat.

But Sara scoffs again as if it's her favorite reaction. "What're you? A witch?"

I laugh like a dork struggling through a bad date. "No, of course not."

In the living room, I perk up when she asks for the Wi-Fi password. But when I tell her it's Nevermore99, as a nod to both Edgars, she groans. "You're one of those sad nerds, aren't you?"

I don't know how to answer. Worse, her thumbs fly over her phone screen, like she's sharing my sad nerdiness with the world. Or my Wi-Fi password. Or both, based on her satisfied smirk.

Mira bounces on her feet and releases a heavy sigh. "Sara, why don't you take your bag to your room and get settled? Remember what we discussed about making the best of things, huh?"

After a mind-blowingly intricate eye roll that would cause an aneurysm in most people, Sara heaves her suitcase down the hall.

I lean against the back of the couch, pained. "I shouldn't have bought the Squishmallow."

"Yeah, *that's* the takeaway... You're trying too hard. Just relax. Give her space, and she'll warm up to you. Eventually. *Maybe.*"

"Sure she will," I say, mustering my confidence. "She'll love it here when she gives it a chance."

Mira eyes me skeptically. "You want to cry, don't you?"

"No." I swipe the dampness under my eye. "A little. She's a smidge meaner than I expected."

"She's had a rough few days. She's close to her dad. It wasn't easy seeing him off to jail... Remember how sad you were when Mom left on deployment?"

"Of course."

"Well, you had your grandparents. Imagine being stuck with a stranger." Mira helps herself to my cucumber and cream cheese sandwiches. "Rolling out the red carpet probably feels... overwhelming."

"Of course, you're right. Understood. I will pull back the red carpet and play things cool."

"Just be normal. You do your own thing. Let her do hers. Take it slow."

Mira puts Sara's number in my phone. "She might be more willing to communicate with you this way."

When she hands it back, I send off a quick text to her. *This is Rowan. Text or call whenever. Happy to have you here.* *house emoji, nerd emoji*

Mira shakes her head. "That's not playing things cool."

"I said *whenever*."

After a short talk with Sara alone, Mira leaves. The house remains quiet but unsettled, like restless spirits are afoot, but they don't know what to do with themselves.

I follow Mira's advice and give Sara space. This makes me think of Dean. Why do people need so much space from me? If he were here to support me, he'd have Sara talking and laughing by now. And I'd feel like a woman in a solid relationship instead of wondering if two weeks of silence falls into the ghosted category.

I stare at my phone, debating. Should I add another text to the lingering messages I've already sent?

No. Tucking my phone into my pocket, I clean the kitchen and put the cookies and sandwiches away. Then, I break out my laptop to catch up on work emails and continue researching for my Inspiration Project. There's nothing like to-dos to stave off an emotional breakdown.

I start a list in my work notebook. *#1: Stock up on extra school supplies & pantry items*

I wonder if Sara will want to go back-to-school shopping. What teenage girl doesn't like a trip to the mall? With the stipend provided for Sara's care, she'll have her own shopping spree. I almost text her the idea before reminding myself to give her space. That brilliant plan can wait for tomorrow.

In the kitchen, I make dinner. I play music while cooking, hoping to lure her from her room to see what's happening. *Maybe she'll want to help. Or talk. Something.* But she doesn't take the bait. Over an hour later, I pull steaming enchiladas from the oven, set the table, and head to Sara's door. She hasn't come out of her room once since Mira left, and I hope that means she's enjoying her space.

But when I knock, she doesn't answer. I try again, louder this time. Nothing.

Heart racing, I check the bathroom and the rest of the house. But I only find Edgar chittering at birds through the back window.

At her door again, I pound. "Sara, this isn't funny. Open up, please."

When she fails to answer, I try the doorknob. It's locked. In my panic, I jump to frightful conclusions. *What if she's unwell? Or she took something? Or tried to hurt herself?*

I bolt to the kitchen, grabbing a fine-pointed knife from the utensil drawer. With shaking hands, I work it into the keyhole on her door. The knife slips, slicing a three-inch gash into my right palm. But the lock pops and the door swings open.

Sara's room is empty. Her suitcase sits unpacked on the bed. The window's open, and the screen's been popped out. Checking the front porch confirms that her bike is gone.

First, I'm relieved not to find her unwell or unconscious. Thinking drugs or suicide is a harsh conclusion to jump to, but not knowing Sara well and being fully aware of the desperate lengths teenagers will go to, I couldn't help it.

With a paper towel pressed to my bloody hand, I text her. *Sara, dinner's ready. Where are you?*

No answer, and ten minutes later... *This is Rowan, and I'm worried. Text me, please.*

Twelve minutes and nothing, I call. It goes to voicemail. "Sara, this isn't funny. Please call or text me immediately."

Seventeen minutes pass. I sit at the kitchen banquette with a glass of water, tapping my fingernails on the Formica like I'm composing a frantic song. As the sky darkens, I wonder how long I should wait before calling the police.

I call Mira instead. When she answers, I blurt, "Sara's gone. She snuck out the window and took her bike. Should I call the police?"

"Rowan, take a breath. How long has it been since you saw her?"

"Not since you were here. I was playing it cool, giving her space. She didn't leave a note. She won't respond to my texts or calls. What am I supposed to do?"

"Stop freaking out, for one thing. She's fifteen. Not three. She's not in danger. She's just being an asshole."

"How do you *know* that?"

"Rowan, it's okay. She's probably at the park or her house—that's the downside of placing her in her neighborhood. She's too close to home. I'll reach out to her. Maybe she'll answer my call."

"If she doesn't?"

"Let's give her until nine... then, we'll freak out and call the police."

I don't like this plan, but I trust Mira. "Fine. But I want her home address."

Reluctantly, Mira gives it to me. Leaving the front door unlocked, I hop into my VW Bug and weave through a dozen neighborhood streets before arriving at Sara's house. Her bike is propped against the stoop of a cluttered rancher with a neatly manicured lawn. There's no garage, but a decrepit-looking carport limping on one side houses rusty bikes, a pile of hubcaps, and other random metal objects. An old green truck boasts an advertisement for Sweet's Lawn Service on the door, and the trailer hitched to its back end holds an industrial mower and other lawn tools. I wonder what a three-month hiatus will do to Mr. Sweet's business.

My first instinct is to pull into her driveway, storm up to the door, and demand she return home. But I don't. Anger only makes everything worse. Besides, it's enough to know where she is and that she's not in danger. For now.

I text Mira with an update and wait for her at home.

Sara climbs into her bedroom window at 8:56. She finds me at the kitchen table with my phone, my hand neatly wrapped in gauze, and the uneaten enchiladas cold and unappetizing beside me.

She grunts at the sight of me and bypasses me for the fridge as if nothing's happened.

I straighten my back and take a breath. "Look, I know this is tough. You don't have to like me—"

"Good because I don't."

Her words burn a hole through me. "Fine. But here we are, like it or not. I want to make this as pleasant as possible for us both. For me, that means knowing you're okay."

"Well, for me, that means dealing with you as little as possible. This place is a shitty hotel to me."

"This little house is friendly, comfortable, and safe—three things you may not have gotten elsewhere." My words come out with surprising sternness, given how weak and disappointed I feel. "I promise to give you space as long as you tell me where you are... and you always come home by nine."

"Whatever." She snatches a banana from the fruit bowl and goes to her room.

After tidying the kitchen and putting the food away, I scoop up Edgar, my new Squishmallow Danielito, and go to my bedroom, locking the door behind me.

Fourteen

ROWAN

"Have time for me?" Jack says when I answer the door. He holds out a bottle of wine with an expression half-worried and half-pleading. His fuller bottom lip curls under his upper teeth, awaiting my response.

"I have nothing but time." My answer drips with disappointment.

"It can't be that bad." He moves inside, shutting the door behind him. "Where's your ward?"

A scoff blusters out. "My ward... that fits since she views me as her warden. She's out. It's been four days, and I've barely had a conversation with her. She hates me."

"She'll warm up."

Doubting it, I eye Jack's wine like it's the Holy Grail—I need a wine night. I produce a corkscrew while he gets out two glasses.

Sara isn't my only source of despair. Mom and Mira have been pushing me to stand up for myself with Dean—either give him an ultimatum (because that *always* goes over well) or break up with him altogether. His silence makes it harder to argue.

Two days ago, Dean FaceTimed from a bar with his RV mates. He looked reddish and warm from alcohol but giddy. "Honey, there you are. I've been meaning to call. Just had the most amazing day—got to say a line. A real line!"

He super-annunciated his words and awkwardly introduced me to his acting buddies. "I told them all about you."

Then, he introduced the girls they'd met at the bar.

"He's been talking about you all night," said one, making me wonder what he says when he describes me.

"Yeah, you're so pretty," the other said in a tone that suggested the opposite.

The camera panned to Dean—wide-eyed and grinning, and I thought... *this is punishment. This is Dean making sure I suffer over my botched answer.*

A familiar uneasiness took hold of me at what I thought I saw hiding behind his eyes—disdain, meanness, anger. I told him to call me tomorrow. He laughed and said, "Yes, no, maybe" before hanging up.

I lay in bed that night, unable to latch on to all those things I love about Dean. Instead of a comfort I long to wrap myself up in, he's become a chisel, breaking me apart in little pieces.

He didn't call the next morning, not that I would've answered.

With little else to do but feel sorry for myself the last few days, I reread Jack's book. Twice. This time, I didn't withhold my annotations, making all the highlights, notes, and stickies my bookish heart desired. Annotating *The Other Us* felt like squeezing a stress ball.

Now, in the kitchen, Jack notices the sticky-filled book on the counter. I half-wonder if I've offended him—riddling the precious ARC with notes and tabs. But he says nothing.

I grab a leftover platter of grapes, cheeses, and crackers scored from Trader Joe's that I'd hoped to share with Sara over a movie. *That* didn't happen, of course.

We settle into the living room—wine and cheese plate on the coffee table. When Edgar saunters in, stretching from his long afternoon cat nap, I sit on the floor and play with him. Jack copies me, stretching his long legs before him while nibbling the cheddar.

"So, what's on your mind today?" I prompt as Edgar circles, emanating his sultry purr.

"Why doesn't Christine believe in love?"

Taken off-guard, wine drizzles awkwardly down my throat, making me cough. "What happened to the cozy questions, huh? Favorite color? Biggest celebrity crush? You know, the easy stuff?"

His brown eyes narrow curiously. "Okay, biggest celebrity crush?"

"It's a toss-up between Keats and Shelley. Don't get me started about Shakespeare and his iambic pentameter."

"You're such a dork." Jack's laugh dwindles fast, though. "Is your mom's love life a difficult question?"

My hand slides over Edgar's arched back. "Mom doesn't date. Not since my injuries. And I don't talk about that."

"Never?"

I shake my head, refocusing on Edgar. But it's a lie. My mac-n-cheese story gets told at least once a year when brave students ask—so I *do* talk about it, just not the real *it*. Even sharing the fake story seems risky with Jack.

"Hmm, what about your no-romance rules? Is that fruit from the same off-limits tree?"

"Um, no. Not exactly. Indirectly."

"Care to share the reasoning behind them?"

"I have nothing against sweet gestures or romance, *theoretically.* But at the beginning of a relationship, the goal is to get to know someone. Romantic gifts and the expectations behind them could cloud a person's judgment—they've clouded mine. It's funny. Parents teach children not to take candy from strangers, and yet, young women not only accept roses, dinners, and drinks from men they don't know but are impressed with the gesture—as if it's an epic quest, going to a florist and pulling out a credit card."

Jack chuckles. "Note to self—never buy Rowan roses."

"I love flowers," I say, dreamier than I intend. "I just don't want them from someone new. I'd much rather have them from someone who knows me and what I like. Not someone trying to impress me... not that men generally try to impress me. Most avoid me."

"Fuck them. They're idiots."

My brow creeps up. "Not all of us are lucky enough to have a contact list full of sex buddies."

"You consider that lucky?" He leans up, petting Edgar, who has plopped between us.

"What would you call it?"

"Routine maintenance," he says in a breath. "Fucking lonely, if I'm honest. I wouldn't buy any of them flowers."

His confession shocks me. The hot guy with a constant rotation of back-yard parties and overnight romps—*how is he lonely?* I can't fathom the *every-body-wants-me* attention he's used to, but part of me leans into what he's saying like a plant toward sunlight. I *know* loneliness.

"Then, that's how you'll know," I say after several silent sips between us.

"Know what?"

"When it's real—you'll want to buy her flowers."

His boyish smile returns like he might be picturing it—a proud stroll into a florist shop for the woman he loves. He'd turn it into a creative mission, choosing only the most meaningful and unique flowers.

Even my sweet imaginings make me sad these days.

"Nice thought, but unlikely," he says, clearing the air. "So, tell me. Did your rules help? And how did you establish them?"

"My rules were part of my dating profiles on the sites Mira made me join."

"Made you? Not a fan of online dating?"

"Not a fan of *dating*... I've had an embarrassing number of no-shows, turn-arounds, or never-call-agains."

He doesn't seem surprised. "You mean, guys that don't show... presumably because they see you from afar?"

"Right. My profile pics always showed my scars, too, but seeing me in person still surprised them. A few made it to the table before turning around. One guy saw my face and said, 'hell no' before leaving."

"Pricks like that aren't worth airspace, let alone your time, Rowan."

"I only signed up for the sites because Mom and Mira were worried about me—*I* didn't want to do it. I thought having rules would weed out idiots—they probably helped. But a few snuck in, anyway."

Jack sits up, crisscrossing his legs and turning toward me. "There's so much to unpack here, I don't know where to begin... Why were Christine and Mira worried?"

"I hadn't dated in a while."

"What's a while?"

"Few years."

"Why not?"

At my hesitation, he pops up, rushes to the kitchen, and returns with the wine bottle. He tops off our dwindling glasses before resuming his position on the floor.

I take a long sip. "I was in a bad relationship, and after, I didn't want to date."

When I don't continue, he stares at me over the tops of his eyes. "It's okay. Tell me about the prick."

These are things I don't talk about. *But you should*, I hear Mira saying like a little devil by my ear. But it's Jack's loneliness confession that eases me into it. His vulnerability tugs at strings I keep tied tightly, loosening them.

"I've had my... *features* since I was fifteen," I say, stealing Renita's word. "When everyone else was going out and getting boyfriends, I was stuck in surgeries or at home recovering." I pause as a memory resurfaces—vague like a ghost rounding a corner. "There was one time... in recovery after a skin graft. The boy in the bed next to mine flirted with me."

Jack's head cocks curiously. "Given your cheesy grin, he must've had a nice bedside manner."

"It's funny—I didn't remember until now. Isn't that weird?"

"Memory is a mystery, elusive sometimes. Tell me about it."

"I don't remember much. He had shockingly red hair. His name was... Caleb. He'd had a skin graft, too, for burns on his hands and arms. A botched arson, he claimed, but I didn't believe him. He was funny. Talking about movies, music, and books with Caleb was the most normal thing I'd done in months. Gosh, I can't believe I'd forgotten... I thought about him for so long after. Every time I went to the hospital after that, I looked for him. Sounds silly, but I hoped I'd see him again, that fate would give us a re-do so I could do things better."

"Like what?"

"Uh, get his number, give him mine, find out where he went to school... basic, I want-to-know-you things." I take another long sip, wondering about Caleb. "Sorry, you want to know about the prick."

"No apologies. I love a good diversion."

"Mira and her wife, Jane, introduced me to Trent. He worked with Jane in real estate. He was an exceptional charmer. He'd seen me before, visiting Jane with Mira, and he liked me, anyway." A light smile perks my lips, remembering how that felt.

"Trent loved romance—he was all roses, wine, dinners out, and surprises. He lavished me with gifts and attention—he said he was making up for lost time and the previous idiots who missed their chance."

"Yikes, he was a charmer."

"I was a sucker for it. I'd never had that before. I'd also never known to look for red flags."

"Like what?"

"Small controlling things at first, like him always choosing the restaurant or making suggestions. *You should wear more green—you look stunning in green. Or flats are okay, but heels are sexy. Why don't you wear your hair up more? If a skirt goes below the knee, it might as well be pants.*"

"An order veiled as a compliment."

"Exactly. But I didn't see it. I thought I'd hit the jackpot—a good guy who didn't mind being seen with me."

"Wait, you call that a jackpot? Sounds like base requirements to me."

A wine-bolstered chuckle blubbers from me. "You sound like Mira—yes, I have self-esteem issues. Do you blame me?"

His eyes roll while he nods. "Fine. So, when did you realize Trent wasn't Prince Charming?"

"He'd get bothered by strangers *supposedly* staring at my scars. At first, I thought he was being protective, but it got weird."

"How?"

"I know when someone's staring—I can't help it. It's a side effect of this." I motion to my face. "But he started noticing the stares and whispers before me, and sometimes, when I didn't believe they were staring at all. He pointed it out everywhere we went, angry at the injustice of it. I feared he'd do something—confront these people or pick a fight."

"Did he?"

"No. No matter how close he seemed to the edge, I always managed to pull him back. Usually, that meant leaving the restaurant or wherever and me spending the rest of the night calming him down, making him feel better."

"Oh, shit." He leans forward, hand to his mouth like he's trying to keep himself from talking.

My head droops as I stare into my wine, ashamed. "You know where this is going."

"He manipulated you into being the damsel in distress so he could play the hero… and reap the rewards of your gratefulness."

"Sick, right? I fell for it, over and over. I stopped going out. Covered up more. Eventually, the anger he directed toward others reversed to me. He'd say or do something horrible, and the next day, I'd get roses or candy or, if it was really bad, jewelry. The worse the offense, the greater the gift."

After another gulp, I say, "Mira dragged me out of the relationship and to a therapist. But endings aren't easy. He couldn't accept that the damaged girl had rejected him. He stalked me, hacked my social media, got creepy…"

I set my glass aside to run my hands over my face as if to wipe the memories away. "A restraining order ended it—most women don't get so lucky. Without Mira's law enforcement connections and Jane making things hard on him at work, things would've been worse for me. He backed off and later moved. And that's the story of the prick."

Anxiety waves over me with the story out there, lingering between us, and my creepy Trent vibes resurface with it. Trent slamming my head against the wall and digging his fingers into my scarred cheek as if trying to peel off the marks makes me shiver. My face itches with the memory, and my fingers fidget with the urge to scratch it. My eyes close as if I can block out the images.

"What are you remembering *right now*?" His voice is soft, but it jolts me.

"His anger. He was violent once. That's when I got out." The words come out with surprising ease, like I'm under hypnosis. I fear he'll ask more questions and want details I don't want to give.

Instead, a strange sensation on my fingertips peels my eyes open. Jack softly eases my jittery hands into his from across our laps. His thumbs roll over my outer palms, grazing my scars like they aren't there, before moving to my fingers. He touches me like he knows me, and maybe now he does a little, but it makes me breathless and confused and mesmerized all at once.

"I'm sorry." He takes me in with an intense stare. "There are certain things in this world that should *never* happen. I hate that some of those things have happened to you."

A pinched smile breaks through. "This is why I prefer the easy questions."

"I get it." His eyes fall to our linked hands as his fingers curl with mine. "But be proud of your scars, Rowan. Inside *and* out. They tell stories—stories worth sharing. You survived something difficult. You're still surviving it. Your worldview is forever altered and unique. That doesn't make you less than. It makes you badass. A *beautiful* badass. I feel *more* connected to you knowing you've been through shitstorms—maybe that's why I'm writing again."

His hands are strong, like the rest of him, and calloused where he's held a pen for too long—he writes *and* types to create his books. I have the same callous on the inner side of my right index finger from hand-grading thousands of essays, and he smirks when he finds it.

Absorbing his words, I smile. "Well, since you put it like that... then, sweet are the uses of adversity."

Lacing his fingers through mine inspires a heat wave through my core.

"Which, like the toad, ugly and venomous, wears yet a precious jewel in its head," he recites dramatically, his grip tight as he caresses my hands. "And this our life, exempt from public haunt, finds tongues in trees, books in the running brooks, sermons in stones and—"

"Good in everything," we say together. Laughing brings us closer. I catch the piney scent of his cologne and the sweetness of his breath. Our foreheads nearly bump, bringing on more chuckles.

A shameful fantasy stirs—me tackling him to the floor with wild kisses, sex sparked by wine and Shakespeare. But I come to my senses. That road would only lead to a dead end and absolute humiliation. This thing between us isn't like that, anyway.

I tug my hands from his.

Amused, he says, "There you go again. You and your dead white guys. But this time, I think Shakespeare would—"

My phone rattles on the coffee table. Dean lights up the screen, but I make no move to answer.

"Should you get that?"

The aftermath of Dean's last call comes over me like a dark shade—I don't want to feel like that again. "I should, but I don't want to."

Jack's face twists with sudden discomfort. "Um, Rowan, I—"

"No, Jack, not because of you." A chuckle bumbles out at his obvious distress. "Don't look so horrified. Save your *let's just be friends* lecture for your bed bunnies—I have no ideas about us."

"Wait. What?" His discomfort switches to confusion. "That's not what I was going to say—"

"It's okay." I flip the phone over as it stops ringing and take the food into the kitchen. "You don't need to explain. I'm engaged, *sort of*, and you're... well, Jack Graham."

"What's that supposed to mean?" He follows me with our empty glasses.

"It means I'm not your type." I sort some plastic containers to put the leftovers away.

"Why not?" Looking amused and curious, he leans against the counter beside me, nudging me with his shoulder.

My eyes roll at the question. "What difference does it make?"

"For research purposes. Tell me... Why aren't *you* my type?" His hand lays over mine, fiddling with containers, forcing me to look at him. "We're around the same age. Unmarried. Accomplished professionals. And we're both hot—"

"Not exactly," I argue, tugging away from him again. But his words roll over mine.

"—So, either you think I'm too shallow to want you as you are, or you're too insecure to think it's possible."

I stop my work and stare at him, feeling uneasy. "I don't like these questions."

"No shit," he laughs. "But those are the most interesting questions to ask. Come on. Why aren't you my type?"

"Fine." My eyes narrow to slits. "You have a very lackadaisical attitude toward sex that I could never have. I'm not judging—just observing. Sex is just another fun party for you. But it's a milestone for me. To get to that place where I feel close enough with someone... it means everything." I shrug lightly, feeling childlike with my admission, like I'm flashing my badge of inexperience. "That probably sounds—"

"Don't assume you know what I'm thinking." He looks pensive—the amusement has vanished from his face. "You don't know me."

"Did I say something offensive? I'm sorry—" My phone rattles from the other room.

"You should answer it." He takes the food container from my hands. "I'll finish this and let myself out."

Unsure and uneasy, I do as he says. Moments later, Jack's gone.

121

Fifteen

JACK

I don't know why I'm pissed. Rephrase—I *know* why, but I don't like it. It's jealousy—the familiar pangs of discontent I've felt lately over other authors pumping out new books and my friends talking about their kids' games branches into new territory. And I don't like it at all.

Rowan takes the call, her voice lifting into feigned cheerfulness as she answers—she doesn't want to talk to him. I shouldn't have pushed her. She paces the living room, head lowered. Whatever he's saying to her, it's bullshit, but she listens, giving him attention he doesn't deserve.

I'm not jealous of that. Unlike the rest of the neighborhood, I've never doubted the existence of Dean. Her semi-engaged status has been stuck on repeat in my head ever since striking our deal. *Neighbor. Engaged. Off-limits.*

It's what she said—everything she said—that upsets me.

From the living room, I hear a weak, "...yes, Dean, but..." Her words linger in the air, unfinished.

My anger upticks. Where does she find these asshole fuck-heads who won't even let her finish a sentence? I can't listen anymore.

I put the food away and eye my book on the counter with its bent spine and sticky-note-rainbow. I tuck it into my waistband under my shirt and make a quick exit.

At home, I toss the book on the kitchen counter—I'm in the wrong headspace for that right now. I pour Jim Beam and watch the liquid swirl in my glass.

Rowan's dating history makes my blood boil. I *hate* how she's been treated. And tonight's revelations aren't the worst of it—her reluctance makes it clear. She blames her face. I blame fucking men—the entitled, manipulative, twisted pricks who leech onto her because they think she's an easy target. Her words to Mira make more sense now—dating *is* torture for her.

But that's not entirely why I feel like shit right now. If anything, I should be thrilled that she shared something so personal—she's dropping her iron shields around me. That's a momentous win.

"Then, what's the prob, Bob?" Devin's voice brings a light smile. I picture him on the barstool, eyeing my drink with nostalgia for the days we'd sneak Dad's bottle and get stupid-drunk with Corey on boring Saturday nights.

"The *prob* is she racks up assholes like she's curating a collection for a dickhead museum. She could do so much better."

"Like you?"

"No, not me." I toss back my drink. "I'd just be another asshole."

"Then don't be another asshole." Devin challenges with his goofy grin. "Be a friend, and see what happens."

Scoffing, I pour another drink. "I'm off to a good start with the novel. I don't need her."

"Then, why are we talking about her?"

"I don't know. She's... got me flustered. Intimacy means everything to her—I wonder what that's like. To slowly ease into her heart until she gives all of it. *That's* what I'm missing. Meaning. Substance. Real affection."

"I believe the technical term for that is love. But in book jargon, it's the slow burn neighbors to friends to soulmates story—I know that one well," Devin says deviously.

"I'm talking theoretically. Rowan isn't interested. Or available. Or a good idea."

"Excuses, excuses. Who are you trying to convince, huh? Be honest—" He leans over the counter, locking eyes with me like he's a human lie detector. "You want to be the one easing into her heart and getting to her everything. Right?"

"I want..." My brow pinches in futile deliberation—what I want doesn't matter. Still, I give imaginary Devin an answer, if only to keep the conversation going. "... her to have the love she deserves. She's earned it."

"I dare you to give it to her," he says as if we're playing a game. "Who knows? You might get love, too."

I scoff again while my phone chimes. Jennifer, the sexy optometrist and roller derby maven, sends a suggestive text before asking to come over.

"I prefer my usual happy endings, but thanks anyway." I send the thumbs-up emoji. When I look up, Devin's gone. Not that he was really there in the first place.

Twenty minutes later, Jennifer's pinned against the foyer wall, my tongue plunged into her mouth, and my hand between her legs. I didn't even say anything when I answered the door.

But despite the gusto of our good time, our reindeer games don't play out like normal. I'm distracted. I keep thinking how different this would be with Rowan. Slower. Softer. Sexier. Intimate. I imagine her legs wrapped around me, her fingers on my arms, my hands lacing her hair. And that smile—delicate, wanting, hopeful.

Rowan's face shows up whenever I close my eyes like she's a virus fucking with my normal programming.

Keeping my eyes open isn't better, because I can't pretend I'm with the girl next door.

So, I keep them closed and let my head go wherever it wants. I imagine Rowan's hands and mouth all over me, my lips devouring her, my fingers exploring her warmest places. We don't even make it to the stairs before she's naked and quivering.

"Holy shit, Jack. What's got into you, huh?"

I answer by making her come, and her question is lost in her outcry. Then, I take her against the kitchen island, hard and fast. It's the best sex I've had in ages.

Still, I'm glad when she leaves. I feel empty. Pissed, though I don't get why. Since when is amazing sex not enough for me?

A long shower washes Jennifer away but does little for my irritation. So, I return to what's been going well. I'm 47,323 words in, but still missing a crucial element—the inciting incident. Incredible scenes with complex, wounded characters have cued up in no particular order, but not what sets off the string of events in the first place. I need the original domino.

Harper Lee meows and hops onto my desk, sauntering across my keyboard and notebooks in a not-so-subtle plea for attention. I pick her up, rubbing her back as she hooks over my shoulder. Her paws knead into me as she purrs. I breathe into her fluffy orange fur, and that's when it comes to me.

Caleb, the boy with the shockingly red hair, and my version of Rowan searching for him wherever she goes...

Harper Lee protests with a sharp meow when I release her for my keyboard, but it's okay. She lives a lovely cat life and understands that my books are partially responsible. Pencil tucked against my ear, I switch on a random playlist, volume relatively low, and invert my hands over my keyboard, cracking them, before I start typing. The scene plays in my head with striking clarity—a late-night hospital emergency room and two injured teenagers who don't want to go home.

I don't look up until the sky is gray, and I hear Rowan's front door shutting as she goes on her morning run. I watch her from my front window—it's not stalking if you live next door. I consider texting her something funny about her always running away from the neighborhood or a random good morning. She opened up to me yesterday in ways she rarely does with anyone, however shitty it made me feel after. I want to reach out. Assure her. Thank her, even.

But as soon as my eyes drift from her face to her tight running outfit, I turn away.

Distance, asshole. Distance.

Sixteen

ROWAN

Dean's apology feels half-hearted, but I accept it anyway. He vents about long hours, the discomforts of sharing an RV with three other guys, and the stress of being a grunt on set—it's unusual to hear him complain. But, of course, everything between us is unusual these days, like my botched answer was an iceberg, knocking our ship off course, and we're struggling to set it right again.

Or at least, I am.

I do all the hopeful fiancée things—I listen, validate his troubles, and offer encouragement. But he doesn't return the favor when I finally tell him about Sara. Rather, he huffs and says, "Don't you get enough of other people's kids at school?"

"If you can't be supportive, then maybe you shouldn't call. Whenever we talk, you make me feel horrible, and I don't deserve it."

"Well, that's how I've felt all summer," he retorts before ending the call.

"You and me both," I breathe out.

I knew I shouldn't have answered. But Jack was insistent. I consider marching over there, asking him what went wrong. I even step out to my front porch, armed with an innate desire to fix *something*.

But when I see the busty brunette at his door, I stop. His Amazonian princess is another version of perfect, reminding me of my place and proving exactly what I tried to explain—I'm not his type. Envy ripples through me when his hand hooks into her cleavage to pull her inside—my toes curl *for* her.

I retreat, feeling hurt all the way around without completely understanding why.

Days pass. Dean goes silent.

I don't hear from Jack, either.

That conversation should've drawn us closer. Mom and Mira nearly exploded from shock when I told them I opened up about Trent. Now regret grows with his silence. There's one obvious conclusion—he got what he needed.

Home upkeep keeps me busy. Maintaining the grass monopolizes several grueling hours a week with the rough push mower in life-draining heat and humidity. The overrun beds, front yard and back, grow more unruly, and I don't have the energy or know-how to tackle them. So, they become visible to-dos, mocking me.

More problems arise—neglected gutters cause drainage issues, the smoke alarm in my bedroom needs replacing, and one of the skylights in the living room leaks in heavy rain. Cleaning the gutters and replacing the alarm I do myself—a comical but effective enterprise that brings Vernon over to supervise. He has a keen sense of home repairs, like a Jedi noticing disruptions in the force, but I don't mind his help. But I fear the roof leak and ignore it for the same reason I ignore Jack's tree—money.

Meanwhile, I stick to a routine for my sake and Sara's. Routines are comforting, and I want to give her stability if nothing else. I'm up early and running by six. My morning coffee is usually combined with FaceTiming Mom or project work. When Sara emerges, I suggest things we can do together. Shopping. Library. The aquarium. Putt-putt. The beach.

She responds with sharp derision. "I'm not going anywhere with you."

She snubs the healthy breakfasts I fix, but after my shower, I find it eaten. And her gone—a sticky note slapped on her door indicating her single-worded plans.

Park.

Home.

Friends.

Or once: *Anywhere but here.* On that day, she amended her note via text. *Park.*

She makes minimal effort, though. She's home by nine every night. The dinner I save for her is always gone from the fridge the next day. When I'm not around, she washes her dishes, does her laundry, and, I suspect, plays with Edgar, for his toys are often spread out, and he leaves some outside her bedroom door like peace offerings.

This every-woman-for-herself living arrangement isn't unfamiliar. Living with Mom built my quiet independence, so I understand and respect it in Sara. I tell myself—this isn't so bad. She's safe, clean, and fed.

But the cozy comfort of the little house is hindered by the tension—I can't relax. I feel like I should constantly make an effort, as if something magical will turn her to my side, like buying the right color of Mountain Dew or making her favorite dinner by accident.

I know that's not true. Like with Dean, I can't *make* someone care about me or do what I expect. So, I imagine we both feel like her father, each serving our sentence and desperate for escape.

Sara falls in with the rest of my summer fails, making me second-guess everything—very unlike me. Acquiescing to Dean has only made everything worse. Buying the little house has demolished my bank account. My tried-and-true lesson plans face unwanted extinction. My budding friendship with Jack seems rocky, given the terse way he left the other night and his silence since then. I can't seem to get anything right—a feeling I hate.

Saturday evening, Sara comes into the kitchen while I'm feeding Edgar. I force an upbeat smile. "Hey, how about a movie tonight? Your choice."

Hovering over the open fridge, Sara scoffs. "We're *not* going to be friends. Will you give it up already?"

"Sure ... in three months. Until then, can't we try to get along and have some fun?"

She slams the fridge shut. "You want me to have fun? My dad's in jail. His cousins want to rob the house while we're gone. We'll probably end up losing the place because Dad's not working and won't be able to pay the bills. I'll reserve my fun for when this nightmare is over, and I don't have to look at your ugly, fucked-up face every day."

I recoil with a sharp exhale, like I've been gut-punched. She looks pleased.

Turning toward the living room, she hesitates at the threshold. "Mr. Maddix feels sorry for you. That's why he asked you to marry him. That's what everyone at school says, and you freaking humiliated him. Why do you think he's stayed away all summer? He can't stand looking at you, either."

Her door slams a moment later.

Any other day, I might take a deep breath and shake off her horribleness like I'm made of stainless steel. I've heard worse. I've felt worse.

But today, her verbal assault shakes an already unsteady foundation, and my strong barriers crumble.

I duck out of the sliding glass doors by the kitchen and curve around the house, where she can't see me. Between the hedges and screened-in porch, I break into a pathetic sob with choking gasps and fat, hot tears, drowning out the soft thuds of music coming from next door. Her viciousness shoves me into a mental replay of my *'ugly, fucked-up face's'* greatest hits—from walking the halls of my high school for the first time after it happened to Renita's drunken display. I want to scream like I'm doing in my head.

She's a kid lashing out—I get it. Common sense tells me not to take this personally, but I can't help it. It *is* personal.

I slide my phone from my pocket and call Mira.

"What happens to Sara if I don't want this anymore?" I say, unable to hide my weepy voice.

"What's wrong?"

"Just tell me. What happens?"

Mira sighs heavily. "There's a group home downtown that has a spot for her. She'll share a room with a dozen other girls, some there for behavioral and criminal issues, and she'll go to New Castle."

"Right, with its welcoming metal detectors and frequent gang issues..." The words come out shaky and irritated. "There's no other option?"

"No. But she'll survive... and she'll regret losing her spot with you. Tell me what's happened."

"She's just... mean, Mira."

"What'd she say?"

With a deep breath, I blurt out, "Oh, the usual... about my ugly fucked-up face and how everyone at school thinks Dean feels sorry for me. And my face has kept him away all summer."

"I'll come right now, pack her ass up, and take her downtown."

"No, Mira. I can't do that to her."

"Well, how about I come over and talk to her? We'll set more ground rules."

"No, I don't want that either. I'm not... tattling. I'm not backing out. I'm venting."

"What then? Tell me what you need."

"I need... a good cry, some alcohol, and about fifteen minutes away from her so I can figure out what I'm going to say when I go back inside."

"Well, how about you and Sara come to our house for dinner tomorrow night? She'll loosen up around other kids."

"Mira, how the hell would I get her in the car? She doesn't want anything to do with me."

"Then, we'll bring the party to you. Dinner, too. And alcohol. Tomorrow night at six."

"Okay. That might help."

Mira offers other encouragement, but her words run together with my tears. Still, I assure her I'm fine, promise to text later, and get off the phone.

I lean against the porch siding, taking deep breaths. But when the tears don't stop, I bury my face in my hands and just let them come like a necessary detox of all my bad feelings.

"Rowan." Jack appears at the hedge corner.

I blurt an expletive and consider running away to spare myself another indignity. I *hate* that he sees me like this. I can't even look at him, but I keep my head low and my puffy, wet eyes fixed on the dirt under my bare feet.

He moves next to me, so close I smell pine and coffee. "Sorry. I wasn't trying to listen, but my study window was open, and... well, a woman bawling her ass off is hard to ignore."

My uneasy laugh creates a weird mash-up with my crying that doesn't quite work. "Then, I'm sorry. It's a new workout I'm trying—bawling my ass off."

"It's working for you."

An awkward beat passes before he moves in front of me. Unable to look at him, I fixate on his bare feet, closing in around mine. His hands rise slowly between us before gently reaching my chin. His fingertips slide along my cheekbones, lifting my face until our eyes meet.

He's touching me? Not just me, but my face? And I'm letting him? These events don't make sense like a crazy dream without a storyline.

Still, I can't look away when his boyish smile and thoughtful eyes land on mine. He takes me in, studying me, my lines, my marks, everything, never once revealing anything but admiration. His hands are warm, tender, and surprising, cupping my cheeks like they're simply two sides of me, one no different than the other.

I can't remember the last time someone touched me like this, and certainly not in kindness or affection. More tears surface over his sweet acceptance and how beautiful it makes me feel.

He thumbs my tears away, and his smile grows like he knows what I'm feeling.

"Rowan... This is the beautiful face of a woman who can handle anything."

I laugh out loud. First, because he's right—this *is* the face of a woman who can handle anything. Second, because his sweet joke and enchanting acceptance have me thinking—just for a second—that he might kiss me, an idea so preposterous that it's funny.

He hesitates before letting go and reaching for my hand. "Come with me."

My hand drops into his like he's put me in a trance. He leads me around the hedge, up his deck, and into a cozy wicker chaise.

"Stay here."

He returns with liquor in a crystal tumbler and a box of tissues. He sets both on the small glass table and crouches beside me. "Stay here as long as you need. Cry as much as you want. Do whatever makes it better."

My face pinches, and more stupid tears drip from my puffy eyes. "Really? I thought you were upset with me."

"Never. Myself, yes, but it doesn't matter.... Um, help yourself to more whiskey if you need it."

"Thank you, Jack."

"Anytime. I mean that." He stands, heading toward his sliding glass door. "Oh, and Rowan..."

He catches my gaze, holding it in his. "When you're ready, go back in there and tell that asshole you're not putting up with her shit. You're a good person doing a good thing. You deserve... better."

He leaves me. More tears plummet from my eyes like crying is a new invention, and the novelty hasn't yet worn off. It's a double relief—getting alone time to pull myself together here and Jack not pressuring me to talk about it. His words resonate, too, mimicking what I said to Dean—I deserve better. I put those words on repeat as I soak up the dying sun, sip whiskey, and spend twenty minutes gathering myself.

The tender way he touched me, his fingers on my face, replay in my thoughts, and it's a memory I hope I never lose.

When my eyes are dry and my glass empties, I leave the luxurious chaise, not bothering with cleanup or needless thank yous. Jack isn't waiting for that.

I march home, bypassing Edgar's meows to pound on Sara's door. It flings open, and she stares at me daringly as if this is her house and I'm the invader.

"If you ever talk to me that way again, I'll make *one* phone call. Within the hour, you'll be moved into a group home with a bunch of pissed-off girls, like you, only angrier and more violent, and you'll be their new target. Let me tell you, it sucks being someone's target. I hate that these things have happened to you, Sara. I wish I could wave a wand and make your world better. But I can't. The best I can offer is this." I wave my hands around my cozy little house. "And if that's not good enough, then go, try your hand with the group home and the inner-city school. Or stay. And have a decent life for three months. Either way, you will *never* talk to me like that again. Understood?"

The stone-cold expression under her lavender hair fades into one of worry. "Fine. Sorry. I shouldn't have said shit about your face or Mr. Maddix."

"*Never again*," I reiterate, sternly.

"Okay," she says, just as sternly. "Can I watch TV?"

Edgar saunters between us, rubbing himself against my legs and hers like he's forging a friendship.

"Um, sure." I leave her to it, retreating down the hall to my room, where I splash my face with cold water and take cleansing breaths. My relief mixes with my surprise—standing up for myself came easier than I expected and instantly made things better.

When I return to the living room, Sara's watching a ghastly horror movie. Edgar settles onto the couch beside her, and I do the same, taking the other end.

My phone buzzes in my pocket. It's Mira asking for an update. I type out a quick—*Better now. Call me tomorrow.*

Then... *P.S. Jack Graham isn't the spoiled playboy I thought he was. He's actually a little amazing. I'm... befuddled.*

Mira: *Befuddled = a distant cousin to desperate. We should talk more about this.*

Me: *The only thing I'm desperate for is a wine night. Maybe tomorrow night you can help me with that?*

Mira: *Absolutely, as long as you elaborate on your befuddlement. What's happening with your neighbor?*

Me: *If I knew that, I wouldn't be befuddled.*

Mira: *Fair enough. See you at 6.*

The next night, Mira, Jane, and the kids bring wine and pizza, successfully luring Sara out of her room. Though she still keeps her distance from me, she plays with the kids and pleasantly socializes long enough to give me hope.

And strangely, thinking about Jack gives me hope, too.

Seventeen

ROWAN

After a long day of errands, I putter into the driveway at home to see Jack bolt from his front porch waving *The Other Us* in his hand—*my* copy of *The Other Us*, I realize, seeing its multi-colored mohawk of sticky notes.

"That's my book!"

He opens the car door for me. "Unrealistic? Ridiculous? A guy's version of a woman? What the hell, Rowan?"

Rising from the car, I shut the door and lean against it, my notes coming back to me as he spouts them off. "A few *tiny* things didn't ring true for me, but you're a guy writing a female character, so that's to be expected. Didn't you see all my positive notes? In my *torturous* annotations, which you *stole* from my house?"

A heavy sigh raises his broad shoulders, accented by a navy-blue t-shirt that somehow brings out brown flecks in his eyes. Or maybe that's the afternoon sun. He runs a hand through his unruly hair, which draws my eyes to his motley collection of tattoos. I catch glimpses of a raven, random books scattered like confetti, and fire. *Fahrenheit 451*, I think. His other arm boasts a rocky island, eerily dark and disturbing. Could it be *And Then There Were None*? He moves too quickly to make everything out.

But I want to, I think, with growing unease.

His brown eyes find mine—he looks amused, like he can read my inner Jack-thoughts. "Would you mind explaining what you meant, please?"

I move to the front of the car, open the trunk, and grab bags. He does the same, tucking the book under his arm.

"Well, a down-to-earth girl like Jasmine wouldn't care about designer shoes—that's a *Sex in the City* cliche. Not all women are shoe crazy," I say as we shuffle inside.

He groans, looking almost murderous. "Do you know how much time I spent researching fucking Jimmy Choos and Louboutins?"

I laugh—can't help it. "No. Don't want to know, either. Those shoes don't fit her character. She has enough to worry about, anyway. Someone who's been through trauma wouldn't be so... happy-go-lucky with a strange man in her apartment. Most women, traumatized or not, feel uneasy about it."

Jack looks perplexed as he sets his bags on the counter. "What? You mean the plumber?"

"Yes. You accomplished your goal in the scene—to show how her OCD tendencies appear to outsiders. That part's good. But what you don't capture is her inherent vulnerability in that situation. Just the fact that he notices her peculiarities would unnerve her. Instead, she's way too relaxed about it, even talkative. She'd be reluctant to open up."

"Like you." His dark eyebrow cocks slightly, looking skeptical. "So, you feel vulnerable with repairmen?"

"Vulnerable with anyone at my front door." My voice trails off weakly. I've wandered into a conversation I don't want to have.

"Why, exactly?"

"Um, it's hard to..." I take a breath, remembering this is about his novel—not me. "Letting a stranger in is always overshadowed by what-ifs for a woman." My shoulders slump in a sigh. "Men are inherently free of half of a woman's worries, and ignorantly so."

Avoiding his quizzical glare, I put the groceries away, hoping he doesn't notice my unease.

In a quiet deliberation, Jack's hands go to his hips. He looks upset, and I worry that this might kick off another one of our cordially volatile arguments or an interrogation.

"Jack, these are small, incidental things. The story is beautiful, regardless. Why are you so bothered?"

A light scoff putters from his lips. "Nearly every adult woman on this street beta reads for me, and they never pointed this out."

"Yes, but my critical thinking skills are banging. You've seen what I do to books. Besides, these are only my opinions. My *private* opinions—not notes for the author. If I'd known you'd steal the book, I probably would've gone easier on you. Could it be that they don't want to discourage you?"

His response is a mild groan.

Sara pops into the kitchen, grabbing a soda from the fridge. A quick introduction brings a pleasant exchange, baffling me since I never had the same courtesy.

"What's for dinner?" she asks.

"Um, let's see..." I haven't thought about dinner yet.

Jack whips out his wallet and hands her a credit card. "Order whatever you want."

My mouth bobs open to protest, but Sara's face alights in a smile—the first I've seen. She bounces as she leaves the kitchen. With a sigh, I let that go and refocus on Jack.

"You really shouldn't have helped yourself to my *personal* annotations. Those notes were for me. Not you. I probably went too far."

His brows scrunch into a pocket at the top of his nose. "No, you... You're exactly right. Not only did you spot my *few* flaws, but every nuance, device, trick, and even my convoluted metaphors. Hell, you saw things that even I didn't. Nothing got by you."

"Well, it's what I do. But I read it for pleasure first. You were right, too. Once I relaxed into the story, it was the immersive experience it should be. I'm grateful to you for that."

Jack stands there, hand going through his hair periodically like he's unsure what to do or say. I reach for the book still tucked under his arm and battle his tight grip to repossess it. He lets it go but in a catatonic way. Then, he leaves, taking my stack of folded paper bags with him.

Damn it, I've upset him. Again.

Sara announces the imminent arrival of Thai food while I plod down the hallway. A maroon T-shirt and sweat shorts replace my blouse and dark jeans. My hair goes up in a loose bun before I pour a glass of chardonnay. I meet Edgar Allan Poe in the living room, where he saunters up with a soft meow before collapsing at my feet and pawing the air in my direction. I plop beside him, delivering belly rubs and playful tugs to his ears.

The doorbell rings, followed by a quick pound. Sara rushes to answer it.

"Food's not here yet," she announces dryly.

Jack wears the same bothered expression as moments ago. He sets a full paper bag on the floor beside me.

"What's this?"

"Books. My books. Will you read them?"

I smirk, confused. "Sure. I was planning to, anyway. Just haven't checked them out from the library yet."

"No, I want the full dissection. Every muscle. Every vein. Every nerve. Critique each word if you want to. Hold nothing back."

"Um, okay."

"For your trouble, I'll take care of the tree." His pinched face reminds me of frustrated students bargaining for extra credit.

"What's with you and that tree? You're obsessed with it. No need to do anything except meet my classes, as we agreed. Reading and annotating your books to death will be my pleasure." A coy grin stretches over my cheeks at the last word, *pleasure*, a not-so-subtle I-told-you-so over him valuing my annotations after all.

"Don't worry, Jack. I went all out with dinner. It's going to be a feast." Sara hands him his credit card with a devious smirk.

My smile joins hers as I peek inside the paper bag. *Cape Moon* sits on top—the one I want to read next.

"Jack, do you have other books I might borrow? Contemporary books?" I say tentatively. "I want to read other genres my students might be drawn to. I'll read the hell out of these, but I'm having trouble scoring recent bestsellers at the library. There's a waiting list for everything good."

He holds out his hand to help me up. "Come, check out *my* library."

We traipse across the lawn to his house barefoot. His study is an add-on—a sunroom with long windows, tacked onto the side of his house closest to mine like an afterthought.

Upon entering, I gasp. It's something out of a whimsical Instagram post. Books wrap the room like wallpaper. All available wall space is a bookshelf, even the few inches above the window frames. Books form funny stacks in odd places like stalagmites in caves. Three pieces of furniture occupy the room—a rustic wood desk in the middle with a matching chair, and an oversized cushy red chair tucked into a corner with open books perched upside down along the armrest and back to save his place. He reads multiple books at a time.

I peruse the shelves like a quaint bookstore, starting with the nearest to my left. *The Magic Treehouse Books, Little House on the Prairie, The Hardy Boys,* Tolkien, *Choose Your Own Adventure Books,* Shel Silverstein and Dr. Seuss—the shelves are a timeline, starting with childhood, moving into classics and college books, then a mystery and horror phase, and wrapping around the room to current reads—including every book I'm waiting for at the library. Contemporary romances share the space with thrillers and science fiction, as if he indiscriminately pulls books from shelves without noticing the genre. From the looks of it, Jack Graham has never met a book he didn't like.

Funny bobbleheads, including one of Edgar Allan Poe, decorate the shelves. In front of *The Hardy Boys*, I pick up a small framed photo of him and his brother in their Coastal baseball uniforms. Devin shared Jack's devious side grin and thoughtful eyes, and seeing them together makes me sad. My finger traces over their faces before returning the picture to its perch.

The desk is scattered with Moleskin notebooks and pens—*good* pens. Pilot G-2s and expensive gel pens sit beside heavy gold pens—the kind I see in cases in antique stores. The other paper bags from my earlier stack remain on the desk's corner. He snatches one and whacks it open.

"I hit a few local bookstores every month for whatever looks intriguing." He motions to the shelves with the latest titles. "Take whatever you want... except the ones on the chair. I haven't finished those yet."

"It's amazing." I'm a little breathless. "Where should I start?"

My question makes him smile—he wanted me to ask. He picks books from the shelves while delivering elevator pitches like he's been dying to talk about them. The bag fills quickly. He goes for another, but I stop him.

"Jack... thank you. That's enough for now. I promise I'll return them in pristine condition."

His brow furrows. "No, don't do that. Do your fucking worst on them. I'm actually hoping they get worse marks than mine. Counting on it, really."

Through the open window, I hear Sara giggling into her phone in my kitchen just across the hedges.

My eyes return to Jack's. "Come back and have dinner with us."

He heaves the stuffed bag into his arms. "Definitely."

Eighteen

JACK

Keeping my distance isn't working. Keeping *her* at a distance isn't either.

Reading her neurotically detailed annotations felt strangely like being with her, letting her wriggle into my brain and root around... in a good way, like an earthworm in the dirt letting in air. Her comments got my creative neurons firing. She enlightened me, as she does every time we're together.

I'd be an idiot to give that up over fears of us getting too close.

We're already too close.

Touching her the other day made me feel like her hero, the Superman to her Lois Lane (even though she hates that kind of thing). Touching her scars isn't off-putting, either. The opposite, really. Beautiful in a strange way. It's like running fingers over a canvas with thick swirls of expressive paint.

And worth the risk for the two truths it revealed—that she's rarely if ever, touched there, and I like showing her that not every guy is a heartless prick.

This isn't too bad either—sitting around the kitchen banquette with her and Sara, feasting on Thai food. Sara is talkative with a dry sense of humor, and it's a relief that she's pulled the stick from her ass. Whatever Rowan said to her when she returned inside must have been spot-on, the exact thing she needed to hear.

Mid-dinner, the doorbell rings. Fear spikes that it could be Dean showing up to ruin whatever this is. *What is this?*

But it's the neighbors. They shuffle into the little house armed with wine, desserts, and their usual neighborly persistence.

"We can't stand it any longer," Rose announces as they stream into the living room. "We must meet Sara."

"Seconded," Vernon says. "I need to tell her the air pressure in her back bike tire is low."

"I need to tell her how much I love her purple hair." Marcy's face scrunches in delight. "It's my favorite color."

"Purple Haze," Tom mentions calmly. "Jimi Hendrix."

"Come in," Rowan says, though they've already invaded. Her hand goes to her hair tie, releasing her messy bun to let her hair hide her scars, and I wonder if it's subconscious, automatically covering up.

Introductions circle, and Sara takes it in politely, even the interrogation portion. Rowan tenses beside me like she doesn't know whether to intervene or let Sara handle herself.

"Don't look so worried," I whisper. "They'll figure each other out."

Her shoulders relax. "You're right. I'll sort some wine glasses and start pouring."

She disappears as Vernon asks, "Did you know Rowan before you moved in?"

Helping Rowan in the kitchen seems the more interesting of my two options until Sara's answer stops me.

"I haven't had her as a teacher yet, but everyone knows Miss 'Mac-n-cheese' Mackey."

She says it so matter-of-factly that I imagine it's attached to a funny story involving a trip-and-fall in the cafeteria and Rowan being stuck in a cheesy blouse all day.

"Mac-n-cheese Mackey? That has a funny ring to it," Marcy says.

Vernon folds his arms. "I hope it's not a derogatory nickname, young lady."

"How exactly would it be derogatory, Vern?" Tom asks.

"Well, I don't know, but surely calling your teacher cheesy—"

"Sara, tell us. Why on earth would you call her that, love?"

"You don't know her mac-n-cheese story? It's why she's covered in scald marks," Sara says with a *duh* tone.

"Maybe we shouldn't talk about that," I say.

"It's no secret," Sara says. "Everyone at school knows. She talks about it—no big deal. A dumb accident while making mac-n-cheese. She splashed herself with boiling water—"

"That's right." Glasses clink together on Rowan's tray as she stops abruptly beside me. "Not my best move." A weak laugh accompanies her deer-in-the-headlights expression, and I know right away—that story is bullshit.

She clears her throat before moving again. "Um, I had an after-school hankering for mac-n-cheese, and as Burns wrote, *best-laid plans oft go awry*." An uneasy chuckle escapes as she sets the tray on the coffee table. "Let me grab the wine."

Vernon holds up a finger. "Household accidents are a silent killer—no one talks about them. My Uncle Lou died after an unfortunate scuffle with a toaster…"

Rowan whips by me, her gray-blue eyes catching mine. Her forced smile and her fidgeting fingers give her away. She's not only uneasy but downright nervous.

And I get why. Her no-big-deal story for her students is her way of controlling the narrative. It's practiced and delivered in a space where she's in charge. That it happens here, around her new neighbors, and without her leading the story, derails her tried-and-true explanation. She didn't plan for this.

She returns, bottles at the ready.

Rose chides Vernon for rambling while Tom agrees, "Most people die close to home."

"Um, red or white?" She holds up the wine.

"Red for me," Sara says.

"Nice try. You can have yellow... as in Mountain Dew."

"Wait, I don't get it, love," Rose says as Rowan fills her glass. "How did the water get from the pot to you?"

Her practiced smile returns. "The pot was too small, Rose. It happened when I turned from the stove to the sink—I did it too fast."

Vernon seems about to argue the logistics of it, so I jump in with, "Hey, um, Sara, what's the deal with the purple hair? Do you identify mermaid or something?"

"I want to know what brand you use because it's awesome," Marcy adds, twiddling with a wayward lock of Sara's hair like they're already best friends.

"What could you do with mine?" Rose asks.

Rowan plays hostess, filling everyone's glass, and the tension in her shoulders immediately releases with the subject change. Stepping away from the group, her eyes close tightly, as if blocking out the lie.

She brushes by me again, careful not to make eye contact as she retreats to the kitchen. She serves the donated desserts, staying busy, while Sara keeps the group engaged. She talks about her father's lawn care business, which I joke Rowan should hire as soon as possible, earning a small smile. Sara relates that she loves crystals, horror movies, and RPGs. Rowan seems to relax the more she learns about her roommate.

The party dissipates once Sara promises to visit Rose for crocheting tutorials and Marcy's for hair dyeing, as if that had been the main goal for them descending on the little house in the first place. The neighbors leave. Sara retreats to her bedroom.

In silence, we address the leftovers and dirty dishes. I hand wash the wine glasses—all but ours, which I promptly refill. She seems somewhat perplexed that I'm helping in the kitchen, but she doesn't question it.

When the work is done, I take my wine to the living room and play with Edgar on the floor. She takes a spot nearby, not seeming to mind our informality. She tugs the hair tie from her wrist and recreates her messy bun—I take this as a sign that she's becoming more comfortable with me.

Since everything with Rowan feels like an experiment, I test the waters. "A kitchen accident isn't the real story. Is it?"

She stares into her wine glass like it might generate an answer for her. She wants to smooth out the lie, and I expect her fake smile and a suitable deflection. Perhaps she'll claim I'm so desperate for drama that I can't accept that there isn't any. *Not everything's a book-worthy spectacle, Jack*—cue laughter.

Her words don't come, though. Instead, she releases her hair again like a curtain, ending the show.

"It's okay, Rowan. We don't have to talk about it."

"Good because I *don't* talk about it."

Her defensiveness surprises me. "First rule of Fight Club?" My attempt at humor falls short. "There's no judgment here. It's smart to have an answer ready for an inevitable question, and I bet teenagers can be rude about it."

"Adults are worse."

"It's an awful situation to be in. The thing that affects your life the most is the one thing you don't want to talk about. I get it, but does it hurt less holding it in all the time?"

"Some stories don't belong to you, Jack."

"If you don't share your stories, what's the point of having them? How can anyone truly know who you are?"

Again, she doesn't answer.

"But Dean knows, right?" I edge closer, peering through her hair curtain with skepticism. "Surely the guy you let into your heart and bed knows these fundamental pieces of your history?"

Holy shit, he doesn't. Her irritation gives her away.

"That's exactly how we've gotten this far—keeping the past out of it. Dean doesn't care about my scars—"

"He meets the minimum requirements—I get it."

Her eyes narrow. "It's more than that. He doesn't see me as a victim. He's a fresh start... or he was. I don't know anymore. I don't want to talk about him, either."

"Fair enough. But I'm here… if you ever *want* to talk about it. Might make you feel better. Talking about Trent did, I think. I promise—I won't use it."

I hold up my fingers in a Scout's honor gesture, making her laugh, and it's a relief to hear it.

Her eyes roll. "You can't make that promise."

"Seriously—I do. Trust me. We're friends, right?"

"Ha! Friends? Friends don't steal each other's annotated books. Besides, our conversations wouldn't be so one-sided if we were really friends. *Enough* about me."

"Ah, are you suggesting a *quid pro quo* arrangement for conversation?"

"You realize you're Hannibal Lecter in this scenario, right?"

I smirk deviously. "I'm okay with that. Instead of being on a cell block, I have writer's block."

"And instead of catching a serial killer, you're hunting for killer ideas."

"It's the *Silence of the Keys*." My embarrassing snort-laugh makes her giggle even more.

"Oh, damn," she laughs. "If the cheesy jokes have started, we've definitely had too much wine."

"No, this is good… What do you want to know, Rowan?" I stare over the tops of my eyes, drawing out her name to make it sound like Lecter saying, *"Clarice."*

After a wine-induced giggle, she shrugs. "What upset you the other night?"

I'm not the only one with good people perception. Given what she did to my book, I shouldn't be surprised. I pour more wine. "Damn, you're making it tough on me."

"Well, you made me talk about Trent, so…"

She says it like she's kidding, but I feel bad for putting her through it. "Yeah, that was hard for you… Fine. I was jealous."

"Jealous? Of what?"

"I don't know. Jealous of…" My frustration returns with the subject. "Of the idea that when you give yourself to someone, you mean it—heart, mind, and body. I've never had that."

"Sure, you have. What about your muse?"

I laugh. "I don't have a muse."

"That's not what everyone else says."

"I stopped writing. They needed theories to explain it. I didn't argue. Letting them think I've lost my muse felt easier than the alternative."

"Which is?"

I shake my head, gnawing at my bottom lip in debate. I don't want to talk about my shit either. But she's been so honest—every time I give, she's given something back. And for once, I don't want to be emotionally stingy, not with her.

My answer spills out in a belabored breath. "I'm abysmally unqualified to write love stories. I cared about Evie. Still do. But I never loved her—not the way I once wanted, not the way I *write* about. She inspired my heroines, loosely, and she's exactly what you might picture a muse to be. Beautiful in an ethereal way, accomplished, intelligent. Perfect. She came into my life when I needed someone most. Losing Devin devastated me, and if not for Evie... I don't know that I could've gotten through it."

I pause, closing my eyes. "I took it hard when Ben died. It was like reliving everything that happened with Devin. I reached out to Evie—the one person I thought would understand—and she... blew me off. That's not what we're about, she said."

I laugh at the irony. "She used my spiel against me. Guess there's poetic justice there."

"That doesn't make it hurt any less. I'm sorry."

My head hangs in her sincerity. "She's in love with someone else. She has been for a while. He's good for her—I don't have a problem with it. But when things get rocky with him, she comes to me. Old habits, she says. It's easy with me because not being in love means I can't hurt her. And I've never minded being her safety net."

"But she couldn't be yours. Not anymore." Her hand rests atop mine and squeezes gently before leaving again, and I miss the warmth of it as soon as it's gone. "That must've broken your heart a little."

"Yeah, *a little*, but I shouldn't have been surprised. Evie and I haven't been truly close in years. *Even* in high school, I knew it wouldn't work out."

"But you stayed with her?"

"I was a teenage boy with a hot girlfriend. Of course, I stayed with her. But there were red flags. She isn't a reader. Can you believe it?"

The revelation makes her chuckle half-heartedly.

"Worse, she's *ambitious*. I don't mean to say it like it's a bad word. I love career-minded women. But Evie's too... Lady Macbeth. She'd do anything to get the crown. She hates this neighborhood. She thought my writing was a fad I'd get over to make a real career in journalism. It's a wonder we ever clicked at all." I shrug again. "I mean, it was more physical than anything else. That's all it is now. All it'll ever be."

Rowan looks surprised, maybe disappointed, when she asks, "You'll keep seeing her?"

"I don't know. Probably." Truth is, I don't want to, but I don't expect anything to be different when she shows up at my door—a fact that's hard to explain since Rowan puts so much emotional value in sex. Being with Evie is easy for me, too.

"But everyone says you're miserable after she leaves, even before what happened with Ben. If it's just a sex thing, then why does she, in particular, make you sad?"

I consider holding back—our talk has detoured into a minefield. I don't talk about this with anyone. But I think of those elegant hands of hers trembling when she told me about Trent, and I can't refuse her.

"She's the one semi-serious relationship I've ever had. Seeing her reminds me how... alone I am... and makes me feel like a fraud. Who am I to write about love?"

She laughs, and my eyes flick to hers in offense. "Sorry, I'm just surprised—"

She delivers a soft punch to my arm, an innocent, playful move that rouses not-so-innocent thoughts.

"—You're as close to perfect as any man I've ever met. It's a bit jarring to discover that the great Jack Graham's just as insecure as the rest of us."

"I'm touched that my inner pain amuses you."

"No, I get it—imposter syndrome. I feel like that every time I walk into my classroom. Who am I to teach kids? Or foster one? But that feeling makes me work harder. So it's not a bad thing."

She reaches over again, resting her hand atop mine, and damn if my heart doesn't do somersaults for how fast it's beating.

"You're not a fraud."

This is the woman from the restaurant—confident, poised, perfect. My eyes fix on hers, enchanted.

"You are not a fraud," she says again. "So you haven't had your great love yet? That doesn't mean you can't write about it. The Brontës wrote gorgeous love stories without finding love themselves. Mary Shelley didn't animate a dead body to write *Frankenstein*. Lewis Carroll never stepped foot in Wonderland, nor did he ever meet the Cheshire Cat..."

Her eyes drift to the cat's toothy grin peeking under my shirt sleeve. She wants to see my tattoos, a realization that brings on my Cheshire Cat grin. But she quickly returns her eyes to mine, pink-cheeked.

"—A writer's best resource is his imagination, and you use yours so beautifully."

I chew my bottom lip, watching her like I'm under a spell. She matches my stare like a dare she wants to win.

"Careful, Rowan," I say, my voice soft and raspy. "Encouragement like that will bring me to your doorstep a lot."

"I'm okay with that." She pulls her hand away, but with a twist of my wrist, I catch it, holding it there.

"You're pretty close to perfect, too, you know. I mean, when you're not planning everything or dissecting books. No—actually, I take that back. You're perfect then, too... I hope Dean knows how lucky he is."

She exhales sharply. "I hurt him. He needs a little time to remember his luck, I think."

"He shouldn't need time to remember that."

"What would you have done? You finally find the woman you want to spend your life with, go through a gorgeous, public proposal, and she blurts out a non-answer."

"What would I have done? That's easy. I would've kissed you like you've never been kissed before, until the only answer was yes."

An insistent tug releases her hand from mine. She looks bothered. Flushed, even.

So, I push further. "Course, I never would've proposed to you like that. On stage in front of everyone—that's not romantic. It's a fucking circus. No, you're more of a beach-at-sunset kind of girl. No, wait... I'd tie the ring to a bookmark and tuck it into whatever book you're reading. Then, I'd circle relevant words on the page—love, lovely, sexy, whatever—a romantic annotation that only you could appreciate. Then, I'd slap a sticky note in there... *Marry me, Rowan.* See? Nothing forced or nervous. Just you, about to do the thing you love most and being quietly delighted by the person you love most. Perfect, right?"

Her face tells me all I want to know. Not only are her heartstrings pulled, but yanked hard enough for her to imagine it. A quiet, lovely, bookish proposal. Sweeter still, I don't think it's Dean she imagines.

The serene look on her face holds me in place. I mean every word, like a memory that hasn't happened yet. I see myself peeking around a corner, waiting for her to discover it, waiting for her *yes* like it's my first breath.

Shit, what the fuck is happening to me?

She quickly comes to her senses, clearing her throat and setting her glass aside. "Um... another sign of too much wine—Jack Graham dishing out marriage proposals." Her laugh emerges half-heartedly.

"Admit it—that would get a *yes*."

"Yes, no, maybe. You never know with me. I don't care how it happens, only that Dean asks me again. I'll give the right answer next time."

"Really? The guy backpedaled on his proposal and abandoned you for the summer—he doesn't seem like much of a Prince Charming."

"Oh, I don't need a prince. A squire will do fine. Or a duke. Hell, even the local bookbinder could make me happy."

Her joke falls flat this time. I shake my head at her, saddened by how little she thinks of herself. "Damn, Rowan. If you're going to bother being with someone, why not hold out for someone who at least makes you happy?"

"He does. He will." A light shrug stops her useless convincing. "Mom and Mira have given me a hard time about Dean from the beginning, but they don't get it—he's a good man who wants to be with me. Or did. Is it wrong to hope that everything will be okay? That this one mess-up won't be my sliding door to a miserable, lonely life?"

"It's not wrong to hope, but are those your only choices? Dean or misery? You should hope for more doors."

Nineteen

Rowan

Hoping for more doors is a romantic ideal that makes sense for Jack Graham. He's picture-perfect, bite-my-lip sexy, and has a heart-racing way with words—doors open for him automatically. Marcy's remark about Jack and book signings—too many women hitting on him at once—probably isn't an exaggeration. In a different life, I'd be one of those women desperate to catch the eye of the man behind the amazing love stories, and wishful that such a thing could happen.

But things like that *don't* happen to me. Romances make promises that reality doesn't keep—it's an unfair genre. Spending time with Jack feels unfair, too. The way he looks at me, touches me, talks to me, tickles hope that shouldn't be there. I can't hope for more doors, but I must try to reopen the one I have.

Tonight's the night! Rose's text alert arrives as I cross the gully into our neighborhood from my morning run. It's barely eight, but rental trucks, caterers, and event planners descend on Jack's place like bees to a hive. I catch my breath on the grassy knoll and let out an embarrassing screech when firecrackers pop and squeal from Tom and Marcy's backyard.

My phone alights again. *WECT mentions Jack! TOU gets great reviews!*

"It's tradition," Rose explained the other day over tea. "Whenever Jack releases a book, we set off fireworks and airhorns when he's mentioned on TV or jumps up on the bestseller lists. It's an all-day celebration."

A cleansing breath relieves my sudden tension at the noises, and I stretch-walk the rest of the way home. At the door, my phone chimes again, this time from Jack.

Is it okay to say "disabled person?"

Put people first. "A person with a disability."

I tuck my phone away, smiling, and trudge inside. The last two weeks have been quiet. Jack and I have occasional book talks as I work through my long reading list, and only then when we run into each other at the mailbox or in the driveway. He's been writing nearly nonstop.

But he texts often. Questions like, *Is gregarious just a pompous way to say friendly? Don't you hate easily confused words like exasperated and exacerbated?*

Yes. Yes. And just two days ago...

Please say you're coming to my party.

Again, I answered *yes*. Attending Jack's book release parties is an unwritten requirement in this neighborhood. But I want to anyway.

Airhorns sound from down the street—his release must be a hot topic on the morning talk shows.

The tradition started with Jack's first book, *Cape Moon*, and a small gathering of family and friends in Tom and Marcy's backyard. But as books kept coming, sales grew, and so did the celebration. Jack goes all out to thank the neighborhood that supports him. Black tie, book swag, live music, and catering—it promises to be a ritzy caviar and champagne party for an otherwise hot dogs and hamburgers crowd.

From the front window, Edgar and I watch Jack in his front yard, wearing his usual shorts, old band t-shirt, and flip-flops, directing the deliveries while occasionally picking weeds from his flower beds.

Another popping explosion echoes from Vernon and Rose's driveway. Bothered by the noise, Edgar chirps and races down the hall, probably to hide under my bed.

I look up, shaking my head, to lock eyes with Jack from his yard. A timid wave passes between us, waking the butterflies in my stomach. Jack does strange things to me, like he's a full moon, disrupting tides, altering moods, and inexplicably crowding emergency rooms. I don't quite know what to think about him—only that I am. *A lot.*

Stranger still, he and I are becoming very good friends.

My phone buzzes in my hand—a text from Jack. *Need help with those notebooks?*

With a light laugh, I text back. *It's party day. You have much better things to do.* I breathe out a sigh as I hit send. Though I've given Dr. Evelyn Tate a vague semester-long plan, I now need to fill in the gaps, not with traditional lesson plans outlining lectures, activities, and assignments but with what I'm calling Weekly Guides, material to have on hand and share based on each week's theme. The first week, I plan to discuss genre to help them make their first book choices. *What makes a book timeless… what makes a bestseller… what books appeal to them individually.* Though I won't dictate what we do, I need something to inspire them and fill awkward silences.

Not really. It's too chaotic to write. Let me hide out with you?

If you're here, I won't get anything done. It's a truth that pains me to admit—I'd rather hang out with Jack. But with school starting soon, I can't procrastinate any longer.

I'm looking forward to tonight, I add on as an afterthought. I even know what I'm wearing—a sleek black dress with a swan-necked collar, which minimizes my neck scars without requiring a cumbersome scarf. In case there's dancing, I think, hopefully. I'm not even nervous—a shocker, given that the oyster roast had me swearing off neighborhood parties and contemplating moving altogether.

Besides, as Mom rightly pointed out, it's a *book* party. It'll give me a cool story to tell my students when school starts. Dean sounded excited, too. "I hear Tom Holland's starring in *Cape Moon*... you know, from *Spiderman*? They're talking to Elle Fanning. Do you think they'll be there?"

I had no idea. But it was a nice change having an upbeat conversation with Dean. He even said he loved me at the end, raising hope that things will return to normal when he's home.

I head down the hall to my room, passing Sara's door. A sticky note slapped to her door reads, "My house."

My phone chimes. *I'm looking forward to you being there. Text me immediately if you change your mind about the notebooks.*

Annoying Jack-tingle-shocks release in a cleansing breath.

Sara arrives home just before the party while I put the final touches on my smokey eyes. I call out a greeting, but she doesn't answer—the typical response.

So, I jump when I catch her reflection in my bathroom mirror behind me. "You, um, you look nice."

I smooth out the sides of my dress. "Thanks. Do you really think so?"

She nods, plopping beside Edgar on the bed.

"It should be fun. Rose and Vernon said that sometimes Jack does door prizes." I turn to face her. "Aren't you going to get dressed? You said you'd come—"

"Something's come up." She gnaws on her inner lip while worry lines clutter her forehead. "I was hoping you'd be okay with me staying at my place tonight."

"Why?" My strappy black heels click across the wood floor as I sit on the opposite bed corner.

"Um, I miss home... It'll just be for one night—I think. Maybe." She fiddles with her fingers uneasily.

"Sara, whatever it is, just tell me. Maybe I can help."

Her intricate eye-rolling ability makes a stunning return. Still, it ends with resignation as she slumps and blurts out, "My cousin Shaina says that my other cousins—the ones responsible for Dad being in jail—are planning to rob our house tonight. It's like the perfect crime with no one there. I thought if I'm there with the lights on and the TV going, they'll think he rented it out and won't risk it." She holds up her phone, tapping on a soundtrack of barking dogs that scares Edgar from the bed with a shrill meow. "See? I'll play this if I see them coming. They hate dogs."

"How sure is Shania that it'll be tonight?"

Sara's green eyes widen. "Nearly a hundred percent. They've been talking about it all day."

A deep breath brings me to my feet. "Then, we better get over there."

"We?"

"Yes, we. I can't let you do this alone. Besides, with my car in your driveway, they might buy your ruse. Maybe Shania could off-handedly mention that she heard there's a renter?"

She texts Shania before I finish speaking.

Outside, cars line the street. Well-dressed partygoers overflow Jack's yard and driveway. "Pour Some Sugar on Me" plays loudly from Jack's backyard. Intoxicating food smells waft through the air—Asian barbecue—and my stomach growls.

Sara and I hurry to my car. But seeing Jack at his door greeting guests makes my heels scrape the concrete in a sudden pause—he looks incredible. His shaggy dark hair is tamed away from his eyes. The light stubble on his face is neatly trimmed. And his black suit makes him seem like he should be on a red carpet somewhere—not in a normal neighborhood hosting a house party.

Our eyes meet long enough to mouth a quick "Sorry," and point to Sara before getting in the car.

Pulling into Sara's driveway, my phone pings. *Is everything okay?*

I have to do something with Sara that can't wait. Sorry.

Can I help? A short pause brings another ellipsis as he keeps typing. *I have no qualms about leaving my own party. It'll make me seem like a rebellious badass.* *smirking face.

A heavy sigh escapes, and I realize, confusingly, that I believe him—he'd come if I asked. *Thanks, but we're good. Enjoy your party.*

I expect questions, but he texts back. *I'm here if you need me. Take care of Sara.*

As streetlights flicker on and night takes over, nothing moves, and we hear crickets ramping up their evening activities.

"Shania says they're having a few beers first." Sara unlocks the front door and leads me inside a tidy living room with mismatched second-hand furniture adorned in cozy accents. A crocheted blanket drapes the couch, reminding me of Grandma Betty's handmade quilts. Colorful beach artwork featuring thick brush strokes in the style of Van Gogh liven up the brown paneled walls.

"These are gorgeous," I say, peering into a beach at sunset painting.

Sara shrugs and starts turning on the lights and fans. It's stuffy inside since the AC's been off. But she gets that going, too, and I follow her lead, clicking on table lamps as I find them.

The living room feeds into an updated kitchen with white cabinetry and clean granite countertops. Sara's room down the hall, with its walls covered in art and taped pictures, contrasts greatly with her father's bare-bones minimalism. Everything is clean and well-kept.

We settle into the living room, where the street view through the picture window alerts us to traffic. She puts on *Antiques Roadshow* on PBS while we keep a cautious lookout.

Sara's nervous eyes dart from her phone to the window like she's on high alert. I order Domino's, hoping to lighten the mood. We picnic in her living room and devour pizza between outrageous value reveals on the show.

"There isn't much to steal," she admits, mouth full. "But it's ours, you know?"

"I understand wanting to protect your home. But you know, you can't always be here."

"I know." She sighs heavily.

"Do you have other family who might help?"

Her lavender head shakes. "They're garbage people. That's why I'm with you. Dad didn't want me with them—a stranger was better. When his parents left him this house, they were all jealous. He wants to believe the best about people. He employs half of 'em in his lawn business, and they still treat him like shit. Maybe now, he'll learn his lesson."

I don't say anything—what's there to say? Sara needs no validation that her life is complicated. Nor does she need platitudes about things getting better. What she *really* needs is a solution.

"You have Wi-Fi, right?" I prompt my phone, thinking about how Jack answered his door before I rang the bell.

"Yeah."

"I'm ordering two Ring doorbells. They have motion-sensor cameras that alert you if anyone comes near your front or back doors. That way, you can watch while you're not here."

"I can't pay for—"

"Sara, the state gives me a stipend for you. You *are* paying for it." With a few swipes, I announce, "They'll arrive tomorrow."

Her brow pinches like she doesn't understand me. "Um, thanks."

"Oh, I have another idea." I scroll through my contacts until finding Lt. Ben Wright—the police officer Mira asked to help with the Trent situation years ago. His calm but authoritative demeanor diffused a few tense situations, and he helped me secure the restraining order. "I know a police officer. I wonder if he's working tonight."

I type out a quick text reminding him who I am and explaining the situation. He answers almost immediately. *I remember. ETA one hour.*

I smirk—he's not one to use more words than necessary. "He'll swing by soon. Let's try to relax, huh?"

Still, the tension mounts with each passing second. We take turns pacing and staring out the window. When Shaina texts to say the cousins have left, our anxieties skyrocket.

"What are they driving?"

"A beat-up white van, like losers who learned crime from TV." She shrugs, expressionless. "They're not exactly masterminds."

A growing sense of dread creates a knot in my stomach. *What will I do if they show up? How can I protect us against three criminals? Am I so desperate to connect with her that I've lost all common sense?*

I find my phone under the pizza box. Three missed texts from Jack light up the screen, asking for updates. A surprised smile breaks through my unease—why is he thinking about us when he should be enjoying his party? I type out a quick *we're fine,* wondering if I should tell him the truth.

Sara goes to her father's room and returns with a wooden baseball bat.

"Give me that." I muster up my most reassuring smile despite trembling in my four-inch heels. "Your job is to call *9-1-1*. That's it. Okay?"

She nods weakly as I prop the bat by the door.

"Headlights," she says suddenly.

I peek through the blinds to see faint white lights cutting through the darkness. "Everything's okay. They'll see the lights and the car and won't stop. Do you have your barking dog ready?"

She prompts her phone and tests the sound effects, weirdly making us both jump even though we expect it.

The lights curve the block, slowing as they approach. As the vehicle nears, she grips my arm in anxious suspense, and I squeeze her fingers with mine.

The white van pulls to a squeaky stop at the curb. When a broad, bulky man exits the passenger seat, carrying a crowbar and looking at his surroundings as he lumbers up the lawn, I know I've made an enormous mistake. Adrenaline surges, bringing with it an onslaught of bad memories.

I drop Sara's hand and grab the baseball bat.

"I'll keep him distracted. Go out the back door to the neighbors. Call the police and wait there. Understand?"

She nods, gripping her phone like a lifeline. Her whole body shakes, and her fear keeps mine under control. *Mostly.* As the man's footfalls land on the short stoop, I feel like I'm living in two nightmares simultaneously, this one and the one from long ago.

Sara prompts her barking dogs, bringing his clunky boots to a stop. He bangs on the door anyway, and through the peephole, I see him hiding the crowbar behind his back. I mouth a quick "Go" to Sara over my shoulder.

"Go away," I yell toward the door. "I've called the police."

"Who the fuck are you?"

"I'm the armed resident of this house. Who the fuck are *you*?" I shout back. I hold the bat on my shoulder, my hands strangling its handle. "Leave! Now!"

His boots shuffle on the concrete outside the door as if he doesn't know what to do. I hear voices egging him on across the yard. My heels pull along the carpet as I step away. He tries the door handle. Finding it locked, he wedges the crowbar between the lock and the frame.

My heart thunders in my chest. I know I should run. *Why aren't I running?* Wicked memories cement me in place. *Always make sure the door is locked. The door is your best defense. Don't turn away.*

The wood splinters and cracks. His shoulder bangs against the door. The noises echo, merging with memories. *Bang, bang, bang.* My heart beats so hard and fast that there's no separation between them—just one long, agonizing beat.

It's the strangest time to think about Jack. Heart racing. Feet immobile. Perpetrator nearly through the door. Jack breaks through my brain fog like he's suddenly my comfort animal. He's texted all night. I should've asked for help.

The door cracks again. It's only held by the chain now.

I inch backward, my heels catching roughly in the shag carpeting. Then, I turn to run—*I shouldn't be here.*

Sirens and screeching tires prevent the last break through the door.

"Oh, shit!" The crowbar clangs against the concrete.

I run into Sara, rushing through the back door. "It's okay. The police are here."

The bat falls to the floor, my legs wobble, and she holds onto me.

Blue lights flash through the front window. Gun drawn, Lt. Wright orders the men to the ground. They quickly obey, and two other officers pat them down and put them in cuffs. He finds us in the house once the men are safely in custody.

As Sara and I gush our thanks, Lt. Wright calmly explains the charges and takes our statements. Then, he promises to add Sara's house to his nightly patrols.

Everything's okay. Only I'm not.

Twenty

JACK

"Nice shindig." Devin leans against the railing beside me. He wears a tuxedo t-shirt, jeans, Converse, and an amused expression, taking in what's left of my dying party. "Why are you hiding over here?"

I don't answer. I'm parked on the fencing at the pool's edge, near my study, where I can peek at Rowan's driveway.

It's nearly midnight. She's still not home. Though her texts have been vaguely reassuring, I'm worried.

Frustration plays a close second. Something must be wrong for her to leave so quickly and not be here by now. I wish she'd get over the anti-damsel-in-distress thing and ask for my help. Or, at least, tell me what's going on. I reread her texts. She might as well be giving me her forced smile, shields up.

"You've been watching for her all night," Devin says. "She's not coming."

"I don't care about the party," I say into my whiskey before gulping it down.

Rephrase—I don't care about the party *now*.

Earlier, I did. I bothered the hell out of the caterers and decorators, making sure everything was just right. I added her favorite chardonnay to the menu at the last minute. I had the mini-basketball court turned into a dance floor. And remembering how much Rowan liked the twinkling lights at the oyster roast, I had the decorators add them everywhere—draping the trees, the railings, and the arbor over the outdoor kitchen.

I imagined her showing up, looking fucking amazing. She'd be nervous at first—parties aren't her thing. But I'd stay by her side, loosen her up with wine and my quick charm, and introduce her to all the important people in my life she hasn't met yet. My friends. My agent and editors. Even my parents. I imagined whispering in her ear and making her laugh over my father's tipsy ramblings about grocery prices these days and my mom's uncanny ability to find fault with the food. We'd take a bet on how early they'd leave—whether it'd be because of Dad's tipsiness or Mom's unease driving at night. They left by nine for a new reason—Mom's designer heels hurting her feet. Maybe Rowan would've guessed it.

I'd sign books and divvy out door prizes while she'd linger with the neighbors and Sara, and I'd catch her eye from afar occasionally. She'd smile, her gorgeous blue eyes twinkling under the lights, and I'd make every excuse to get back to her.

She'd meet my agent, Lynn, and hear her gush about my latest pages. "It's your best work yet," she said before explaining everyone's relief. "The publisher is already talking about renewing your contract. *The Other Us* is exceeding expectations. Your writing hiatus worked for you... but never do it again."

My idiot friends would be on their best behavior, partly because of their wives but also because I forewarned them to behave. They'd warm up to Rowan just like I have, and she'd laugh over their best and worst stories about me.

I'd get *The Hurricanes* to play "November Rain" and lure her to the dance floor, where she'd slip her arms around my neck and hold on to me a little easier than last time.

At the night's end, she'd linger, and at the right moment, I'd tell her—

"Tell her what?" Devin chimes into my thoughts.

It's the only part I haven't figured out yet. It'd be easy to tell her how I feel—at my keyboard, where I transform pivotal moments like this into fucking art that has my heroine falling into her lover's arms.

But *this* is Rowan. Romance doesn't work. Plans don't work—she's not even here. Even if she were, what would I say?

"Tell her the truth. Tell her you're falling for her." Devin cocks his brow at me. "And just go with it, even when it's hard."

I peek at Rowan's empty driveway. "It's already too hard. She's hellbent on marrying the world's worst fiancé and convinced she's not my type."

"Change her mind, dumbass. Or give up and go back to business as usual." He motions to a newbie on my editing team, a twenty-something redhead in a skin-tight black dress. She catches my eyes and nibbles her bottom lip—the same come-hither look she's been giving me all night.

"If you *can* go back to business as usual. Can you?"

"Of course. It *is* business as usual. Rowan's a no-show and off-limits, any-way."

"Prove it... Incoming."

The redhead beelines toward me as if making eye contact was an invitation. Pursing her lips and watching me over the tops of her eyes, she looks determined. Sexy, too. *Definitely your type*, I imagine Rowan saying.

I check my phone. Nothing. I lean to see Rowan's driveway. Nothing. Only a few guests linger over half-finished cocktails, and the staff is already cleaning up. My best hopes for tonight are over.

The redhead arrives with two whiskies. I down the one in my hand and accept hers. Her sparkly fingernails graze my hand as she gives it to me. "Mind if I join you?"

I give her a once-over, catching the way she shimmers—her dress, her eyes, her glossy lips. "If you want."

Her lips curl. She leans next to me, her thigh brushing against my hand. "Should we talk about your books and how much I love them? Your party? The weather?"

"No. None of that."

"Good." She tilts closer, practically begging me to look at her breasts, which I do, of course. Her hand falls on my thigh and squeezes. "I've exceeded my limit on chitchat for one night. How about you?"

"I don't do chitchat."

She laughs, though I'm not kidding. Her fingertips dance along my inner leg. "What *do* you like to do?"

A minute later, she follows me inside.

Though I have a dozen rooms in my house, I take her to the downstairs guest bathroom. She hops up on the sink and sets a condom on the counter beside her ass.

Her dainty arms drape over my shoulders. Her red lips hover close to mine, daring me to kiss her.

I want to. To forget this night and put my feelings for Rowan in a discard pile of shit-stupid ideas. She doesn't want me, so why not feel better with someone who does?

When I hesitate, she tugs down her sleeveless dress, revealing the lacy get-up pushing her breasts together. *Come on, Jack.*

With my hands clamped to the counter on either side of her, I still do nothing. I only loiter, close but not touching, taking her in but not taking her.

She wriggles out of the bra next, letting me see her, and I wonder how far I can take this without doing a damn thing.

Her legs spread wide, inviting me in. She goes for a kiss, but I recoil.

"Playing hard to get?" Her whisper dances over my lips, tickling me. Then, her hand travels slowly over my chest, tugs at my belt, and slips over me.

We're both surprised at what she discovers. This woman does nothing for me.

"Sorry, honey. Too many whiskies."

"Too bad." She slumps, pulling her bra up. I help her from her perch. She puts herself back together, not hiding her irritation. Then, she leaves. And I feel like shit for all sorts of reasons.

I exit the bathroom and stagger down the hall into the open kitchen. Devin sits cross-legged in the center of the kitchen island, shaking his head at me. "So, *not* business as usual?"

"Fuck off."

If this were a novel, this would be the lightbulb moment when the hero realizes his dead brother is right. Maybe I am falling for her. The evidence is there, whether I want to admit it or not.

I don't.

I don't see the redhead again. The remaining guests say their goodbyes. The staff finish their work and leave.

Finally, alone, I shed my jacket and tie, kick off my shoes, and get another drink. Irritated, restless, and feeling the alcohol, I grab my laptop and carry it to a table outside.

But thinking of what I *can't* do resurrects my writer's block. I can't write anything.

I smash my whiskey glass on the concrete. Breaking glass sounds like strange music, especially as the shards clink and ping against the floor. I grab a wine bottle from another table and break that, too.

Broken glass slithers into the bottom of my foot. Another lightbulb moment—this is a bad idea. Blood dots the pavement underneath. I'm stupid-drunk.

So, when I hear my name, I think it's my imagination.

Hearing it again, I catch a tremor in her voice. Something's wrong.

Turning scrapes the glass deeper into my skin, but I don't care. She's here. And drunk as I am, I know she needs me.

Twenty-One

ROWAN

It's after one when we return to the little house. The party has ended, leaving a quiet, sleepy street. Sara slugs inside, exhaustion catching up with her.

"Good night, Rowan," she says before disappearing into her bedroom.

The game face I plastered all night vanishes with the click of her door closing. Deep breaths keep my heart from racing, but I can't do anything about my shaking fingers or the nervous energy now pulsing through me. A home invasion was nearly the death of me once, and tonight, I almost let it happen again. The two events replay in an endless loop, clashing with each other and all the what-ifs. We were lucky it ended well. It almost didn't.

What was I thinking?

I try making tea, but the teabag rips apart. My nerves, my body, my head—everything is rattled. I step outside the sliding glass doors, hoping the cool night air might bring some relief.

It doesn't.

Movement catches my attention through the hedges in Jack's yard—he's still awake. I think of how he consoled me after Sara lashed out, and I long for his comfort again. With him, I won't have to explain unless I want to. I won't have to worry that he'll ignore my call. He'll just let me be with him as long as I need.

My shoulders buck at the sound of breaking glass as I take the path between our houses. Jack stands at the pool's edge, holding a bottle and stumbling over his feet. He's drunk and irritated.

I hesitate, but only for a second before saying his name.

He pauses until I call out again. He whips around, nearly falling. "Rowan? You made it."

His frustration vanishes like butter melting into warm toast. It's a wild relief, the change in his disposition, and a surprise, given my previous experiences with drunk men. I go to him, stopping short of walking straight into his arms.

Glassy-eyed, he looks me over. "Something's wrong. What is it? Is it Sara?"

"She's fine." My voice trembles with the words. "Just... a rough night."

"You're shaking." With this discovery, he gently pulls me to his chest, and I press my ear against his heartbeat. A trapped breath sputters out as I latch on, and he curls me up—his arms tight around my shoulders and back, his head resting on mine.

His warmth and comfort are exactly what I need. *He's* exactly what I need. His tight hold feels like a shield, us against the world. I can't remember the last time I felt so safe. He says nothing and lets me linger. Secret tears emerge while I clutch him, leaking out with the released tension. He strokes my hair with his fingertips like he knows I'm crying. As drunk as he is, as late as it is, he doesn't let go, like he might stay this way all night, if that's what I needed.

A lovely but dangerous idea that I can't entertain for many reasons.

Still, I retreat slowly, lingering in our collected heat. He hovers over me, his breath in my hair and fingers pressing me to him. It's like he doesn't want me to pull away. Or it could be my wishful thinking.

Meeting his eyes, I force a weak smile. "Um, how was the party?"

"Fucking awful."

"Why?"

"You weren't here." He shrugs like it's obvious.

A weak laugh rumbles out. "Sorry." I glance at his white button-down, now smeared with damp mascara. "Oh, shit... and for that." Quick swipes under my eyes remove the leftover evidence of my breakdown. "Guess you were right about me. I *am* needy."

"I don't care about the shirt." Awkwardly, he yanks it off and tosses it in the pool. A boyish smirk plays at his mouth as he stands there in his plain white t-shirt. "See? And forget what I said that night. You aren't needy. You're human. A perfect human. With your perfect smile, your perfect lips, perfect ass, perfect legs, perfect face. You're perfect, scars and all."

"No, Jack. I'm not."

"You are to me."

It hurts to hear him say these things. He feels sorry for me, *that's all*. He's overcompensating for what he knows isn't true, just like Renita did. I'm no one's 'beautiful, no one's 'perfect.' Jack's too drunk to see it.

He stumbles slightly, catching my arm.

"You're perfectly drunk... And bleeding. Here, sit down."

I ease him into the nearest chair, careful of the glass and glad for the distraction. The sparkling mess around us almost works with the decor—his backyard shimmers with gorgeous twinkling lights. They canopy the deck and circle the pool, reflecting off the gold and black balloons holding up every corner. I spy the empty dance floor with regret.

"I missed a beautiful party, Jack. I love the lights."

"I knew you would." He leans closer, lightly twiddling my hair. "Rowan, can't believe you're here. You look amazing. Holy shit, that dress."

"Thanks, I really wanted to be here."

"I really wanted you here," he says slowly. "Want to talk about it? Your rough night?"

Part of me does. But I shake my head. "No... just grappling with some old ghosts."

"Yeah, me, too." He looks sad but doesn't elaborate.

"Let's take a look at your feet, huh?"

"That's weird, but whatever you say."

I prop his injured foot into my lap and tug off his sock. The gashes aren't deep, but I extract two glass shards. Then, I rinse his feet with a nearby water bottle.

"Sorry, I'm a mess," he says.

"It's okay. I'm a mess, too."

But my mess takes a hard backseat to helping him. I'm no longer shaking or nervous, as if all my anxieties left me during our long embrace.

I help him to the expensive sectional in his gorgeous living room. He tells me where to find the first aid kit in the kitchen. He lays on the couch while I dab his wounds with an alcohol swab and wrap them in gauze.

By the time I finish, he's drifted to sleep.

Outside, I turn off the excess lighting, clean the glass, and get his laptop. I find aspirin in the kitchen and leave it on the coffee table beside him with two water bottles and a small trashcan, just in case. I ease a throw pillow under his head and cover him with a thick blanket I find draped over the plush side chair.

While bringing the blanket up, his tattoos catch my eye. I chuckle, raising the edge of his sleeve higher—the Cheshire Cat.

As my fingers trace its wide, devious grin, Jack wakes and says, "*How puzzling all these changes are! I never know what I'm going to be, from one minute to another.*"

His Cheshire Cat quote makes me laugh and gratefully hides my embarrassment for touching him like that. "*I'm stranger. You're stranger. Together, we are... strangers.*"

"Strangers together. I like that." His dark eyes lock on mine, lips curving like the cat on his arm.

I smile, too, relieved that he's a pleasant drunk and grateful I'm here, helping him, just as he's done for me. *I really care about this man.*

He lifts his fingers to my face and, cupping my scarred cheek, his thumb softly traces my skin's uneven texture. And I don't stop it.

Trent used my scars. Dean avoids them.

Jack's gentle affection makes me think it's possible to love *all* of me, even the rough parts. And why shouldn't I be loved completely?

"*A rose is still a rose, even hidden under different petals...* You are... absurdly beautiful, Rowan. In the strangest, most intoxicating way."

My breath catches and holds, a little enamored. "Um, you're quite drunk."

"No! Just drunk enough to say what I *really* think. He doesn't deserve you, you know."

My eyes catch his, almost surprised at how serious and lucid he is.

"That's the real, ongoing travesty in all this." His fingers slip over my cheek and tickle my neck. "The stories people tell you, and you believe... that you're not enough. That you're damaged goods. That it's okay for everything else to come before you. It makes me sad. Sad that you aren't loved the way you're meant to be loved. You should be ravished, Rowan." His goofy smile returns. "And cherished. And fucking adored."

"Spoken like a true romantic," I mutter through the lump in my throat. I tug his hand away from my face, holding it against his chest. "No one lines up to do that." *Not even Dean.* "But don't worry about me, Jack. I'm okay with it."

"You shouldn't be. Don't you want to be ravished?" He asks like I'm an alien species, yet to learn human ways.

"Who doesn't?" I say, not hiding my sarcasm. "I appreciate the sentiment—I think. But everything will look different tomorrow. Promise me you'll stay here and crash?"

"Only if you make me a promise, too."

I sigh, giving him an expectant look.

"Promise me... you'll tell me the real story one day—when you trust me enough. Not for me to write or to satisfy my curiosity. But because letting it go will make *you* feel better—I *know* it will. Like tonight. Like it always is with us."

His sincerity breaks through his drunk facade easily, like a train through a tunnel—*he truly wants this for me.*

"Okay, I will— *When* I trust you enough." It's not hard making the promise, not with that disclaimer. *When.* It's like saying *when* hell freezes over or *when* pigs fly. But still, I imagine it wouldn't be difficult. He is like wine to my inhibitions, sweetly able to lessen my defenses.

Satisfied, he leans against the pillow. "Okay, Rowan. It's a deal." He pulls the blanket up while I tuck the edges around him. A fat, orange tabby jumps into the space between his legs, startling me.

"Ah, who's this?"

"Harper Lee. We both have author-cats."

I laugh, surprised he hasn't told me before. "Aw, I love *To Kill a Mockingbird.* That's the perfect name for a cat. She's gorgeous." I lean over and rub her back, initiating heavy purrs.

"So is Edgar Allan Poe. I got tattoos for both. Wanna see?"

"Not tonight. I should go."

He grabs my hands. "Please, Rowan. Stay. I'm trying to tell you something."

"I'm listening. What?"

His brow kinks like he can't remember. "I really like... holding you. We should do it more often. Make it a thing."

"A thing?"

"*Our* thing," he says. "This isn't drunk-Jack talking. This is real-Jack."

A chuckle sputters out, knowing exactly which Jack I'm talking to. "It *was* nice, but it can't be a regular thing."

"Why not?" Then, he grunts and rolls his eyes as he realizes the answer. "When's your acting friend coming back?"

"Next week."

"Straight into your open arms, right?" His tone shifts to frustration. "Like he hasn't abandoned you all summer. Like he hasn't put you in purgatory and made you feel like shit. I see it all over your face. It amazes me what desperate women will put up with for a ring on her finger and a kid down the hall."

"That's what you think of me?"

"I get it. You're marrying him because he's safe. Well, can't get safer than a guy who's gone half the year." His mocking laugh hurts my ears. "If he cared about you at all, he'd be here to get you out of that dress."

"Mind your own business, Jack." I head to the sliding glass doors, suddenly anxious to escape him.

"Everyone thinks I'm alone because of the one that got away, but you're alone because he *stays* away. I don't know which is worse. Or more pathetic."

My feet stop on the word *pathetic*. "Telling me I'm beautiful one minute only to cut me down the next? Lecturing me on how I should be loved as if you know best? As if your sex buddies aren't flawless Barbie dolls? Spare me your condescension—you would *never* want someone like me, *not like that*. Not *sober*, anyway. You don't know Dean... or me and Dean. And you're the one who got shit-faced at your own party—that's pathetic."

I never should've come over here. Never should've entertained ideas of being anything more to him than an arrangement. Never should've let him hold me. I leave without looking back.

Twenty-Two

ROWAN

Days later, a honking horn sends Sara and me into a scattered hurry, dumping dirty dishes into the sink and grabbing our things—beach bags, chairs, and a small, pink Igloo cooler. The horn goes off again, longer this time.

"Ugh, he's so annoying," Sara huffs.

"You're the one who wanted to join them," I remind her.

I *did not* want to join the neighborhood beach day. Multiple invitations arose after the party—I refused them all. Rose's 'biscuits' didn't sway me. Neither did Marcy's wine.

But Sara said our neighbors made her feel like she could truly be herself. So, how could I refuse? We've only just connected—I don't want to lose our tenuous bond. Still, if she hadn't asked, I never would've agreed to go.

Besides, the last few days have been rough.

Dean arranged more gigs to carry him through next weekend, meaning he won't get home until the day before school starts. "A last hurrah," he explained during an exasperating FaceTime call, which means no *hurrahing* for us before work begins—a point I didn't have time to make before he had to rush off.

But strangely, my indifference bothers me the most. What's another weekend? Jack's drunken remarks don't help. Have I put up with this because I love Dean or because I so desperately want a partner and a family?

I stifled my confusion with work. I spent a full day at school, setting up my classroom and fine-tuning my weekly guides. Meanwhile, the Ring cameras arrived, and by the time I got home, Vernon and Jack had already installed them at Sara's house.

As Rose explained that evening after I gushed my thanks, "Sara is a peach! Isn't it funny? I bring over tea, and she tells me about her cock-up cousins and how you foiled them. Meanwhile, that cute UPS delivery man brings cameras, and hop, skip, jump, the boys take care of it. Poor Jack was a little perturbed that you went through that alone, love."

I want to say he also perturbs me, but don't for fear that it'll end up headlining the *Daisy Chain*.

So, with two weekends until school starts and almost as long until Mom and then Dean arrive, summer circles the drain like an unfinished cocktail, wasted.

I don't know what to think about Jack, either. I dream in his embrace but can't live there. Words like *absurdly beautiful, cherished,* and *adored* mix with *stays away, purgatory,* and *pathetic,* creating a curdled potion in my head. I'm not proud of what I said to him either—who am I to judge his sex life or drinking habits? Or argue with an intoxicated person? Or let what he said in that state bother me? I hope the gods of drunkenness do me a favor, and he doesn't remember. *Please, don't remember.*

The horn goes off again as we trudge across the lawn. Jack meets us at the back end and loads Sara's chair beside the others. She promptly skips to the sliding door.

Our eyes meet for the first time when he reaches for my chair. He looks morose—the Jack I first met that rainy night in the little house.

I offer a weak smile. "Thanks. Are you okay?"

His hard features soften with the question. He shuts the back door, blocking us from the passengers. "Not really. I was a dick. But I'm pissed at you for dealing with those fuckers alone. Do you realize the danger you put yourself in? Anything could've happened. You should've told me, should've let me help."

My shoulders slump. "I know. I'm sorry. It was a stupid mistake."

His anger dissipates with my confession. "I fucked up, too. You aren't desperate or pathetic—that's not what I think of you, Rowan. You're the best person I know. I was being... protective, I think. I'm sorry."

My gaze drops to the space between us. His beautiful compliment gets tainted by the word *protective*. It's a nicer way to say he feels sorry for me, like he's a pseudo-big-brother, critiquing my choices like Mira and Mom always do. "I don't need protecting. Can we just reset to cordial again?"

"You're still pissed at me?"

"Yes. No, ugh." Flustered, I lock eyes with him. "I'm not pissed, just confused. When you can't handle something, you turn into a jerk—*that*, I understand. But *why* when it comes to me? What about *me* can't you handle?"

He looks stumped. Pained, even. Like I've given him a pop quiz, and he hasn't studied.

"Have I done something?" I try again. "Is it me?"

"It's not you—"

"If you say *'it's not you, it's me,'* I'm banning you from writing, Jack Graham," I say, hoping to ease the tension. He allows a short smirk but keeps his eyes pinched.

"As you should. Thanks for saving me from a career-ending mistake." He leans against the van, arms folded. "I, um, what I meant to say was... I'm sorry for being a dick. I'm working some shit out. I'll do better."

I sense he wants to say more, but his lips clamp shut. Maybe I'm reading into it, anyway. "Back to cordial, then?"

He nods. "Or something like it."

"We should go." I dart around him.

Leaning into the van, I size up the seating options. A long-lensed Nikon hangs from Vernon's neck while binoculars droop from Rose's. Tom and Marcy wear matching wide-brimmed hats in the back. Between the couples, Ed and

Renita look flashy—her in a long, flowing floral cover-up and Ed wearing a Bermuda shirt and aviator sunglasses. Sara plops between Vernon and Rose.

I'm left with the front passenger seat beside Jack.

"Lovely day for the beach," Renita coos as the van rumbles from the neighborhood.

"Dad would be so jealous," Sara says. "He loves the beach. We go every weekend. Or um, used to."

I twist to see her. "Have you heard from him?"

"He calls once a week." She glances up from her phone. "I miss him."

"We should visit him. I mean, if you're allowed. Are you?"

She gives me a funny look. "Yeah, but it's on the other side of town. What? Are you going to take me?"

"I don't mind taking you. Just me—this isn't a community field trip," I say, turning to the rest of the van.

"Understood, love," Rose says.

Catching Sara's eyes again, I ask, "Are you sure it'd be alright for you to see him like that? It might be difficult."

"Better for me to see him in a tacky jumpsuit than not at all. You really don't mind?"

Her pleading look softens any hesitation. "I should've offered sooner. He's your dad. Of course, you should see him. We'll go tomorrow."

"Thanks, Rowan."

I shrug lightly—no big deal—but turned around in my seat, I can't help my wide grin. I fold my arms over my chest to shield myself from the blasting AC.

Jack leans over and taps the vents away from me.

I'm about to thank him when Marcy asks, "Rowan, summer's almost over. When do we get to meet your fiancé?"

I nearly cringe at the word fiancé like it's a title I haven't earned yet. "Soon. He'll be home on Labor Day, I think."

"Working actors comprise the majority of the entertainment industry," Vernon says. "It's harder than it looks—the magic of—"

"Vernon, no. What's he working on this week, Rowan?"

"I can't keep up, Rose. A Hulu production, I think."

Jack rams on the horn at a lifted truck that cuts him off. "Asshole!"

"Oh, Hulu—we have that." Rose glances at Vernon for verification. Sara giggles at Jack's cursing, though no one else seems to notice.

"We should plan a welcome-home party."

Rose claps at Marcy's idea, and I offer a weak, "Um, he'd like that."

Jack weaves around slow cars in the left lane only to give them a wave of irritation as we pass and mumble curses under his breath.

"We must do a cinema theme," Rose says, spurring more ideas from the group, and plans for a Dean party unfold.

Jack turns the radio up, drowning the conversation, and within moments, the entire van is rocking out to Taylor Swift. Sara and I share a bemused look at the unharmonious cooing. I curl into the seat, a headache nipping at my temple. I imagine a lifetime of this—me reporting on Dean because he isn't around to tell them himself.

Rose's words from the night I met her circle into my head. *If you love something enough, you find a way to make it work.* They mix with Dean's. *This is why we work... we're independent people who want to be independent together.*

Only it sounds hollow now, like a bargain basement consolation prize to *ravished, cherished, adored.*

We arrive at the Carolina Beach boardwalk and set up base camp near the lifeguard stand. Jack and Tom erect a family-sized beach tent while we unfold our chairs. Jack acts as a porter, making multiple trips to the van for more gear and helping with set-up. Like a dutiful son, he doesn't mind when Vernon hands him money for a donut run or when Marcy asks him to clean her glasses.

Vernon goes off to take photos in the morning light. Ed and Renita tour the boardwalk, hunting for mimosas. Rose and Marcy wade in the light waves. Tom and Jack get the surfboards strapped to the van's roof and head out to catch waves. Sara settles with a sketchbook, angled away so I can't see what she's doing.

I pull out *Cape Moon*—Jack's first novel. I'm halfway through, and he's spun a thick, sticky web around me, pulling me in and holding me tightly. It's the story of Tyler and Rachel—childhood sweethearts who share a devastating secret that slowly tears them apart. Told from a shifting perspective between the past and present, he leaves the reader desperate to discover what the secret is and, even more, if their love can withstand it. It's dark, sometimes funny, strange, and sexy, but best of all, the love story is addictive. Every time I look away, my eyes zip back to the page like it might disintegrate in my hands if I stop reading—and I can't let that happen.

I vaguely notice Sara going for a swim and keep a distracted eye on her. I hear Rose and Vernon talking. At one point, Renita's high-pitched laugh makes me think they scored their mimosas. But otherwise, I'm oblivious to everything but the world Jack's created—one of aching, desperate love, eerie sadness, and suspense.

Thunder breaks the spell. The dark sky at sea is split by lightning hitting the water. Our group eyes the approaching storm, except for Jack—he's watching me, stretched out, long and lean, on a towel near my chair.

"Better head for cover," Tom announces calmly. "Just a summer storm. Won't last long."

"Sara, come!" Rose waves her hand. "Let's go buy you a proper sunhat."

She races with them toward the boardwalk.

Renita and Ed dash up the beach in a giddy but ungraceful run toward a bar. Tom and Marcy follow, hand-in-hand, as fat raindrops pummel our tent. When I turn back to the stormy ocean, Jack's on his feet, his hand reaching for mine.

"Come on." His words come softly but sound demanding, like he's responsible for me. *Protective.* But I won't quibble. Lightning streaks the ocean behind him, with thunder quickly crashing, and my heart races. I tuck the book in my beach bag, sling it on my shoulder, and take his hand.

The rain picks up, making it hard to see. But Jack pulls me along, never loosening his grip as we weave through the evacuating crowd.

Lightning electrifies the sky, separated only a second from ear-splitting thunder. Barefoot, we kick through sandy puddles and cross over the boardwalk toward the shops.

But we don't stay with the crowd, ducking into stores and restaurants. Jack leads me behind the boardwalk steps and under the platform with an insistent tug. Over our heads, the long slits between boards provide cuts of gray light, but it's mostly dim. It's a makeshift cave, shaded and safe. The rain and sudden coolness bring on a full-bodied shiver, and my heart races with the excited effort to get here.

But meeting Jack's eyes, I laugh, even as another explosion makes me jump. Stuck in his story, I feel giddy, even drunk on it, like a teenager crushing on a book for the first time.

"I was at the part in the woods with the moss and the wet leaves under their feet," I explain breathlessly. "When the rain comes, Tyler takes her to their old lean-to. And they kiss for the first time."

Saying nothing, Jack sorts through my beach bag at my feet and pulls out a towel.

"When I looked up and saw the storm, I thought I'd conjured it from my imagination... Or, I mean, *your* imagination. Weird, huh?"

The beach towel circles my shoulders, dry and warm from the heat it captured on the beach—I didn't realize I was shivering. Jack holds the ends together between us like he's afraid I might not have the wherewithal to keep it on.

"And that kiss, Jack... ah, if only kisses could feel so magical. I don't think a kiss can be *that* good."

His intense stare falters slightly into curiosity.

I suddenly realize how alone we are. And close. Gripping my towel between us, his hand is fisted at the top of my chest. The other dangles loosely beside my right hand, a mere inch apart. It'd be easy to drag my fingertips across the tattooed world on his exposed chest—books and scenes spilling into each other like different chapters in the same eclectic story.

My eyes stop on the tattoo over his heart—a *Calvin and Hobbes* version of him and his brother wearing baseball uniforms and toting gear toward the field. I think of his office picture and the letters $C + D$ etched into the closet door in Sara's room, how sweet and sad it is. I long to touch him, hold him, offer some comfort in hindsight.

"Um, not a first kiss, anyway." Inexplicably nervous, I focus on his face instead. "Those are always clumsy and awkward in real life. Don't you think?"

Why isn't he saying anything? Rain slaps against the wood planks over our heads, slipping through the tiny gaps. Thunder rumbles, and Jack stares at me like I'm a puzzle he can't figure out. His free hand mingles with my left one, dangling at my side—tips to palm, and then his fingers roll over the outer side, where my marks cover half my hand. *Why is Jack Graham touching me?*

His grip on the towel edges me closer before his lips land softly on mine. My hands fall against his chest. I think to push him away—I *want* to push him away. But he does this wicked, teasing thing with his mouth, taking my bottom lip first and sliding his tongue across it before kissing me full-on in this soft, sexy, playful move that enflames my cold body in a second. He is salty, warm, and intense, like a crucial comfort—an addiction—that might make my heart explode in my chest for the crazy things he's doing to my body all at once.

I can't resist him. It's the kiss I've always wanted but didn't think existed. A unicorn kiss.

The towel falls to my feet, and we're practically skin-to-skin. His hands go to my face, cupping my cheeks and fingers lacing in my wet hair. He hesitates, pulling away just enough to run his thumb over my lip and take me in. He is *so* close to me, studying me, pressing into me like he's on top of me, and making me feel that nothing exists outside this hidden nook, our lips, hands, and magical touches. And strangely, I want to cry for the Pandora's box he's cracking open, making me see what I didn't know was there. He's a black hole ripping open my universe, sucking me in.

Breathing hard against him, bodies tight, hands gripping, lips close, and eyes locked, we kiss again—maybe I start it this time—and I'm swept away like a boat lost at sea that capsizes under a powerful wave. This is no clumsy first kiss. My hand circles his neck, runs through his hair, and over his rough cheek, keeping him there, savoring him. My legs twitch to wrap around him, especially with his hands kneading down my back, lower and lower, until I can't help it. My right leg raises just enough to bring his hand to my thigh. He grips it so tightly that I feel all of him against me, and I ache for more. Ache for him.

Lightning flashes and thunder cracks, jolting me back to reality. *What am I doing?*

"I can't do this," I whisper, still close to him.

"Yes, you can," comes his stern reply. His hands lock around my waist, holding me in place.

"No, I'm not like you." My words are weak, almost whiny, but I can't help it, like I'm crashing after an adrenaline rush. "This means something to me. I'm not a plot line or a plaything. Or a cheater. I can't do this to Dean."

"Break up with Dean. Be with me."

I yank free of his tight grasp. "Damn it, no. How dare you even say it or even think it. No, I-I can't be one of many, Jack."

"Fuck, that's not what I'm asking." He looks confused, angry even. "Rowan, is it so hard to believe I want *you*? *Only* you?"

"Yes! You never *only* want anyone. I'm... just the wounded girl next door. I'll run out of stories to tell, and the words will stop flowing. What then? I'll never be enough. Not when you can have anyone you want. Not with... so many pretty faces. Damn it, Jack. How could you do this to us?"

I grab my things and rush into the rain, desperate to get away from him.

Twenty-Three

JACK

Fuuuuuccccckkkkkk! Pissing her off wasn't my plan.

I didn't have a plan.

But kissing her felt necessary. Like blinking or breathing. And she didn't stop me.

Everything between us has built like a wave at sea until it had nowhere else to go but to crash at her feet. That kiss was my confession.

And who wouldn't want a first kiss under the boardwalk in the rain?

Maybe the woman with rules against romance? *Damn it.*

I think to chase her, but I can't. I need a solid few minutes to calm down. I'm too turned on to go anywhere—she is so much more than I expected.

I lean against the piling, take deep breaths, and think about baseball. Or anything but her tender lips, her warm, sun-kissed skin, or the moment she got over her surprise and opened up to me. I still feel her lips parting against mine and the hungry exploration of her hands. And ah, she was so close to wrapping those gorgeous legs around me. So achingly close.

No—that kiss wasn't a mistake. No matter what she says.

Those incredible five minutes brought more insight than some of our longest conversations.

For starters, all the women I've been with suddenly seem like opening acts for the *real* show. Rowan is beautifully intense. It's like she's an overflowing well of heat and desire that's gone untapped by the selfish pricks of her past. I want to fucking drink her up *and* be the rain that makes her full again.

Damn it. I *am* in love with her.

More distressing, she has a shit opinion of me. *Plot line. Plaything. I'm not like you.* Her words twist together into an ache in my stomach. She thinks I'm playing games, toying with her. That's what she thinks I do. That *is* what I do.

At least, that's what I *used* to do. There must be a way to convince her that she's different.

The rain comes to a slow stop. I step from our hovel to find the crowds emerging from their shelters. Ed and Renita stumble from the corner bar. Good thing I'm driving.

I return to the beach and sit in Rowan's chair, determined to talk to her. The neighbors trickle back to home base, but over an hour passes, and Rowan doesn't show. While the others are distracted with food and swimming, I nudge Sara's shoulder, pulling her away from her sketchbook.

"Seen Rowan?"

"Nope."

"Text her. See if she's okay."

Sara's eyebrow pyramids on her forehead. "Something wrong with your phone?"

"Please, Sara."

Her eyes roll at my pleading expression. *This fucking kid...* but she relents, her thumbs flying across her screen.

A moment later, she reads the reply. "Fine."

That's the answer I should've expected. I lean forward, and maybe it's immature to pry information from a teen, but I ask, "What do you know about Dean?"

She side-smirks. "Mr. Maddix? Why do you want to know about him?"

"Don't fuck around. Either you have an opinion of the guy or not."

She laughs. "He's alright. Theater geeks love him. I'm taking his class as an elective this year, which I wouldn't do without hearing good things. His project with Rowan was the highlight of last year—a trans retelling of *Taming of the Shrew*. It's on YouTube. You should watch."

"Including the proposal?"

"Yep... That's the part people watch most. The project's highlight reel is also cool—seeing how they put it all together, how Rowan and Mr. Maddix worked together."

"Hmm," I grunt, searching the app on my phone. "What else?"

She wags her purple fingernail at me. "Nope. Not until you tell me why."

My shoulders slump in resignation. "Fine. I kissed her. She... reacted badly."

"What do you mean? Reacted badly?"

"She was into it, and then suddenly, she wasn't."

Sara nods—nothing surprises her.

"—Tell the neighbors, and I'll switch my playlists to folk ballads, Barry Manilow, and fifty-year-old country songs," I tack on quickly.

"Who's Barry Manilow?" She laughs. "Fine. I won't tell."

"Good. Now, have any insights?"

She takes a deep breath, glancing at the ocean. "Well, Mr. Maddix is a good guy. Dorky, but he means well. The thing is... everyone knows that Rowan hates crowds and attention. So, I get why she was nervous. He put her in a tight spot. But messing up her answer put him in a tough place, too. Still, everyone's surprised that he's bailed on her all summer. There's a school group chat about it. Team Mackey. Team Maddix." She huffs and rolls her eyes. "Shows how boring we are, huh? Group chatting about our teachers?"

I shrug. "What team are you on?"

"Definitely Team Maddix at first. He's always so funny and friendly, and she embarrassed him."

"What about now?"

"Team Rowan—don't tell her that. She'd probably want to start braiding each other's hair or getting mani-pedis together."

A light chuckle comes out, knowing it's true.

"She tries so hard, you know? And she's sad. All the time. I think Mr. Maddix is the type to run away from his problems, like not dealing with the real reason behind Rowan's answer. It's easier than the truth."

"Which is?"

"She doesn't want to marry him," Sara says dryly, like she's remarking on the weather. "But she will."

"Really?"

"Rowan doesn't run away from problems. She fixes them, even when she shouldn't. He's practically ghosted her, and still, whenever he calls, she puts on her happy voice and pretends it's okay. It's sad, really. He'll come back, and they'll be just like before—she'll make sure."

"You think that's okay?"

"Look at me—I have purple hair and piercings. I like getting noticed. I can't imagine what it's like to be Rowan, with people always staring for the wrong reasons. She probably thinks Mr. Maddix is as good as it gets. Maybe she's right."

She isn't, but I don't argue. "You're pretty smart for a teenage dumbass."

Sara chuckles. "You're pretty dumb for putting Rowan in another tight spot. No wonder she reacted badly."

"Couldn't help it."

She gives me a skeptical look. "Are you... *serious* about her?"

"Is that so hard to believe?"

"Ah, *yeah*. You're a man-slut. Plus, she's your *neighbor*. Your *engaged* neighbor."

"You've stopped being helpful. Do me a favor. Find her and see if she's really okay?"

Before she answers, Vernon and Rose stroll up, hand-in-hand, and he says, "More storms approaching. Might be time to pack it in."

"I'll find Rowan," Sara says, setting her sketchbook aside.

By the time Sara returns, our base camp is mostly dismantled. Rowan looks bothered and guarded—brow pinched and arms folded over her buttoned cover-up.

Renita says, "Rowan, you're as pale as a ghost. Feelin' alright, sugar?"

"Oh, love, what's wrong?" Rose coos, latching onto her arm.

"Headache came back," Sara answers for her before dealing with Rowan's chair.

"Should we pop into a market for some Tylenol or BC Powder?" Tom asks dutifully.

"No, thanks. I'll be fine. Too much sun, that's all." She picks up her little pink cooler, trying not to look at me.

"What the heck is BC Powder?" Sara asks.

"Pain medicine in powder form. You dump it on the back of your tongue and then chug-a-lug," Marcy says.

"Gross." Sara winces.

"My mother, God rest her soul, swore by BC Powders," Vernon says as we trek up the beach. "Quicker to work. She was a teacher for decades, and those powders saved many a—"

"Vernon, no." Rose cuts in softly.

"I prefer Advil," Ed says, and the group launches into a conversation about pain medications and ailments.

I zone out, focused only on her. I see exactly what Sara meant—she sees me as a problem.

A wedge between her and Dean.

An obstacle to the life she's planned.

An impossible risk, no matter what her heart tells her.

The longer she refuses even the simplest eye contact, the more I fear I've lost her. Backseat conversations create a constant hum behind us on the way home. In the front seat, no one else sees the worry on her face. It kills me that I made her feel this way.

"Fuck!"

Her shoulders jerk, but she doesn't look over. I shake my head, strangling the steering wheel.

I drop Renita and Ed off first. They make a stumbling production, exiting the van, that would normally have me laughing my ass off. Not today.

I park on the road between our four houses. "Everyone out. Unload your stuff."

She's already out of the van and speed-walking across her lawn before I get my orders out. *To chase or not to chase.* Glancing at Sara in the backseat answers my question. She gives me a stony look—*not to chase.* Maybe it's best to give her time.

Course, that doesn't help my frustration. I write shit like this all the time—it's *always chase.* On the page, I know *exactly* what needs to be said: the perfectly swoony, desperately needed words that will make her melt.

But with Rowan, words battle too harsh a reality—mine *and* hers. I can't seem to string the right ones together.

Inside, Harper Lee joins me and my tall whiskey on the couch. I stream the YouTube videos Sara suggested to the big screen. As rain pelts the back deck and pings against the windows, I watch *Ten Things*, the Shakespearean spin-off she created with her students. Not only is it well-written, but packed with meaning and humor. I couldn't have done it better.

The play ends. Dean takes the podium, looking self-important and pseu-do-humble. He's like a poor man's Greg Kinnear or Carson Daly. He does his spiel about the students, charming the audience into well-deserved applause.

Then, the mood changes.

Roses come out—*idiot. So cliche... and that dumb expression on his face.*

He recites expressions stolen from Hallmark cards. *What an asshole! He's not even trying.*

Then, he calls her up. The suspense grows the longer she avoids him. A laugh rumbles from me as I lean forward in my seat. *Don't do it, Rowan.* Like I don't already know what happened.

She takes the stage, looking beautiful but rattled. Uneasy. Her forced smile looks plastered on like a wax figure, melting in the sun, and her heels drag along the floor like she's not used to wearing them—something I know isn't true. Another red flag—the spotlights hit her wounded side. He didn't even give her the courtesy of picking stage right for his spectacle. It's no wonder she flubs her answer.

But the worst part is how desperately she tries to fix it. For a second, I think she might drop to her knees and propose to him. Anything to save face. To save *his* face. The charming Mr. Maddix does nothing to help her. He even holds back a real kiss. *Prick.*

The highlight reel plays next, counterbalancing his shit proposal. It shows that their students like them, and they like each other. Smiling conversations over the scripts, consulting about costumes, and sitting together in the audience during rehearsals. This thing with Dean started as friends.

It's the kind of love story I'd write about. Unlikely partners to friends to lovers. Two jaded people, resigned to being alone, find each other and realize they don't have to be.

Seeing them together hurts unexpectedly. He isn't the dickhead I want him to be, and I get why she's trying to save it.

Only he can't be the hero of her story.

I send Rowan a text. *Can we talk?*

Nothing.

I shower. Try writing. When that doesn't work, I rotate through my current reads. Nothing holds my interest. I keep thinking of her. That kiss. And her sudden coldness.

The rain stops. Desperate for a distraction, I invite my friends over to enjoy copious amounts of alcohol while watching the Yankees play the Red Sox. It works for a while.

But late into the night, I reach out again. *I couldn't help it, Rowan. You have no idea what you do to me. Please say I didn't ruin us. Please say something.*

Her silence is as telling as her kiss.

Twenty-Four

ROWAN

Early afternoon the next day, Sara and I drive to the county jail. Traffic through the city makes our journey slow and irritating—not that we need anything added to our nervousness. Neither of us has visited someone in jail before, and though Sara assures me she's cool with it, her knee bounces incessantly, and she fiddles with the ends of her lavender hair like she's weaving a purple blanket.

I'm uneasy, too. Distracted. About Jack. About his kiss. I can't seem to get my head out from under that boardwalk.

Within twenty minutes of parking, we sit at a cafeteria-style table, waiting for Sara's dad. Other visitors talk quietly at their tables with orange-clad inmates while guards watch nearby. The cinderblock walls, sterile lighting, and seating resemble school. It's strangely calm and normal despite the bars, guards, and neon orange.

"Think he'll be mad?" Her sudden question comes out with a nervous tremor.

"No, of course not. Why?"

"That I'm *here* to see this."

"Your dad loves you. He'll be happy to see you and know you're okay."

A breath putters from her as she nods.

A clanking door announces a new arrival to the visiting space. Eddie Sweet is tall and lean with a leathery tan, surely thanks to his lawn care business. His salt-and-pepper crew cut matches his clean-shaven face and brightens into a wide, toothy grin at the sight of Sara. He has friendly eyes, especially when his laugh lines tighten. His warm embrace surely eradicates her fears.

"Eddie Sweet." He shakes my hand.

"Rowan Mackey, nice to meet you. Sara's a wonderful girl."

She gives me a surprised glance.

"Thanks for bringing her to see me," Eddie says as they sit down.

"Of course, anytime." I motion to the windowed waiting room where we checked in. "I'll just be over there while you two catch up."

It was a last-minute choice—leaving them alone—but it felt intrusive not to. They're father and daughter and should be allowed to talk without me hovering. I return to the waiting room, where I retrieve my phone and stand near the window.

They talk for nearly an hour. I try not to watch, focusing instead on my group chat with Mira and Mom, which has been ridiculously active since last night when desperate for advice, I opened the discussion with: *Jack kissed me, and I kissed him back. *mind-blown emoji, anguished emoji, broken-heart emoji. ??? WTF *face-palm emoji**

Mom FaceTimed right away. The entire story gushed out in a frustrated purge, ping-ponging between Jack and Dean like a tennis match. Only there's no competition here—at last check, Dean wants to marry me, and I made a promise.

Then, there's Jack. He's motivated by what? Lust? Curiosity? Sympathy? Book ideas? I don't understand why he did it—not sure I *want* to because there's no good reason for someone like him to play with my feelings like that. I'm with Dean, but even if I weren't, Jack would never be *with* me, and I'm no charity case to add to his sex rotation.

"Rowan, being with you isn't charity!" Mom said, aghast. "You've been together all summer. He cares about you. He said so. Why is that so hard for you to believe?"

"Because it's not true. You don't know him or his revolving door of perfect women. If your advice is to dump Dean for a shot at Jack—"

"No. My advice is not to settle for anything less than what you deserve. You deserve a man who is there for you, someone who excites you and makes you a priority, a man who loves you *wholeheartedly*... Does that sound like Dean?"

It didn't, but I couldn't answer. The two were split on whether I should tell Dean about the kiss. Mom thinks I should be honest, while Mira worries it'll be another thing he holds over my head.

I couldn't argue with either.

I lean against the waiting room wall as last night's Mom-lecture replays in my head. She doesn't get it. Dean wants me as a partner, or he did. Jack wants me for a toy. There's no comparison.

My phone chimes.

Has Dean texted you back yet? Mom's text lights the phone as I scan our past messages.

No. Not yet.

This morning, I texted Dean. *We need to talk. Not a quick call between takes but a real conversation, face-to-face. I want you home sooner than the day before school starts. Give me the entire weekend. I've been patient and understanding all summer. Now, I expect you to show me the same courtesy.*

I wonder if I sound too demanding. He read it hours ago. A disconcerted ache grows in my chest the longer it sits there, unanswered.

Then, like bad karma is playing a wicked game, my phone pings again—Jack's third text since the beach.

Just tell me you're okay. His latest text expands the ache in my chest.

Gnawing my inner lip, I consider my answer. *I'm fine. Please stop texting.* My finger hesitates over send.

A knock on the glass breaks my concentration. I look up to find Sara waving me back inside. My finger falls on the screen, sending my message. I give up my phone to return to the main room.

When I approach, Sara huffs and leaves.

"Is she okay?" I ask Eddie.

He nods, motioning for me to take a seat. "Ms. Mackey, I apologize on behalf of my daughter for her terrible behavior toward you."

"Oh, that's unnecessary. She's apologized, and I understand she's in a tough situation."

He gives me the same serious look he gave his daughter. "No, it's unacceptable. She's headstrong, yes, but being in a tough spot is no excuse for meanness and unkind words."

"She told you about that?"

His long head bobs again. "I pressed her about it, and she's not one to lie."

"I appreciate the apology, but we're past that now. She's warming up to me... slowly."

A light smirk corners his thin lips. "It's not you, understand? It's me she's angry at. She likes you a helluva lot more than she lets on."

"Really?" The word comes out in a high-pitched gasp like a doe-eyed child permitted to have my pick at a toy store. "Are you sure?"

"Definitely. You came to her rescue with the house. Thanks for that."

"No problem. I'd do anything for Sara." The realization strikes me funny. Sure, it's true. It's also true for my hundreds of students.

But Sara's different. I feel innately drawn to her. Maybe it's my long-dormant maternal instincts kicking in or that I see so much of my childhood in hers—that stubborn and independent spirit, most of all.

"Yeah, I can see that. It's much appreciated. She's a good kid, and she needs someone like you in her life. Though I'd advise against tangling with my cousins in the future," he says. "They ain't running on all cylinders. It's not worth putting yourselves in danger."

"Understood. No more stakeouts. Any other advice for me? Sometimes, she sees me as the enemy, I think."

He leans his sinewy arms on the table, linking them in front of me. "She's not quick to trust anyone. Her mom left when she was little, and she's never had great role models—"

"Except you—I mean, one stint in jail excluded."

He chuckles. "Yeah, stupid mistakes kinda run in the family. Sara's like a crepe myrtle. She doesn't need much and will do fine on her own, but things will go a lot better for her with cultivating and the occasional pruning. You're a nice person—I can tell. But don't be too forgiving. Don't let her get away with bad behavior."

His words kick up the dust of my entire summer, scattering annoying particles into the air. *Have I been too nice? Too forgiving?* The longer my text to Dean goes unanswered, the more I wonder if he always meant to spend the summer away, and messing up his proposal gave him an easy out with less guilt for leaving. Was his spontaneous wedding proposal his way of ensuring I'd be here, waiting with open arms, after he left?

Focusing on Eddie, I sit up. "I won't."

"She likes space..."

I think I hate that word.

"—And horror movies, though, they scare the bejesus out of me."

I chuckle lightly. "Me, too."

"She's an artist. Paints, ceramics, pencil drawings—there's nothing she can't do. If you show an interest in that, she'll warm up to you right quick."

A lightbulb goes off in my head, remembering their art-filled living room and Sara hovering over a sketch pad at the beach. "Ah, *that* I can work with. Thanks."

Sara rejoins us, and we chat casually about her awful taste in movies before the guards tell us that visiting hours are over. Our conversation ends with a long embrace for Sara and a handshake for me, but I promise to make it a weekly thing.

Driving home, the first ten minutes go by in a windy silence. With the top down, the late afternoon sun kisses us goodbye as the coastal breezes sweep the day away.

Nearing a congested red light, I downshift, slowing the VW and quieting our windy serenade.

"Rowan, I've been kind of a jerk. I'm sorry for the bad things I said. Thanks for taking me to see Dad."

"Anytime. I'm glad that he shares my opinion of your movie preferences. Do you ever watch anything without slashing or haunting or torture?"

She sputters out a light chuckle. "Um, not really. But it's your house. You should pick the next one."

I nod in quiet victory as the light turns green, and we roll into action again. "It's the first Sunday of the month this weekend—free for residents at Airlie Gardens and Cameron Art Museum. I thought maybe we could take advantage?"

"Art museum sounds fun," she says with a mild shrug.

I play it cool, but I'm beaming inside.

"Rowan, is it okay if I take a few driving lessons with Jack? He offered yesterday. Well, he and Tom."

"Oh, um, sure. Or, um, I could teach you."

"What happened yesterday?" She side-eyes me critically. "You and Jack were acting weird at the beach."

Excuses and denials cue in my head like my relationship drama is something I need to protect her from. But I think of my students and how they hate it when people treat them like children and assume they won't understand.

"Jack kissed me... and I didn't stop him right away. So, now I feel horrible, and I don't know what to do."

Her cheek bubbles with her smirk. "It's no secret that Jack has the hots for you... or that Mr. Maddix has been a dick. You should be with whoever makes you happy and not feel horrible about it."

"What would make me happy is someone I can trust. Right now, that's neither of them."

Sara nods. "Then don't do anything. Let time figure it out for you. They'll either build your trust or wreck it. It's like with Dad. He thought he could trust his cousins, but they proved him wrong. He won't give them another chance after this. But you could do a test if you wanted to move things along."

"A test?"

"Yeah, I just did one on you," she says, laughing.

"Really? Did I pass?"

"Yep. I already knew about Jack's kiss. He told me."

I groan. "He shouldn't have bothered you with our... mess."

"I'm good with messes. Trust each of them with something important and see who disappoints you. I did that with my so-called friends in the eighth grade. Someone was talking about me behind my back, but I didn't know who. So, I told each of them I had a crush, but I told them different people. When the rumor got back to me, I knew who'd told my secret."

"Wow, that's clever... and a little devious."

She shrugs. "I take friendship very seriously, and I don't have time for anyone who doesn't."

"Fair enough. I'll think about it. Thanks."

"If it helps, Jack sounds serious about you."

"Jack's serious about material for his book, serious about whatever he wants at the moment, but not serious about me. He's... we're not... the same."

"Hmm, not exactly, but different might be better. Can we order Chinese for dinner? And can I invite Ella over?"

"Sure," I say, handing her my phone so she can place the order and grateful for the subject change.

Twenty-Five

ROWAN

Sara and I stand outside the front entrance of the Cameron Art Museum five minutes early, waiting for the doors to unlock. She hugs her sketchbook tightly and bounces back and forth on her Doc Martens.

"Did we get the time right?" Her phone says 12:01.

"Yes. They'll open any second now."

Movement inside quickens Sara's excited dance. The door opens, and the security guard greets us with a bearded smile. "Good morning, ladies."

About to enter, Sara turns toward a loud rumble and squeal in the parking lot. "Oh, good. They're here."

The old white van taking the space next to my VW makes my heart rate spike. "What're they doing here?"

"I invited them. Art then Airlie Gardens." Sara looks devious. "You can't ignore him forever."

"It's only been a few days. I wish you'd asked me first."

"Consider this a chance to rebuild some trust. Don't worry—I texted him to be cool."

I square my shoulders and take a deep breath as the neighborhood posse lumbers across the parking lot.

Rose's floral dress waves as she walks. "You lasses look sun-kissed and lovely!"

We smile, looking at each other's outfits. Independently, we opted for sundresses. Sara's American Eagle white linen babydoll dress brushes her knees and somehow works with her black boots. My blue boho dress with a low back and spaghetti straps is more comfortable than fashionable. Still, it's artsy, especially with my watercolor silk scarf loosely covering what my shoulder-length hair doesn't.

"Pretty as a picture," Vernon confirms, snapping one with his Nikon.

Rose starts a train of cheek kisses, as if everyone naturally follows her British customs.

Jack doesn't, though. Aside from a short wave to Sara, he stays focused on me, his brown eyes filled with unusual trepidation. His affection rushes back over me like a warm wave, his hands on my face, and the way he studied me between kisses. I feel a bit breathless.

And guilty. I shouldn't feel like this. His kiss shouldn't shuffle through my head like a ghost, haunting me, or like a song I can't forget, warming me whenever it plays. His kiss has turned cruel—like test-driving a car I could never afford or trying on a designer dress I'd never have an occasion to wear. That damn kiss transformed me into a fake Cinderella, but now the party's over, the spell is broken, and based on the uneasy way he stares at me, I imagine he's as regretful as I am.

Sara orders the group inside, but it's with such excitement that no one seems to mind. They form an awkward line, streaming in mid-conversation.

Jack and I don't move from the sidewalk. The door clanks shut behind them, leaving us alone.

I say exactly what I'm thinking. "Let's just forget it happened. Please."

His eyes narrow, taking in my words and desperate tone. "That's what you want?"

I nod before he finishes his question. "Of course, that's what I want." I choke out an awkward laugh, trying to sound dismissive. "Wild kisses under the boardwalk... bet that happens to you all the time. But it's a first for me. It must've been storm madness or your beautiful book or, I don't know, you being you. It doesn't matter—it was a mistake."

"No, it wasn't. How can you say that?" He takes a short step forward, closing in on me as other patrons circle us to go inside. "This shit doesn't happen to me all the time, damn it. Wanting something real with a woman I truly care about is a first for me, too."

I nearly laugh. "I'm not a damn toy for your amusement. I'm offering you an out. Take it. I want to let it go and focus on having a nice time with Sara."

I twist toward the museum door. His hand gets there first, opening it for me.

Contemporary artists Jan-Ru Wan and Willie Cole feature in the long first room. Prints of ironing boards and antique irons make for a gorgeous, if not unusual, display. A drape of white collared shirts fills the middle, and I'm instantly drawn in by the textures and feelings these pieces create—everyday objects turned into powerful art. I long to catch up with Sara, but our party is nowhere in sight.

We stand in front of the intricate tapestry of colors in Jan-Ru Wan's *Longing*—made from her father's dress shirts. We're silent for a long minute before he says, "Beautiful and sad. It makes me think of funerals, of life and death. Mom made a quilt out of Devin's old t-shirts. She keeps it on her bed. I weave him into my stories. In small ways. No one catches it."

"The boy down the hall from Jasmine in *The Other Us*... and the over-friendly guy running the concessions in *Cape Moon*?"

Jack faces me abruptly. "How'd you know that?"

I edge around him and into another exhibit. "You give your Devin characters baseball imagery. The boy wears a baseball cap. The guy has a baseball team's sticker on his phone. Plus, he's always joking around. Sounds like Devin."

He follows me to a different room. The dim lights highlight a ceiling installation—blue, white, and gold colors on what looks like plastic sheeting form waves around us, like an artsy fun house—or another galaxy, I think, landing on his eyes again.

"Rowan, I don't want an out."

"What?"

"An out—I don't want it. That kiss wasn't me playing, plotting, or trying to prove anything. I kissed you because I wanted to. I *still* want to. Every day. For as long as you let me. *You*, Rowan, and no one else... And that scares the hell out of me—*this* is what's been hard for me to handle, wanting you. But I don't care. I could easily fall in love with you, you know. Hell, I may be already." He looks disappointed like he's gone too far.

"Is this a joke? You can't possibly mean that."

"Why not?" He steps closer, sizing me up. "And don't you fucking dare say your face. I happen to love your face."

A labored laugh mixes with a sharp gasp as tears spring to my eyes. These are words I never imagined someone saying to me—they're words I can't say to myself. And yet, the sincere look in his eyes assures me—he *could* love me. In this blue haze, *I know* I could easily love him, too. *Maybe.* If I could trust it to last.... If things were different.

"I'm with Dean," I mutter weakly. "He's coming home. I can't just—"

"I know." Jack's hands slide into the pockets of his dark pants, and his head hangs, his shaggy hair falling over his eyes in lazy wisps as he watches me. He lets out a trapped sigh. "I'm sorry for the terrible position this puts you in. It's a risk for me, too. The whole neighborhood might turn against me if I screw this up."

A laugh rumbles out between tears. "I'd be ousted altogether. The headlines alone make it a risky endeavor."

"To hell with them. It's worth it. All I want is a chance for us."

A chance for us. The words repeat like an unbelievable discovery that requires convincing. He's not one to take his words lightly—I *know* that. Despite his playboy persona, he'd never say this without meaning it. My trust in him upticks with each vulnerability, like shards of glass bonding together to form a mosaic.

He adds color when he says, "I wake up wanting to spend time with you and go to bed thinking about things you've said. You occupy my thoughts like no one ever has, and I welcome the invasion, Rowan…"

A tearful chuckle slips from me.

"—And that kiss… I know I write that shit all the time, but until you, I didn't think it could be that good, either. It meant everything to me."

His words liquefy every hard part of me. I reach for his arm like I might wobble under the weight of what he's saying.

"Sorry. I didn't mean to make you cry."

Another laugh emerges. "I knew moving next to you would be trouble… just never expected this kind."

"That makes two of us."

Other patrons enter the blue room, and Jack moves us to a corner, shielding me as I pull myself together. His thumb brushes away the wetness under my eyes. And for the first time, when it comes to Jack, I think… *maybe.*

"Rowan," Sara's voice bounces off the hazy display, and she waves us in her direction.

The nearest opening leads to a room of intricate dioramas of old school buildings, homes, and churches. Tom, Marcy, Vernon, and Rose peer through the tiny windows, debating the tools needed for such an enterprise.

Sara sits on a central bench, legs crossed and sketchbook open. Her eyes catch mine as she flips the page.

I sit with her as Jack melds in with the others.

"You okay?" Sara asks in a small whisper as she eyes my hands. I'm strangling my dress hem.

Rose announces to the others, "I like the bits and bobs of it, but it's not like we can hang one of these over the hearth, is it?"

Their animated discussion turns to home decor.

A chuckle breaks through my unease. "Don't worry about me. This place is amazing."

She runs her charcoal stick along the sides of her textured page, roughly capturing the lines of the diorama. Watching her pencil strokes is meditative, calming me the more I focus on the picture she's creating. That she lets me watch feels like another long-fought victory.

"What's been your favorite so far?" she asks.

"The blue room." *That's* where Jack Graham said he could fall in love with me. His words roll over in my head like rocks in a tumbler. "How about you?"

"The shirts. They make me think of Dad's lawn care t-shirts. He's forever going through them; they're always dirty no matter how much we wash them."

"Wonder what you could make out of them."

She grins. "Me, too."

We tour the remaining rooms together, discussing each piece like amateur critics. Sara's knowledge of mediums and techniques is impressive for an adult, let alone a fifteen-year-old. I plan to take advantage of my guardian status and discuss extra opportunities for her with my colleagues in the art department.

With the inside rooms exhausted, we rejoin the others. They sit at a long table in the museum's café, enjoying tea, cold drinks, and bistro-style sandwiches.

"Rowan, let's go see the pieces outside." Sara waves me along.

Jack Graham professes his hope for us, *and* Sara's made me her new best friend? It's a banner day for Rowan Mackey. Maybe I should buy lottery tickets.

We take a side door to the lavish outside, where art mixes with a garden and wooded pathway.

"Thanks for bringing me here." Her hazel eyes narrow as she side-glances me. "For what it's worth, I'm glad you and Jack are talking."

"Um, yeah, me, too." *I think.*

When the first sculpture outside inspires her, Sara plops onto the grass to capture it in her sketchbook. I take a bench nearby, watching her with a strange joy. Sara's sprawled out, sitting on one leg while the other is extended on the grass, indifferent to her white dress or anyone seeing her like this. She bites her bottom lip in her lovely concentration. Holding the charcoal and softening her strokes with her finger makes black smudges on her hands and fingers, even a small gray mark on her cheek when she scratches it. I take secret pictures, sure her father will want to see them and to add to my family album after she's gone.

In the contemplative silence, I ask myself a long-forgotten question—*what do I want?*

Someone I can trust with anything—my stories, my past, my heart. When Dean asked for my future, it's no wonder I flubbed the answer—I hadn't trusted him with the rest yet. I can't even trust him to return my calls, so I'm not sure I want to now, either.

But I do with Jack.

Twenty-Six

JACK

I feel better. Rephrase—I'm fucking ecstatic. I don't cuss once on our drive to Airlie Gardens, even driving behind a shithead doing forty in the passing lane. Things are complicated—*I get it*—but confessing my feelings opens her up to the possibility and brings us closer. And she didn't refuse me, not entirely.

Besides, we're here. Together. Admiring the gorgeous oaks draped in Spanish moss, the delicate gardens that remind me of manicured estates from old books, and the water views, where boat and bird spotting becomes a peaceful game to play.

Ahead, the group halts when the paved path ends, debating where to go. Unable to agree, they split up. Tom and Marcy take a right toward the pier to spot oyster beds and herons. Vernon, Rose, and Sara opt for the butterfly house and glass mosaic garden across the vast lawn on the left.

Rowan trails behind Sara. I fall in beside her. In a silent partnership, we cross the crisply mowed lawn with its thick-bellied grand oak in the center. We maze around picnics and families. Rose, Vernon, and Sara disappear into the butterfly house, but she detours to a shaded bench. I ease into the space beside her. We say nothing, like we're simply the chaperone and driver awaiting our passengers.

Finally, her big blue eyes catch mine. "Parts of my mac-n-cheese story are true. I used to tell myself I was protecting my students from something horrible, but they can handle anything. I'm the one who can't handle everyone knowing. But I think you should."

"Only if you're ready." Her uneasy smile indicates that she isn't ready, simply willing. Perhaps baring my heart has lessened her tight defenses. "You don't have to."

"I want to." She straightens her shoulders with a deep breath. "I was fifteen, just home from school, and hungry. Boxed mac-n-cheese was a typical go-to when I was alone. I started the water in a pot that was too small because I was too lazy to wash the one I should've used."

"Your mom was at work?" Throwing in a benign question is a journalist's trick to relax someone into talking, and I want to help her through it.

A weak smile flashes over her face. "Yes. She usually didn't get home until six or so. But that day, she was coming home early."

"Why?"

"I won an essay contest," she reports sheepishly. "A thousand words on preserving the sanctity and beauty of our parks for environmental science. Mom insisted on celebrating. She planned to take off work early for mani-pedis, dinner out, and *Baskin-Robbins* for dessert."

She stops, head lowered like she's peering over a cliff's edge and bracing herself for the fall.

"What happened?" I urge, my voice gentle.

"Mom had been dating a fellow officer. She rarely dated. I used to tease her that she was an army nun, but I understood, too. She was exceptionally cautious. I mean, as careful as she could be... I *never* thought it was her fault."

"Tell me about the fellow officer."

"Rick... Richard Warren Linkous, the third, to be precise." Her eyes plead with mine. "I don't tell people this story."

"I'm not people."

She glances at the butterfly house, where a family spills out from the double-doored exit. A smile crosses her lips watching Sara through the screened windows, arms laced with resting butterflies and Vernon snapping pictures.

"They've adopted each other," she says. "At least Sara's scored pseudo-grandparents out of this."

"She's scored more than that."

She turns to me. "Can we go somewhere else?"

We stroll side by side like any other couple, *almost*. We're missing the absent-minded hand-holding and automatic touches others naturally drift to. We aren't there yet. But for the first time in my life, I want that. Someday.

We pass heavy-laden strollers, parents carrying backpacks, and toddlers stopping to examine every leaf, bug, or flower petal on the path. Ready to spill her story, she looks bothered by revealing something wicked in such a lovely place.

I get it. The setting is wrong. Not that there's a right place for this.

On the opposite side of Airlie, a small church and graveyard bridges the gap to the final garden—well-shaded with fountains, elaborate oaks drenched in Spanish moss, and a circular walkway covered so well in vines that it's ten degrees cooler inside and almost dark.

She leads me through the vine-covered walkway to a secluded bench. A cocoon of greenery-wrapped columns serves as a cool, dim stage. It smells like dew and honeysuckle. Sitting, she glances around as if worried her story might wilt the white petals and turn the air sour.

"How did you know it wasn't the true story?" she asks.

I lean forward, elbows to knees, and smirk lightly. "You're a terrible liar."

"Yeah, so I've been told. Mira's put it on repeat since Grandpa Ro confronted us about pilfering his whiskey at fifteen, and I couldn't lie. At least my students buy it... or pretend to."

We fall into an awkward silence as she fidgets with her scarf.

"Let's make a pact," I say, "This is a safe place. Ours and no one else's. No matter what's said. No matter what happens. When we leave, we leave it all here, too. We never have to talk about it again if that's what you want."

She laughs a little. "What happens in Airlie, stays in Airlie?"

"If it helps... You never have to be afraid to tell me anything, you know."

"I know."

I nod and say, "Richard Warren Linkous, the third."

"Mom dated him. He seemed nice enough, but a few months in, she broke it off. It was an amicable parting to hear her tell it. We were moving again soon, and, I don't know, she didn't want any complications. After my deadbeat father and having a daughter in the house, Mom always kept men at a distance. After Richard, she didn't date at all. That's why she stopped believing in love. She still doesn't date. That makes me sad."

She straightens the rumpled fabric of her dress around her thighs and twiddles her fingers. "So, that day. A Friday. Home from school. Hungry. Mom coming home soon. The doorbell rings, and it's him."

Her eyes shut tightly, and I imagine her memories flooding back, his face permanently branded there.

"He was the kind of guy you wouldn't look twice at—in the park watching his kids play or in Home Depot buying caulk. He was disturbingly normal. But you never know what's going on under the surface."

"What happened?"

"He asked for Mom. I said she wasn't home. I heard the water boiling over and hitting the burner. So, I spouted off a quick *I'll let her know you stopped by* before closing the door and rushing to the kitchen."

Her hands are shaking now, so she tucks them under her legs, and rocks back and forth. "I missed every sign of trouble, did everything wrong—it all happened so fast."

"How could you have known?" I ask softly.

"The alcohol on his breath. His flushed, bothered face. Jittery hands. Me vaguely remembering then that they'd broken up weeks before. And... that he must've blocked the door from closing."

She rocks faster, energy pulsing. "He never said a thing. I still don't really know why he did it. Because he could, I guess. And he was angry."

"Tell me what he did."

"He snatched the pot from my hand. The water splashed and burned my fingers. I screamed, so he knocked me to the floor and poured it on my face."

She holds her left hand high on her face, covering her eye, and the lines of her injuries match—burned hand and lower cheek—where she tried shielding herself.

"He laughed when he did it. Laughed at my agony. I still hear it sometimes."

Our pleasant cocoon feels pressurized now, full of tension that builds in our silence.

She fills it quickly, like she can't help it. "I remember everything—what he wore, the grime under his fingernails, the bitterness of his breath. I remember wanting to die. But then it stopped hurting. He melted my nerves. I still don't have feeling in some parts. When the water ran out and my screaming slowed, he pressed the bottom of the hot pot to my face and neck like he wanted to crush me with it. Him on top of me... pressing... my skin sizzling... him laughing... my jaw cracking..."

Her fingers press into her marks, massaging the base of her neck, like she's experiencing phantom pain just by retelling it. I want to stop her—she shouldn't have to relive her horror to keep a promise to me. And I never expected how much it would hurt to hear it.

But I see she wants to get it out, like it's a stone trapped inside her, weighing her down. She's not even crying, as if she reached her tear quota for this years ago and can't produce them anymore. Or perhaps, shielded from the sun and surrounded by honeysuckle in our safe place, she doesn't need tears.

"And, um..." Her eyes lock on her feet, and her voice cracks. "I blacked out. He didn't like that. The screaming and fighting seemed important to him, so he slapped me awake again and again. That part—hardly anyone knows that part."

Her voice trails off. I want to touch her, hold her, but that isn't what she needs. Not that I *really* know what she needs. There are no words, no magical touches, no combinations of sympathy or anger that could even put a dent in the pain she's suffered. And still suffers.

She twists toward me and looks surprised to find me crying. It shocks me, too. Soft streams trickle down my cheeks and merge into my stubble like I can't physically contain the pain of what she's telling me.

That she went through this...

That someone did that to her...

I have so much rage for her agony and love for the woman she is that my quaking emotions need some release, and tears are all I can do.

I haven't cried since Devin, and never like this. It strikes me how alike they are—both unfairly poisoned with what they can't change or ignore.

And Rowan is reminded of it every time she looks in the mirror.

She releases a trapped breath and, twisting in my direction, brings her hands to my face. Her warmth softens me, like her touch naturally releases my pain for her. My cheek presses into her hand as she wipes my tears with her fingertips. I've never felt more emotionally connected to anyone before, not even Devin. The world could go to shit around us, disintegrate into ash, fall into the seas, implode or explode, and I wouldn't care because everything I need is here. With her.

A gentle smile perks on her lips. "A man who cries—I thought that was a myth."

"You've never seen a man cry before?"

"Haven't been around many. I saw Grandpa Ro get teary once—never cry. For years, the people I loved most shielded me from their pain like it would only add to my own. Even Mom stopped crying in front of me, afraid it would hurt me more to see it."

"Does it?"

"No. Strangely, it makes me feel better. I wish we'd been friends then."

I flash her a funny look.

She shrugs. "It's a weird thing to say, I guess. We were at Fort Hood. I had friends, but none were close, and it was an awful situation anyway. People keep their distance when they don't know how to comfort someone. I spent weeks in the hospital—the worst pain came when I was healing."

"I couldn't have helped that," I say weakly.

"No. But you never would've let me suffer alone—that's who you are. It would've been a relief—someone not being skittish around me. Someone telling me jokes or stories or pulling out a book to read. Someone to share my anger, fear, or whatever else—to feel it with me. No holding back."

"They've been talking to you about Devin."

"Yes, they gush about you two. I'm sure he was grateful to have you at his side. I would've been."

"He would've loved you, you know." My head droops and tears spill onto my pant leg. "I still see him sometimes, talk to him."

A light smile plays on her lips. "Good. You should hold on to him as long as you need."

Tears flow heavier now like she's granted me permission to feel normal. And I do—for the first time, I think. It's as if all the shit I went through with Devin prepared me for her. I couldn't be the guy she needs now without understanding real suffering, real pain. She gets me and trusts I have at least half a chance of getting her. Every word she gives me ties us closer together, tightening the threads of our connection.

But her story isn't over. A quiet moment later, I ask, "In the kitchen... how did it stop?"

"Mom came home."

"What happened then?"

"Mom was an Army colonel at the time, a division chief. She shot him with her service weapon." Her shoulders pop up twice in quick succession, like she hears the gunshots in her head.

"Dead?"

"A man attacking her daughter in her own house? Yes. Dead. She didn't even warn him."

"Good."

"Yeah. Apparently, he was on drugs, pissed at something that had happened at work, and maybe still angry over the breakup—there was a lot of conjecture after. In the news. With the police. With his family. Not that it mattered to me. Reasons and excuses couldn't heal me faster or take away the damage. I felt like my life was over. It was for a while... But that's another story."

A long silence ensues. I wrestle sharp feelings—hatred for Richard Warren Linkous the third, agony over her pain, but, above all, love for this incredible woman who rises above it every day.

I wipe my eyes on my shirt sleeves. Then, standing, I reach for her, and the second she drops her hand in mine, I pull her into my arms. She fits me perfectly. Head against my chest, she relaxes there, just as she did the night of the party.

"I wish we'd been friends then, too," I whisper into her hair as I hold her.

A deep breath seems to release what's left of her tension and anxiety, as if she's expanding the tight bubble she usually keeps around her, giving her more room to breathe. "You're right. I feel better."

I edge away to see her face and run my fingers along the goosebumps on her arms. "I can't take away what happened or erase the pain. Hell, I'll never even understand what you went through, still go through. But I'm here. And every day from now on, I'll be here, loving you, wanting you, hoping to make things better."

"You *have* made things better." A light shrug precedes her weak smile as she pulls away. "But trusting you with this is all I have to give you right now. Today has meant so much to me. I never thought someone like you... I wish things were different."

"Things *are* different. It's just a choice, Rowan."

"It's more than that. It's me at a crossroads I didn't expect, and desperate to do what's right. I need you to trust me, Jack. I'm glad we had today, but I need you to stay away for a while."

"What? Why?"

"You know why."

Her voice shakes again, and her body tenses. My fingers tighten against her back, holding her in place. She cups my damp cheeks with trembling fingers, and for the first time in all of this, tears speck her eyes.

"Jack... something about you strips me bare... and that's hard for me. And unfair to Dean. Please, promise me you'll keep your distance until I'm... ready."

I *hate* this plan. Every nerve in my body pulls to her like a damn magnet, now more than ever. Distance is torture when what I want is to scoop her up, carry her home, and wrap myself in her for as long as humanly possible.

But I can't deny her anything, either.

A weak nod makes my hair fall over my creased brow. "I'll be waiting."

My fingers drag over her as she pulls away.

Twenty-Seven

ROWAN

I feel like I've been living under a huge chandelier hanging by a fraying rope that barely holds it in place. I'm not only spotlighted by my trauma, but it hangs over me, threatening to crash, keeping my shoulders scrunched and my head low. Strangely, sharing it with Jack edges me out from under it. I breathe easier, knowing that should it fall, I have a better chance of being pulled to safety because now he's there with me.

As an educator who studies analogies, I get that's a weird one.

Mom arrives at the little house Thursday before school starts, days before originally planned. She insisted on coming early after I unloaded everything that happened with Jack. She told me that I'd done the right thing, asking Jack for time, and that she was proud of me for being so vulnerable with him. *"You can't let things go without letting anyone in, Rowan. I love that you're opening up to someone."*

Mira and I greet her in the driveway, and something is different about her. She's tanner—yes, probably from spending her summer touring. Toner, perhaps, though she's always been fit. But her laugh lines and crow's feet no longer look hard-earned but friendlier. She wears lip gloss and a light summer dress, highlighting her shoulders and showing more skin than usual. Her softer look makes her seem gentler, too, like her rough edges have been filed away.

Her thin-lipped smile grows as she embraces us.

"How are my sweet girls?" Her pixie head rests between us.

"Good," we say in unison, and Mira adds, "How are you, Christine? You look... *really* good."

"She's right, Mom. Are you doing something different?"

A mild chuckle escapes as she turns to Sara, standing awkwardly nearby. Mom grabs onto her as if they've already known each other for ages. Sara, amazingly, accepts the affection.

Rose and Vernon gently interrupt our sweet reunion, approaching cautiously from the street.

"We had to meet your mum in person, Rowan."

"Thank you for your service." Vernon shakes her hand and then salutes. "My father, God rest his soul, served for—"

"Vernon, no." Rose takes Mom's hand, holding it between hers. "We love Rowan. She's a breath of fresh air. I hope you're staying awhile."

"A few weeks. Then, California before going overseas again for a consultancy. I'll return for Thanksgiving and, hopefully, Christmas, as always."

As they chat, Tom and Marcy peek out their front door like skittish meerkats, taking in the unusual activity. A moment later, they join our growing circle, introducing themselves, telling her how much they love me, and asking about her plans—as if they're operating from the same script.

"Your neighbors are weird." Mira grins at my side. "But I kinda love it."

"Yeah, me, too. Mom seems different, right?"

"She looks... happy," Mira says.

"Oh, you must meet Jack." Sara bolts across his yard before I can stop her.

"Dean returns tomorrow?" Mom asks.

"That's the plan," I say with a noncommittal shrug.

She gives me a knowing look—I can't make promises regarding Dean. I've reached out every day, but most texts go unanswered. He calls randomly, and it's always the same—a quick report about him.

Sometimes, I wonder if he's afraid to let me talk. The more I try, the quicker he is to end it.

"Won't that be wonderful?" Marcy says. "Together at last."

"Romance is in the air," Rose coos.

"I'll say," Mom says, her blue eyes honing in on Jack as Sara drags him across the yard. He's wearing khaki shorts, a black t-shirt that hugs him just the right way, no shoes, a pencil tucked in his ear, and more scruff on his face than usual. But his smile is warm and expansive as he beelines in her direction. They don't shake hands but embrace like old friends. My chest tightens.

"Oh, my!" Rose giggles. "You really are a fan."

Mom pulls away—a beaming grin still planted as she takes him in. "I am. I love his books, too."

Rose looks as confused as everyone else, but Jack laughs. "I'm a fan, too."

Their instant connection hits me strongly—with what, I'm unsure. Love and sadness, like one of his books.

The quiet girls' night I planned disintegrates when Jack announces, "Dinner and drinks at my place?"

Everyone cheers—Mom the loudest.

I cringe. Not because I don't want to spend time with him—I *really* do. The entire week's been an exercise in self-control—me staying away from Jack so I can deal with this the *right* way because I sure as hell haven't so far. My guilt compounds the longer it goes unresolved. I'm the worst fiancée ever. Not only have I betrayed Dean by entertaining thoughts about Jack, but I never really let Dean know me in the first place.

So, my guilt grows, and every time I relive Jack's words, his touch, and that kiss, I feel even worse.

This isn't me—I'm no cheater.

Also, not me—letting guilt about ruining Dean's proposal and everything since then take over my confidence. I've spent the week red-penning my relationship and brainstorming how to fix it—if I *should* fix it, that is. I don't know what to do.

So, a Jack party isn't what I need right now.

Still, he goes out of his way to make everyone feel at home. He engages with Mom and Mira nonstop, as if it's his only chance. We congregate in his kitchen and living room first, where he makes everyone drinks and raids his fridge for fruits and cheeses. Sara helps him make pizzas. Then, he moves the party outside.

Laughter and conversation flow easily—I'm the only quiet one. It's the kind of evening I once wished for Dean to win over my loved ones. Only he didn't. His attempts to woo my family dissipated after Grandpa Ro's funeral when Mom was too sad to notice, and Mira didn't care for him at all. He gave up after—I don't blame him. But it's another thing adding to my guilt.

"Do you have spontaneous neighborhood parties often, Jack?" Mom asks as we lounge around his outdoor dining area, nibbling on pizzas.

"Yep." He slides the next pizza into the hot brick oven. "Growing up, Mom always freaked out about guests, like they might give her house a white-glove inspection. It was even worse when Devin, my older brother, got sick. Germs and a weak immune system prevented her from letting too many people in—she was right not to. But Devin made me promise not to be like that... after. He didn't want us to close people out."

"Jack has an open-door policy," Vernon says. "We're welcome anytime, as long as he isn't writing."

"Sometimes, even then, if he wants the noise," Rose giggles.

"Are you writing?" Mom asks. "Rowan mentioned writer's block."

Jack shrugs, turning the pizza with the peel. "Writer's block isn't a problem anymore. I'm writing better than I have in years. I'm days away from sending the final pages to my editor."

"Good. What's this one about? Or am I allowed to ask?" Mom says, sitting up curiously.

"Ask me anything, Christine." Jack pulls out the pizza. "It's about two home-insecure teenagers, outcasts for different reasons, who fall in love after spending one night together in a hospital emergency room. They're separated the next day, so the story is about how they survive and get back to each other. It's two people at their most vulnerable and also at their strongest. I'm calling it *Bare*."

My hand covers my mouth, hiding a gasp. Tears threaten, too. *Something about you strips me bare.* With his eyes on me, a soft heat rises, joining the tightness in my chest.

"Wow, that sounds harsh and beautiful," Mom says, "and I like the title. *Bare*."

Jack leans over the table to refill Mom's wine. "Join my team of beta readers. I'd love your opinion."

"I'd be honored! So would Rowan—she's totally fallen for you."

"Mom!"

"I mean, as a writer, of course." Mom's devious blue eyes twinkle as she flashes her wry grin. "Wouldn't you like to beta read for Jack?"

"Rowan stopped reading Jack's books," Sara reveals, earning a stern, pinched look from me. Her eyebrow creeps up daringly as the rest of the table stares in my direction, astounded.

With a light shrug, I say, "I'm taking a break. That's all."

"But what about preparing for your classes?" Mom asks, her smile bent. "Aren't Jack's books the inspiration behind your project?"

"I have enough notes on *The Other Us* to last all semester. I need to try out other writers." I lean back, twiddling the paper towel in my lap. The neighbors are aghast, as if I've just announced my intention to become a sister wife. With all eyes on me, I feel hot and uneasy.

Jack smirks at their forlorn faces. "Don't worry, guys. She'll come back to me in the end."

The rest of the table relaxes. His playful expression meets my worried one.

"How are your non-plans coming along, by the way?" He slices the new pizza. "Ready for school to start?"

"I'm nervous but ready. I think. But, of course, I plan to go wherever they lead me, so who's to say? I have to be prepared for anything. It's a little overwhelming."

"Don't look at it that way. You're not teaching. You're talking books. It's fun. If you get lost, all you have to do is talk about what turned you into a reader and the books you've loved." He smirks, catching my eyes in his. "Just don't try to say it was your English classes. They'll see right through you."

I smile. "No, I wouldn't dare."

"When in doubt, read them one of Jack's sex scenes," Rose advises. "That'll keep them interested."

"Those are my favorites," Marcy admits.

"Ah, me, too. They're always fraught with emotion, so full and rich and unyielding," Mom chimes in, making me blush, wide-eyed with shock. "How do you do it?"

Jack blushes, too. "Um, I don't know—it's love as I imagine it... and it's not such a great mystery anymore."

His eyes land on mine. I half-wonder if he says things to get a reaction—a type of click-bait with words. The chair screeches against the deck boards as I rise from it.

I find the downstairs bathroom, a charming half-bath with an R2-D2 soap dispenser and a framed cross-stitch that says, *"You should've brought a book."* I run cold water over my wrists and take deep breaths. Guilt about Dean compounds. *I miss Jack.*

He waits for me outside the bathroom, leaning against the wall with his hands in his pockets. "I'm not being creepy."

"Feels a little creepy." I shrug.

"I just wanted to see if you're okay. It's been hard not talking to you."

"Hard for me, too." With a deep breath, I lean against the wall across from him. "But I'm okay."

His head droops, sending his dark hair over his creased brow. He offers a weak smile. "Your mom's everything I thought she'd be. Funny, formidable, warm. I'm glad she's here."

A small smile edges my lips. "Me, too."

"Sorry we crashed her homecoming, though."

A chuckle escapes. "I should've expected it in this neighborhood. We'll have time to catch up, and I need to—something's different about her."

"She's in love."

"What? No. Really? Why do you think that?"

"She said 'we' instead of 'I' a half-dozen times, and... there's an unexpected lightness about her. She's sharing her world with someone."

"Just not sharing it with me." Tears pop into my eyes like strangers crashing my *I-have-it-all-together* party. "Why wouldn't she say?"

When he hesitates, I step closer, my hand resting on his black t-shirt like I can't help but touch him. With a gentle tug of the soft fabric, I say, "Just tell me. Please."

"She blames herself for what happened to you. That's why she didn't date afterward. Now that she's found someone, she feels guilty for being happy when you're..."

"When she thinks I'm not..." My eyes close, as if I can block out this new information and push away the sadness I suddenly feel. More guilt heaps on my shoulders. "I've always encouraged her to date, always assured her that she's not to blame."

"*None* of this is your fault," he says sternly. "You know how it is, Rowan. We all take on burdens that we were never meant to carry. They weigh us down and make us believe things we shouldn't."

And once again, Jack Graham edges me out from under the chandelier. "What should I do?"

"Nothing. Be happy for her," a playful smile perks on his lips. "She'll come clean about her sexy, fun times with her new boy toy when she's ready."

"Ah, gross. Sexy fun times? Now, I'll think *boy toy* when I meet him," I laugh.

"And blush just like you are now." His thumb sweeps my cheek. "You're welcome."

His hand lingers until I take it in mine and hold it between us, unable to let go just yet.

"I hope you know how much you mean to me, Jack."

"I do." He grows serious. "I miss you."

With emotions rising again, I release his hand and nod.

"How are you about Dean coming home?" he asks hesitantly. "Have your break-up speech ready? People say I'm a decent writer... I could help if you want."

My soft chuckle veers into a worried sigh. "I don't have a speech. It's hard for me to even think about... I don't want to hurt him. Or lose him... though it feels like I have already." Jack's gaze falters at my admission, making me regret it. "Or hurt or lose you. I'll know how I feel when I see him. We were *really* good together once, and I haven't been fair to him. Please understand, I want to be sure."

"I get it."

The concerned stitch between his eyes makes me wonder.

His hand drifts to the small of my back as we rejoin the group, the soft press of his fingertips sending Jack-tingle-shocks through me. I should mind, but I only want more. Talking to him, touching him—I haven't felt this relaxed since Airlie.

We find them laughing hysterically over Rose's admission that she only goes to church to hear Jack's impressive cursing on the way there and spends her church time asking for forgiveness for enjoying it so much.

I'm about to share a discussion I had with my students last year when they called curse words "sentence enhancers," equal to adjectives and adverbs when a voice cuts through our laughter.

"Hello? Rowan?" Between our houses, Dean appears.

Twenty-Eight

JACK

The laughter stops instantly, like an old record player screeching to a halt. My hand tightens against her, nearly fisting her shirt to hold her in place. But she pulls away and rushes straight into his arms, taking my confidence with her. Dean should be a formality, and dumping him just another item on her to-do list between paying bills and getting an oil change. But as they collide into an all-too-familiar embrace, I see it's not that simple. She looks almost happy to see him.

"Dean, you're here."

"Missed you, Rowan. Left as soon as filming ended. I couldn't wait any longer."

Just all summer. This guy... this fucking guy.

She relaxes in his embrace but snaps back when he goes for a kiss.

Atta girl. Stay strong. There's hope for us yet.

She waves over her lackluster response by taking his hand and leading him up the deck.

He approaches like a car salesman circling the lot, a cheesy grin plastering his stupid face.

Christine stands and offers him a limp embrace—nothing like the one she gave me. "Welcome back, Dean. It's good to see you."

"Ah, Christine. I didn't know you'd be here."

Rowan's brow pinches at this. She probably told him, and he didn't listen. *Strike ten for Dean.*

Mira doesn't get up, but he pats her shoulder. "Mira, always a pleasure," he says, with questionable sincerity.

He introduces himself to everyone amid a round of *how-was-traffic* and *what-have-you-been-filming*. Rose gets him a glass of wine while Tom fetches another plate. Vernon grabs a chair, and everyone makes room at the table.

My table. My wine. My fucking backyard.

For once, I regret being so damn cozy with the neighbors.

I'm a stone, immovable, leaning against the brick counter. My eyes lock on Rowan. Her forehead creases with worry lines while her eyes plead with me to behave.

Tom presses a whiskey glass into my hand. "You won't win her heart with anger," he whispers.

He's right, more than he knows. I down the drink and extend a hand to Dean.

His gray eyes widen when I introduce myself. He grips my hand with both of his, shaking vigorously.

"Wow, it's an honor," he says. "Everyone's been talking about filming *Cape*—"

"The absentee fiancé," I cut in, unwilling to listen to his bullshit. "Or boyfriend or whatever. We were starting to wonder if you were real."

"Here I am, *fiancé*, in the flesh." Dean smiles good-naturedly. "I'm grateful for your hospitality. And to all of you for taking such good care of Rowan and Sara while I was away."

"Well, someone needed to be there for them," I huff.

"It's our pleasure, love," Rose jumps in. "They're part of the family now. Have something to eat. You must be famished."

Dean obeys, thanking her as he picks up a pizza slice. *My fucking pizza.*

An awkward silence is broken when Christine clears her throat. "So, what's this I hear about driving lessons for Sara?"

Tom leans in with cutthroat seriousness. "We begin Friday at noon. Automatic *and* manual. She'll be able to drive any vehicle by the time we finish with her."

Sara grins. "Jack said I can learn on his Tesla."

"That's generous," Mira says. "Don't think I'd let any teenager near my Tesla, if I had one. Not even my own kids."

"So, did you get your big break?" I stare at Dean like a sniper on a rooftop. "A whole summer away—I hope it was worth it."

Rowan mouths *"Stop it"* over Dean's shoulder. I don't want to be a jerk or disappoint her, but saying nothing isn't an option. Sara's words from the beach stick like a bad song in my head—*she doesn't want to marry him, but she will.* He's treated her like shit—if Rowan won't call him on it, I sure as hell will.

Dean clears his throat. "No, it wasn't worth it. I have the most amazing *fiancée* on the planet. But I've neglected her, and even the role of a lifetime wouldn't make up for how I've hurt her."

He twists in his chair, facing Rowan, his hand slipping over her knee under the table. "No dream is worth being apart from you—it won't happen again. I'm sorry that it took so much doubt and disappointment for me to realize that I've had my dream all along."

Rowan gapes at him like she's breathless. But it's the most ridiculous thing I've ever heard, forcing a vitriolic laugh to rumble from me.

"Sorry," I say, as everyone glares at me. "It's just—wow—"

"Thanks, Dean. That's nice to hear." Rowan to the rescue, again. At least this time, she looks unnerved.

"How sweet," Rose allows.

Marcy mutters a soft "aw" while Mira groans.

"Dean, what a lovely speech," Christine says, pouring more wine.

"*Speech* is the operative word. So, no big break then?" I repeat, dragging everyone into silence again.

Dean's smile falls, finally catching on to my animosity like a fish hooked through its gullet. "Not for lack of trying. I landed an agent, and I have a few promising auditions coming up. Minor roles... but there are no small parts, only small people."

Almost imperceptibly, my head shakes. *This fucking guy.*

He puts on his best fake-humble smile and squeezes Rowan's knee again like he wants me to challenge him.

"We can't all be as lucky as you, Jack. Didn't I read somewhere that you dated your agent before she took you on as a client? In the article, she joked that she's always wondered if that's why you went out with her—to get her to read your manuscript."

Rose looks aghast. "Is that true, love?"

"A coincidence. That's all. Weird that you'd be reading up on me."

"I read all the news from the entertainment industry," Dean explains. "You're a hot topic lately with the book release, the Netflix movie, and your usual exploits. Aren't you dating a Victoria's Secret model?"

I flash a coy grin—a flimsy jab straight from the tabloids. I hope Rowan sees his pettiness.

Marcy rebuffs him first, "Oh, Beatrice or Inga? Doesn't matter—they were ages ago. So, what if Jack's had a robust dating life?" She tips her glass toward me.

"No judgment here." Dean puts his hands up submissively. "But that's where *I'm* the lucky one... I have Rowan."

His words hang in the air like an arrow in suspended animation aimed at me. The only thing keeping me from pouncing on this asshole is Rowan—she looks genuinely pissed at his smugness.

I scoff, raising an eyebrow. "You *have* her? Interesting word choice. You don't even *know* her."

Rowan jumps from her seat, sending her chair scraping across the deck. "I'm done. Tired. It's getting late. Mom and Dean have had long trips today. Right, Mom?"

"Oh, yes. I'm exhausted." She rises, widening her eyes at Mira.

"Better get home to the family," Mira says with obvious reluctance.

"Yeah, this is getting... weird," Sara says slowly.

As the *it's-been-lovely* and *we-should-do-this-again* remarks line up, Rowan's eyes lock on me. She looks defeated and disappointed. My anger vanishes into regret. I've put her in a tough position and made it worse by being an asshole. Stepping toward her, I'm determined to put it right, even if it means apologizing to the prick beside her.

But then Dean says, "All night in your bed is exactly what I need, Rowan."

Son of a bitch, I want to hit this asshole. Only I can't. Not after what she's been through. I remember her words. *Anger is destructive.*

Still, I stop, afraid I might do it anyway if I get closer, especially with the daring look in his eyes as he hones in on me. Rowan winces at him, taking in his cocked brow and sly grin. He's proud of himself for getting the last word in. He should be—he gets to go home with the woman I love.

Mother fucker.

No choice—I storm inside the house. I can't look at him anymore. I can't watch her leave with him. This is why no one should ever fall in love.

The party comes to a quick end outside, and thankfully, my neighbors know me well enough not to expect any more of my hospitality. Shadows move across the living room as I pace, new drink in hand, and then vanish altogether. I try not to think of them together, but Dean's sabotaged me. I can't think of anything else—his hand on her knee and slithering upward, his mouth leeching hers, his fake-ass platitudes in her ear. *Damn it.*

Why would she give herself to a man who doesn't even see her? She's only a ghost to him.

"What's with you and ghosts, huh?" Devin appears, sporting jeans, Nikes, and a FanBoy Comics t-shirt.

"Not now."

"Calm down."

"Can't."

"That won't help." He nods to my drink. "If you hadn't been wasted after your party, things might be different now."

I slump. He's right. Sober, I would've pressed her to tell me what happened, and she would've opened up to me then—I'm the one she came to, after all. Not that asshole. And any loyalty to Dean would be long forgotten. "You're not helping."

"Fine. How can I help?"

"How do I get her to see that he's not right for her?"

"Maybe she sees that already, and she's simply trying to end things the best way she can."

I groan. "He'll weasel his way back in like he never left."

"You don't know that. Why don't you trust her? She trusts you... or did."

"Did you hear his bullshit? Not even the role of a lifetime could make up for hurting her?" I scoff, downing my third glass and going for another.

Then, a villainous laugh bellows from my depths. "Let's put him to the test, huh?"

Devin locks eyes with me. "Don't."

I yank out my phone and scroll through my contacts.

"She asked for your trust. Do this, and you'll lose her."

"If I don't do this, I'll lose her, *and* she'll end up miserable with that guy." I glare at Devin, begging him to argue, but he can't. Sure, my actions might seem underhanded and immature, but not when considering Rowan's happiness. Her yes to Dean translates to a lifetime of no's for what she wants and needs. I'm doing this *for* her.

My agent, Lynn, answers on the first ring. "Did you finish it? *Bare*? I've been dying to read those final scenes."

"No. Almost. I need a favor."

"Oh, my, that sounds intriguing," she says in her sultriest voice. I *did* once date her so she'd read my manuscript, but she knew what I was up to and never complained. "Name it."

I explain what I want with as few words as possible, and she doesn't press me with questions. A good thing since the more my excellent idea rolls around my head, the less confident I feel in it.

"Done. Easy," she says. "Give me a few days."

"I'm doing this for *her*," I say once I'm off the phone, but Devin's gone. Not that he'd believe me, anyway.

Twenty-Nine

ROWAN

I can't leave fast enough. I remember stories of this phenomenon—a wonky love triangle with two men interested in the same woman—but I've never even dated two men in the same month, let alone considered myself a candidate for this awkward catastrophe. It's not the ego-boost it should be—I feel almost sick.

But Dean lingers even after his last shot at Jack like he's taking a victory lap. He dishes pleasantries to the neighbors, shaking their hands again before I coax him away.

Mom, Sara, and Mira stroll ahead of us, curving around the corner of Jack's house and taking the shrubbery-lined path. Mira grabs Mom's luggage, and Sara leads them inside to give her a tour.

I stop Dean at my front door. "What was that?"

"He's got a thing for you. Can you believe it?" Dean laughs. "I know he's a womanizer, but I'm surprised. Aren't you? It was fun playing the protective fiancé's role against *the* Jack Graham, huh? I wonder if he'll use it in his next book."

Five seconds ago, I couldn't have imagined feeling any worse. But now, I do. It's a double hit to my pride that Dean's astounded that someone else could have a thing for me, especially *the* Jack Graham, and that he's giddy like he might brag about it to his acting friends. *Yeah, you know the* New York Times *bestselling author Jack Graham? He's in love with my fiancée. He's got a contract with Netflix.*

Worse still, I detect no jealousy or concern. "Doesn't that bother you?"

His eyes roll like he's about to explain something simple. "Honey, a man like that is all about conquests. You'd never be so gullible. He probably only wants you because he can't have you. Or he's bored with shallow supermodels. Besides, this summer apart proves how committed we are. So, why should I be bothered?"

I sink into myself further like unsettled ground, shifting to fill in invisible holes. "You shouldn't have taunted him. Or mentioned being in bed together. You embarrassed me."

His hands land on my upper arms, rubbing up and down—a move I once liked but now makes me cringe. It feels more condescending than affectionate. "You're right. I took it too far. It was such a surprise, you know."

"So you've said. I want you to stay at your place."

His genial expression changes into disappointment, but he nods. "Yes, it might be awkward with Sara and Christine here."

"No. I mean, yes, but that's not it entirely." I latch on to my growing unease like a life vest in rough seas. "I'm not as confident in us as you are. Not anymore. I've tried to tell you, Dean. We need to talk. I don't want to be *together* until I'm sure we're *staying* together."

"Wow, okay. I'm a little blindsided, Rowan." He runs a hand through his hair. "But we should reconnect. It'll be like we're dating again. I'll plan a nice weekend for us, and you'll see. Everything will be perfect."

Our *perfect* weekend doesn't happen until Monday night, back-to-school eve. Everything else has taken strange priority. Me opting to keep my shopping plans with Mom and Sara on Friday prompted Dean to catch up on schoolwork and errands on Saturday and Sunday, which felt like retaliation for me not dropping everything for him. He claimed to be overwhelmed, but I suspected he didn't want to hear what I had to say. He avoided me, just like he had all summer.

But not tonight—I made him promise. I'm carrying his engagement ring in my purse. I will put it on or return it by the night's end.

Even so, Dean embraces date night with his usual optimism. He wears a dark suit and tie. He looks almost like a movie star—I tell him so. And he beams as if it's the best compliment I could offer.

"You're gorgeous." He pulls me into a warm embrace after wide-eyeing my outfit. It's a two-piece dress that I bought after finally agreeing to date again and at Mira's insistence that I looked "banging" in it. The teal silk halter top wraps around my neck, accentuating my shoulders rather than my scars, and cuts off just below my belly button, exposing an inch of skin before the matching skirt hugs my waist and hips and shows off my legs. Mira calls it my *fuck-me dress*.

But sex isn't what I'm after. I *need* the confidence a 'banging' outfit provides. Is tonight a break-up date or a reunion? I don't know. The other night's backyard fiasco has only worsened my confusion. At least in this outfit, I can feel good about something.

Getting into Dean's Honda, I hear Rose shout, "Have a nice evening, you two," from Jack's front porch, where she and Vernon sway in the swing, Marcy and Tom lean on the railing, and Jack stands like a sentry at the top of the steps, arms folded, and his usual brooding eyes pinched and dark as they trail me to the passenger side.

Jack apologized for the other night, and I understand why it was hard for him. But his words feel watered down, meaningless. *Another day, another apology.* Dean could be right—Jack might want me simply because he can't have me.

But Dean's words feel watered down, too.

Dean's hand slips easily around mine as we approach the restaurant he's picked for us. It's a ritzy downtown bistro with linen tablecloths, tuxedoed servers, and a view of the rippling Cape Fear. I would've been happier somewhere quiet, even his place, where we could've *really* talked, but Dean insisted on going out.

It's a gorgeous night. With the sun setting behind the silhouetted peaks of the USS North Carolina across the river, orange beams add a gold tone to everything. We're given a table in the corner, and Dean offers me the inner seat against the wall. Now, the dying sun warms my scars while keeping them hidden—a double-sided comfort.

His blue eyes sparkle in the sunlight. "Tell me what's on your mind."

I pull the engagement ring from my purse and set it on the table between us. "When you gave me this, I meant yes. Truly, I did. But that yes has wavered the longer you've been away, with every unanswered call or ignored text. You had no right to abandon me over one mistake. My mess-up was an accident, but you hurt me on purpose."

He eyes the ring, forlorn and confused. "You're right. I was angry. Everyone witnessed your uncertainty about me—I was so heartbroken and embarrassed."

He leans forward, blue eyes landing softly on mine. "I'm sorry. For everything I put you through. Leaving wasn't the right choice... Nothing was easy for me, either, you know. Working as a grunt on productions, twelve or thirteen-hour days, most of the time waiting, being yelled at by assistant directors itching to make a name for themselves... it was humbling. Exhausting. But I kept thinking about you, wanting to make you proud, wanting to come back to you a better man, and fearing that you'd end up thinking me a hack for trying—"

"Never. I never thought that. I still don't."

"I know, and your support has meant everything. What I'm trying to say is... you weren't with me, but you were always *with* me." His eyes dart to the ring before fixing on mine again. "I want you with me forever, Rowan."

My heart skips—a sudden, shocking putter that takes me back to the first time our eye contact lingered too long during play practice, our first touch when we traded scripts, and the night we stayed after practice long after the kids went home because we were too engrossed in conversation to call it a night. We fell for each other so sweetly, so honestly. *That's why I love Dean.*

His hand slips over mine from across the table, stroking my fingers. Warmth rises with his touch. "I won't make a big show of it, but please, wear the ring. Marry me."

This is it—the redo I wanted. But once again, my *yes* gets caught in my throat. I long for the security I had with him before all this, but at the same time, I understand that it wasn't real. How could it be? He doesn't know me—I never gave him a chance to.

He picks up the ring and edges it closer, a soft but hopeful smile lifting his cheek.

My hand slips over his, pressing the ring to the table's surface again. "Wait. There are things I need to—"

A shadow looms over our table, turning us toward a large man with a boyish grin.

"Hey, Dean."

"Ryan!" He stands and greets him with a hug. "Rowan, this is my cousin Ryan. He's thinking about subletting my condo. Ryan, this is my stunning fiancée, Rowan."

He looks shy as he shakes my hand. "Nice to meet you finally. Dean talks about you all the time."

I want to say the same, but Dean hasn't mentioned him or subletting his condo. "Nice to meet you, too. What a coincidence."

"Ryan recommended the place," Dean says.

"I live nearby. Popped in for happy hour and carry-out."

Standing side by side, Ryan is the spitting image of his cousin, only heavier.

"Wow, you guys could pass for twins."

Dean laughs, play-punching Ryan in his stomach. "Until middle school, anyway."

"Yep, I've always been more of a wide receiver than a cheerleader, like Dean here," Ryan grins. The barman catches his attention, setting a to-go bag on the counter. "Ya'll have a nice night. Good to meet you, Rowan."

He heads to the bar for his takeout. Watching his thick fingers reach for the bag strikes me as familiar. "Have I met him before?"

Dean sits, shaking his head. "No. He's new to the area, hoping to escape a bad roommate situation. I mentioned we'd be moving in together soon." He eyes the ring, middling the table like a condiment. "You wanted to tell me something?"

Those *somethings* scatter like dried leaves under a blower. *Why am I so bothered by meeting Dean's pleasant cousin? Or am I just nervous about what I need to say?* I had a plan for tonight—to finally trust Dean with my past, see how he reacts, and measure our relationship accordingly. My love for him would either return full-force or dissipate altogether.

But his intent gaze and expectant smile don't comfort me into talking—quite the opposite. I'm nervous. I excuse myself for the restroom, hoping to refocus. Rinsing my hands in cold water, my distress pieces together like a mental game of Tetris. I *have* seen Dean's cousin before. My plan fades while my certainty grows—I know what I want for the first time in months.

I find our dinners and the ring at the table but no Dean. I spot him outside through the picture windows in an animated phone call. I sit, refill my wine, and text Mira.

Can you pick me up? I send her my location.

Be there in twenty.

Napkin in lap and fork in hand, I dive into my pasta dish like tortellini might soften the hardness now lodged in my gut. I'm angry and hurt, but more than anything, anxious for this to be over. I want to go home.

More than that, I want to go home to Jack.

My plate is half-empty when Dean returns. He rushes in on a wave of excitement.

"You'll never guess what's happened," he says, oblivious to my angry face and speed-eating. "My agent got a call from casting on Jack's movie. I'm going to play an inspiring guidance counselor in *Cape Moon*! Can you believe it? I'm getting my big break after all!"

His news breaks me, shattering my inner hardness into a million sharp pieces. My would-be fiancé is a liar, and Jack's a controlling manipulator—why did I ever trust either of them?

"Jack's behind this," I say with calm indifference.

"He probably feels bad about being a jerk the other night. I have to take it—this could be it for me."

"What about school? Your students?" *What about me?* I almost tack on at the end.

He shrugs carelessly. "Eh, I'll take a leave of absence. Or quit. It's too good to pass up."

But I'm not. I stare dumbfounded that his promise not to let anything come between us again fails to register. Nor does the underhandedness of it—that Jack's used his connections to bait Dean into breaking it.

Dean leans in as if seeing me for the first time. "What's wrong, hon? Too much wine?"

"Not enough. The picture hanging in your office—heavyset, high school Dean—that isn't you. It's Ryan."

Surprise hits him first, followed by a mild chuckle. "Technically... yes. So?" His head cocks in a strange amusement, like I'm a child overreacting to something I don't understand. "Are you upset? It's not a big deal."

"Lying to your students? Lying to me? That's not a big deal? How?"

He takes a breath, still smirking. "It's a prop. I use it to inspire my students. You won't believe how many pounds have been lost thanks to that story. And it gives the kids confidence," he adds, almost as an afterthought.

"But it's a lie."

"What? You *never* lie to your students?"

"I don't invent personal struggles I *never* went through!"

"I do it to help them, Rowan."

"Then, why lie to me? Did you want *me* to shed a few pounds?"

"God, no! It's like being immersed in a role—I didn't want to break character and put you in an awkward position if your students mentioned it."

"Oh, so you lied to *me* to save *me* from lying to them?"

"Um, yes. Why are you upset? It's one little lie for their benefit. I would've told you eventually." He forks his fish as if the argument is over.

But *that* was why I loved Dean. It was the foundational story of our friend-ship, the load-bearing wall of our relationship. Removing it makes what's left of us crumble into dust and tears.

"I believed you'd gone through something truly difficult. Your weight loss story drew me closer to you—and you let me believe it because that's what you wanted."

"Are you listening to yourself? You're pissed because I wasn't a fatty in high school?"

"You manipulated me."

"I wanted to be with you! I'm sorry, Rowan. I didn't think it mattered. Why should it? That stupid story doesn't change anything."

"It changes... everything. You play a role for your students, a role for every audience, a role for me."

I stand up, dropping my napkin over my plate. I tuck my purse under my arm. "I love you, Dean. Even *with* the lie, I love you. But we aren't right for each other. My answer is no. And that you'd even consider a part in Jack's movie tells me your answer is no, too."

As I climb awkwardly into Mira's mini-van, she says, "Aw, you're wearing your *fuck-me* dress. You okay?"

"Fine." I lump in the passenger seat. "Dean and I are over."

The *I-told-you-sos* I expect don't come. She only nods.

I rest my head against the cold window, and several silent minutes pass before Mira clears her throat. "Um, there's something I should tell you. Can you handle more bad news?"

I sit up. "Tell me."

"Eddie Sweet's release has been moved up. He's getting out."

"When?"

"End of the week. It's thanks to you. Well, you *and* Lt. Wright. He went to see Eddie after his cousins were arrested and talked him into not covering for them anymore. Eddie's trading information for an early release. It's good news, really."

"You're right. Sara will be thrilled and relieved. We need something to celebrate. Let's tell her when we get home."

Mira nods, side-eyeing me. "You're freaking me out with your whole deadpan thing. Sure you're okay?"

"I'm tired. Pissed. But for the first time in months, I have clarity. I'll be fine."

The words come out confidently, like a mantra I'm programming myself to believe. I long to be home, snuggling with Edgar and watching mindless TV with Mom and Sara over bowls of ice cream.

But pulling into the driveway, the little house doesn't offer its usual relief—it's not home anymore. My neighbors occupy Jack's front porch almost exactly as I left them—it hasn't been long.

All eyes follow us as we exit Mira's minivan. I feel on stage again, under scrutiny, especially since it's obvious that the night went badly.

Well, obvious to most of them.

"Oh, Rowan, how'd it—"

"Vernon, no," Rose snaps.

Mira wraps her arm around me as we walk to the front door, and I lean against her like I've done hundreds of times before.

But Jack misses the unspoken understanding that I should be left alone—or thinks it doesn't apply to him. He reaches us halfway up the walk, bounding into our path.

"Rowan, are you okay? What happened?"

His concern feels like manipulation, somehow layering irritation atop my cold disappointment. Discovering Dean's lie leaves me questioning everything between us. Consoling me after Grandpa Ro died was probably him gathering material, vampire-biting my grief. Then, I think of that damn proposal. A packed auditorium, bigwigs, TV coverage, and Dean—the hero, *generously* loving the woman who isn't easy to love. It'd been all about him. Before him, it'd all been about Trent.

With Jack blocking our path, insisting on talking, I realize—*I have a type.*

"It's not a good time, Jack," Mira says.

Her soft warning only encourages him. "Let me help. I could—"

"You've done enough." My freaky calmness makes a stunning return. I lock eyes with him, determined for my words to sink in. "Dean sends his heartfelt thanks for the part in your movie. How clever and entitled of you to plot the demise of my relationship like that. How could you be so selfish and under-handed? You made everything about you—*that's* what you do. That's what all guys do, I guess. Maybe that should be the theme of your next novel. *Bare* is what women *want* to feel with someone if only men didn't wreck their trust *every* time. Leave me alone."

"Go home, Jack," Mira says more sternly as she pulls me around him. Mom meets us at the front door, and we lock it behind us.

Thirty

ROWAN

It's the first day of school, and I have no choice but to pull myself together. Gathering my books into my large purse on the kitchen table, I take inventory.

My fully annotated copy of *The Other Us*.

My thin file folder of Weekly Guides.

And *The Little House* by Virginia Lee Burton. Jack's advice recycles in my head—if I get lost, I'll talk about my origins with reading and books I've loved.

Damn it, Jack. I take a breath. My sadness dulls my first-day jitters like an all-natural anxiety medication. I no longer have the energy to be nervous or the will to be excited.

Mom's arm circles my shoulders. "What can I do to help?"

"Do something fun today. I hate the idea of you sitting here, waiting for us to get home."

"I'm hitting the beach. I'll be fine."

I turn to her suddenly. "But you'll be here this morning for Jane and the sign, right? She wants new pictures featuring all the work I've done."

Mom slumps. "Yes, I'll be here. But I wish you'd wait. You're in no shape to make a big decision like this."

239

"Actually, for the first time in months, I know *exactly* what I want. It's nice having a problem I can solve. The sooner it's on the market, the sooner I can move. I don't want to be here anymore."

"Wait until the weekend, at least. Give yourself a chance to—"

"Mom, I've decided." I force a smile before planting a kiss on her cheek. "I know what I'm doing."

Sara rushes into the kitchen. "Ready, Rowan?"

Walking into my classroom twenty minutes later has an instant calming effect. I *love* my classroom.

Large windows feature the gangly pines and thick-leaved magnolias outside in the courtyard—evergreen all year. Over the years, I've gathered cozy thrift store finds to create an eclectic and colorful vibe—a patchwork of mismatched rugs, a reading corner with plush chairs, pillows, and bean bags. The desks face each other, a wonky round table that centers attention on them, not me. In the center, a large wingback chair, black with red and orange daisies, will serve as our sharing chair as we jump into reading.

But the room's most unique feature was created by the students themselves. A comic-book-style mural covers the cinderblock walls—artistic odes to the literature we've read. Frankenstein's monster peeks over the whiteboard next to an imagined Pecola with distorted blue eyes and withered marigolds from Toni Morrison's *The Bluest Eye*. Dark moors stretch across the tops of the windows and feature a glowing hound and a brooding Heathcliff. A long ocean scene along the back wall shows *The Old Man and the Sea*, *Moby Dick*, *The Rime of the Ancient Mariner*, and *The Odyssey*. A nearly translucent *Invisible Man* hovers in an underground room covered in lights. Harry Potter, a black cat for Edgar Allan Poe (my idea), Percy Jackson, Katniss Everdeen, *The Ranger's Apprentice*, *The Hate U Give*, and *Howl's Moving Castle*—whatever literature the class loves finds a place.

It's the ideal setting to launch the project, I decide as the bell rings.

Seniors filter into the room with the casual ease and confidence of students ready for graduation. We launch into a round of *how-was-your-summer* as they settle, oddly taking the same seats they had the year before, as if no real time has passed.

"How's Mr. Maddix? Any wedding plans yet?" Ashley Morrow asks, looking coy.

My head tilts to my notes. "He's fine... I think." They exchange looks but, thankfully, don't press for more information.

A shy-looking redhead named Benny whispers to Eddie Speck—the star of the play last year—and Eddie laughs and raises his hand, much to Benny's dismay. "Ms. Mackey?"

"Yes, Eddie."

"Benny wants to hear your mac-n-cheese story," he reveals with a devious look, hazing the new kid, though it's clear they already know each other.

I glance at the wall clock and lean against my desk. "Only three minutes into class... It might be a new record."

But for the first time in nine school years, my pre-planned explanation doesn't spill out like usual. *If you don't share your stories, what's the point of having them?* Jack's words cause an unexpected swell to my typically calm mental seas. Thinking about Dean does, too. I don't feel ready for this.

Julio says, "You don't have to tell us again, Ms. Mackey. We all know you got too excited making mac-n-cheese."

"Right. Yes. Um, I was fifteen and hungry after school. So, I went for my favorite—boxed mac-n-cheese. I got the water boiling in a pot that was too small..."

Usually, I joke about hungry teenagers or how my cheesy noodle addiction led to destructive behavior. But the story falls flat when I can't deliver a soft transition. Instead, my brow pinches as the memory replays. I pop up, holding my notes, *The Other Us*, and reaching for *The Little House* from my desk, knocking into my travel mug of coffee. It plops over, hits the desk's edge, and dumps onto the floor.

"Shit!" My expletive makes the students laugh. Julio retrieves paper towels from the freshly stocked classroom pantry while Ashley grabs the trashcan.

"You okay, Ms. Mackey?" Julio asks while we clean up the mess.

"Fine, thanks. Just reliving my teenage clumsiness, I guess."

But turning to their expectant faces, regret crashes over me. I feel like a hypocrite for my anger over Dean's lies when I do the same thing and a fraud for making them believe it was my fault. What happened to me *wasn't* my fault. Just like it wasn't Mom's fault. Or anyone else's except *his*. Lying and shouldering the blame isn't fair to anyone, especially not me.

I hug my materials to my chest and lean against my desk again. "Actually, that's not the real story."

The room goes silent. I forego my usual *all-is-well* smile and take a long breath. "It's been a strange summer. I've been reminded that teenagers can handle anything," I say, thinking of Sara, my fifteen-year-old self, and the faces before me, "and that our stories are meant to be shared... *when* we're ready to share them. I'm not there yet. But I can't go another minute perpetuating a lie I never should've started. My injuries weren't sustained in a kitchen accident but during an assault by an angry, disturbed person, and nothing about it was *my* fault."

Their stunned, gaping faces cue me to move on quickly—this isn't how I want our year to begin. Even so, my back straightens, and my shoulders align like something heavy that I didn't realize I carried has been lifted. A genuine smile emerges, moving out behind my fake ones like the sun from behind clouds. "It feels good to say that out loud. I hope you'll forgive me, and we can put Mac-n-Cheese Mackey behind us, huh?"

"I never liked that nickname anyway," Julio says. "And there's nothing to forgive."

"Oh, my God, Ms. Mackey. You truth-bombed us," Ashley says, green eyes wide. "I, for one, love your honesty."

"It's like you're coming out of the closet," Eddie says with a wink. "There's no shame in that."

"Thanks for making it easy on me." I take my notes and picture book to the winged chair. "Now that we've established that things will be different this year, let's talk about our Inspiration Project. I'm ditching my lesson plans, and we're reading for pleasure."

After explaining the plan and how they'll be graded, I tap the armrest of the wingback chair. "Every day, in this chair, someone will share something that speaks to them. Weekly writing assignments will allow you to elaborate on your reading experience and our classroom discussions. I encourage you to make bold, personal choices that challenge and excite *you*."

"Does it have to be published?" Julio asks.

The question surprises me. "Um, no. If you want to read the work of an *'inglorious Milton,'* then so be it." No one gets my joke. "But you may need to provide me with a copy."

"Can it be a comic book?" Benny smirks deviously.

"Sure, if you can talk and write about it. Whatever you choose to read, you must share the journey it takes you on. I'm reading *The Other Us* by Jack Graham. So, this week, your assignment is to choose your first read and explain why you picked it. Leading up to your decisions, we'll talk about books that have meant something to us in the past."

I hold up the blue and white picture book in my lap. "This is one of my favorite books from childhood. I was an army brat to a single mother. We moved a lot. This story gave me comfort and a dream for the future when I'd have my own little house."

One I won't have much longer, I think sadly, clearing my throat.

I read the story aloud, showing the pictures on each page. I thought this might be a dumb idea—seventeen and eighteen-year-olds aren't toddlers, and reading them a picture book might be insultingly simple.

But they're transfixed. They even applaud at the end.

"It's because they moved the house, right?" Julio asks. "That's why you loved it?"

"Yes, I wanted a house that moved with us, to have something that was always the same."

"I like the part where the house felt out of place and neglected in the city," Eddie says thoughtfully. "I think people feel like that—alone in a crowded place."

"It's also about finding the place you truly belong." Mia Danvers pushes her glasses up on her nose. "The house didn't belong in the city. It wasn't right for her."

"Or perhaps it *was* right for her, but her environment changed beyond her control," I say. "Themes matter, even in picture books, and it can be unique to the person reading it, too. A sense of belonging for Mia, alone in a crowd for Eddie, and the value of a comfortable, reliable home for me."

"Wow... that's actually... deep," Ashley says with her valley girl twang. "Can we bring in our favorite picture books to share this week while we're deciding?"

Twenty hopeful and engaged faces lock on mine, forcing me to smile. "Absolutely."

At the day's end, Sara meets me for a ride home. I share what I told my students earlier in the day—she's already heard—and she's just as understanding. It's weird—I expected the day to be full of questions about my revised story. But that didn't happen. Telling one group sufficed for telling everyone, and the rest respected my privacy.

"They're more interested in what's going on with Mr. Maddix," Sara reveals. "Avoiding the question makes everyone talk."

Our phones chime in unison. A *Daisy Chain* text alert begins with a series of shocked, heartbroken, and mind-blown emojis preceding a close-up picture of a *For Sale* sign perched on a lawn (presumably mine) with a second sign behind it.

A groaning sigh escapes me. "What's he doing?"

Sara chuckles. "The same thing you are."

Thirty-One

JACK

Putting my house on the market may be retaliatory and immature, but who cares? If she goes through with selling the little house, then I've lost her.

I *can't* let that happen, even if it costs my house. If it comes to that...

Eyeing the old-school clock above the printing counter at Staples, I imagine Rowan arriving home from school about now, already pissed and frustrated that I've hijacked her bullshit plan. I'm even using her sister-in-law as my agent. I smirk, imagining the family conversation over that tidbit.

"Sir? Can I help you?" The young employee gives me an indifferent glance. *Did he call me sir?* "Pick-up for Jack Graham."

He fingers the computer before searching his workspace. He pulls out my manuscript, freshly printed and bound with plastic rings. He eyes the scrawling title on the cover, *Bare*, and my name underneath.

"Is this it, sir?"

My eyes narrow. I long to give a sarcastic answer or send him searching for another bound manuscript with my name on the cover. But I don't have time to play with this young-as-fuck Staples employee. I have things to do.

"That's the one."

He rings up the printing cost and the colorful pens—*good pens*—and sticky notes I've dumped on his counter.

Walking to the car, my phone chimes. *Motion at the front door. Doorbell. Doorbell. Doorbell.* Rowan stands on my porch, tapping her high heel on the concrete, arms folded over her silky blouse.

My voice over the doorbell's speaker makes her jump. "I'm not home."

Her brow pinches as she leans into the tiny camera. "We need to talk."

"No shit. I'll be by later."

She grunts and storms away from the door. It may not be the smartest move—irritating the woman who's already pissed at me. But I'm pissed, too. My attempt to get rid of Dean was misguided, yes, but done out of love—why can't she see that?

Leave it to me to fall in love with the most untrusting, jaded woman on the planet.

I show up after dark when Sara assures me that Rowan's calmed down and all I'm interrupting is them binge-watching *The Walking Dead*. Apparently, Rowan has claimed Darryl as her rebound guy. I set my peace offerings on the porch swing, out of the way, before knocking.

The wind is knocked out of me when Rowan answers. She looks gorgeous. Her Cleopatra hair holds soft waves and artful crimson tips, making her look fiery and badass. A long, thin white sweater covers a pink cotton tank and soft gray shorts, but barely. My eyes drift over her lips, down her neck, and across her bare collarbone, where her scars spread before ending just over her heart.

She doesn't smile and pulls the edges of her sweater closer together.

"Um, you look amazing," I say.

Her hand goes to her hair. "Sara said everyone gets break-up bangs, but I shouldn't follow trends. We settled for break-up hair dye."

"It's working for you."

She leans against the doorjamb, looking expectant.

"Take the fucking sign down, Rowan."

Stepping onto the porch, she closes the door behind her like she doesn't want Sara and Christine to hear us.

"My sign isn't coming down. Take yours down."

"You first. Why are you selling? You love this house."

She takes a breath, seeming to center herself. "I don't want to be here anymore."

"Be angry at me. Fine. But don't make a bad decision because you're pissed. Selling before you've built any equity means losing every penny you've sunk into it and taking a huge tax hit."

A sardonic laugh escapes her. "Are you mansplaining my finances to me? I know exactly what this will cost me, asshole."

"Then, why do that to yourself?"

"To get away from you!"

That hurts. My jaw hangs in stunned limbo while my brow contorts into a thousand devastated creases. "Um, that's a shit reason to move. I'm sorry for what I did. It was a dick move, and yes, fucking selfish. But you went to him, Rowan, like he never left, like nothing between us mattered. I've never been in love before. Aren't I allowed one fuck-up? You gave Dean a thousand chances—"

"Yes, but I shouldn't have!" She dares to meet my eyes and brings her voice down to a soft, desperate plea. "Staying here terrifies me. I could never be enough for you, not for long. I can't be the woman next door to your... to what would happen when we fall apart."

"When? How can you have so little faith in me?"

"Easy. You had zero faith in me. All you had to do was wait and trust me. I was seconds from breaking up with him when he got that damn phone call. How could *you* try to control me like that after everything I told you?"

"You walking off with the wrong guy, getting into bed with him—how could I do *nothing*?"

"I didn't get in bed with him. You hurt and humiliated me to prove your point. You wanted Dean to choose a part over me, and he did. Do you have any idea how shitty that feels?"

"No shittier than him ghosting you all summer. He could've said no. After what you said about not wanting to hurt or lose him… I got worried, okay? I'm sorry."

My pleading apology stirs an exasperated sigh. She motions to the sign on my lawn. "And what's this, huh? Another manipulation? Is pretending to sell your house supposed to make me feel better?"

"I'm not pretending. Ask Jane. We're looking at properties in Landfall tomorrow, and she's already booked three showings."

Her arms fold. "Why are you doing this?"

"So you don't have to. You shouldn't have to leave the place you love because of me. If one of us has to go, I want it to be me."

She softens instantly, but watches my expression like she's hunting for insincerity.

But I mean every word. "I've priced it under market. My place is all upgrades and fun times—it'll sell fast. When I have a signed contract in hand, you'll know I'm not kidding and trust me enough to take your sign down."

Her head tilts, and a tear escapes. She wipes it away quickly as if embarrassed. "But you can't move, Jack. What about the neighbors? What about Devin?"

"Devin's with me wherever I go. As for the neighbors, I'll bus them to Landfall once a week. They'll love it."

She shakes her head. "No, I can't let you do that. Please, take your sign down."

"The only way my sign comes down is if you want us to be neighbors again. Otherwise, I'm leaving as soon as possible to save you from doing it. I'm Sydney Carton."

A spurting laugh breaks through her quiet tears. "You're no Sydney Carton."

"Course, I am. I'm sacrificing myself for the woman I love—Dickens couldn't write this scene any better."

She laughs again, music to my ears. "This is hardly *A Tale of Two Cities*."

"It's *A Tale of Two Neighbors.*"

More laughs. "Sydney Carton would never *tell* Lucie his plan to sacrifice himself—he'd just do it. Stop trying to seduce me with books."

"Do you have a better idea of how I might seduce you?" My eyes circle her face, stopping at her lips. Damn, I want to kiss her. And the way she looks at me, I suspect she entertains the idea. Her arms fall to her sides, and her cheeks flush pink. Leaning closer, I trace her hairline with the tip of my finger before tucking a wayward lock behind her ear. "I fucking adore you, Rowan... forgive me. Please."

A struggle ensues behind her eyes. Her trust has taken a double hit between me and Dean, and lumping me into her overfull memory bank of shit-boyfriends probably seems like the safest plan. Moving, too. If she stays and we're not together, it'll be awful for us both. When another tear slips, I brush it away with my thumb.

She clears her throat, glancing with a pinched brow from her feet to my eyes again. "I don't want you to give up anything for me... but I'm not ready to take my sign down, either."

"Fair enough. How about a compromise?"

"I'm listening."

"The signs stay up, but we agree not to sign anything until we finish what we started."

Her head cocks in curiosity while I grab two items from the porch swing. I hand her the manuscript first, and another tear slides down her cheek as she looks up at me.

"You finished it?"

"Yep. I want you to be the first to read it cover to cover."

She holds it like a baby, letting her finger run over the oversized scripted title on the front page, and she smiles.

The cat mug stuffed with good pens and sticky notes comes next—I set it in the crook of her arm. "Like we agreed, you have full veto power over any of it. Mark it up to your heart's content."

Nodding, she smirks. "I will... as we agreed. I'll need a few days."

"I have to visit your class, too. That was the deal."

She chews her bottom lip. "Monday, then. Be there at eight."

"Done. How did today go?"

Another smile breaks through. "Um, really well. They loved the plan, and um..." Her brow pinches like she wants to tell me something but can't put the words together. "Um... Congratulations on finishing your book." She taps the manuscript and turns toward the door.

"Rowan, wait." I reach for the last item on the porch swing—a vibrant array of flowers. "I selected them myself: the full blue hydrangeas to match your eyes, friendly yellow Gerber daisies to go with your smile, delicate lilies and soft dahlias for your gentleness, and lavender sprigs for your calmness. I frustrated the hell out of that florist."

I lay them atop my other gifts, watching her expression bounce from them to me.

When her bothered brow creases even more, I say, "You said that's how I'll know, right?"

"Um, I have to go." Arms full, she awkwardly ducks inside her door, leaving me wondering if I went too far.

Thirty-Two

ROWAN

He went too far.

Inside, I lean against the door and inhale the eclectic bouquet. I can't believe he bought me flowers. I also can't believe that I've gone from angry to sad to... I don't know anymore.

I almost wanted him to kiss me. Falling into Jack Graham's arms would be so easy—he is the sexiest, smartest man I've ever met, let alone been close to. Seeing his bedroom eyes in their natural habitat and exploring his tattoos up close alone are incentives enough to give in and let him do whatever he wants. Why not take advantage of such a rare opportunity?

Oh, right—the devastating heartbreak it would cause. It's clear in the way he touches me, the way he kisses, that it wouldn't be anything less than the kind of mind-altering sex that drives a stake through time—before Jack and after. The *after* scares me when I am whole-heartedly his, and his interest dissolves like fog baked in sunlight.

I can't handle being with him, knowing I'll lose him. Or living next door to the consequences.

Through the peephole, I see that he lingers, brooding on the other side, his arms braced on the doorframe like he might sling himself inside if I open it again. Our talk has dulled my sharp edges, though. Maybe I'm holding on to the wrong impression of him, like it's an out-of-date map leading me astray. I *know* he isn't the selfish playboy man-baby I first thought he was. But guys like Jack Graham don't settle... and certainly not with someone like me.

"You okay?" Mom calls from the living room amid groaning zombies.

I hold up my gifts with a short eye roll before heading to the kitchen. I arrange the flowers in a tall vase with water and bring them to the coffee table.

"Gorgeous! Jack gave you those?" Mom says as if it's a mystery. I nod.

Sara chuckles. "He's making an effort."

"Anyone can buy flowers." I plop beside her, grab my unfinished glass of wine, and whimper, "More zombies. More Darryl."

Sara obliges, but she scoots over and puts an arm around me. "It'll be okay."

It's late when I finally crawl into bed, but I bring Jack's manuscript anyway.

Bare begins with two injured teenagers in neighboring beds in a hospital emergency room. They connect instantly, like old friends. Jack's teenagers are waiting for the same on-call doctor, a specialist in serious burns. Caleb has burned his hands in a botched arson—Kate thinks he's joking. Kate says she fell in the kitchen, hitting her cheek against a hot coil burner. Only one story is true.

Jack pulls me in and wraps me in his story like a warm blanket. Caleb conspired to burn his house down to end the abuse inflicted by his tyrannical father—without walls, he couldn't lock Caleb in for days or beat his mother in secret. Kate didn't fall in the kitchen—her stepfather pressed her face to the burner when she wouldn't do what he wanted. These horrific scenes play out in segmented flashbacks as they talk to each other—nothing is said except for what they tell everyone else, their version of mac-n-cheese stories. But it's like they know. By the night's end, they scoot their beds together and make a risky promise—to do whatever it takes to make it back to each other again.

When I stop reading, it's nearly three, and I'm crying over the story and my memories as they link together. Jack's done it again.

I put the book away—*I have to*—and go to sleep thinking about love and risks.

The next day, Dean peeks into my classroom after the final bell, like a new student, unsure if he's in the right place. I manage a weak smile to usher him inside. He carries two to-go coffees and a bag slung over his shoulder.

"Truce?" he asks timidly. "I can't stand that you're mad at me."

A sigh flutters out. "I can't stand it, either. And I'm not mad. Just… sad and disappointed."

He nods, moving closer to my desk. "Me, too—in myself. We had it so good, and I wrecked it. I'll never forgive myself for how badly I've treated you."

Though *never* feels like a strong word, I accept his apology with a shrug.

He hands me a coffee. "Thought you might want your usual pick-me-up."

"Thanks." It's like old times, and I realize how much I miss him.

He releases the tote bag, setting it on my desk. It's one of mine—a reusable sack for library books or groceries. "I gathered what I could find from my place. It's not much, but I thought…"

Peering inside, I find laundered and folded clothes, a toothbrush in a plastic baggie, hair ties, and my black cat mug because Dean's stark white mugs felt too boring for me. "Thanks. I forgot about these things."

He leans against the nearest desk, sipping his coffee. "Um, I'm going to turn down the part."

"Dean! Why?"

He glances at his brown Oxfords, looking sheepish. "I'm an idiot, Rowan. I was so excited about the part that I ignored why I shouldn't take it. Jack Graham played me like a puppet. It feels wrong, taking it."

"This is your chance. Who cares how it happened? Take it and be the best damn inspiring guidance counselor the world has ever seen, and make Jack regret allowing you to steal the limelight."

He chuckles. "You really think I should?"

"Absolutely. Don't feel bad about it, either. Jack isn't why we aren't together."

His eyes droop to his shoes again. "I know that, too. I'm sorry. How are you holding up?"

A laugh erupts, though nothing is funny. "Well, Mom, Sara, and Mira are treating me like I'm terminally ill, my neighbors keep showing up with reasons why I should stay—I'm selling the house, by the way—and my students suspect we've broken up, given their sympathetic looks and veiled condolences. Ironically, my Inspiration Project is the only good thing happening right now."

"I've heard great things. The kids love it. Giving students educational free will is a dangerous precedent, though."

I laugh. "You'd think it'd invite chaos, but it's been amazing."

"Tell me about it," he prompts, sipping his coffee.

This is why I love Dean—we were always good at being friends. I share my classroom successes like he would his acting highlights. I'm practically giddy, telling him about it.

"What about you, Dean? How are you holding up?"

His genial smile dips into a frown. "Um, been better. School's fine... I'm just...Thank you for not outing me to the students about Ryan."

"I'd never hurt your reputation with your kids, and I-I feel like a hypocrite for getting so upset about it anyway."

"Don't. I lied. I never should've done that, especially not to you." His eyes catch mine, holding me with a pained, quizzical look. "I, um, heard some of the kids talking about your scars. They said you were assaulted?"

The lead weight I'd carried holding all the things I should've said returns, hard and tight in my chest. I move out from around my desk and lean against it so there's nothing between us. "Yes, I was. When I was fifteen."

"I always assumed it was an accident. That's what everyone said. That's why I never asked. I wish you'd told me." He's breathless, concern and hurt etched on his face.

"I should have. I wanted to. But everything between us was always so... *nice*. I haven't had a lot of *nice*, and I stupidly thought that telling you my real story might hurt us somehow." Tears slip from my eyes, and I hang my head, ashamed for keeping him at a distance. "I was so worried about losing you that I never really had you."

He stands, sets his coffee aside, and meets me where I am. "It's okay. Trauma doesn't have rules or etiquette. The only right answer is whatever you're comfortable with, and I didn't make it easy for you."

My arms wrap around him, and he lets me bury my face in his neck while he holds me. Just like old times.

"Thank you, Dean," I whisper into his neck. "I didn't make things easy for you, either."

"Any chance for us to start over?" With his question, he pulls away just enough to see my eyes. And in the warm space between us, for a moment, I consider it.

But when I don't answer right away, Dean softens his disappointment with a smile. "Even if I go on to become a big-time actor in Hollywood, I will *always* regret leaving you for the summer."

"I'll always regret it if you don't take that part. Tell me you will."

His hands fall from me, and he takes a step back. "With your blessing. It's the best revenge, right?" His smile fades into curiosity. "Is that why you're moving? Some sort of passive-aggressive revenge? I thought you loved that house."

"I'm... angry," I admit, like Dean's my priest suddenly. "What does love matter if I can't be happy there?"

"Here's something you've definitely taught me. Everything's fixable. Have you talked to him?"

"Yes, but he's..." I don't know how to voice my opinion about Jack if I even should. "How will I ever feel safe with a guy who..."

"Can have anyone?"

"Right."

"Rowan, the last thing I want to do is push you toward someone else, but... you are beautiful, intriguing, and everything any guy could ask for. Don't let a few scars make you settle for anything less than what you want."

"Damn it, Dean. You're making me miss you so much."

He breaks away from me, tossing his empty coffee cup into the trashcan. At the door, he turns around. "Rowan, take a lesson from me. Don't let *anything* come between you and something you love."

A light smile cuts through my tears. "Look at you, inspiring guidance counselor, already in character."

We share a brief chuckle before Dean disappears into the hallway.

Thirty-Three

ROWAN

Mira arrives at the little house Friday afternoon to take Sara home. I would've done it myself, but Mira said it had to be official.

As we load Mira's SUV, the neighbors skittishly emerge from their dwellings bearing gifts. Tom and Marcy bring their delicious homemade barbecue sauce. Vernon gives Sara a pink toolkit to properly care for her bike while Rose hands over a basket of yarn in every conceivable shade of purple.

"What about Jack?" Vernon peers across the yard.

"Oh, he already gave me his gift." She holds up her phone. "A year's subscription to *Chiller*. He gets me."

I smile at their generosity and feel slightly bad that Jack's staying away because of me.

"Your gift is in your bedroom," Sara whispers when I hug her goodbye. "Don't be mad. I can't help what inspires me."

Once they drive off, the neighbors offer a few soft words before leaving me with Mom. My tears surface when Sara's out of sight. Mom wraps me up and whispers assurances—things I know are true. *I'm not losing her.*

But I'm already heartbroken, and perhaps being a secondary wound makes this cut feel deeper.

Alone in my bedroom, I find Sara's gift. *I'm not mad.* But it's a gut-kick when I'm already down, however beautiful it is.

It's an abstract painting of Jack and me in the blue room at the museum. The soft sheets of the mobile appear to be moving, the way she's painted them. We are black silhouettes, arguing based on his hand reaching toward me and mine set in a stopping gesture.

But between our silhouettes, ghost images of us—me in my boho dress and him in his dark pants and lighter polo—float toward each other. Hands mingled, chests pressed, foreheads touching. Small patches of color from my dress speckle him as if I'm flowing into him, and his grays and darks merge into me, too.

Her painting inspires an unexpected longing to be the ghost couple, merged together and sharing pieces of ourselves. But fear mixes into it, too. The ghost couple could be an illusion.

I haven't seen Jack since the night he came to my door, and he's been quiet. No loud music. No late-night parties. No texts or awkward encounters around the mailbox.

But house hunters have streamed through his place since the sign went up. Jane reports three offers so far and predicts a bidding war once our Monday deadline expires.

She's shown the little house once, but to clients who called it too small before heading next door. So, it sits unloved and in limbo, just like the house in the story.

In the war over our houses, Jack will win. I feel pressured to do something—he can't lose his beloved house and neighborhood because of me. But I'm conflicted, too—he can't trap me here, either.

Mom does her best to distract me over the weekend. We go shopping and splurge on out-to-eat meals. We spend time at Mira's, playing with the kids. Finally, on Sunday, she makes dinner for us at the little house.

And she invites a guest.

When I first see Reggie Tucker, I think *boy toy*, but immediately compose a more accurate label—*lovable nerd meets tired traveler*. He reminds me of Idris Elba with his salt-and-pepper beard, probing eyes, and easy smile. Like Mom, he's toned and in his fifties, but he's a head taller and hunches slightly, as if to be closer to her. He's a doctor from Boston specializing in childhood cancers, and is endearingly nervous.

He shakes my hand without glancing at my scars—Mom's prepped him, and he's invested enough to adhere to her rules. He calls me and my home lovely and admires my eclectic mix of art on the walls, gifts from students over the years, claiming he has a similar gallery of his patients' drawings. He graciously listens to me gush about Sara and her art.

Reggie helps Mom serve steaming lasagna, garlic bread, a Caesar salad, and wine, and I love watching them move together. It's a symbiotic dance, with them shifting positions to serve or pour while finding gentle ways to touch each other. Hand to waist. Hand over hand. Hand to arm. They overflow with smiles whenever they make eye contact and carry lingering smirks when not.

I love seeing her like this.

Mira, Jane, and the kids arrive, squeezing around the kitchen banquet.

Mom and Reggie have a moment amid the chaos. With their hands dangling at their sides together, he gives her a look that says, *"See? Everything's fine."* And she smiles with relief that these pieces of her life are finally fitting together. I envy their silent love language.

"How did you two meet?" I ask when we're settled.

With a loving glance at each other, Reggie tells the story. A busy Italian café, one empty table, and two singles deciding to take a chance and share it.

"It was love at first sight," Reggie says, "at least for me."

"For me, too, though I never believed that could happen," Mom says.

"When? How long have you two been together?" Surely, not long, considering their new relationship energy, and this is the first time I'm learning about him.

They share an awkward glance before Mom says, "Since last summer, actually."

I gape in dumb surprise. *Before I started dating Dean?*

"I'm sorry I didn't tell you. It's been forever since I've considered dating. I didn't want to bring it up until I was sure it would last—"

"I went through a rigorous vetting process," Reggie jokes, "and background checks."

"I wasn't that bad," Mom argues lightly. "Then, when Dad got sick... the point is that first, I wanted to be sure, and once I was, I... never found the right time."

"I never wanted..." My voice trails off as Jack's words about taking on burdens we were never meant to carry recycle in my head. "Never mind. I'm thrilled for you, Mom. It's perfect telling me this way. Checking Reggie out in person is way better than on FaceTime."

The tension visibly lessens on her shoulders as her smile grows.

They share their stories, and we linger at the dinner table long after the leftovers go cold to hear them. They are full of laughter and hope and beautiful familiarity—this is exactly what I've always wanted for her.

For me, too.

It's late when everyone disbands. Mira and the family go home, and though she argues, I insist Mom goes with Reggie. He's rented a beach cottage for his stay, and there's no reason why she shouldn't be with him.

"I'm fine," I tell her for the millionth time.

And it's true—I realize, reentering the little house. Mom and Reggie's connection makes me think of mine with Jack. He touches me like that. We laugh like that. He's willing to give up the house he loves *for me*. He's spending the day with my students tomorrow *for me*. The confused fog I've been in finally breaks.

Sara's painting holds me captive once again—Jack and I in our ghost forms coming together—*that's* what I want. His creative brain. His bookish tattoos. His perfect kisses. And the way he sees right through me. He is where I belong.

It's late, but I don't care. I slip out the sliding glass door and race along our houses, barefoot and breathless.

My feet skirt up the deck planks with light thuds. Goosebumps cover my arms from the chill night air and probably from what I'm doing, too. *Am I really doing this?*

Yes. Most definitely, yes.

Desperate to see him, I nearly trip over my feet. Under the drooping Edison bulbs and around the luxurious chaise, I rush by his dark office. Light spills onto the deck planks from his living room and kitchen windows.

But shadows move inside, and voices slow me down.

Edging the first window, I peer inside, nervousness rising in my gut. *That's* a woman's voice. My eyes lock in breathless disbelief—Jack with Dr. Evelyn Tate.

He leans against the kitchen counter, drink in hand, hair disheveled—he looks amused. She's perched on a barstool, a tight, black dress hiked up on her thigh. She looks nothing like she does at school. Her head tilts back, laughing, and she raises her glass to him. Behind the island, she makes herself at home by kicking off her heels.

My stomach twists into jagged knots—I might be sick. *Evelyn... Evie.* His first love. His muse.

The woman he'll never turn away.

All smiles, they chat, probably about their amazing sex or equally hot, flawless bodies. Jack gives her a sheepish grin, folding his arms over his chest. She leaves her seat, slowly, seductively making her way to him.

I twist away. I can't watch.

I've been such a fool. *Again.*

Hand over my mouth to keep me from screaming, I return the way I came, determined to shield myself in the little house and have my breakdown privately. I'm not just hurt—I'm devastated. But no good can come from a confrontation, especially not for me at work. And what's the point, anyway?

I knew who Jack Graham was from the beginning, and he's proven me right. I will never be enough for him. And he's not enough for me, either.

Thirty-Four

ROWAN

Jack answers his front door, smiling wide when he sees me. He's wearing a white towel wrapped loosely around his waist because *of course, he is*. I *hate* that my eyes wander over him like I'm on an exploratory adventure. His wet hair drips onto his face, clean-shaven for once—he's made an effort. Shame it's for nothing.

"Rowan, hey, I'm almost ready. Want to ride together?"

Game face, Rowan. "No. I only have a minute."

My forced smile makes his brow pinch. "What's wrong?"

I take a breath, and my plan falters. The short but direct speech I prepared seemed like the right idea, *in theory*. I had all night to work it out and affix the calm, unshakable demeanor I needed to deliver it. I hold his manuscript in my arm and my keys in my hand. My bag and a travel mug of coffee await me in my VW—I'm ready for a quick exit. I'm determined to minimize the damage and hold myself together.

All I have to do is say what I need to say and be done with it. *Quickly.* But my strength wobbles unsteadily.

"Want to come in?" He motions inside, but I shake my head.

I glance around him, almost expecting to see her, even though her BMW accelerated down Daisy Lane two hours after spying them together, taking what remained of my hope and dignity with her.

"No. Definitely not. I need to make this quick." My keys jingle in my hand like proof. "I'm canceling today's visit and ending our deal." I hand over his manuscript. "But I finished this. It's amazing, but you already know that. I'm glad you got what you needed."

"What I needed?" His face scrunches. "I don't understand. What's going on?"

"The other thing is that I'm moving regardless of what you do. Sell your house if you want to, but the point is, our deal is off."

"Why?" His hands go to his hips. "Did something happen? Why are you upset?"

A tear slips through my rigid facade. I swipe it, scraping my cheek with my keys. "I don't want to argue. I'm not even mad—"

"Are you kidding me? You're seething. What's wrong?" His eyes burrow into mine, his face stern and just as determined for me to answer as I am to run away.

"I came over last night, hoping for... I saw you with her, Jack."

"You didn't see me *with* her," he refutes. "You saw her *here*—that's all."

"I saw enough." My eyes catch his. I force another smile, shaking my head and letting the tears fall—there's no stopping them now. "For the record... *That* woman doesn't deserve you. Not your love, your pen, or your dick. She's my boss, one of them, anyway. The kids call her the Ice Queen. She's all about money and appearances and getting ahead. Your books sit on a shelf in her office, propped up by old swimming trophies. *That's* what you are to her, Jack—a trophy. I would've walked through fire for you. She doesn't even read your books. But you're so enamored by her *fucking perfection*—"

"No. I ended it with her. That's all. If you'd walk through fire for me, then *listen to me*. I did not sleep with her. I did not kiss her. All we did was talk. I swear."

"Right, and I'm just supposed to take your word for it, huh? Ignore what I *know* about you, ignore what I *saw*, and believe this time was different than *all* the other times she's popped in?"

"I expect you to believe the truth."

"You must think I'm..." So many derogatory words line up that I can't pick the best one. In all my plans, I never expected an argument. Not *really*. I expected to barely get the words out over my incessant blubbering and hating myself for letting him see me like that. Facts are facts—how can he deny them? Despite what he might think, I'm not so pathetic that I'd turn a blind eye to his extracurricular love life or let him charm me into thinking he didn't have one. I'm not that gullible.

Desperate to get out of here, I stumble down the stairs. My heel catches, twisting my ankle. Hard. I curse as I grab the railing to keep from falling. Pain shoots up my left leg.

"Rowan, stop. You okay?"

I ignore my throbbing foot. "We're over—that's all I need you to understand. I have to go to work."

"Fuck work. You don't get to drop this on me and bail." He bypasses the stairs altogether by hopping down the stoop and jumping in front of me. "You don't get to control *this* narrative like you do everything else—I *deserve* a chance to explain."

"As if there's anything to explain—" I take a breath, stopping. "I don't want to do this."

"Tough shit. I did not sleep with that woman. Or any woman. What can I do to prove it to you?"

"Nothing!" The word comes out loudly, making me look around, afraid I've woken the neighbors. I take a breath, desperately trying to stay calm but wincing as I put weight on my leg.

"You're hurt. Let me help you," Jack says, a little calmer.

"No, I'm fine. You don't have to prove anything—*we aren't together*. And you don't want to be. You know what Evie's about, why she shows up... she was here for hours, Jack. *Hours*. How can you reasonably expect me to believe nothing happened? If you care about me, how could you let her in?"

His face contorts with bothered creases. "I shouldn't have let her in. You're right. But I didn't touch her. I didn't even want to. I'll tell you everything."

I take a breath, unable to believe him or put myself through any more of this. "I have to go. I'll be late."

"You're pissed—I get it. This is exactly how I felt when Dean showed up and put his fucking hands on you. But you have to believe me—nothing happened. I want you—"

"And every other engaged woman you can find! Don't come near me again! Not today. Not in my class. Not ever! I wish I'd never moved here! You are the worst thing to ever happen to me, Jack Graham!"

I hobble at full speed to my VW, hands shaking as I put the key in the ignition. I jerk the car onto the street and head toward school. Though I want to call in sick and initiate a pity party with Edgar, I can't. My students expect the great Jack Graham, and I need to explain why he's not coming. Or, at least, give a watered-down version that doesn't incriminate any administrators before popping in one of their favorite movies or anything that will soften the blow and get their eyes off me. Driving with the top down dries my tears.

But in the silence of my pre-bell classroom, I nearly crumble again. My ankle throbs and aches. But worse, the replay of our fight and images of him with Evelyn rip through me like a jagged blade. It shouldn't hurt this much—not when I expected it to happen. My head falls into my hands—I've been such a fool.

"Ms. Mackey, everything okay?"

An exasperated huff lifts my head, bringing my eyes to Julio's. "I don't know anymore."

Nodding, Julio sits next to my desk. "Rough morning?"

"The roughest."

"How can I help?"

I sigh, glancing at my swollen foot. "Ice from the nurse?"

"Coming right up."

The first bell rings. Ashley, Mia, and Eddie enter, carrying armfuls of Jack Graham's books.

They eye my leg, now propped on a stack of dictionaries.

"Oh, my gosh, Ms. Mackey!" Ashley rushes over. She sees the dark purple and bluish bruise left by my awkward tumble and says, "Ew."

"What did you do to yourself?" Eddie asks.

"A little misstep, that's all."

"It's a good thing you don't have to do any teaching today with Mr. Graham coming," Mia notes with a sparkle in her hazel eyes. I take a deep breath, trying to hold myself together.

Eddie brings two throw pillows from our circle-time collection, propping one under my foot and the other behind my back. "We should probably come up with a better ottoman than a stack of dictionaries."

"It's nice seeing them put to use," I joke.

When the second bell rings, my leg is much more comfortable in a cushioned folding chair and covered with a bag of ice. The students take strategic positions around the winged-back talking chair—some on the floor and others at desks, but all carrying Jack's books and hopeful expressions as they await their revered guest.

The class quiets and their excited faces turn to me.

A teacher must always keep her shit together—it's the foundation of teaching. And leave her personal drama at home—it has no place in her classroom.

But for the first time in nine school years, my sturdy and reliable classroom demeanor cracks like a glass table under too much weight. Flashes of Jack and *that* woman mix with his devastated expression when I said he was the worst thing to ever happen to me. I didn't mean it—I could *never* mean that. The worst thing to ever happen to me is as clear as the scars on my face. I let Jack get to me, and anger get the better of me. *Me, of all people.* Shame settles on my shoulders along with everything else, splintering the cracks.

"Is he running late?" Mia's voice shatters my mental shield.

Two tears slip out, one on either side, so I can't play it off. "He's not late. He's not… I messed up."

Julio stands while everyone else stares in mass shock, waiting for me to explain. He fetches the nearest tissue box and brings it to my desk. "It's okay, Ms. Mackey. Happens to everyone."

"I appreciate that, Julio." I take a breath and force a smile. "But this time, it impacts all of you, and I hate that, especially since you've taken such good care of me. Don't tell the others, but you truly are my favorites."

They laugh, and Eddie says, "Oh, honey. We already know that."

"What happened, Ms. Mackey?" Mia asks quietly.

"I got angry, and it must've short-circuited my wires because the things I said…"

"Uh, oh, Ms. Mackey. Did you say some choice words?" Eddie asks, grinning coyly.

I chuckle. "Ah, yes, you'd be proud, Eddie. I used some colorful sentence enhancers."

"She sounded like an angry rapper," a voice says, entering from the hallway. "Woke the whole neighborhood, and the funny thing is, she was talking to her damn foot. That's the last time her foot will ever betray her like this."

Shock precedes laughter as attention diverts to the man strolling into our classroom. It's good they're distracted, because my flushed face and gaping mouth prove unequivocally that I'm not keeping anything together.

Thirty-Five

JACK

Letting Evie in was a bonehead mistake. I told her we were done at the door—something I should've said when she brushed me off after Ben's death or, hell, *any* year previously—but she played the damsel in distress card and brought out the tears—fiancé troubles. I didn't want to be her safety net, but maybe I wanted to test myself. If her kryptonite didn't weaken me, I'm better than Superman at this love thing with Rowan. And I am—I didn't touch her, even when she tried.

It just looked bad.

The shocked and relieved look on Rowan's face assures me that showing up here, despite what she said earlier, has worked in my favor.

Always chase.

She practically melts. And my love for her swells like a universe expanding. She is brainy and complicated and fucking gorgeous, no matter what she thinks. I can't let her think the worst of me.

But I get it. She's been hurt so many times, in so many atrocious ways—it's no wonder she expects it.

I approach her desk, set down the cardboard cup holder I'm carrying, and take out the contents. Two coffees, a water, and a bottle of ibuprofen. I tried to think of everything she might need, like she did for me after the party. I tried with my appearance, too—dark skinny jeans, Adidas, a white polo, and a black blazer create a fitted, author-y look, and for the first time since she's known me, I'm clean-shaven.

With my back to my awaiting audience, I crouch beside her elevated leg, resisting the urge to touch her. Instead, I grab the medicine and tap pills in her hand.

We lock eyes, and I whisper, "Rowan, I swear on Devin's memory and everything I love, nothing happened."

She softens, her distrust vanishing like a tide being pulled to sea. "I know," she mouths. "I'm sorry."

My hand tops hers, to hell with the kids, and my grip tightens. "Sorry for putting you through that. It won't happen again."

The tension in her shoulders releases with a smile.

I rise, grabbing the second coffee. "Sorry, I'm late. Parking's a bitch around here." I turn to the crowd. "I'm Jack Graham, by the way, and... holy shit. This is the coolest classroom I've ever seen."

They practically hop from their seats to introduce themselves and give me a tour, explaining the books represented on the walls and their plans to add to the mural this year. It's clear—Rowan has made this *their* classroom, and they're damn proud of it.

A blonde with a valley twang—Ashley—offers me water and food from a stocked pantry. "Ms. Mackey says we learn better with calories."

"I know I do. Who keeps this stocked?" They motion to Rowan. "No surprise there. She thinks of everything."

When the tour ends, Julio leads me to the winged-back chair to the right of Rowan, and a Q&A begins.

Mia timidly asks, "Why romance?"

I launch into my usual spiel about journalism and chasing human interest stories. "I'm surrounded by beautiful, tragic, messy, complicated, and daring love stories. So, I started writing them down and asking myself *what if*. That's a writer's best tool—asking what if. *What if this had been different? What if they'd met then? Or later? Or what if she'd married someone else?* But even though I loved stories like these, it took me a while to call myself a romance writer."

I chuckle. "Guys are supposed to write about spies or cops or murderers or sports legends. How could I tell my basketball buddies I'm writing romance without it becoming a joke?"

The class laughs with me.

"Did they tease you?" Ashley asks, already offended.

"Of course, they did. But they also helped convince me to do it, indirectly."

"How?" Benny asks.

"One night, after too many beers, my friends were complaining about their girlfriends making them watch romantic movies all the time. That got me thinking—why *do* women love rom-coms? My drunk self concluded, with the help of my idiot friends, that romances offer a bit of everything. That's what I wanted for my books. Most genres are one-note when it comes to emotion. Horror books are scary. Thrillers are... thrilling. Mysteries are mysterious, and, well, you get the idea. A good romance is everything—scary, thrilling, mysterious, happy, sad, funny, dark. I wanted a genre with an emotional depth that could be anything I wanted it to be. Romance fits me best."

I smirk deviously. "And it has the highest readership of any other genre, so now my friends come over and drink *my* beers, swim in *my* pool, and ask me how to romance their wives, so they don't tease me much anymore."

Laughter fills the room again.

"Where do you get your ideas?" Julio asks.

"Everywhere." My eyes return to Rowan's. "My neighbors feature in my stories often."

"Oh, does that mean Ms. Mackey will be in your next book?" Eddie asks.

"We'll probably all be in the next one," she says, smiling.

"Yes. I pull from real life all the time. When I write a love story, it's almost subconscious for me—putting the people I care about in it."

The class moves on to literary devices, techniques, and my process—I just try to be honest. I admit that every first draft sucks and has to be rewritten. I confess to getting angry at salesmen and Jehovah's Witnesses at my front door when they interrupt my writing and being an asshole generally when words aren't flowing. I talk about my music playlists and how I organize them by writing moods—pissed off, sexy, upbeat, ominous, beast mode, love sucks, and so on. I even share my insecurities about imposter syndrome and anxiety when someone first reads my work.

Turning to Rowan, my eyes narrow. "Tell the truth. What did you think of *Bare*?"

Her soft, easy grin answers my question. "It's my favorite Jack Graham romance to date."

"Really? Your *favorite* Jack Graham romance?" My brow cocks, and she blushes. Hard. This is turning out to be a very good day.

Always chase.

She clears her throat. "It was the extensive annotating that did it."

Her students groan, but I laugh.

Then, almost like she catches the vibe between me and her teacher, Mia speaks up again, her doe-eyes huge behind her glasses. "How do you know if you're in love?"

Now, I'm blushing. "Damn, Mia, you've brought your A-game today."

She giggles.

"Okay, how do you know if you're in love..." I square my shoulders as the class leans forward for the answer. "I've asked this question often, and everyone has different answers. A neighbor knew he was in love when she laughed at a terrible joke to make him feel good. My Aunt Susan fell for Uncle Rob because he kept showing up to her tennis matches even though he hated tennis. My parents claim love at first sight—not sure I buy that—but they've been together nearly forty years, so anything's possible…

"But my favorite answer is what my brother Devin told me when he was your age. It's love when home is no longer a place but a person, and that's where you always want to be."

A long, silent beat breaks when the bell rings. Students moan with irritation.

"Ms. Mackey, if we get permission from our other teachers, can we come back?" Julio asks.

"Of course, if they agree. But you have to give up your seats for the incoming class."

Satisfied, they file out, promising to return. The classroom empties.

Rowan stands, kicking her cushioned foot-chair and losing her ice pack. I rush to her side, bracing her as she winces.

"Where do you think you're going?"

"To you. I owe you a huge—"

"No. You don't."

"I said things I didn't mean," she says desperately. "It's just seeing you with her—it was a shock—"

"You had every right to be angry. I should've considered that you might see us. She came over late, upset about her fiancé. We talked—that's all. There is nothing between us anymore. Hell, we spent half the time talking about you."

"Me? Oh, no."

"No, don't worry about it. This is my fault—"

"But I'm grateful you're here, anyway. I didn't think you'd—"

"Rowan."

Her pleading face relaxes when she meets my smile.

"I will *always* show up for you."

She gapes breathlessly like I've said the perfect words. *Finally.* This morning's drama dissipates into nothing, like a meaningless spat from ages ago that we can't remember, ghost memories that no longer matter.

I slide my hands to hers. "Let me back into your life. Please, I'll do anything. Keep the sign up if you need it, but rescue me, Rowan—my love, my pen, my dick."

She blushes again—she's pretty in pink. "I can't believe I said that."

"*That* will definitely feature in my next book."

"Not my best moment," she groans.

"Go out with me tonight—just you and me."

"Yes," falls from her lips with barely a thought. "After we take our signs down."

"Really? Signs down?"

"Yes."

Heat rises in my gut with the way she looks at me—her blue eyes fix on mine, deeply and wholeheartedly, like there's magic there that no one understands but us. It's a very good day.

I ease her into her chair, re-situate her foot, and grab her water-logged ice pack.

"Which one of your minions can we send for more ice?"

She chuckles at the way I say it and finds a willing volunteer from the students filtering in.

Some of the same faces return, which happens for every class until it's standing-room only. I answer their questions until my voice is raspy and sign their books until my fingers cramp. And finally, I turn the questions on them, asking about reading choices.

The first period kids are quick to tell me about Julio's grandfather's poetry.

"He's like... deep and wordsmithy," Ashley sums up.

"It really makes me think how lucky I have it," Eddie adds.

Curious, I ask Julio to share a passage, and he picks one he's read to the others already—when Dominic Martinez first sets eyes on his family after being apart for two years. First in Spanish and then in English, Julio recites the narrative to seventy mesmerized students, and even I tear up at its conclusion.

"Is he still alive?" I ask boldly.

"Yes."

"He should publish. Think he'd be interested in talking with my agent about getting his work out there?"

Julio's shock changes to excitement in a blink. "Yes, I'll call him this afternoon. Thanks, Mr. Graham."

I don't need thanks. Dominic Martinez has a powerful voice that needs to be heard.

When Tom first suggested this classroom visit, I didn't like the idea at all. I thought it might be too hard, being back here. Coastal High is where Devin secured his kingship as the coolest guy in school, and I went from his nerdy, awkward brother to the angry loner who lost him. The walls could've felt haunted.

Rowan seems to understand this the same way she reads between the lines of my books. During her planning period, she insists on hobbling to the gym, where Devin's picture still perches beside our regional baseball championship trophy.

"Tell me more about Devin. What was he like?"

"He was an asshole. Sometimes. He pantsed me in the eighth grade in front of the cheerleading tryouts. Embarrassed the hell out of me and made me undatable for about... two years... But most days, um, he could bring out the best in anyone. He had this annoying Andy Samberg vibe, which made him stupidly popular. He was everyone's friend."

"Kinda like you."

My wry grin appears briefly. "Eh, I grew into being a good person, sort of. For Devin, it was... automatic."

She lets me ramble on about how we wouldn't have won without Devin's double play in the bottom of the ninth. We detour to the library, where she pulls Devin's senior yearbook off the shelf, prompting more stories. Not that I need much urging. Revisiting good memories feels like being in them again.

Talking about him to Rowan feels even better.

Her last-period class fills beyond capacity, but no one seems to mind being shoulder-to-shoulder. It goes by fast with questions. The final bell rings, bringing on applause and thanks from students as they leave.

Parents flood the room next in a not-so-subtle ploy to combine pick-up with a book signing. Teachers show up, too, hugging my books like treasures. It's been so long since I bothered with a book signing, but now I wonder why I stopped—it's damn cool that people resonate with what I write, and definitely more of an ego boost than a hassle. Rowan jumps to the rescue, ready to shoo them out, but I tell her it's okay. I sign every book, pose for a thousand selfies, and even get on a FaceTime call with a fan's mom in another state.

When Julio is the only one left, we call his grandfather and get permission to share his work. Then, Julio hands me a thick-tipped Sharpie. "Sign our wall?"

I glance at the homage to timeless classics, unsure. "Really? I'm not—"

"Yes, you are," Rowan counters sternly.

I pick a space on the sandy beach near the black cat that looks like Edgar. I bookend my signature with an off-centered heart, like the one scratched into the closet door by Corey and Devin.

When Julio leaves, we stand alone by the mark I've left, me bracing her with my arm. She looks as exhilarated as I feel. We latch on to each other, and I whisper, "Thank you for today. I've never been happier to call myself a writer."

This sudden truth makes me realize how closed-off I've been, pumping out manuscripts while limiting my life to one small block for inspiration—no wonder I had writer's block. I need more. Not just more of Rowan—though, yes, her, too. But more purpose. More... *life* in my life.

And now that my head is finally out of my ass, I plan to keep it that way.

Thirty-Six

JACK

"Sure you're up for this?" I ask, eyeing her wrapped ankle as she hobbles out her front door.

"Yes, as long as we aren't taking a walking tour of Wilmington. Or going anywhere fancy. Flip-flop casual?"

"Like urgent care?" I grin.

"I promise, it's only a sprain."

"Fine. A casual dinner, and I'll do my best to keep you off your feet."

Blushing, she drops her keys while locking the door. Both bending over, we bump heads and then blurt out laughing like teenagers in a rom-com.

"Never put this moment in your books, Jack," she warns as I retrieve her keys. "Too cheesy."

"Oh, a classic head-bump situation is too simplistic for my books. I prefer my meet-cutes in rehab or along roadside ditches."

"I believe those are called meet-rough-and-toughs." She giggles. "Or meet-streets? Meet-mean-streets? Meet-creeps?"

"You're a dork," I say, though I'm laughing.

"Oh, a meet-dork is what's happening right now. I'm an expert at those."

I extend my elbow for her to latch onto. "Come on. I promise you can be as dorky as you want. I'll even encourage it."

"Oh, I never hold back when it comes to dorkiness."

I open the passenger door, holding her hand as she lowers into the seat. "You look gorgeous for a dork, though. If it helps."

She eyes her outfit—a breezy little skirt, revealing enough of her legs to make me happy, a teal top that brings out her sea-blue eyes, and flip-flops. It's nothing like the dressy get-up with heels she sported on that first date I witnessed years ago, but softer and sexier. It's what she picked for me, unguarded and easy.

"Thanks. Oh, you could grab your book. We could talk about it over dinner if you want."

"No, that's okay. Tonight's about you and me. No book talk."

"*No* book talk?" She repeats, wide-eyed. "That might be hard, but I'm game."

I close her inside the car just as my phone pings—another alert from the *Daisy Chain*. Rose and Vernon have been active since we arrived home, posting pics of our signs coming down and the subsequent reply-alls of relief and happiness from the neighborhood.

I groan, getting in the driver's seat as I eye the newest alert—it's us five minutes ago at her door. Of course, that's nothing compared to the one they sent this morning—me in a towel on my lawn arguing with Rowan. I must talk to them about boundaries.

Rowan sighs, switching her phone to silent. "Let's add no neighborhood talk to our shortlist. Huh?"

"Agreed." I flip my phone to silent, too.

I take her to Billy's Cape Side, tucked alongside the Cape Fear River on the outskirts of downtown, with ample parking out front, so she doesn't need to walk far. We're seated on the back deck under wide-reaching oaks draped in swaying Spanish moss that crowd the riverbank. Sunset glitters on the calm water like it's been gone over with a gold-tipped brush and mimics the glow of the small lantern on our table. A lone blue heron stands regally at the edge of the bank, on guard, it seems. Or perhaps, just enjoying the view.

"Does this qualify as flip-flop casual?"

"It's perfect." She sips her frosty beer and ponders the menu. "So, no books. No neighbors. Whatever will we talk about?"

"Sex?" The word pops out as a joke, but I immediately regret it. Yes, it's on my mind—it always is when I'm with her—but I feel like an ass for mentioning it. "Shit. Sorry. That's inappropriate first date talk."

"No, it isn't." Her crystalline eyes narrow, and her head tilts in a question. "We should be able to talk about anything, right?"

"Yes, but I was only joking. We don't have to go there yet."

"Too late to take it back now." She leans forward, peering at me with a daring grin. "What do you want to know?"

"Everything. Anything," I say honestly, hunting for the right question. "Let's start with something easy. Best sex ever."

She laughs before taking a healthy chug of her beer. The waitress appears, pen in hand.

"Want to share a pizza?" I ask when she seems puzzled over what to order.

"Absolutely," Rowan says.

I order a margherita pizza and another round. The waitress bounces off, and I take in the other diners on the patio—a family of five takes the long table in the far corner, an older couple eyes us from the middle, and two twenty-somethings laugh over mixed drinks at the bar. It's a slow weekday night.

"Robbie Jones," she announces, bringing my eyes to hers. "I was seventeen. We were stationed at Fort Eustis in Virginia then. Robbie and I would sneak out of our houses and meet at the park. He was clumsy and awkward but was the first guy who didn't mind this."

She motions to her face with a light wave of her hand. "One night, we talked until late. It started drizzling. Lying in the damp grass, looking up at the stars, it happened so naturally that sex seemed part of our conversation, gentle and easy. He was also... attentive, not what I expected." She glances upwards in consideration. "I often wondered if he studied for it like he would a test."

"Probably. All teenage boys *study* for it," I say, putting the word *study* in air quotes.

She laughs. "It paid off for me—I had the best time. Those two months with Robbie are still the best relationship I've ever had. So, I'm one of the few weirdos alive who can say her best sex was her first time."

"That *is* a rarity. What happened with Robbie?"

"Oh, what always happened. We moved." She shifts her leg under the table, wincing.

"Give me your leg," I say, motioning under the table. "It needs to be elevated."

She looks suspicious. "Are you sure?"

"Definitely."

She kicks off her flip-flop and gingerly eases her foot against my leg. I rest my hand over it, letting my fingers run gently along the top, massaging her. She looks as surprised by my attentiveness as she was by Robbie's.

"I haven't had the best partners," she admits, shrugging. "Trent was... rough and angry, triggering, and had me running to a therapist, where I discovered that in a good relationship, I'm actually hyper-sexual because it makes me feel beautiful, and few things do."

I shut my gaping mouth as soon as I realize I'm doing it. Not only is my girlfriend—*is it all right to call her that?*—truly amazing, but the alluring confidence that drew me to her in the first place has returned with renewed energy.

Her eyes narrow as she studies me. "Too much information?"

"God, no. I love your openness."

"After Airlie, I feel like I can tell you anything," she says with a crease on her brow as if she's only just realizing it.

"You can. And you should. Tell me more about this... hyper-sexuality and all the ways I can make you feel beautiful."

"No, no. It's your turn. Best sex ever."

Our beers arrive with our pizza, but despite the interruption, Rowan's eyes stay on mine in a curious challenge as my hand drifts slowly up her soft leg, tightening around her firm calf. *Ah, these legs.*

As soon as our server leaves, I say, "This might sound trashy—I don't remember her name."

She lets a relieved sigh escape, probably because it's not Evie. And it really isn't, not that I'd dare bring her up. Evie's a lazy lover.

"It was my junior year of college. My roommate dragged me to a frat party. It's cliche—I know—but I met a girl. A senior. We connected over cheap beer, loud music, and *Harry Potter*, oddly. She asked me to her room and told me *exactly* what she liked. I listened and paid attention. The more she was into it, the more I enjoyed it. It made me better at it, frankly. No matter how much *studying* a guy does, a confident woman is his best teacher. Turned out to be the most useful thing I learned in college."

"A *real* life skill." Then, she blushes as if she's imagining us—I know I am. "Um, can you believe we're talking about this?"

"Look, I promise I had perfectly acceptable first date conversation cued in my head, if not for my Freudian slip."

Another chuckle rises behind her bite of pizza. "Oh, like what?"

"Like... how is it with Sara gone?"

"Quiet, a little sad, but okay. BFFs for life."

"Ah, there's that dorkiness you promised. I thought you were a crazed do-gooder adding a foster kid to your life of service. She was such an asshole in the beginning. Are you going to put yourself through it again?"

Based on her pinched brow and staring off into her beer, this question seems to challenge her more than talking about sex. "I'd love to do it again."

"It's difficult—letting a stranger into your home and hoping for the best, but when I imagine it from the other side—the kid who lost a parent or stability, whatever the case, I think... damn, that's so much worse. You're good to take the risk."

"The best things require the most risk. Besides, I think I got more out of it than she did."

"You and the rest of us." A cheesy grin wraps my face as I tilt my beer toward her.

The twinkling lights overhead reflect in her eyes like specks of gold as she peers into the river's darkness. "You were right about Mom," she says after hesitating. "She met Reggie at a crowded café when they shared the last table. Love at first sight, they say. They've been dating for over a year."

"*Over* a year? That's a long time. You okay?"

She shrugs lightly. "He's wonderful, and they're annoyingly sweet together. They're the newest old couple you'll ever meet. I'm a little sad she couldn't tell me sooner, but I'm thrilled for them. I have you to thank for that."

"For what?"

"Preparing me for it. If not for our talk in the hallway, I would've gotten hung up on her not telling me instead of what matters—Mom finding love."

"You would've handled it fine." My finger traces the curve of her knee.

Her back straightens as she sits up. "It's more than that, Jack. Your books helped Mom believe in love again. Without them, I wonder if she would've been open to sharing a table with a stranger at a café. It's like you prepared her for meeting Reggie."

"I can't *possibly* take credit for that."

"You should. It's more proof that writing love stories is what you're meant to do, and your work matters."

Her words and the sincere gleam in her eyes stir something in me I can't quite describe—me, the fucking wordsmith. My work has always mattered to my fans and especially my bank account. But that she believes it contributes to a greater good brings on an emotional surge in me—a complicated mix of pride, hope, fear, and determination. I want to pen a thousand books just to keep her faith in me.

"Um, you're definitely giving me too much credit, but thank you. And cut it out. I can't get choked up on our first date. I'll never live it down."

She laughs and leans forward again. "Fair enough, but there's one more thing I need to thank you for—just one."

My eyes narrow with angsty suspicion.

She rubs her bare arms, leaning closer. "I told my students the real story. Not the whole story, of course. But that it was an assault, not a kitchen accident."

Once again, I gape at her, impressed. "How'd they take it?"

"You met them. They're amazing. I came clean about lying, and they offered instant forgiveness. I even think they put the word out to the rest of the classes not to bring it up because no one has since. It's such a relief for me—I hate lying."

"You're really bad at it, anyway," I say as her hands run up and down her arms again. "I'm proud of you."

"Without our talks, I never would've been ready."

"Again, too much credit. But you're welcome... And you're cold. I have a hoodie in the car. I'll get it."

She opens her mouth to argue, but I'm already out of my seat, gently placing her foot on my empty chair. Walking away, I take in the patio. Kids run around the corner table and their tired parents. The twenty-something breaks into a delighted cackle as she rubs her date's thigh at the bar. I weave behind the graying couple at the middle table and hear the bearded man say, "God created make-up... She should do more to hide it... damn ugly..."

Anger spikes in me like a fever, nearly rendering me delirious. It's only out of consideration for Rowan that I continue my mission rather than yank the asshole from his chair and beat some manners into him. I want nothing to ruin our night or erase that gorgeous smile from her face.

On my way back, our eyes lock across the patio, and her light side-smile matches mine. But hers falls when the middle couple laughs, drawing her eyes to them. I wonder if she heard them, but she probably didn't have to—she said herself that she's hyper-sensitive to staring. She runs a hand through her hair, combing it downward like she feels exposed.

Edging around the older couple, the wife gives me a grinning once-over, whispering something to her husband before laughing. I hear only one word—*opposites*—as I go by. Assholes.

Rowan's visibly relieved when I reach the table. I slip the zippered hoodie on her shoulders, leaning close to her ear. "Everything okay?"

"Yes, thanks for the hoodie."

"No problem." Instead of taking my seat and resuming foot duty, I steal another chair from a table nearby and set it next to hers.

As I move my plate and beer to my new side, she asks, "What're you doing?"

I sit, completely blocking her view of the nosy couple. "I want to be closer. Easier to charm you like this, and the way things go with us, this may be my only chance."

Her uneasiness dissipates with a laugh. "Not your *only* chance, I think."

My leg brushes against her thigh under the table as my fingers skirt her knee. "That's the third-best thing I've heard today."

"Third best?"

"Well, after you agreeing to go out and your awful attempts at renaming a meet-cute." I chuckle, tickling the soft skin under her knee. It's fun—watching her flush. If the hoodie doesn't warm her, my touches will.

The waitress approaches and asks if we need anything. I turn to Rowan. "Want to get out of here?"

She nods enthusiastically.

"We'll need a box," I say, pointing to the leftover pizza. "The bill... and we'll take the bills for the couple at the bar and the family in the corner. Don't tell them until after we've left, but make sure they know it was us."

The waitress looks stunned, slightly confused, as she bounces away.

"What are you doing?"

"Creating a scene." I lean closer, and she follows my gaze to the dining room. "The kids look tired, so the family will leave next. They'll ask for the bill, and the server will say, *'Oh, the hot couple in the corner took care of it.'* They'll be fucking ecstatic, attracting attention because, well, it's a stretch eating out for them anyway. But they'll leave, and the other couples will be like, *'aw.'* Then, the bar couple will go next—she's already giving him the 'come hither' look. Again, the waitress will announce that it's covered. They'll fucking go berserk, taking pics and posting on social media about paying it forward and shit like that... Following the scene so far?"

She nods, her brow pinched.

"Okay, good. Then, the couple in the middle will catch on to the vibe and ask for their check, already thinking it'll be covered. When the waitress delivers their unpaid bill, they'll be like, *'Why didn't the hot couple treat us like they did the others?'* One of them—probably the wife—will say, *'Maybe it was because you were staring too much, Gerald.'* Or better yet, they'll think they were overheard talking about us and feel bad about what they said. Doesn't matter. From this day forward, they'll remember the night they could've gotten a free meal but didn't because they stared and whispered like assholes. So, maybe they won't be so shitty next time. The end."

Her pouty lips part like she's breathless, and the lights in her eyes sparkle more as they fill with tears. Is it anger? Frustration? Sadness? I can't tell. Only I expect she's pissed at me for interfering like volatile is our default. We started this day with anger—is that how we'll finish it?

I move so close I can feel her breath on my lips. "I promise I'll never embarrass you or make you uncomfortable like with Renita again... but doing nothing isn't always the answer, either."

I start to say more, but it's too late.

Her lips torpedo mine before another word comes out. And holy shit—it's a desperate, smiling kiss that makes me want to ravish her right here on the table. Her tongue slides against mine like a curled finger saying, 'Come here.' She grips my bare cheeks and does to my mouth what I hope she does to the rest of me—explore, play, love. I fist the collar of the hoodie, dragging her closer. Every nerve in my body twitches with energy like her lips are a pleasure epicenter, switching me on.

Until I have to stop. "First best thing to happen to me today." I'm breathless this time.

"That may be the sweetest thing anyone's done for me."

"Not too romantic for you?"

"Well, you can't buy half the restaurant's dinners every time we go out."

"Why not? We'll change the world, one dinner at a time."

She stays close to me, giggling at the idea. But slowly, her eyes pinch together like she's working out a math problem. "It's strange... this has actually happened to me before."

"What? Amazing kisses? I should hope so. You're really good at it."

Confusion edges out her soft smile. "No, a stranger paying for my dinner. On a very bad night for me. Weird, right?"

Good at playing dumb, I lean away, looking for our server. "Not really. Shit like that happens all the time."

"No, it doesn't, and definitely not to me."

"Sir? Your bills?" The waitress edges the narrow notebook onto the table before boxing our leftover pizza. Under Rowan's contemplative scrutiny, I scribble across the bills, glad for the distraction. It's not a life-changing secret or anything, but I don't know how she'll take it, knowing I've kept something from her since day one.

As soon as I close the notebook, she gets up to leave, and I follow her lead. On our way out, the middle-aged couple eyes us critically as we pass.

Rowan plasters on her best fake smile. "Have a good night," she tells them, earning a devious grin from me. She hooks her arm in mine as we exit the building.

"What now?"

"Home."

There's no tone in her voice, but I'm disappointed and a little worried that her wheels are still turning over that night two years ago when she got a free meal, and I nailed my final scene for *The Other Us*.

Once home, I help her hobble to her front door, under watchful eyes. Shadows move in Rose and Vernon's window, and Tom sits on his front porch, facts that seem to annoy her as she glances from them to me.

Under the soft porch light, she faces me. "It was you, wasn't it?"

"Yes."

"Why? You felt sorry for me?"

"That asshole treated you like shit—of course, I felt sorry for you. But I was drawn to you before that."

"Why? My face?"

"First, your legs." I step closer, shoving my hands in my pockets to keep them off her. "You have the sexiest legs I've ever seen. Your poise held my attention, too—with your dark hair and your little green dress. After the asshole, I admired your confidence. You stayed for a good meal—that alone should've earned you a free one. And better wine. Your soulful eyes drew me in next—they're so blue and beautiful. Then, I saw your scars, but for me, they were a footnote to a much better story... and still are. I've never had a better day than this one."

She gnaws at her bottom lip, and I fear I've messed up. Again. Worse, she digs out her keys and then extends her hand, looking pensive. "Thank you for a nice time."

A fucking handshake—I can't believe it.

As my heart damn near breaks and our hands rise and fall in business-like formality, she glances at the street before her eyes return to mine.

A smirk perks on her mouth. "Meet me at the back door in five minutes."

I'm there in three.

Thirty-Seven

ROWAN

Jack says nothing when the door slides open but steps directly into a full-on kiss that makes my breath hitch and my lower half alight with electric tingles—a power surge through my spine. Pressed tightly together, every muscle in his chest tenses under my fingers, and his veins pop as his hands move over me, arms to back to face like he can't decide where to touch me. I can't decide either—my hands cross with his in a strange tangle as I move from his biceps to his neck and then over his cheek. Our intensity causes me to stumble and sends pain jolting through my bum ankle, breaking our kiss.

"You okay?" He hovers near my lips like he doesn't want to venture too far away.

"*I'm so okay.* I've never had a better day, either. Stay with me."

"Always." His forehead rests against mine, and his dark eyes penetrate me. "I'm yours. Whatever you want."

"Is this the part where I tell you *exactly* what to do?" A breathless chuckle escapes, teasing about his best-sex-ever story.

He laughs, pressing further against me while his fingers slip under the hem of my shirt. "If you wish. I promise to be extremely *attentive*."

The word inspires a giggle. His fingertips dance over my stomach, making my heart race and forcing a sharp inhale.

"Tell me what you want," he whispers, his hand rising under my shirt, his fingers edging lightly over the top of my lacy bra.

"You already know," I gasp as his finger delicately brushes the hard tip of my breast.

His brow cocks curiously as I untuck his shirt and hook him closer by his waistband. His muscles tense under my touch, and his lips curl as they close in on mine. "Do I?"

A coy grin rises on my flushed cheeks. "I want to be ravished, cherished, and fucking adored."

He laughs, his fingers sweeping across my chest like feathers. "Anything else?"

"Yes... I want to *see* you." Even admitting that aloud arouses me.

With a low rumble like a purr, he pushes me against the back of the couch in a wild, tongue-laced kiss. A soft moan ekes out when I wobble on my leg again.

He leans over and scoops me up. "Hold on to me."

My hands loop around his neck, and my head rests against his shoulder. It feels like a damsel-in-distress moment, but one I definitely like. I'm weightless as he swings me across the living room and down the hall, careful of my dangling feet.

He sets me on the bed's edge, and standing before me, he kicks off his shoes and pulls off his shirt. The soft bedroom light illuminates his form and the artwork across his chest. Lifting to my knees on the bed's edge, I run my fingers over the fiery books on his arm before kissing them. Vines with thorns and wilting flowers travel over his arms and torso, connecting the images together. My mouth slowly travels upwards, whispering the book titles between kisses.

"*Fahrenheit 451.*" My fingertips trace the next ones—The Cheshire Cat, a triangle with a Big Brother eye and a hand holding the skull of Yorick. "*Alice in Wonderland, 1984, Hamlet.*"

He watches me intently, submissively, letting me do just as I want. I switch to his other arm, resting his hand against my hip as my tongue follows the artful patterns. "*The Lord of the Flies, And Then There Were None, The Black Cat,*" I whisper. I smile as goosebumps appear under my breath.

He moans sharply when my kisses grow more intense over his neck and collarbone. Nibbling him. Tasting him. Letting my tongue drift over the veins popping across his chest. His hands wrap around my thighs and up my skirt, kneading me with his fingers.

Over his heart, I trace the outline of the *Calvin and Hobbes* version of him and his brother headed toward the baseball field before resting my head against it and giving it a soft kiss.

My lips travel lower on his chest. "*To Kill a Mockingbird, Harry Potter, The Hunger Games.*"

The images end over his rippled abdomen. "Turn around," I say. His hands drag over me as he obeys.

The vines and flowers wrap around him, framing his largest tattoo like a window.

"The Lonely Mountain from *The Hobbit.*" Silhouettes of the ragtag dwarves, Bilbo, and Gandalf climb up the side while Smaug hovers at the top. The dragon is red with yellow eyes, and the detail is exquisite—each scale, every tooth, the red and orange fire escaping his mouth.

"Devin's favorite book," Jack says as I trace the images. "When he was at his worst, it was the only book he'd let me read to him. *The Hobbit* was Devin's heaven... or at least, what he hoped it'd be like. I hope he's fighting orcs right now."

"Or being ravished by a hot elf," I say with a small laugh, missing someone I never met.

Jack turns in my hands, and I look up at him. "Yeah, he'd probably enjoy that more. Sorry, I didn't mean to—"

"No, don't. You're beautiful." It's all I can think to say. He is all muscle and art and slick warmth. The longing in his eyes grows as I undo his pants and pull them down. He kicks them away at his feet, leaving only his boxer briefs.

"You have no idea what you're doing to me," he says, breathless. His hands grip my legs, dragging me against him until I'm on fire.

"Your turn." His voice is barely above a whisper, breathy and desperate. "I want to see you."

He kisses me. Lips parting mine. Tongue teasing mine. Until I'm breathless and wanting, and him pulling my shirt over my head is the only reasonable next step. He eases me out of my skirt, too—my lacy black Victoria's Secret bra and panties aren't so secret anymore.

Only that's not what draws his focus, not at first. In the warm light with no collar or scarf to hide them, he takes me in, studies me, lets his fingers trace the rugged marks along my cheek, down my neck, and cresting my heart. There's more feeling in those places than I remember, at least under his touch. Softly, sweetly, his gentle exploration has me breathless and moaning and eager to take him. His lips follow. His tongue. Touching the untouchable. Loving the unlovable. Wanting me as I am.

"*You're* beautiful," he counters, lips sliding over my heart. He unhooks my bra one-handed and pulls it away. Then, eases my panties around my hips and down my legs as I lean backward to the bed. I'm bare. And given the breathless, desperate, loving look in his eyes, beautiful, just as he said.

He meets me on the bed, and my legs wrap around his midsection, pulling him to me. He devours me, neck, chest, breasts—wild and gentle at once. His fingers graze the warmth between my legs—his touch alone might be my undoing.

Only I'm not ready. In a swift maneuver, I flip him on his back. My fingers travel along the sandy roughness of his cheeks, down the wave of his broad chest, and over the tight ripples of his stomach. A moan rumbles from him as my hand slips under his boxers and finds him deliciously hard and ready for me. I tug the last of his clothes away.

"Fuck, Rowan," he groans as I take him in my mouth, his voice desperate and surprised. I'm surprised, too—this has never been my go-to. Trent made it a requirement, ruining it for me. But now, with Jack, it's as if he holds the secret combination that unlocks the *real* me. And the real me enjoys ravishing *him*.

His hand threads through my hair, moving with my rhythm, but only for a moment before he stops me. "I'm too close."

He twists me around this time, lavishing me with wet kisses and teasing touches like he can't get enough. Face between my legs, his hot tongue makes me rake my hand through his hair and cry out—a first for me.

Another first—his *attentiveness* doesn't stop until I come. *Twice.*

One thrust inside me elicits moans from us both. It won't take much more for either of us.

"Damn," he growls. "You're perfect, Rowan. Fucking perfect."

He watches me from the bed as I shift my hips against him for the final ride. I'm quivering and aching for him—I *knew* it would be like this. A stake has been driven through time. Before us. And after. Sex like this is practically a new discovery that'll require decades of study and exploration—a prospect that thrills me to no end.

Nearing the end, he sits up, holding me tight against him as explosions and tremors overtake us. Even when they come to a slow stop, we remain entangled. Breathless. Clinging. Happy.

"You're shaking," he whispers, pushing hair away from my face.

"So are you."

He smirks. "First best thing to happen to me today... or any day. This. You. Us."

"Me, too." A chuckle slips out. "This. You. Us... sounds like a book title."

"Uh-oh. I'm definitely rubbing off on you if you're starting to think in book titles." He lays his head against my chest, holding me closer. "There's something I have to know."

His sudden seriousness surprises me. "What?"

He edges away, locking eyes. "Tell me the truth—was I better than Robbie?"

I curl into him, laughing. "Was I better than no-name college girl?"

"Fuck yes. Worlds better. I'm seriously considering marrying you just to secure a lifetime of that."

"That better not be a proposal."

"Hell no. I've already... well, you'll see. Stop distracting me. The question was—"

"Yes, better than Robbie."

"Thank God." In a swift move, he twists me onto the bed and hovers over me, kissing my face and neck and making me laugh hysterically.

Laughter moves into talking and, later on, another sweet and sexy round in the shower—my idea—that leaves us trembling and tired but blissfully content.

Then, sometime, late into our first night together and still damp from our shower, we fall asleep, wrapped against each other like we're afraid one of us might slip away during the night.

The gray morning arrives. My eyes open against Jack's bare chest just as I remember falling asleep. He's propped up with pillows, one arm draped around my shoulder and one hand on Edgar, curled to his other side. We are addictively warm and cozy. I want to watch him sleep, but my shift causes him to stir.

His eyes flutter, and he smiles—the easiest, most affirming smile—and my heart swells with elation like I've climbed a summit to see the gorgeous view everyone raves about for myself. *This* is what I've always wanted. To feel beautiful at first glance.

He brushes my smile with his fingertip. "Rowan... good morning. Come here and kiss me."

Edgar stands, stretches, and jumps from the bed as if cued—he doesn't want to see that.

I lean up, planting kisses on Jack's chest and neck before reaching his lips. He laughs as my hands wander over him.

"Let's stay in bed all day," he says between kissing me.

"Can't. I have a job to get to, remember?"

"Hmm, is it take-your-boyfriend-to-work day again?"

I smirk over his joke and the word *boyfriend*. "Afraid not. But after yesterday, I'm sure you'll still be our main topic of discussion."

"Aw, I won't see you blush whenever you hear my name."

A laugh rumbles out, and I blush just thinking about it. "No, but you can spend the day thinking of ways to make me blush when I come home."

He moans in delight, pulling me closer. "I won't be good for much else today with you occupying my headspace. I'll never shower again without thinking of you."

"Me, neither. We should just always shower together—make it our thing."

"Oh, we'll have *many* things," he assures me. "But yes—never showering alone sounds like a good plan. So, how about I help you get ready for work, huh?"

I agree with a deep kiss, and he carries me to the bathroom.

Thirty-Eight

JACK

Damn... this woman. I can't describe what she's done to me, what she *means* to me—*me, the fucking wordsmith.*

Rowan drifts to sleep on my shoulder, her breathing soft and rhythmic. It's late. I'm wired. But more content than I've ever been. Her gorgeous leg is draped over mine. My fingers lightly strum her bare lower back. Her arm lays across my stomach, fingers over my heart. We're warm against each other, though we're naked and still damp from the shower.

Ah, the shower.

I replay the memory, fiddling with the damp ends of her hair on my chest.

"Tell me what you're thinking," I asked her when our after-sex conversation drifted into silence.

She laughed, her cheeks reddening. "I can't say."

"How come?"

"It might seem... I don't know... like too much."

My eyes must've widened to the size of chestnuts because she giggled at my expression. "Now, you have to tell me." My arms tightened around her while I tickled her with quick kisses—cheeks, neck, nose. "Tell me now, or I'll do this forever."

"This isn't so bad," she snickered.

I vampire-bit her neck, turning her laughs into playful screams. Then, I went for her lips, my teasing kisses turning into serious ones. "Tell me."

"Shower. Let's get in the shower," came out in a breath.

"Damn. You. Me. Shower. I love it... and I fucking love you for saying it." My breath caught on the words as they spilled out, relieved and surprised at myself. "I do, you know. I love you, Rowan."

I almost winced when I said it, fearing it was too much. But the love for her that I'd been toying around with had suddenly strengthened. A tidal wave rushing over me. A confession, once again, crashing at her feet.

But I doubted she was ready for it.

In her silence, I scrambled for the right words to get us to the other side of this—to free her from any pressure. I didn't need her to say it back. I didn't need anything beyond her.

But the words came anyway—soft, sweet, smiling. "I love you, too."

I expelled a breathy sigh—I couldn't help it. Those words crumbled the last of her walls, and I loved her even more for saying them.

Still, I played it cool. "It's settled then. Shower it is."

I used shower time to study Rowan's geography like there'd be a test afterward. I memorized her slopes, curves, plateaus, peaks, ridges, and valleys first with my eyes and then my hands as I washed her with a soapy cloth. She moaned with every touch like each hit her erogenous zone. And *that's* what she wanted—for me to see all of her, there, where neither of us could hide. I read her nakedness, her openness, her confidence, like a promise between us. *I trust you. I want you. I love you.*

Then, with those glorious legs of hers wrapped around me, I pinned her against the tiles, hot and cold together, and took her. Deep. Wet. Hard-pressed.

Damn... this woman. She isn't just sexy and intense and fucking amazing, she's warm and funny and familiar and everything I never knew I wanted until her. My world has shifted onto her axis—I'll never be the same again.

And I don't want to be.

I was serious when I said I'd marry her. I'd ask her today if I didn't think it'd scare the shit out of her.

Morning arrives. She foregoes her run because of her leg, and that means more shower time with me. I fix her breakfast as she hobbles around the kitchen, shoving things into her bag.

"Your career is putting a serious dent in my playtime," I tell her, handing her a plate of eggs and toast.

She smirks. "What're you doing today?"

"Gutters and drains with the boys for Hurricane Nadine," I report, eyeing the texts from Vernon and Tom. "Fantasizing about you... oh, and writing."

"Don't do the fantasizing while you're with the boys, huh? That'd be weird."

"Understood. What's your day like?"

She shrugs, grinning. "I'm talking books with a bunch of cool kids. Jealous?"

"Definitely."

At the back door, she kisses me goodbye with a skeptical look, as if parting ways for a few hours might break the spell we're under, and we'll be back to cordially volatile neighbors by the time she gets home. Her default is to expect good things not to last, and I get it—most of the time, they don't. "See you later?"

Damn, this woman. "I'll be waiting for you."

After another lingering kiss, I leave her, crossing her backyard and slipping into my own. Ideas swirl, thinking of Rowan, her class, and all she does for them. Teachers must be so many things beyond educators—managers, accountants, organizers, creators, shrinks. It's a wonder anyone takes it on, especially for so little pay. I think of Rowan's binder bookshelf, her classroom pantry, and her raiding my library because she couldn't get bestsellers at the public one—they should give her a book budget, at least. Teachers give so much and expect so little in return.

Harper Lee purrs at my feet as I feed her. Then, desperate for my laptop, I head to my office.

I started a new book as soon as I finished *Bare*, a paranormal romance called *Strangers Together* about a woman starting over after an abusive relationship. She moves into a condo only to discover that the entire complex is haunted by a ghost—the dead brother of the reclusive man who lives on the top floor. Desperate to see his brother happy so he can finally cross over, the ghost does what he can (which is limited) to bring the residents together—that is, get his brother to connect with other people so he won't take his own life. Only his plans, ranging from mischievous to creepy, continuously backfire. Until the woman comes along. Having been through something horrible, she's more open to the ghost, and soon, she finds herself wanting to learn more about the mysterious man upstairs. It's lighthearted and sad and probably the strangest thing I've ever done, but it's practically writing itself.

Fuck you, writer's block.

"Wait, am *I* the ghost in this story?" Devin plops into my reading chair. "I feel a little typecast. Why can't you make me a professional baseball player? Or a damn superhero, huh?"

I sit in front of my laptop, stirring the touchpad. "Just keeping it real. At least you'll have a starring role in this one."

He shrugs. "Sounds like you do, too. Tell me, does the recluse on the top floor know it's *his* brother haunting the building?"

"I don't know yet. Yes, maybe. Why?"

"If his unhappiness keeps his brother around, he might be inclined to stay that way."

"No." It comes out emphatically as my story mixes with Rowan's words to Mira. *No one wants to be alone.* But Devin catches my eye, looking more serious than usual as he cocks his head at me. With an uneasy shrug, I reconsider. "He'll resist happiness at first. If his brother can't have a happy life, why should he?

He'll try to say he's not *that* guy, that he's better off alone. He'll believe it, too. It's easier being alone. Not letting anyone else in means..."

My brow pinches as I see where this is going.

"Means what?" Devin pushes.

"Nothing changes, and he never gets hurt again. He'll hold on to his brother and his misery, keeping them both in limbo."

Devin leans into the plush red chair, hands latched behind his head. "Until... *dun, dun, dun...* what happens?"

"Until he meets someone who—" A smile slips up my lips as I think about her. "Brings him out of his misery. Then, loving the right person matters more than the risk, heals the emptiness left by his brother, and..."

"He doesn't need him anymore."

Air evacuates my lungs like I've been jabbed in the stomach. He's right—I don't need him anymore. Not that he's really here in the first place. He's definitely a welcome character in my overactive imagination. But, if he really were here, he'd tell me not to hang onto my grief anymore—that's not the damn takeaway from Devin's short life. To love and be loved—that's what he taught me.

And that's what I have now, too.

Devin rises from my reading chair. "It's like me and Corey used to tell you—three's a crowd."

I laugh—he said that a lot. Though I'm bubbling with ideas, I minimize the tab for *Strangers Together*—that's not what I'm writing today.

Devin cracks his fingers at the same time I do. "Well, I'll leave you to it. I have a hot elf to ravish."

I laugh and open a new document that I hope will make it a little easier for the woman I love to do what she loves.

And the next time I glance up from my keyboard, Devin is gone.

Thirty-Nine

ROWAN

Mom cries when I show up with Jack at Reggie's oceanfront rental two nights later. Like, *seriously* cries. Especially when Jack tells her, "I've changed her mind about romance. You owe me dinner, Christine."

She enthusiastically obliges. Mira, Jane, and the kids join us, and everyone dotes on Jack like they're desperate to secure his place in our family. It's a little embarrassing, but he seems to like it. The bad weather coming over the weekend has prompted Mom and Reggie to move up their travel plans—they leave Thursday. Typically, news like this would have Mom teary about leaving us early.

Not this time. She has Reggie. And she's leaving me with Jack.

Friday morning, I pick Sara up for school with the top down. She tosses her backpack into the backseat before waving the newspaper.

"You won't believe what's in the paper today." She looks almost purple with giddiness, but it could be her hair reflecting onto her cheeks.

"You read the paper?"

She scoffs. "No, Dad likes keeping up with the police blotter in case his relatives are arrested."

"Oh, has someone been arrested?" I twist to back out of her driveway.

"Look at this." She holds up the paper, forcing me to hit the brakes before pulling out. It's a grainy black-and-white photo of Jack. *Guest Columnist* is listed under his name next to the title of his piece. *Romancing the Learning Curve.*

My mouth goes bone dry in nervous anticipation. "He didn't tell me he was writing for the paper. What does it say?"

"Ah, it's *so* good, Rowan. He talks about his awesome class visit, your Inspiration Project, and how giving teenagers more freedom has improved their learning. He quotes Julio, Eddie, and Mia. He says teenagers aren't the moody, shallow, disinterested jerks older people often judge them to be. If given the right tools, encouragement, and trust, there's nothing teenagers can't do. He rants about teacher salaries. He talks about your student pantry and that if we seriously can't pay teachers what they deserve, then at the very least, the community should get off its ass and provide supplies. He calls you—get this—'a modern-day Elizabeth Bennett, an intelligent forward-thinker, under-resourced thanks to society, but still bucking against the boring rigamarole of lectures and multiple-choice tests to give her students what they really need—space to fall in love with learning.'"

I scoff while blushing. "If I were his teacher, I'd take off points for hyperbole."

"He challenges teachers to let go of rigid lesson plans and remember what they once loved about learning—and businesses, communities, and leaders to be supporters rather than critics. Seriously, Rowan, it's the best article I've ever read. He's *so* in love with you."

I meet her coy grin with a light shrug. "Um, it sounds... amazing."

I read it in the early morning quiet of my classroom, sipping coffee between gasps over his beautiful words. What he's vying for is nothing new—higher wages and more support. But like everything he writes, there's magic in it.

He starts with a narrative about his nerves and expectations before his classroom visit. *"I didn't want to be back there, surrounded by kids I didn't know and aching for the brother I lost."* He explains his warm reception, and how the students' excitement in showing him their literary mural jolted his preconceived notions—*this wasn't a typical classroom.*

Jack provides insightful quotes from my students and discusses our reading adventures. *Schools are not institutionalized entities that exist in our communities—they* are *our communities. I am a childless romance writer—if I can get involved, so can you.*

The paper drops to my desk as tears pinprick my eyes. His article feels like a love letter, and the nod to Elizabeth Bennett assures me that's exactly what it is.

Dr. Evelyn Tate appears in my doorway when my second-period class ends. She carries a small pink clipboard and a smug, glowing expression. Her pleated purple skirt squishes pleasantly as she sashays to me. She smells like lavender and rich people.

She motions to the newspaper on my desk. "We need to talk."

"Um, okay."

"I would've liked an opportunity to weigh in on that article," she says, not hiding her annoyance.

"I had nothing to do with it."

Her eyes narrow like she doesn't believe me. Then, she looks at her clipboard. "I've been tasked with letting you know that... let's see... a local builder is footing the bill for your field trip buses for your community readings, anywhere you want to go. A book club wants to take over stocking your student pantry—they want a list. The school board has requested a luncheon. I'll go with you, of course, to help you explain your project... The public library has invited your students to do story times, and they want to send some local authors your way for visits. The TV station where Ashley's father works has invited you for an interview. I'll help with that, too. The paper wants to talk about your students writing contemporary book reviews for a weekly column. And the school has received over eight thousand in donations since the article posted last night. So, if you have any wish list items..."

She glances around my eclectic classroom with its thrift store rugs and second-hand furniture. "New decor, perhaps?"

"Um, wow. I-I don't know what to say. That's amazing."

"Well, Jack is full of surprises, but creative types can be very unpredictable. You never know what he might do from one moment to the next."

Is that jealousy? "Oh, I don't know. Jack's lived in the same house all his life. He takes care of his neighbors like family. He's helping me and my students. That's not unpredictable. That's Jack being Jack. But, of course, you don't know him like I do."

She winces.

A spark of pride flashes in me. "I'll get you a list for my pantry. I don't want the TV interview, but I'll meet with the school board. I'll contact the library and the newspaper and have the classes write thank-you's for the rest if you have their information."

She unclips the papers and hands them over.

"Thanks, and we like our classroom. The money should go to stocking more contemporary bestsellers in the library. I'll have my students create a list of suggestions. Oh, and maybe they can write quick notes to put inside, explaining why they loved the book. It'll create connections between the students."

I can't wait to get started on this new extension of our Inspiration Project. But ironically, Dr. Evelyn looks unimpressed as she nods and saunters to the door.

After dropping Sara off that afternoon, I detour to the ABC store and buy the best whiskey my budget allows. At home, I trade my work clothes for a soft sundress and flip-flops. I love Edgar as he meows about his day, chirping at birdies and keeping an eye on things. Then, I carry the artsy whiskey bottle to Jack's.

Stepping to his front porch, music blares from inside. Metallica. And I wonder what mood he's creating for his writing—angry, perhaps? I hesitate to push the doorbell.

But, of course, it's too late.

The door swings open. I jerk, surprised at the movement, and "Nothing Else Matters" loudly hitting my ears. He looks pleased but distracted, like I've cut him off mid-sentence. With a hint of surprise and a light perk on his lips, he says, "Rowan... hey."

"Jack, you're writing. I wasn't sure I should bother you."

"Writing is just what I do until you show up." He smiles coyly, pressing a remote to turn down the music. "Get your ass in here and tell me about your day."

Laughing, I obey and wait for the door to shut behind us before pinning him against the wall. My enthusiastic greeting makes us chuckle through kisses. He tastes like coffee and cinnamon, comforting and sweet. His fingers knead my back as they slip lower, stopping only because I pull away, desperate to free my hand from the whiskey bottle.

"My day was amazing, thanks to you." A little breathless, I thrust the bottle to him. "Thanks for the article."

Confusion twinges his face briefly. "Oh, did that come out today? Wait, what day is it?"

"Friday."

He breathes a heavy sigh. "Right. I used to work there. The editor's been begging me to guest post for years, but I never felt I had much to say. People should know about the good work you do. Not that anyone reads the paper anymore."

"They do, actually. Donations have been pouring in all day." My brow creeps up my forehead. "But a modern-day Elizabeth Bennett, Jack? Come on."

"I had to pull on your literary pigtails a little, right?" He leans down for another soft kiss. "Come, have a drink with me."

With "Enter Sandman" playing softly from the surround-sound speakers, Jack takes the whiskey into the open kitchen, grabbing glasses. I perch on an island barstool. He pours two drinks and hands one over.

"I'm considering more articles... I mean, *maybe*. I liked writing something different, something that matters. What do you think?" His hand goes through his hair before staring into his glass as if worried about my answer.

"Yes, definitely, yes."

He lights up. "I'm itching to do a piece on homelessness. I stayed at a shelter for a few nights, researching *Bare*. It was... humbling."

"Wow, you *really* will do anything for a book."

He shrugs off how impressed I am. "Then, maybe something on the foster care system, with your help and Mira's. I don't know—I could really get into it."

"You should. Your writing inspires people. Maybe more will step up. I love the idea."

His head tilts, staring at me. "It's not all about me anymore. The more I put that into practice, the happier I am. Thanks to you."

Warmth flushes my cheeks—partly from the whiskey but mostly from him. "For once, I'm in the spotlight and don't mind the attention... too much. Work has never been better, and neither has... this."

Shyly, I break eye contact for another sip, which burns in a good way as it slips down my throat. He meets me at my stool, and I grin as he moves between my legs and slips his hands around me.

"*This*... makes me fucking ecstatic."

"*This*... scares me to death," I whisper.

"Me, too, but in the best possible way." He leans closer, nuzzling his head against mine. "Are you freaking out?"

A chuckle escapes me at the smirking way he says it, but I admit, "Yes, a little. You're not?"

"I think in what-ifs, Rowan—of course, I am."

"So, in your what-ifs, everything falls apart?"

"No, the opposite, actually. Even the worst of my worst-case scenarios ends in loving you. If my head games can't break us, nothing will."

"Then why freak out?" I ask, sliding my hands up his chest.

A slow, playful smile eases over his lips as he stares into my eyes. "It's too good not to, right?"

"Right," I breathe out in a sigh.

"Devin's already given me the best advice on this," he says with an air of expertise. "Just go with it."

"Just go with it?"

"Yeah, enjoy it. Trust it. Go with it, even when things get hard."

"Hmm, I like that."

Hands tugging my thighs, he nestles into me, and his soft kiss on my lips goes from sweet to seductive in a blink. When my cool hands hit his hot chest, he nibbles my bottom lip, and I swear, every nerve erupts with tiny aches for him.

But the doorbell combines with a pinging alert on Jack's phone.

With a throaty groan, he edges away from me. "I'm going to fucking murder whoever that is."

I slip my hand into his pocket, retrieving his phone.

He holds up the image—Tom and Vernon on his doorstep in a debate, each holding different sprinkler heads.

I laugh. "Looks serious. I should go anyway. I have a hundred essays on the stylistic differences between classic and contemporary lit waiting for me. Continue this later?"

"As soon as possible. Let's hunker down at your place for the storm, huh?"

"Sounds like a plan," I say, not hiding my cheesy grin.

Forty

ROWAN

Late the next night, I stare at the TV weather map, where red lines band their way into our region. Hurricane Nadine has been downgraded to a tropical storm. But winds rattle the trees and whistle through the woodwork of the little house. Rain pours in thick sheets, underscored by low rumbles of thunder.

It's my first significant storm in the little house.

But hunkering down with Jack has eradicated anxieties over what's happening outside. Cards from abandoned games are strewn across the coffee table next to empty glasses of wine and nibbled cheeses and crackers on a snack tray. An empty popcorn bowl sits there, too, from the movie we watched earlier. It's felt like a sexy slumber party, only it's gotten late. He dozes on the opposite side of the couch, our legs entangled under a blanket.

A crack of lightning stirs him. He sits up, rubbing his tired eyes. "Shit, I should check on Harper Lee. She hates loud storms."

"Bring her back here. Edgar won't mind."

"I'll grab my laptop, too. Feeling inspired," he says coyly.

"Oh, by dreamland? Because you were snoring a minute ago," I chuckle.

His brow knits. "I don't snore, liar." He leans over me, giving me a soft kiss. "Back in a minute."

His words are bookended by winds howling across the chimney top. A shiver races through me as the front door shuts behind him.

I take our dirty dishes to the kitchen to clean up before bed. With the rain coming down in sheets against the sliding glass doors, I get a towel from the bathroom—Jack'll be drenched when he returns.

Several minutes pass. I resettle on the couch, eyes glued to the storm coverage.

An explosive crash and a bright light make me scream and curl against the couch. The power flickers out. Cracking comes next, and a low whistle before the ground shakes in a massive thud with a raucous explosion that rips through the house. Though I can't see the source of the noise, it sounds like a tank has taken a slow detour through the walls and over the floorboards, crushing the little house under its belted wheels.

The tree!

Edgar darts like a gazelle from the couch to my bedroom, surely hiding under the bed. Grabbing my heavy-duty flashlight from the kitchen, I go in the opposite direction—to the laundry room and converted garage. Opening the door reveals the tree, splayed and broken in brittle bits across the converted garage. The outer walls and roof are gone. A rainbow of notebooks, books, and art supplies forms a debris bed, presently soaking in the pouring rain. To the left, netting from the screened-in porch wraps around its trunk like an odd blanket, and to the right, my car's hood acts as a pillow for the tree's piney tips.

But this damage is nothing compared to what my flashlight reveals across the gap between our houses.

"Jack!"

I shut the outer door, securing the main house. I race into my rubber boots and raincoat. The wind and rain hit me like a wall. Through ankle-high water, I circle my car and the tree to get to Jack's front door.

It's locked. I pound on it, waving my hand over the doorbell sensor. When a minute passes without a response, I border the house, bracing myself against it, and go around back. Lightning cuts the gray sky like a jagged knife. I cringe inside my hood. I climb the deck and find the tree trunk split into two pieces. One has shattered the outdoor kitchen and sliding glass doors, spreading tree bits into the living room. The other, larger section holding the majority of the thick branches has scraped through the side of Jack's house like a rake and made a path through his study.

Oh, my God, he wanted to get his laptop!

I cut through the broken doors, carefully avoiding the large glass shards dangling from the threshold.

"Jack!" The wind takes my voice away, so I yell louder. "Jack!"

There's no response but my pounding, racing heart banging against my chest. My flashlight bobs across the room as I rush toward his study. Wicked imaginings form in the seconds it takes to get there—Jack hurt, Jack crushed, Jack... I am gasping and desperate when I examine the space, the flashlight shaking.

There's too much debris—I can't even make out his desk chair for the broken tree limbs, busted furniture, and fallen books. Bracing myself on the stable wall to the right, I lean in, shining my flashlight everywhere. I see no sign of him, but the silver corner of his computer peeks through the clutter like a beacon.

He's buried underneath! I must find him. And fast. I scream for him over and over. But the windy silence lures me onto the broken floorboards. My rubber boots feel too heavy for such an unstable surface, and I slip on the damp decline with my second step, scraping my leg against the splintered tree trunk. I fear falling through to the crawlspace and getting stuck. It's dark and difficult to know where to put my weight. But I inch closer to the center, finally giving up my grip on the stable wall to reach where I'd imagine he'd be. I miscalculate my next step, and books give way beneath me, making me fall to my knees. The surface ahead looks even more precarious—I'll never get to him on time.

I scream his name, but it gets caught in my throat as something strong hooks my waist, yanking me up to the solid floor again.

I turn into Jack's arms, and he curses in my ear. "Damn it, Rowan. You scared me to death. What're you doing?"

"Finding you!" My voice—my entire body—shakes. "I thought you were..."

He leans into me, his breath hitting my lips. "I'm okay. We're okay."

I latch onto him, desperate and tearful. "I love you, you stupid jerk. Never do that to me again!"

"I love you, too." A smile crooks the corner of his mouth. "You were about to claw through rubble for me? You must mean it."

"I-I do. I... We stay together from now on!"

"Fine. But we can't do anything here," he says, shining a flashlight around the open space. Seeing the cloudy night sky through the broken roof and rain pouring inside the walls chills me—it's weird and unsettling. "It's too dark and unsafe... What about your place?"

"The damage is contained to the garage and porch."

"Good. I'll find Harper Lee, text the neighborhood that we're fine, and we'll stay there until the storm passes."

Scanning the floor, my flashlight fixes on something on the floor near my rubber boots. I lean in, bracing myself on the intact threshold to grab it. Devin and Jack's baseball picture. I swipe it across my shirt and tuck it into my pocket.

Jack grabs my hand, pulling me away from the mess. On the other side of the house, he flips the power off at the breaker. Then, we find Harper Lee hiding in a closet upstairs. Jack gently coaxes her into her carrier. I cover it with a throw blanket.

Wind swirls through his living room like ghosts, rattling what's left. Jack examines the broken glass door to his deck as if he might want to secure it.

"Motherfucker!" Glass protruding from the door jamb slices into his arm.

"You can't do anything about that now," I shout over the storm noise. "Let's get Harper home, huh?"

Back into the rain and howling winds, we make a slow but hurried trail through our water-logged yards and around the broken tree. We reach the little house, drenched and cold. With the power out, everything is dark, but I quickly set up lanterns and candles, creating a warm glow. Jack covers the broken kitchen window with plastic trash bags and duct tape. We clean the glass together before releasing Harper.

Edgar approaches with caution, but Harper's quick to bat her honey eyes and give an affectionate head butt—she's a pacifist. Wearily, Edgar accepts her with suspicion, keeping an eye on her.

With the cats settled, the last few minutes do vicious circles in my head. *This is my fault.* Tears flood my eyes with the realization of the damage.

"What's wrong?"

"I should've listened to you about the tree. Your beautiful house is ruined, your study, all your books. This is my fault."

"Stop. I don't care about the house. We're safe. We're together. That's all that matters."

He's right—a fact I've never felt entirely confident about until now. *This moment.*

Dodging cats, I fall into his arms, snuggling against his chest even though he's damp. He smells like wind and rain and feels clammy cold.

"There's nothing more we can do until daylight," he says, his voice soft. "How about you wrap the cut on my arm, and then you let me wrap you up, huh?"

Smirking, I look up at him, my blue eyes widening. "Oh, wordplay… I like it. How 'bout we ride out the rest of the storm with me riding you?"

"Damn, Rowan." He laughs. "Forget the arm. Let's do your plan. Right now." He squeezes my ass, bringing me tighter against him.

"Cut first." My hands slip to his waist, where I roll up the hem of his hoodie, slowly taking it off him. It's not a bad cut, just messy. I retrieve my first-aid kit from under the kitchen sink and get to work.

He works hard to distract me—fondling things, vampire-biting my neck, grazing sensitive spots with his fingertips—but I stay focused on my task despite my laughter and flushed cheeks.

Finally shutting the lid of my kit, I laser in on him, practically throwing myself on him. He lifts me, wrapping my legs around him like they were made to fit there. I kiss the soft skin under his ear—he loves that. Then, my lips trail lower, biting and licking him as he carries me to the bedroom.

"The storm surge will be... impressive," I giggle between kisses.

"So will the tides," he breathes against my neck, smiling. "Cresting high tide will be... orgasmic... I mean, cataclysmic."

I laugh again as we strip out of our damp clothes, and he lays me down. Maybe it's the dorky wordplay that does it, but I know *this* is it. *He's* it. He's my forever romance.

Forty-One

ROWAN

At daybreak, we emerge to see the full extent of the damage. We stand at the edge of my driveway, mouths agape. My garage and porch are crushed like a can underfoot. My VW Bug is dented, and the windshield cracked—easy fixes. But Jack's house looks like a slice has been carved from it, leaving his office demolished and the upstairs exposed.

"Damn," he breathes out as we stare at the devastation.

"I know you said it doesn't matter, but I'm sorry anyway. I should've listened about the tree."

"Rowan, no apologies necessary. Anyway, the tree was hit by lightning." He points out charred sections where the tree split. "So, I wasn't entirely correct about what would bring it down."

"Hmm, just like in *Jane Eyre*—the lightning split the tree to foreshadow the ruin of Jane and Rochester's relationship."

"No chance of that with us. I promise I don't have another wife locked in my attic like Rochester did," he jokes.

I chuckle. "If you did, she would've escaped last night."

He mock-laughs and runs his hand across his forehead. "Whew. So long, Bertha."

"Yoohoo!" Rose's voice draws us back to the subject at hand. "Coffee, anyone?"

My hand shoots up.

She carries a fat thermos, and Vernon holds mugs hooked around his index finger. Tom and Marcy appear, offering donuts from a pink box.

"Well, Jack, you were looking for a new project," Tom says.

He perks up. "I know. I can't wait to get my insurance guy down here. There's a new contractor I want to try. I saw on social media how she restored an old farmhouse, turned it into a café, and converted a barn into a home—amazing stuff." He turns to me with sudden excitement. "Who do you have for insurance?"

I tell him, and he slaps his hands together. "Perfect. Same as mine."

After sipping my coffee, I look quizzically at him. "Do you always get so excited about insurance?"

Marcy snort-laughs. "Nothing makes Jack happier than dealing with insurance adjustors, contractors, or house projects."

"Almost nothing." He grins at me.

Ed's golf cart skids to a stop at the road. Renita eyes the damage from the passenger seat. "Holy Toledo! I can't believe no one's hurt!"

Ed steps out, adjusting his pants by the belt as he takes in the destruction. "It's the only significant damage in our neck of the woods, but it's a real doozy. It'll take months to put it back together again."

"You're welcome to our guest room, Jack," Renita coos.

"Our basement's free," Marcy chimes in. "And we're closer."

"Nonsense. Jack'll bunk with us," Vernon says.

"He's staying with me." My overly loud declaration brings all eyes to me. "Moving in. Permanently. Or for as long as it takes. I mean, if that's okay. If you want to... it's the least I can do."

He flashes an amused grin at my sudden discomfort. "You heard it here first, folks. Rowan Mackey just asked me to move in with her. Sounds serious."

I match his daring smile. "It *is* serious. And not just because you're homeless." I push into his arms and kiss him. A long, sexy kiss that shouldn't be seen by the neighbors, which makes him laugh and blush at once.

"Damn, Rowan. I can't say no to that. We're moving in together."

"And rebuilding your houses together," Tom adds as the rest cheer.

"I'll send a text alert. Does a half-hour work for everyone?" Rose prompts her phone.

I lock eyes with Jack, looking curious. "For what?"

"To start working. Whenever there's storm damage, the neighborhood comes together to help clear out debris, salvage what we can, and secure the holes and gaps."

"Took us a week for Hurricane Florence," Vernon says. "Went house to house like the Amish with barn razing."

"Ask that everyone brings work gloves. Wheelbarrows and tarps if they've got 'em," Ed instructs Rose as she types. "I'll secure trucks and trailers—we'll have much to tote away."

Vernon holds up the camera strapped to his neck. "I'll start documenting."

The group disbands to complete their assignments. Jack jumps on his phone, pacing our lots as he describes the damage to the insurance adjuster.

Inside, I care for the cats, grateful that Edgar and Harper are getting along. I text Mom, Mira, and Sara to tell them what's happened. I learn that Mira and Sara are fine—no damage to their places. They promise to help when they're able. Then, I dress in sensible work clothes and join the crowd assembled outside.

Everyone shows up to help. Neighbors from Daisy Lane and Daffodil Avenue. Mira, Jane, and family. Sara and her father, Eddie, bring his lawn care truck and supplies to help cut the tree into manageable pieces before loading his truck and taking the debris away. He promises to help with my lawn and overrun garden beds when the madness calms down.

The news of our storm damage spreads, and by lunchtime, my students arrive—four or five packed in each car with the music blaring as they come down the road. They park along the street and get out wearing work boots and gloves.

I meet them in the driveway. "You're here?"

Julio grins. "Heard you could use some help with the little house."

"Mr. Graham's house, too," Mia adds quickly.

"I'm totally getting service hours for this," Ashley announces, "but I want to help, anyway."

Eddie shrugs. "You've fixed enough of my problems. Remember the pimple from hell? I owe you."

"Thanks, guys! That's awesome!"

Jack comes over and says, "Holy shit! The party has arrived! Perfect timing, too. I just ordered a hundred pizzas."

We FaceTime with Mom and Reggie over our makeshift neighborhood picnic. Tom asks what I plan to do with the little house.

I shrug. "I don't know. I guess I'll put it back the way it was."

Jack shakes his head before I finish the sentence. "No, Rowan. Upgrades are the only upside to storm damage."

Tom's arms fold over his bulky frame. "He's right. If you don't upgrade, Mother Nature wins."

"I'm upgrading the hell out of everything," Jack says.

Tom claps his hands together and hoots like he's just won tickets to his favorite sporting event. "We'll use my senior discount at Lowe's and Ace. A wraparound porch would be nice."

"That's already on my shortlist," Jack says.

"I'd love a gazebo," Marcy says dreamily. "People don't have gazebos anymore."

"Vernon and I will binge-watch HGTV for design trends," Rose says. "Will you let me help with the paint colors?"

Jack's eyes narrow with obvious skepticism. "I'll consider it."

"I can help with that... and any artistic projects you want," Sara says. "I've always wanted to do a mural."

Rose questions Sara about murals while Marcy and Tom launch into a gazebo discussion. Mom and Reggie voice their opinions on gazebos—they're split. Deep in conversation with them, Vernon takes over my phone, moving it across the debris-filled lawn as they discuss the pros and cons of gazebos.

Meanwhile, I lean on my VW, taking in my chaotic yard with warm delight. Who knew that the best feature of owning the little house would be the family that came with it? *Hardwood floors, fireplace, family*—it should've been listed amongst the amenities.

Like he's reading my mind, Jack slips his arm around me, smiling as he tugs me close as if saying, *"This is good, right?"*

I grin back to say, *"Yes, very good."*

"Since we're living together now," Jack says, "how 'bout you let me handle your renovation?"

"You want to take on my renovation?"

"Absofuckinglutely." He nods toward my students, currently playing a makeshift football game with a water bottle on the street. "Focus on them. They need you right now. You need them, too, I think. I'm here, and I live for this shit. I'll even upgrade for you."

"I don't want an arcade, Jack."

"You will once you see it." I scoff, and he says, "Fine. No arcade. I'll only do what I know you'll love. This way, you can worry about whatever you do—inspiring the next generation, shaping young minds, saving the world, whatever—and I'll take care of the tough stuff like haggling with plumbers and replacing windows. It'll be fun for me, and it'll take stress off of you. Win, win."

I don't even have to think about it. "Yes."

He looks surprised at my quick answer. "Yes?"

"Yes. The little house matters to you, too. I trust you to take care of her. You're all the home I need, anyway."

He draws me closer. His brown eyes circle me, studying me. I love it when he looks at me like my face is the only one he ever needs to see. "Damn, I couldn't have written that better. I'm going to make you so fucking happy."

I don't doubt it, but laughter is my only response as he attacks my neck with delicate kisses.

Epilogue

ROWAN

Summer, three years later...

Checking myself in the mirror, I half-heartedly approve the emerald green dress with scalloped sleeves and a light collar. It will have to do. My wardrobe goal is simple—to look friendly. Surely, the four outfits I tried first accomplished that. It's nerves making me so indecisive. A universal truth about teachers (and anyone, really) is that we all have first-day jitters.

I return the discarded dresses to the walk-in closet and tidy the unfinished books on Jack's bedside table. Edgar Allan Poe and Harper Lee trail behind me, meowing curiously—they know something's up.

I give the bedroom a final once-over. So much has changed since I first moved in. Jack insisted on upgrades—recessed lighting, a walk-in closet, and, of course, a gorgeous, extra-large shower. But the main difference to my cozy bedroom retreat is that Jack and I share it. That, and everything else.

The changes in the rest of the house are much more drastic.

318

Edgar and Harper skirt around my feet as we take the short hallway next to Sara's old room, which will either be a nursery or another guest room, depending on where life takes us. I step into what used to be my living room and take a soothing breath. It's a massive study now—a book lover's dream. Jack writes on a desk in the corner by the fireplace. Scattered cushy chairs invite all-day reading. Small tables are equipped with study lights, notebooks, and, of course, good pens. I do my homework around the kitchen banquette—I had to keep it—and refuel on snacks and drinks from the small kitchen. Like a cool, cozy library, every free space in between is filled with books.

The little house no longer has a converted garage or screened-in porch. Instead, Jack built what we affectionately call the book tunnel—a long, wide hallway of floor-to-ceiling books broken up only by window seats for reading. The tunnel links our two houses into one—a plan I never thought would work. But Jack had a vision—and few things show true commitment than literally joining properties.

Well, that and getting married, which we did last fall.

A stranger to the neighborhood wouldn't know it had been two separate homes looking at it from the street as the tell-tale signs are gone. No divisive hedges. No separate driveway. Even the bricks have been whitewashed to match. We merged houses like we did our lives—relatively seamlessly—at least once we were together.

Jack crosses the living room, fiddling with remotes and gaming systems. "Honey, what do you think? Mario Kart or Luigi's Mansion? Or, wait, would Super Mario Galaxy be better?"

My head spins. "You're playing video games?"

"No, I'm setting something up as an icebreaker."

"What if he doesn't like Mario?"

Jack's eyebrow shoots up. "Rowan, *everyone* loves Mario. If he doesn't, we should worry."

I ease the remotes from his hands and slip my arms around him. "Don't worry. He'll love you. Let's try to relax, huh?"

"Says the woman who's changed her clothes *again*." His lips curve into a smile as he kisses me. "It's okay to be nervous. I'm sure he is. You look gorgeous."

What begins as a peck deepens as he lingers. A familiar heat rises between us that time hasn't softened. Rather, it's grown more intense—we *are* always desperate for each other.

Even so, he breaks away. "I almost forgot... I have something for you."

He dashes across the kitchen, pulling a wrapped box and a bouquet from the pantry. With a giddy grin, my high-energy husband practically jumps over the couch to present the gifts.

My words from ages ago filter through my thoughts. *That's how you'll know... when you want to buy a woman flowers.* And that's what he's done every week since. No plastic-wrapped gas station roses, either. He drives thirty minutes to a wholesale distributor and handpicks the arrangement. Although I've told him a thousand times that he doesn't need to go through the trouble, the flowers keep coming, and I adore it. It's another one of our *things*.

Today's bouquet is an understated arrangement that fits easily in my hand, short-stemmed, and tightly wrapped in brown paper. Deep purple Gerber daisies and sprigs of lavender create an artful contrast to bright orange lilies and bold yellow mums. I lean into the blossoms, catching their soft scents.

"They're beautiful. You may have missed your calling."

"I'm only a florist for you. It's one of many services I provide."

As I laugh, he tugs the flowers from my hand and gives me the box. I open the lid to find the second edition of *Love Story* by Dominic Martinez, Julio's grandfather and a classroom favorite for sharing during our Inspiration Project years ago. Thanks to Jack's influence with his publishing company, the first edition came out over a year ago, launching Mr. Martinez's late-in-life career as a great American poet. This new edition features Hispanic artists to tell his story in art alongside his words.

"It's an ARC." He grins.

"No annotating, then. It's... breathtaking."

Jack opens the hardcover to reveal a message scribbled on the title page. *Rowan, To teach is to love. And love is a gift. Always Give, Dom.*

A tearful sputter emerges as my fingers trace his message. "A signed ARC... Thank you, Jack."

His arms wrap around me, smushing the book between us. "You're my favorite person."

"But what about Mario?"

The doorbell interrupts our sweet giggling moment. Our eyes meet, and we take a simultaneous breath as our nerves rise again.

Jack leans in, resting his head against mine. "I will love you forever, Rowan." His words come slowly, in a whisper.

"And it won't be long enough," I finish with a kiss. "I have something for you, too. Later."

His brow peeks in interest, but the doorbell chimes again, luring us to the door. I expect Mira, but it's Mom and Reggie, carrying tote bags and iffy expressions.

"I couldn't wait." Mom pushes inside.

"The more, the merrier," Reggie spouts cheerfully, following behind her. "Hope you don't mind."

Jack and I share a glance—Mom showing up on a whim has become a welcome norm since she and Reggie married and moved to Wrightsville.

"Ah, Mario," Reggie observes, motioning toward the TV screen. "Excellent idea."

Jack jumps into his previous question with someone who clearly is better informed to give him an opinion while I meet Mom in the kitchen. She sorts through the totes on the expansive island, pulling out everything from chocolate chip cookies to Legos to three different types of apples.

"What's all this? Did you raid Target?" I reach for a vase and fill it with water.

She sighs, her shoulders bobbing. "I got a little carried away."

"Definitely. We have groceries... and toys. We even have flowers." I set the arrangement in the middle of the island.

"Yes, but you heard what Mira said. He's had it rough, and he'll be here a while. We should do extra to make him feel at home."

I couldn't fault her logic, though I worry he might find us overwhelming. Since we finished construction, teenagers like Sara have come and gone from the Mackey-Graham household. Some stay only a week or two before relatives step in. Others stay a few months as their parents sort themselves out. We consider ourselves a haven for teenagers in transition.

But Mom's right—Adam is different. For one thing, he's not a teenager but a child—the youngest we've fostered. Rescued from an abusive household with charges pending against his parents, Adam isn't in transition but recovery with a long road of healing ahead of him. He'll likely be here for the rest of his childhood—we expect, *hope,* that fostering leads to adoption.

"Definitely Mario Kart," Reggie says with authority.

The doorbell chimes. We all go still.

Jack and I lock eyes across the room, and I'm unsure who smiles first.

He claps with celebrity-level excitement. "Let's meet Adam."

We hold hands as we open the door—a subconscious comfort that's become another one of our *things*.

Mira greets us with an uneasy smile. She has first-day jitters, too. I understand why—Adam's blue eyes are angry slits, and his lips form a pinched line as he stares straight ahead.

"Adam, say hello to Rowan and Jack," she says with her soft Mom voice.

"We're glad you're here, Adam," I say.

Jack extends his hand to encourage a low-five or a handshake. "Put her there, Adam."

He hugs his chest, looking toward Mira unsurely.

"Let's go inside, huh?" she suggests.

We move aside, letting them go first. We give Adam space as he looks around. Mom and Reggie wave from the kitchen like giddy schoolchildren spotting their friends on the playground.

Adam doesn't respond to that either. He's eight but doesn't look like it. His body is lanky and thin, and a head shorter than children his age. His blond hair is flat from improper washing. His arms are littered with unruly scars—wounds that have gone untreated. Long, lumpy slashes stand out on his cheeks as if someone Zorro-ed him, and my heart swells with empathy. I suddenly understand why Mira fought so hard to place him with us.

"Well, I'm Christine, and this is Reggie," Mom says, unable to tolerate the silence. "We're your foster grandparents. Are you hungry?"

They rummage over her Target raid, opening cookies and snacks.

Adam ignores them. His eyes fix on me, and his anger switches to curiosity. He follows my scars with a tilt of his head. Instinctively, I want to hide, but I hold my hand out instead, like a discovery for him to examine. Then, I tuck my hair behind my ear so he can see the unusual terrain of my neck.

We have scars in common, after all.

His anger returns, glaring at Jack beside me. "Did he do that to you?"

The tension in the room upticks with the outrageous suggestion, but I focus on Adam and offer a warm smile. Sadly, it's a reasonable question from his perspective.

"No." I ease into the chair beside him, bringing us eye level. "When I was fifteen, a disturbed person took his anger out on me. For a long time, it made me angry, too. We can't help how people hurt us. We can only hope to be better people and for something good to come out of it. Like you... being here. It might be hard to believe, but most people aren't violent. No one here will ever hurt you. I promise."

His arms fall away from his chest, and with an uneasy breath, he latches onto me. His sudden embrace nearly pulls me from the chair's edge, but I firm my position. He feels so small against me, but his relief is enormous, filling me up and spreading through the room.

Slowly, he pulls away and seems embarrassed, as if needing love is a weakness. I meet his sheepish look with an assuring smile. "Adam, you're safe and exactly where you belong. Now, please, tell me you're hungry."

He allows a weak nod, and the room breaks into action.

"I'll heat the pizza oven," Jack says before hesitating. "You like pizza, right?"

Adam nods, staying close and observing the activity like a lost tourist in the wrong country by mistake.

"We have cookies and Cheetos!" Mom pulls bowls from the cabinets.

"Chex Mix, too. That's my favorite," Reggie says.

"Don't worry," I say, leaning near his ear. "They'll calm down."

A tiny smile perks his thin lips. I know then—I love him. He seems to know that, too. He grabs my hand as I stand like he doesn't want me to get lost in the shuffle.

But as the evening continues, he drifts from my side in small doses. To Mom and Mira first. But eventually, to Jack and Reggie when they play Mario Kart. Adam has never played, but it doesn't take long for him to adore that, too.

By ten, our guests are gone. Jack and I lead Adam into his new room—Devin's old room—and though he seems a bit shell-shocked at his new reality, he's also tuckered out. He's fast asleep by the end of our first story—*The Little House.* As my students have taught me, everyone loves picture books.

Jack and I sweep through the house, switching off lights and checking doors, and I feel much like I imagine Adam does. *How can this be my life?* My husband is giddy with getting-to-know-you schemes, mostly involving a basketball or a game controller. Mom and Dad (yes, he's the dad I was always meant to have) live less than twenty minutes away, as do Mira and her family. I'm the English department chair at school, where Julio will be my teaching assistant this year, and Sara will be in my class. We'll be working on her college applications soon. Dr. Evelyn Tate-Kaine has moved on to the school board. Dean Maddix is officially a working actor—we spot him sometimes in police dramas, Hallmark movies, and the occasional insurance commercial. All the pieces have clicked perfectly into their proper places.

Bringing me to Jack...

His first two bestsellers since us, *Bare* and *Strangers Together*, created so much buzz at release that the film rights went up for auction. We would've been set for life even if he never penned another book.

But they keep coming. He's more prolific than ever. He always understood love and how to capture it in his stories, even when he thought he was a fraud. But finding it himself reflects in his writing like a mirror to the strength and depth of our relationship. His stories are even more raw and heart-wrenching than before, but a nice side effect to us is that his books are also happier by the end.

I prop the baby monitor on my bedside table and increase the volume. Harper and Edgar curl into a single ball by the sliding glass doors. Jack pulls the covers back on his side, catching my eyes with his.

"I haven't forgotten," he says.

I give him a fake, puzzled look. "Forgotten what?"

"Don't play games with me, Rowan. You said you had something for me."

I can't hide my coy grin, but I shrug casually. "Did I say that?"

His eyes narrow to dark slits. "Don't make me resort to coercive tickling."

I laugh, moving to his side of the bed. Standing in front of him, I shake my head. "Fine, you win. I got you flowers, too."

"Flowers?" He looks confused. "Well, where are they?"

I hold my arms out. "You have to find them."

He lights up in surprise. His eyes travel over my green dress like it's the only barrier between him and a treasure. "Aw, Rowan. Did you... Are you saying... I mean, really?"

His stunned delight brings a chuckle. "You aren't the only one capable of romantic gestures, you know?"

I reach behind my neck and unbutton the top clasp of my dress. Gently, he tugs the material over my shoulders and arms until it falls to my feet. All skin and black lace, I stand before him. He drops to his knees, taking in the tattoo across my left side, inches under my breast. In newspaper type, his name ends with a crooked heart and sits on a bed of strewn wildflowers in purple, pink, yellow, and blue watercolor hues.

His fingers trace the surface. Then, his lips. "I love it." He looks up at me, sounding breathless. "It's perfect. Does this mean you're *finally* serious about us?"

I laugh. "I'll tattoo your name all over my body to prove it."

"No need. I like it right here, where it's just for me." He almost looks teary as he runs his fingers over it again. "Damn, Rowan, I will have to step up my romance game after this."

"How about we get the next one together?"

His arms wrap around my midsection, pulling me closer. "I still fucking adore you... more every day."

A coy smile stretches over my lips as I run my hand through his hair. "Better show me then."

Between soft kisses, he whispers exactly what I'm thinking. "Always."

Join my subscribers for FREE BONUS CONTENT and read Jack's bonus epilogue.

www.jessicasherry.com/bonus-content

She's always wanted to belong to a family. He wrecks her chance. When these opposites collide, will a tragic accident lead them to what they're missing? Meet Marnie and Grady in *Every Chance After*.

www.jessicasherry.com

From the Author

Yes No Maybe gushed from my imagination in months—the fastest book I've ever written and the most fun. It touches on so many of my favorite fantasies—finding love next door, eclectic found families, wounded people finding hope in each other, just-as-I-am love, the badass Cinderella, taming the bad boy, and, definitely, the bestseller life (I'm seriously shooting for fancy book release parties one day).

But the story also hits home personally. I've been Rowan—the teacher desperately trying to inspire her students. I've been Jack—the angsty writer, sometimes prolific (like with this book), and sometimes not so much. I've also been a nosy neighbor, a pissed-off teenager, and an actress (ish) afflicted with a mountainous pimple the morning of her big theater performance.

Yes! The zit story is true! And yes... a teacher encouraged me to pop it (though she didn't do it herself; an upperclassman helped me, my angelic hero).

Writing Rowan's story made me long for my teaching days and reminisce about the educators who impacted me. My third-grade teacher, Mrs. Brown, encouraged my first novel by letting me and my classmates act it during short downtimes in class, securing my fate as a writer. Later in high school, Mrs. Pierce built my confidence to become an English teacher and encouraged my creative writing. She was also my drama coach, my best friend's mom, and *that* teacher you could always go to for anything.

Teaching is a tough job—intellectually, financially, and psychologically demanding. It's another universal truth that teachers work their asses off. So, when opportunities arise to support them and their classrooms, think of your best teachers, and please be as generous as they are.

Since I'm dishing out thanks and kudos, I need to give a few shoutouts to those who helped me get this story to where it needed to be. Thanks to my editor, Julie Mianecki from Reedsy, for her excellent advice, my beta/arc readers for their amazing feedback, and my Instagram besties for their constant encouragement. Thanks to Alisha and the team at ebooklaunch.com for another amazing cover. Hopefully, green will bring this story luck.

Finally, endless thanks go to my husband, Joe. Every romance I write is a version of us. I'm the moody writer in our house, but he always makes me feel ravished, cherished, and fucking adored. And he's done the most romantic thing of all—he's made my dream of a bestseller life his dream, too. We're another book closer, honey.

Thanks for reading!

Big Hugs,
Jessica

Find me on social media and learn more about my other books
bio.site/authorjessicasherry